The Blacksmith's Daughter

Andrew Mirfin

mirentum.com

Dedicated to Mrs Naylor - My first fan.

In trying to glimpse the elusive truth we decorate history's bare tree with the baubles of invention.

Contents

Chapter One

The sky was a cauldron of grey cloud. It slowly bubbled in the callously, cold wind that was sweeping up the Thames from Plumstead Marshes. The river was an expanse of steely water. Its fast flowing current relentlessly racing towards oblivion in the cold embrace of the sea.

Peregrine Osborne, stood on the quayside in Woolwich naval docks. Nature seemed like a morose metaphor, capturing and reflecting his melancholy mood. It was his birthday, but he had almost forgotten.

His brother, William, was dead.

A chill drizzle swept his face as the heavens wept. Tears were a relief denied to him. An odd lump sat in his chest like a stone and refused all attempts at expulsion.

Dead? Even now, those words seemed bare of meaning. Peregrine was twenty years old, his brother had been twenty-one. They had grown up together, been raised and educated together. Two years ago they had embarked on their greatest adventure, the Grand Tour. They had crossed the channel to the Netherlands, followed the Rhine, crossed the Alps through the Swiss Confederation, then continued to Milan, Tuscany and finally the Papal States and Naples. They had crossed seas, navigated rivers and scaled towering snowy mountains. They had swum together in the Ligurian, Tyrrhenian and Adriatic seas. Climbed the Basilica di Santa Maria in Florence and the Campanile in Pisa. Wandered through the majestic ruins of Rome and ridden gondolas down the Grand Canal in Venice.

Then, while returning home, William had become ill. Recovery had proven so elusive that eventually they consulted doctors in Utrecht who diagnosed smallpox. Over the next few days William's young, handsome features became deformed with malignant pustules. They were assured that most people with smallpox survived. But, for William, this had not been the case and, after twelve days, he had died.

When Peregrine was told, his first instinct was to laugh. How could William be dead? Death was something that happened to other people. A worrisome affliction for ordinary mortals, not for William. He was the Earl of Danby, raised from birth, and at great expense, in the sure knowledge that one day he would be the Duke of Leeds. One of the most powerful men in England. If he was to die...well, what would all that have been for? It would transform the last twenty-one years into an utter waste of time! Where would be the sense in that?

But as the days past he realised it was true. It *had* been a waste of time. There was no sense in it. They had grown up feeling so secure, surrounded by the wealth and power of the family. A family that gazed, like oracles, into the future and planned for it, invested in it as if their earnest hopes and their willpower alone would be enough to make it so. But, all that time some unseen fate had watched, sniggered, and then thrown the stone that shattered the dream like fragile glass.

The Earl of Danby was gone and he wouldn't be coming back.

But the empty husk that had once contained his spirit - that was returning home. Which was why Peregrine found himself standing in the November drizzle on the quayside at Woolwich. His father, the Marquis of Carmarthen, was an admiral in the Royal Navy. The Marquis had made a pretty poor show of being a father, but being an admiral was a role more to his taste, so when he was informed of William's death he found it simplicity itself to dispatch a small vessel to recover the body from Utrecht. Peregrine had had to do very little. The navy people arrived, arranged the coffin, the transport and loading of it onto the ship. Peregrine had simply followed along in a daze, doing as he was told.

During the crossing he had stared, limply at the endlessly churning sea. Like life, the sea could be soothing and bountiful and then suddenly become a raging storm from which they were spat, heaving, onto futures foreign shore. At once relieved to survive, but bearing the unbearable loss of those who did not.

And so he had arrived at grey Woolwich. A hard, uncompromising place on the Thames where England built its navy. The long quay stretched for what seemed a mile along the river, broken by huge stone docks each containing naval vessels of varying sizes in different stages of assembly. Flat featureless yards stretched inland, filled with timbers and rope. The knocking of hammers and rasp of saws was ever present as workmen clambered around or dangled expertly from ropes. None of the ships had sails, some did not yet have masts, but even now they had the appearance of strength and robustness. These would be formidable vessels designed to enforce and project the authority of the nation.

In contrast, the ship that was moored in front of Peregrine was a small gaff-rigged schooner. It was built for speed and the transport of passengers and some goods. A gang plank descended from its deck to the quay. On its deck a group of sailors struggled with William's coffin. They manhandled it rather roughly to the plank. They aligned themselves and began to descend the plank with the coffin balanced precariously on their shoulders.

Peregrine watched tensely. He prayed that the men were up to the job. He really didn't want the coffin to fall and for William's remains to be tipped indignantly onto the quay.

But his fears were unfounded as the men set the coffin on the shore and then started loading it onto a waiting carriage.

Peregrine noticed that the men were being supervised by John Lambert, one of Peregrine's grandfather's most trusted stewards.

"Job done," said a voice behind Peregrine with inappropriate levity. It startled him from his reverie. He turned to see his father stood behind him watching the men load the coffin onto the carriage.

His father, the Marquis of Carmarthen, was a tall man for his time, his thin frame making him appear even taller. He was well-dressed even for this dull weather and occasion with bright ruff, green velvet jacket and sandy brown trousers. The buckles of his shoes gleamed. His brown hair was thin and balding. His face was oval, lacking a jawline, with a sharp, angular Osborne nose. His small mouth and cupids bow lips gave him a slightly feminine appearance. He stood as if oblivious to the weather with all the stoicism of a military man.

"The repatriation of the remains is complete," he explained, as if discussing a delivery of wheat. "The cart will take it into London."

It, thought Peregrine angrily. Take *it*. Take *William,* you mean.

The Marquis knew how to spend money, but lacked the skills, contacts or insight to make it. Initially, the Marquis' father, the Duke, had tried to establish his son as a member of parliament in a series of vacant, and otherwise unconnected, seats such as Berwick-upon-Tweed, Corfe Castle and York. When he lost the York seat after just a year the Duke arranged for him to be elevated to the House of Lords, but the Marquis took no active role there. He had already turned to his other source of income, his wife's, for he had married the daughter of Sir Thomas Hyde and the Marquis relied on her to fund his activities.

In reality the Marquis had only one love in his life – ships. He had chosen a career in the Royal Navy and found his true vocation. Starting as Captain, in two years he was a rear-admiral. He had taken part in the Battle of Camaret against the French.

He had designed his own warships and eventually risen to full admiral just before Peregrine and William had started their Grand Tour. Just as his interests were with the sea, so his vices were those of a sailor. If he had a sense of duty it was to the Navy, not his family.

"And how are you, lad?" asked Peregrine's father casually. "Bearing up?"

No, thought Peregrine. *Not bearing up! William is dead.*

His father carried on as if he hadn't really expected an answer and didn't care that he hadn't received one. "Well, the funeral will be over in a few days and then we can start to put this sorry business behind us."

This sorry business?, thought Peregrine. *Is that all it is?* "The funeral?" he managed to ask brokenly.

"Yes, the funeral. He's to be buried at St Margaret's, in Westminster, opposite the Palace."

"In London?" said Peregrine in surprise.

"Yes, London," scoffed his father. "I know you've been away some years, lad, but Westminster is still in London."

"Not at Harthill?" said Peregrine. Harthill was part of the family's estates in Yorkshire and Peregrine's grandfather, the Duke of Leeds, had created a mausoleum for the family's deceased in All Hallows Church.

"No," replied the Marquis with some discomfort. "Well, Westminster is nearer, it's easier for the family to get to...and there's no need to cart the thing across half the country."

"But William is the Earl of Danby, he should be in the family vault," said Peregrine, limply.

The Marquis huffed, "Well, he won't be. It's just not...practical. Ah, they've got it on the carriage at last. I shall go and make sure they know where they are going."

He strode off before Peregrine could ask any other difficult questions.

Peregrine watched him go over to the carriage, swaggering and enjoying his own importance.

You pompous ass! thought Peregrine. *Why couldn't it be you in the casket being dropped into a hole in Westminster?* He paused and swallowed the bitter taste in his mouth. Like many a son before him, Peregrine dearly wanted to love, or at least like, his father, but the Marquis always made that a very difficult thing to do. As boys, William and Peregrine, had made numerous excuses and searched endlessly to convince themselves that their father cared. Only to conclude he did not.

Peregrine followed, but took care to keep clear of his father. He sidled up to John Lambert who was, in truth, the one really organising things and ensuring all went smoothly. Lambert had started as a page in the employ of Peregrine's grandfather. He had proved himself able, then remarkable and then indispensable. Now Lambert was the man who ran all the family's affairs. While the family members schemed, indulged, partied or busied themselves with the affairs of state, it was Lambert who ensured that the everyday activities of the estates ran flawlessly.

"It's a sad business, my Lord," said Lambert with sincerity. "I never thought I'd be doing this for Lord William. I expected that duty would fall to my successor."

"I am still adjusting," admitted Peregrine.

"It will take time, my Lord. Are you staying at Lindsey House?" asked Lambert. Lindsey House was the Duke's town house in Holborn.

"I haven't really given it much thought," said Peregrine honestly.

"I took the liberty of telling them you would be staying there – all is prepared. It would be convenient for the funeral and the Duke may wish to see you."

"Thanks, John. Yes, you are correct; it would be a good idea".

"I need to go with the coffin to the chapel of rest. But you can take my coach to Lindsey House if you wish and then tell them to come back for me."

"Thanks. That would be good." said Peregrine. As usual, Lambert seemed to have everything under control. It was hard to imagine what the family would do without him.

They went over to the waiting black coach. its doors were adorned with the Osborne arms, a yellow cross on a blue shield and, below it, the family motto, *Pax In Bello*, Peace In War.

Peregrine climbed aboard while Lambert instructed the driver. Then, with a lurch, the coach was away. His gaze drifted down to the floor and he suddenly felt very alone. He shuddered and, before he could prevent it, he wept uncontrollably.

25th November 1711

Peregrine stared wistfully out of the large front window of Lindsey House. The house was situated in Lincoln's Inn Fields in Holborn, the most fashionable part of the city. Sparsely spaced pedestrians wandered down the four streets that ran along the side of the square, carefully dodging the trundling coaches that seemed to run recklessly through the crowd. In the centre of the square was a large open area of grass where large trees stood like sentinels, their bare boughs shifting restlessly in the breeze. Around the square stood the grand town houses of the wealthy. Ornate alabaster porticos adorned giant, four storey, houses whose architecture parodied the temples of Rome. And in the centre of the west side stood Lindsey House. Lindsey House was the Duke's London residence. The Duke's usual home was at Wimbledon House in Surrey, but even though he was over eighty, his political affairs meant he spent much time in London. He had recently been a competitor for the post of Lord Privy Seal. The family did not own Lindsey House, they leased it from the Duke's wife's family, her father being the Earl of Lindsey.

Above the houses and trees the cloudless, late autumn sky was a pale, light blue. The mid-afternoon light was dazzling and crisp. It appeared warm, but the heavy coats of the passers-by betrayed the biting chill that lingered on from early morning.

That morning William had been laid to rest. The service had taken place at St Margaret's Church, overlooking Parliament Square in Westminster. The church was a fine choice. its medieval stones had seemed as solid as the earth. Sunlight had stretched fingers of coloured beams through the stained glass. The family had filled the dark pews between the ancient arches. The Bishop of St Davids, who was the Duke's son-in-law, had given a suitably sombre reading. Finally, poor William had been buried, the soulless coffin lowered gently into the cold earth. Here would be William's resting place, between the Palace of Westminster and Westminster Abbey. Those two axes of earthly authority, man's and God's, reflecting the family's place in society more than any relevance to William himself.

Once it was over, the family had returned silently to Lindsey House where refreshment was provided. And now, drink in hand, Peregrine found himself staring through the window at a world outside that seemed impassive and unchanged while his world inside was decaying with every breath.

On the other side of the room stood Peregrine's grandfather, Thomas Osborne, Duke of Leeds. The eighty year old Duke had lived an eventful and controversial life, rising from a backwater Baron to be someone who had influenced national events. Even now, in his supposed retirement, he was active in London circles. He was a gaunt figure with long face, thin lips that gave him a slit for a mouth. His long, angular, thin nose had become an Osborne trademark. His eyes were dark and narrow, constantly darting. They missed very little.

Next to the Duke stood Peregrine's mother, Lady Bridget. She was a small woman with narrow shoulders. Her face was unblemished, almost pale, and framed with a mass of curly, black hair. Her eyes were wide and disarmingly gentle. Her and the Duke were close, far closer than either of them was with her husband, Peregrine's father. Her marriage to the Marquis had had difficulties from the beginning. For a start, she was already married. Her first marriage was at the age of twelve and there was some debate about whether it had ever been consummated. When the Marquis had come along years later the first task was to arrange for the first marriage to be annulled.

Lady Bridget was the only daughter and heiress of Sir Thomas Hyde, 2nd Baronet, she brought significant wealth to the marriage. Sadly, the Marquis had brought only significant debts. It was a partnership fraught with conflict and, when these arose, the Duke took his daughter-in-law's side in preference to his son's. The gap between father and son became an irreconcilable chasm. They had not occupied the same room for years. The Marquis had not even attended his own son William's funeral that morning. Peregrine had pondered if that was the real reason William was buried in Westminster not at the family vault in Harthill, because a service at Harthill would have inevitably pushed the Duke and his son into a proximity they would both rather avoid.

Lady Bridget stood watching Peregrine where he stood in isolation while the other people in the room bustled around him, but appeared not to notice him at all. She turned to the Duke, "I worry about Pip", she confessed. "Will and Pip were very close."

"I worry about the Dukedom." said the Duke darkly. "My dear grandson's death has placed the family's future on Pip's shoulders now. It's unplanned for and I despise being unprepared. William was always intended to be Earl of Danby, then on my death Marquis and then, on his father's death, finally Duke. Now this burden falls on Pip." He smiled without humour. "Dear Pip, with his gaze fixed dreamily in the clouds."

"He's a sweet child," she said fondly. "Although he has always been obscured. The little one hiding behind Will. The moon can be pleasant, but it is invisible in the presence of the sun."

"He's a dreamer," responded the Duke with a tinge of bitterness. "And he is on course for a sharp awakening."

"It all reminds me of his father," she said with something of a scoff.

"There are similarities," he admitted. The Duke had always intended his eldest son, Edward, to be his heir and, at first this had been the case. But Edward had died childless at the age of thirty-three leaving his younger brother to become the current Marquis of Carmarthen - with all the insurmountable difficulties that had raised. "I don't intend to make the same mistake again. We have to ensure that Pip is in a position to assume his responsibilities when I pass on. Even in his own father's lifetime. " He hurriedly placed a comforting hand on Lady Bridget's arm, "I will make sure you are cared for, my dear, have no doubt. But, to rely on your husband would be, I am sad to say, the gravest error."

Lady Bridget looked again at Peregrine and wondered if he had any idea what was expected of him.

Peregrine did have a good idea what was expected. Like his brother William he had been brought up to know his place in society and the duties that entailed. It was a world of immense privilege for a few, but the entitlement to that privilege was balanced on a knife edge and required continuous adjustment and attention. There were others around who were always alert to an opportunity to acquire what was yours. Hungry mouths were always waiting to bite the hand that feeds.

Peregrine could feel the weight of future obligation on his shoulders. It was just not something he had ever expected to carry and, at the moment, not something he could possibly face.

His mother walked over to him, breaking him out of his thoughts. "I haven't seen you for a long time, Pip. I don't suppose any of us expected to meet again under such difficult circumstances." She paused, her large eyes searching for assurance. "How was your Tour?"

Peregrine smiled politely, thinking back at the great time he had had with his brother. "It was a great adventure." he began. "Just such a pity that it ended as it did."

"You must come to Kiveton for Christmas", she said, hoping to lighten his mood. Kiveton, the estate in Yorkshire, was technically the family seat. At least the Duke had planned it to be so, acquiring the land, having Kiveton Hall built around fourteen years previously and filling it with treasures. The family vault at Harthill, also built by the Duke and currently the last resting place of his mother and father, was also part of his plan to create a dynasty. The reality though was not quite as impressive. The Duke himself lived at Wimbledon and occasionally at Lindsey House. Which left his son, the Marquis, and his family living at Kiveton. Except the Marquis also spent most of his time elsewhere. With both daughters married and William gone, Peregrine could see why his mother might wonder if he would join her for Christmas.

"Will father be there?" he asked gloomily.

"No," she said slowly. "He, uh, doesn't... usually spend Christmas with us."

Peregrine nodded. He knew his father well enough to know his tastes didn't stretch to spending time with his family.

"I have told grandfather that I would go to Wimbledon, but I'll give it some thought," he said.

"Well, I'm sure your grandfather would like to see you. Perhaps you can do both?" She rested her hand gently on his, a rare sign of affection that caught him by surprise. "Please think about it," she said and gave him a pale smile. She pulled her hand away sharply, as if she had touched something unexpectedly hot then hurried away.

He noticed she was hurrying over to where his aunts were grouped together with their respective husbands. While the Duke's sons had proved disappointing, two having died leaving the least suitable to become the Marquis, he had much more luck with his five daughters. He had managed to marry them all off to various earls, lords, bishops and notable people of influence – sometimes more than once. Casting the family's net wide. Peregrine had three surviving aunts who now huddled together, laughing politely, but each one surreptitiously vying to show she was better than her sisters.

Peregrine groaned inwardly and decided he had better avoid them. He turned to get another drink and almost knocked over his sister, Mary.

"Sorry," he said awkwardly. "I didn't see you." Both his sisters were older than him and William, by three or four years. While William and Peregrine had been quickly drawn away by the Duke when they reached their informative years and had been educated abroad, the girls had stayed with their mother at Kiveton.

Mary had a pleasant, round face, even the sharp, Osborne nose seemed subdued amongst her pleasant features. She wore her blonde hair up, something invisible holding it effortlessly in place with just a couple of choice strands falling to her shoulders.

"So, how is the man of the moment?" she asked. She held a drink in her hand slightly too loosely and there was a tiny slur to her speech.

Peregrine grinned, "Me? This is William's funeral, nothing to do with me."

"Ah, but you are the one in everyone's thoughts, not poor Will."

"I don't think so...." began Peregrine who felt like he had been virtually ignored since arriving back from the continent.

"Well, I *do* think so," asserted Mary. "Think about it. There are four of us, right? Bridget, then me, then Will and then you. Well, Bridget and me are both married and, anyway, women don't count," Peregrine opened his mouth to object, but Mary continued. "Will's gone now so that leaves...you." Her eyes suddenly focussed intently on him."They hadn't really noticed you before, but they see you now. They have to."

Peregrine cast a glance round everyone in the room. They were all talking in animated ways to each other. Not a single eye looked in his direction. "Well, they hide it well," he commented sourly.

She also looked round the room. "Yes, they're good at that," she said seemingly to herself. "But there are lots of questions they want answers to."

He laughed, but without humour, "Like what?"

"Like...what kind of man are you? Are you a plotter and

schemer? Do you make friends easily? Can you influence people? Are you a soldier? Or are you more of a farmer? Or gardener? Do you obey the reins...or the whip? No one really knows, you see, and that bothers them."

He sighed, "You seem bitter? And cynical."

She took a slurp of her drink, "Yes, well that's what living with dear Mama has done for me. You and Will escaped all that, at least. You know that even now she'll be preparing a list for you."

"A list? Of what?"

"Of brides. Prospective partners. "

"But I don't know anyone."

"No, but Mama does. She has an eligible young son and so she'll be making a list of eligible young daughters. You're lucky, it's a buyers market. The money follows the male line and a family with sons can pick and choose. A family with daughters needs alliances."

Peregrine realised the possible source for his sister's bitterness. "You got married yourself three or four months ago, didn't you? While we were away. Belated congratulations!"

"Thanks," she said distantly. "That's him, over there in the red jacket. Henry Somerset, Duke of Beaufort."

Peregrine looked over to where a young, tall, handsome, well-dressed man with jet black, thick, wavy hair was chatting to his aunts. His bright red jacket, white shirt, trousers and stockings made him shine while others around him dimmed. As he spoke he waved his arms enthusiastically. Peregrine's aunts hovered round him like moths mesmerised by a bright light. Their attention was fixed on his every word, they grinned broadly and giggled as the appropriate moments.

"You've done well," said Peregrine. "He looks very fine." *Actually, he looks too good for you*, he thought, but he kept that to himself. "Is married life to your taste?"

"I live in Gloucestershire now. Badminton House is very beautiful."

"And love?" asked Peregrine hesitantly. "Are you in love?"

"Well, Henry is," she replied bitterly as she watched her husband talking to her aunts. "Sadly, not with me. He's madly in love with himself."

Peregrine looked at how expertly her husband played to his audience. "I can see that. Still, he is rather handsome. I imagine there are... compensations."

"Indeed," she said looking fondly towards her husband. "He does know how to raise expectations. Unfortunately, that's the only thing that's been *raised* so far."

"Oh," blurted Peregrine in embarrassment.

"Yes, apparently his first wife wasn't particularly understanding about it and told him so, which just made things worse. She died three years later. The second wife fared better, they had two brats, but she still died a few years ago. And now there's me, wife number three. How long do you think I've got?"

He sighed, "Maybe you just need to give it time? And perhaps try and be a little understanding?"

She smiled. "You know what? I'm so glad you are back! You really are the only other human being in this family."

"Mary!" came a shout as her husband, Henry Somerset, came rushing over with, to Peregrines horror, his three aunts following in his wake. "I've been looking all over for you," he said.

"I was talking to my brother," replied Mary tersely.

"Ah, yes," said Somerset, noticing Peregrine for the first time. "Awfully sad to hear about William. A fine chap by all accounts. It's such a damnable waste." Before Peregrine could respond he turned to Mary, "We had better be going. It's a long way back to Gloucestershire." He offered his arm to Mary.

Mary turned to Peregrine, "I'll be at Kiveton for Christmas if you want to get a break from grandfather."

"Mother has already invited me. I'm thinking about it."

"Well, think on. There are worse places to be," she smiled. With some abruptness she took Somerset's offered arm and he led her away leaving Peregrine with his three aunts.

"So, Pip, we've been talking about you," said Aunt Anne.

"Really? That must have been a short conversation," replied Peregrine with unnecessary sarcasm.

"No, not at all," said his Aunt Sophia, appearing not to notice. "We realised we don't really know anything about you."

"It's a sad admission, I know," said his Aunt Bridget. "But we always talked about dear William, you see. You were just William's brother; there really wasn't much else to say."

"He was the heir," said Peregrine wearily. "And I was the spare."

"Quite!" said Aunt Anne without a trace of irony. "But now you aren't any longer."

"And we're all keen to know as much as we can," said Aunt Sophia.

"About what kind of man I am?" suggested Peregrine.

"Yes, yes," said Aunt Bridget, almost clapping with delight. "I knew you would understand."

"So, what would you like to know?"

"Well," said Aunt Anne slowly. "For example, your interests. Would you consider yourself a soldier or more of a farmer?"

Peregrine groaned. "Or a gardener?"

There was a pause and then all three aunts looked at each other and laughed.

30th November 1711

Once William's funeral was over the family had dissipated from Lindsey House to their various homes. Even the Duke himself had decided to leave, there being little business to conduct in London with the Christmas season approaching, and announced he would be heading over to Wimbledon. Lindsey House would be essentially closed until the following year, only a skeleton staff being retained. Peregrine found himself with little choice but to follow the Duke.

The Duke went by coach to Wimbledon with John Lambert. It would take all day to get there. Peregrine decided to make his own way there on horseback. He made the excuse that he enjoyed riding, which was true, but it was also that he really didn't want to find himself spending an entire day in a coach with his grandfather. It wasn't that he didn't like the old man, his grandfather had always been very good to both William and himself. It was just that the Duke was a renowned schemer and Peregrine was in no mood to endure one of the his lectures at the moment.

As it happened, Peregrine did enjoy the ride. Somehow, it was good to be on the move again after days seemingly frozen in London having to endure the funeral and then the family. The winter weather and short days hadn't helped. The walls of Lindsey House had seemed to enclose him like a tight box. Shrinking his world into a series of gloomy, candlelit rooms. Even the London air seemed stifling. It was composed of the smoke of ten thousand chimney's mixed with the inevitable stench of a teeming multitude in close proximity.

The horse's every step put the city a little bit further behind him. Put the darkest of times a little bit further into the past. He crossed the Thames at London Bridge then followed the old trunk road south westwards through Kennington into the open country around Clapham and Wandsworth and finally to Wimbledon.

The Duke's home stood on the outskirts of the village of Wimbledon. It commanded the top of a high hill, looking down upon extensive parkland of woods, tranquil meadows and the grand gardens belonging to the house. To the west the private pleasure grounds merged invisibly with the even larger greenery of the Putney Commons. The Commons were still owned by the Duke but were publicly accessible and where many tenants were granted grazing rights. The Commons extended over an immense area all the way up to the Kingston Road. Then, across the other side of the road, stretched the Queen's significantly even larger Richmond Deer Park.

All in all, Wimbledon House sat amongst a vast rural expanse of trees, woods and meadows. A few years ago, it had been even larger, the Duke having sold a three hundred acre portion of the park in the last few years.

Peregrine approached Wimbledon House from the south. He left his horse at the stables and then approached the house between two large, carefully manicured knot gardens. The house stood two storeys high, but with a lower storey set below ground level. Each floor had nine large, Elizabethan style mullioned windows evenly spaced across the front. At each corner of the house was set a staircase tower with its own windows. The two rear towers rose above the height of the house and were topped with sharply angled conical roofs inset with their own windows. In the centre of the south face a door projection extended forwards in fashionable Tudor style.

A stone balustrade ran round the front of the house, behind which, the ground suddenly dropped like a dry moat to reveal the lower ground floor. The balustrade was broken at regular intervals by three stone bridges that spanned the dry moat to dark, wooden doors.

Peregrine crossed the most central of the bridges that spanned the drop and entered through a large wooden door into the house proper. A large entrance hall opened before him, the walls covered with dark oak panelling and adorned with huge portraits of the Duke, the Duke's father and a pantheon of powerful associates. In pride of place was a giant picture of William of Orange mounted on a white horse arriving in Torbay to a cheering crowd to overthrow the King. An event in which the Duke had played a part in arranging and that, in return, had allowed him to accumulate his wealth and influence. There were no family portraits. It was not that kind of room. The room made a statement to visitors.

This is who I am and these are the people I know.

It was a room designed to project power and authority. The master of this house had had a hand in writing history and would have a hand in writing the future. Amongst all the portraits, standing distinctly aloof, was the Osborne crest and its motto, Peace In War.

John Lambert emerged from a door towards the back of the hall and strode towards Peregrine. "Good evening, my Lord," he said formally and gave an ever so slight bow of acknowledgement. "Welcome to Wimbledon. I assume you had a good journey?"

"Yes, very much. I enjoyed the air," replied Peregrine truthfully.

"His Grace is keen to speak with you, but I'm sure you would like to rest after your journey and, tomorrow, his Grace has visitors all day. It may be the day after tomorrow when he can see you."

Peregrine thought at first he was being asked if this was acceptable, but then he realised Lambert was simply informing him of what would happen. His acceptance was taken for granted.

"Fine," he said. "Is a room prepared?"

"Of course. I'll have one of the staff lead you to your room. If there is anything you require during your stay just ask one of the staff."

"Thank you. I do have one question." said Peregrine quickly. "What are the arrangements for Christmas?"

"Arrangements, my Lord?"

"Festivities? Are any parties or events arranged? Is anyone in the family coming here?"

Lambert smiled as he understood the meaning. "I've been informed that several dignitaries will be visiting in the coming weeks, there are two formal dinners planned, but none of this involves the family. I believe his Grace expects to visit Lady Sophia for Christmas day. You are no doubt welcome to accompany him."

Inwardly Peregrine frowned. Christmas with Aunt Sophia and grandfather was not a prospect he wanted to entertain.

"Thanks," he said gloomily. "I'll see my room now."

"Of course, my Lord," replied Lambert. "Follow me."

2nd December 1711

Peregrine didn't rise early. The winter mornings were cold and dark and his bedroom wasn't much warmer. The servants lit a fire in the evening that kept the room comfortably aired, but by morning that was just grey ashes and the room had an unwelcome nip.

Wrapped in bed clothes he looked through the window. His bedroom looked out towards the north west where the grounds of Wimbledon House stretched seemingly endlessly towards the horizon. Early morning mist hovered over the grasslands, rising only to waist height. In the distance a handful of deer bowed their heads to browse the sweet, dew laden grass. Behind them, the naked bones of ash and sycamore woodlands raised their spidery branches to the sky.

It was a scene of innate peace, thought Peregrine. An artificial haven of tranquillity sealed from the world. This was the real power that the family could deploy. That the world outside could be a place of plots, poverty and miserable degradation where wars could rage and kings be overthrown. But in here, in the family's embrace, there could be security and protection. An unwritten promise that declared all would be well... *if you just play your part.*

Peregrine's stomach clenched so hard it was as if a sink hole had opened and consumed his vitals. He couldn't play that part. He didn't want to. It wasn't his part to play. It belonged to William who had spent twenty years rehearsing for the role. They couldn't change the plan at this late stage. The actor suddenly stepping aside on opening night and thrusting the understudy into the bright lights armed only with a handful of half-remembered lines. It wasn't fair!

He had spent the previous day exploring the House. Only Peregrine and his grandfather were in residence, but the house was anything but quiet. It was a constant boiling pot of fervent activity. Servants were everywhere, continuously lighting fires, cleaning previously lit fires, rushing and buzzing around in every room, straightening furnishings, polishing and cleaning, always endlessly cleaning. Peregrine got the impression that an invisible army disappeared into some secret doorways in every room as he entered, only to reappear as he vacated it and start hurriedly resetting it to a pristine state.

Looking out of upstairs windows he had watched coach after coach arrive outside the house, their occupants rushing into the house on some urgent errand. While at another entrance people emerged, climbed into other coaches and clattering off towards London.

Peregrine concluded that, while his grandfather may be the only family member in the house, he was far from alone. The old man may be eighty years old, but he was as busy as he had ever been. His advice, guidance and instruction seemed to be continuously sought and the Duke was only too glad to provide it. He could not retire, the urge to have knowledge of events and to control them was part of his very being.

Peregrine had wandered idly around the house, finding his bearings, admiring the endless portraits and statues. The house had two long galleries where the treasures were displayed. Each gallery was over sixty feet long, almost devoid of furniture, the idea was to stroll along them, admiring the artworks on display. Peregrine did exactly that. He had seen the pictures before, of course, but now he saw them with a new light... the light of his own experience. The landscapes in particular caught his eye. When he had looked at them before he had appreciated their realism, their use of colour and play of light and shade. He had always been intrigued by their impressive depictions of the exotic landscapes of Rome, Venice, Florence and the majestic Alpine valley's of the Tirol. But now those scenes had a personal resonance. Looking at them he felt the warmth of a sun he had felt months ago and recalled a better, happier time. A picture portraying Rome's Colosseum had invoked the memory of walking those streets, gazing up in awe at its crumbling magnificence. He remembered looking down, seeing his feet walking on ancient marble cobbles before the Palatinate Hill and wondering how many people had stood on these stones over the centuries.

The house also had a large library, filled five shelves high with hundreds of books on mainly geography, history and politics. An assortment of sofas and easy chairs provided a place to read or simply peruse.

Having spent yesterday indoors, Peregrine was determined to venture outside today, so after a light breakfast with some tea, he dressed warmly for the time of year and made his way out through the doors on the north side of the house. If Wimbledon House was impressive from the east approach then the west side was awe inspiring. The house was built on a hill which descended down into the private parkland through a series of high walled terraces and several flights of stone steps.

Peregrine pulled his collar up around his neck and strode boldly down the first flight of eleven steps. This led to the first of the three terraces. This terrace formed a courtyard laid with finely set paving stones. On each side it was embraced by the two wings of the house standing three storeys high. Twin fountains were set to the left and right, in summer they would be alive with refreshing clear water several feet high, but in winter they stood silent. Ahead a balustrade of white marble curved gently inwards creating a balcony nearly ninety feet wide from which to view the park beyond. In the centre, a double set of stone steps went left and right, both flights curving gently down to the middle terrace.

The middle terrace was a large area of grass, sometimes used as a place where coaches could stop if it was wished to approach the house from the park side. The middle terrace sat twelve feet below the upper terrace with a formidable stone wall providing sturdy support..

From the front of the terrace a small flight of stairs descended further before branching left and right, both sides continuing down then turning to join on the small lower terrace. This terrace was almost at ground level and formed a square courtyard flanked by wrought iron gates set between eighteen foot high pillars. Directly behind the courtyard three arches formed an enclosed area usually used to conveniently store a collection of wines for the consumption of guests who would often dine here in the warmer months.

A final set of steps led down to ground level. Peregrine turned and looked back. The ramparts to the first terrace were a good twelve feet high. The wall to the terrace above that another eighteen feet and the upper terrace wall another twelve feet. Above that the house rose a further three storeys in height and the twin staircase towers rose even further. The overall effect was of a gargantuan building, a mighty yet elegant fortress. Peregrine had seen it often, but it never failed to impress. That was what it was designed to do.

Wimbledon House had, at one time, been called Wimbledon Manor and Wimbledon Palace when it had been owned by King Charles I who had purchased it for his queen. It had fallen into disrepair during the civil war years and, afterwards, the newly restored queen had sold it to the Earl of Bristol whose widow sold it to Peregrine's grandfather.

It was quite literally a house fit for a king, a fact not lost on the Duke.

Peregrine looked at it from the park and it struck him as a cold place. Since his wife's death the Duke lived here alone. His daughters were married. His sons were either dead or estranged. His favourite grandson, William, now buried. For all its obvious grandeur the house seemed to lack a soul. There was no love here. For all the people that worked and lived in it, or that came and went, it was not a home. It was a place of work, and the Duke treated it as such.

Peregrine pulled his coat closer round himself, turned and walked out into the park.

A couple of hours later he returned to the House, made his way up through the terraces and into one of the long galleries. One of the man servants was waiting for him to return and said that the Duke would like to see him. Peregrine had expected it, of course, so removed his coat and followed the servant to one of the living rooms where he was shown in.

The Duke was waiting, warming himself in front of a roaring fire. Peregrine winced as the door closed behind him with a loud thud as if to emphasise that there was no longer any escape. The Duke beckoned him over to one of the couches. It swallowed him in a comfortable, if slightly disconcerting, fashion. The Duke remained standing, watching him with the scrutiny of a hawk.

Peregrine was aware that his grandfather was making every effort to appear friendly and engaging. He could have seen Peregrine in his office, but he had chosen more informal surroundings. Now he attempted a smile at his grandson, but it only seemed to come over as a forced grin.

"Ever since William died I've been needing to speak to you, Pip," began the Duke. "There are certain matters that need to be settled. Family matters." He shuffled uncomfortably, "I know this isn't a good time, with dear William only just buried, but I am afraid it cannot wait. Time is a luxury we simply do not have. The future must be… secured." His dark eyes stared at Peregrine as if trying to discern if his meaning was being taken or even if he was making any impression at all.

Peregrine held his face rigidly blank, giving nothing away until he knew what was expected of him. He had grown up in his brother's shadow. William was the one in the light. Peregrine felt uncomfortable under the Duke's penetrating gaze.

"Are you aware you have now become the Earl of Danby?" the Duke asked.

Peregrine was suddenly startled. No, that hadn't occurred to him. "William is the Earl of Danby," he blurted, then wished he hadn't.

"*Was*," corrected the Duke forcefully. "And now that title comes to you. Whether you like it or not, you are on a path that will lead to you, eventually, becoming the Duke of Leeds when I die."

"My father…" began Peregrine weakly.

"Your father!" scoffed the Duke, turning away with obvious distaste. He paused, giving himself a moment to regain his composure and then turned back to Peregrine. "It pains me to say this, Pip, but I am afraid your father is a wastrel. A charlatan. An inebriated no-mark destined for penniless oblivion!" He paused, once again fighting to regain his composure.

He sighed and then spoke gently, "My only concern is that this family's name and fortune does not follow him. I looked to your brother William to ensure this. " His eyes turned to focus on Peregrine, "And, of course now...to you."

"I am not prepared..." began Peregrine then stuttered to a halt. His mind searched for the right words to express his helplessness, but failed. "I was not ever told....I mean...William was always the one."

The Duke nodded in solemn understanding. "Yes, well, things change, lad," said the Duke firmly. He sighed and softened his tone "Undoubtedly, you would prefer circumstances were different. As I do. And, in some corner of Heaven, I am sure William certainly does. But they are not. We are not masters of the times. We do not dictate our destiny. It is handed to us by the contrivance of others or the whims of capricious fate. All we can do is struggle to keep our heads above the waterline."

Peregrine steeled himself, "Yes but some things are certain. Despite your reservations my father will be the 2nd Duke of Leeds...not I."

The Duke smiled, "Technically, yes. Your father will have the title, for a while. But it will be a name without substance. I cannot rely on him, I never have been able to. I need someone that I can rely on to look after the family's interests. Whatever their title may be." He paused and let that sink in.

"To me?" said Peregrine hesitantly. "You expect me to be the Duke, not my father?"

"In essence. Yes."

"Even while he is still alive?"

"Yes. It was always my intention to turn to William, you see, but, well, he isn't here any more..."

"And you expect my father to agree to this?" began Peregrine.

The Duke's friendly façade was dropped, "Your father will not be consulted. I will see that you are elevated to the House of Lords as 3rd Baron Osborne."

"The House of..." spluttered Peregrine.

"Yes," said the Duke with finality. He smirked, "As for your father, well, I'm sure he will be happier at Portsmouth or Greenwich or where ever it is he spends his time these days. Playing with his ships."

"But I know nothing of politics."

The Duke smiled. "You will learn. As we all had to..."

His gaze momentarily slipped as if recalling a distant time. The Duke had played a part in overthrowing the King - replacing James II with Queen Mary and William of Orange. The so-called *Glorious Revolution*. But Mary and William had had no children to secure their dynasty. Then Mary had died, leaving William alone. When William had died the crown passed to Mary's sister, Anne. Despite several failed attempts, she hadn't managed to have any children either and it was unlikely now. The nearest obvious candidate was the old Kings' son.

Focussing back on Peregrine he explained "Queen Anne is ill, oh she won't die this year, or even next, but that time is drawing near. She has no heir and the wolves are circling. They will see an opportunity to place young James Stuart on the throne. If that happens...well, I unseated his father so you can imagine the consequences for this family." He paused, wondering if he had said too much, too soon.

"This is all moving too quickly." admitted Peregrine, his head spinning trying to take it all in.

The Duke sighed and came from the fire to sit in the couch opposite Peregrine. "I understand, and you are right. It is all happening suddenly. But there is time...time to get accustomed to it. Take some time. Think about what I have said and what you need to do. I merely needed to give you some advance warning of how things will eventually play out. So they won't be too much of a shock when they do occur."

He smiled fondly, "Believe me, Pip, I don't intend to die for quite a while yet!" He paused, "And we can't keep calling you *'Pip'*! It's just not appropriate for the Earl of Danby."

5th December 1711

Peregrine had thought about everything his grandfather had said for the rest of that day and most of the night. Sleep eluded him until the early hours when, finally, he was so tired he succumbed without realising it.

When he awoke the next morning the previous days problems had lost their urgency. Even though they still occupied his mind, somehow the new morning brought a glimmer of hope and the future didn't seem quite as daunting as it had the previous day. After all, for the moment there was a pause. The Duke was still very much alive and conducting affairs the same as always. Any responsibilities, or any confrontation with his father when he discovered he was a Duke in name only, were still off in the future.

There was still time. Time to adjust. Time to get things straight in his head. Time to come to terms with the fact that William wasn't there any more to hide behind. That Peregrine was now the Earl of Danby – heir to the Osborne fortune - not his brother. Yes, there was still time... and he needed to make the best use of it while he could.

As he had sat in the great library at Wimbledon House that morning, laying back in a soft chair before a roaring fire, his mind turning the thoughts over and over again, he knew he could not stay there. Although there was comfort and familiarity at Wimbledon, that was really the problem. It was a symbol of the family, of its authority and his looming responsibilities. It was really his grandfather's house, not his. It was close to everything the Duke lived for, power and control, and at the same time far away from all the things he wanted nothing to do with, such as his children.

Peregrine could never see himself ever calling it home.

I've a good mind to sell this place when I own it, Peregrine had thought to himself which had caused him to smile at the outlandish idea. Then his smile had faded, perhaps it wasn't so ridiculous after all. It *would* be his, he could do whatever he liked with it. He abruptly banished the thought, it wasn't a pressing concern.

But it did start a train of thought. Peregrine realised that he didn't really have a home. He lived in other people's homes. The family owned a fabulous collection of houses, but Wimbledon was where the Duke lived, Kiveton was his mother's, Badminton was his sister's, Easton Neston was his aunt's and so on. He was welcome to visit any of them, but be couldn't call any of them his home. He was a guest in them all.

Peregrine had been born at Mymms Park in Hertfordshire. At that time the Osborne family seat had been Thorpe Hall, in Thorpe Salvin, Yorkshire. Thorpe originally belonged to Peregrine's great-grandfather, who had bought the property in 1636. When Peregrine's grandfather became Duke of Leeds, nearly sixty years later, he had decided that the old hall was not grand enough for the important person he had become, so he arranged for Kiveton Hall to be constructed nearby. The family had moved to Kiveton when Peregrine was eight. As the friction between the Duke and his son had descended into downright hostility the Duke began to take more of an interest in his grandsons. William and Peregrine were taken from Kiveton and educated on the continent. In many ways Kiveton itself was unfamiliar to Peregrine, a distant memory.

But Kiveton's rural location, surrounded by small villages - the more he had thought about it the more it began to exert an unfamiliar attraction for him. If his home was to be found anywhere, it might be in the fields and villages of his half forgotten childhood.

By the next day his mind was made up. He remembered his mother and sister Mary inviting him to Kiveton for Christmas.

At the time, it had seemed a pointless expedition, but now, he felt a need to reconnect with a simpler, more carefree time, somewhere from a memory.

At the very least it was away from his grandfather's paternal lecturing. Perhaps going there was a good idea, after all.

Wimbledon House had a range of coaches and a stable of horses available for family use. All Peregrine needed to do was inform John Lambert of his intentions to take a coach to Kiveton and Lambert had made all the arrangements over the next couple of days.

The coach would take Peregrine into London where there would be a change of horses to take Peregrine's coach onwards to the next horse changing post. The horses and post-boys from Wimbledon would return to home. In a series of such journey's, from post to post, the coach would make its way northwards. From London to St Albans, from there to Towcester where Peregrine would spend the night at his Aunt's house, Easton Neston. Then onwards to Leicester, Nottingham and, finally, the area between Rotherham and Worksop where Kiveton was located. If all went well it would take five days.

Chapter Two

Elizabeth Mirfin opened the cottage door and ran out into the yard. A chill wind blew down the hill from Kiveton, blowing her long, black hair back behind her, opening her neck to the elements. She shivered and pulled her scarf tighter. It was a bright, winter afternoon. The sky was cloudless and painted a wonderful lapis lazuli blue. There was dusting of snow on the ground, not that much but the air was cold enough that she knew the snow wouldn't be going anytime soon. She rushed across the yard to the forge and, with relief, got inside and closed the door hurriedly behind.

A soothing warmth engulfed her. The forge was always hot, unbearably so in summer, but now, in December, the heat was almost an illicit pleasure. As a child she had always spent time here when she could. Watching her father manhandling iron, fashioning wonderful shapes from the blistering hot steel that shone like the sun. The warmth and familiarity of the forge invoked a deep comfort that stretched back through Elizabeth's twenty-odd years.

For a moment she paused, watching her father holding some gleaming shard expertly on the anvil while her young brother, Henry, hit it with the hammer. Henry was an enthusiastic eighteen year old, keen to learn the trade and glad to be pulling his weight. They worked well together she thought idly. Father and son, master blacksmith and apprentice. Yes, Henry would make a good blacksmith in his own right one day. She found herself smiling fondly.

"Come on, you two, when you have some time there are some surprises back in the house. "

Robert Mirfin stood straight and looked at his daughter questioningly. "Surprises? I don't like surprises," he said gloomily.

"I do," said Henry with a laugh and put down the hammer he was holding. "Let's go".

"We've work to do," said Robert.

Henry sighed, "Nothing that can't wait a while. And I need a break."

"A break, he says," scoffed Robert. "When we only stopped for lunch a couple of hours ago. My father would say we don't stop till it's done!" But, nevertheless, Robert was already washing his hands.

"Well, from what you and Uncle Jack say, that work ethic didn't make him any happier." said Elizabeth.

Robert shrugged, "It's true. He was a grumpy old so-and-so. I take more after my mother."

Elizabeth and Henry exchanged glances and then burst out laughing.

All three made there way back across the yard to the cottage. Elizabeth thrust open the door. The door opened into the kitchen. Almost everything happened in this room,. This was where food was cooked, where it was served on the large wooden table. This was where the family met, talked and relaxed in the old chairs by the walls. This was even where they occasionally indulged in a hot bath in front of the fire. But that was an extravagance, most of the bathing occurred in the outhouse with cold water. Next to the kitchen was the living room where the easy chairs were and where Robert could sit and have a smoke in the evenings. There were two other rooms upstairs, Robert Mirfin's bedroom and another room that Elizabeth and Susanna shared. Henry slept in the kitchen on a bed that folded away when not needed. None of the rooms were large so heat from the fire easily heated them. But overall, the cottage had a cosy, homely feel.

Their youngest sister, Susanna, turned as they entered. "I think it's ready." said the fourteen year old.

"What is?" demanded Robert.

"Never you mind," scolded Elizabeth. "That's a surprise for later. Now. What day is this?"

"Sunday, everyone knows that," said Susanna excitedly. "We had church this morning."

Elizabeth sighed in exasperation, "It is St Nicholas Day!"

"Oh aye," admitted Susanna. "I think they mentioned that. I don't pay any heed to what's being said. I just like joining in the singing."

"Nah, it's not real music," mumbled Robert. "Not like the psalms when I was a lad."

"Anyway," interrupted Elizabeth before the conversation went totally off subject. "It's St Nicholas Day and so the start of Christmas. And it's time for presents."

Henry and Susanna brightened up immediately but Robert sighed, "I don't hold with these new ways of doing things. Christmas is meant to start on Christmas Day which is three weeks away. St Nicholas Day? What's that? Presents? Hah! When I was young we didn't have any Christmas at all, in fact anyone found celebrating Christmas would have been in trouble. It was illegal!"

"Yes, Pa, we know how much better things were in your day," said Elizabeth sarcastically. "But things have changed now and I am determined to drag this family into the 18th century."

"Where's my present?" shouted Susanna. "Can I have mine first?"

"Yes, yes. Sit round the table and I'll go and get them." said Elizabeth. She reached into a cupboard, pulling out three nicely wrapped parcels and then joined the others at the table. "Now, let me see, I think this is yours, Susanna."

She passed the parcel over to Susanna who took it and eagerly pulled off the wrapping. She held up a bonnet adorned with tiny flowers and finished with pink ribbons. Susanna hurriedly tidied her long, dark hair then pulled on the bonnet, tying the ribbons under her chin. The bonnet framed her grinning face as she ran to the mirror. She stood in front of it, turning this way and that to see how it suited.

"Oh, it's great. Thanks." she enthused. Elizabeth smiled at how the bonnet showed off her sister's round, cherubic face and how her unruly black hair tumbled out of it in such a casual, wanton way. Susanna had always been such a cheerful child, but Elizabeth noticed, perhaps for the first time, that she was becoming a beautiful woman too.

Elizabeth laughed and passed another parcel to Henry. "And here is yours." She got up and went into the other room.

Henry took the small package and opened it gently. Inside was a small, curved, metal hook. He examined it with a frown, "I think it's a fish hook."

Elizabeth appeared, standing in the doorway holding a long fishing rod as tall as herself. "I think it fits on this somehow," she said with a grin.

Henry sprang out of his chair and ran over to her. "My own fishing rod! I won't have to borrow Pa's any more. Thanks." He hugged her briefly, a broad smile across his face.

Elizabeth went back and sat at the table, then passed third package over to Robert. "And finally, yours, Pa," she said quietly.

He looked at her deeply, "How much is all this costing..." he began.

"Shh," she said and held his hand. "Just open your present, Pa."

Robert gently pulled the wrapping off a square package about six inches on each side. Inside was a small, wooden frame and in it, a charcoal drawing of a woman. He looked up, his eyes glistening slightly. "It's Mary, it's your Ma... how did you?"

Elizabeth smiled. "I drew it years ago, just for amusement really. I'd forgotten I had it, but then I came across it a few months ago and thought you might like it."

Robert looked at the drawing intensely, "You've a good eye," he admitted slowly. "You've really captured her there. Thanks."

Roberts wife, Mary, had died about eight years ago. It had been a difficult time, Elizabeth's older sister had died that same year of consumption. And their baby sister, Anne, had died only three years later aged five. But they had pulled through it and things were looking up. Although Elizabeth noticed there was a world weary spectre haunting Robert's eyes that never seemed to completely go away.

Robert drew another parcel out from under the table and passed it over to Elizabeth. "And this must be yours," he said with a smile.

She laughed, "I thought you didn't believe in presents?"

He raised his eyebrows, "I guess I forgot that I didn't."

She tore off the wrapping and there was a book. A real book, with hard cover and everything. She gently turned it round in her hands. Opening it gently to read the illustrated title page, *Il Mercurio Italico, A Voyage Made Through Italy in the Years 1646 and 1647.* "It is wonderful," she admitted. "How did you come by this?"

Robert shrugged. "Our Jack was doing some work for Thurcroft Hall and he asked me to help. In payment I asked him to ask if they had any books about foreign places they didn't want. Is it any good?"

Elizabeth was in awe, "A voyage to Italy... yes, it's amazing." Putting the book down, she went over and threw her arms around him. "Thanks, Pa."

He hugged her back rather uncomfortably. "Well, your mother insisted you should learn to read so you may as well have a book or two or it's all for nothing. Personally, I've never missed it. All I need is a decent drawing. Folks describe what they want, I draw it and, if they like it, then I make it. Who needs to write anything down?"

"Pa, you are so…. traditional!"

"Nothing wrong with tradition," replied Robert defensively. "We all know where we stand if we follow tradition."

"Perhaps some folk don't like where they stand," said Elizabeth which a slight touch of sadness.

"I think those folk will be walking an unhappy path. All these changes take some getting used to, sometimes I feel like I'm not sure what's left or right or what's up or down!"

Henry suddenly piped up, "Speaking of which... what's this other surprise?"

"Plum Pudding," announced Susanna, putting a hot bowl on the table, covering it in a plate and then turning it upside down to reveal a steaming dried fruit pudding.

"What in god's name is Plum Pudding!" declared Robert.

"Apparently it's all the rage in London," said Elizabeth. "I got a letter from Aunt Bett and she said she's cooking it for Christmas and she sent me the recipe. "

"You've heard from Bett?" said Robert. "You kept that quiet." His sister, Elizabeth, had worked as kitchen maid at Hooton Hall. After she married, she had secured a position as a cook at a large house in Taunton in Somerset. Apart from the occasional letter they heard little from her.

"It doesn't seem to have any plums in it," commented Henry upon closer inspection.

"No silly! That's because it's raisins," said Susanna.

"Well, it smells great," said Henry.

"Plum Pudding!" scoffed Robert. "Whatever next? Sometimes I wish they'd ban Christmas again. No good will come of all this...this...giddiness. It's just not Christian!"

"Oh, Pa!" complained Elizabeth. "What's Christmas got to do with religion?"

10th December 1711

Peregrine didn't mind travelling. He had spent months travelling across Europe in boats, on horseback and in coaches a lot worse than the one he now found himself in. In fact, he quite enjoyed the changing scenery and seeing new places. Outside the towns, the entire country seemed to consist of grassy fields and stone and timber villages.

And mud, lots of mud. It filled the yards and streets between the cottages. It turned the tracks they traversed into a relentless mass of puddles and quagmire. There hadn't even been that much rain during the journey, just the occasional snow shower. But the snow settled and, where it did, the traffic of boots and wheels quickly squeezed it down into watery mud.

Thankfully, the horses seemed oblivious to it. They trudged manfully onwards, dragging the trundling coach behind them through the ruts and potholes. Inside, Peregrine relaxed as best he could, but his back had started aching after the first day until now he spent his days switching seats and position in a forlorn effort to get relief.

He had spent the last night in a coaching inn between Nottingham and Derby. It had been comfortable and warm. The same could be said for the food that was available, a simple broth with crusty bread, but it had been surprisingly satisfying.

The next morning, after a light breakfast and with new horses they started again northwards. The coach was beginning to look dishevelled by now. The mud and dirt of the road had splashed it's fine paintwork and obscured the Osborne crests on the doors. The floor inside was getting caked in mud from Peregrine's boots and even the upholstery was beginning to look worse for wear.

As the coach had made it's way north the landscape had changed subtly. They were now passing through rolling countryside, over the tops of hills and down into green river valleys. They followed the main road north from Nottingham towards Edwinstowe. When they were south east of Worksop they forked left onto the Sheffield road, a road that passed through several large country estates. This area of north Nottinghamshire was a pastiche of aristocratic estates, all butting up to each other. To the east of the road was Thoresby, belonging to the Earl of Kingston. Further north the road ran between Clumber Park, Queen Anne's hunting grounds and the Earl of Portland's Welbeck Abbey. Then, finally, as they neared Worksop itself, they passed the estate of the Duke of Norfolk.

Worksop was a small market town on the edge of Nottinghamshire. It comprised a main, narrow thoroughfare leading down a gentle hill from the ducal park lands into the market square. Here the road forked, the right heading northwards, the coach took the left fork towards distant Sheffield.

The houses of the town suddenly thinned out into open countryside and the road turned sharply left onto a wide common. In the distance Peregrine could see the smoke rising from the warm fires of Shireoaks to the south. To the north, a thick wood came right up to the edge of the road as the coach clattered westwards. Here they crossed an invisible border, crossing from Nottinghamshire into the West Riding of Yorkshire. The giant county of Yorkshire was a remanent of the medieval Danelaw, the Danes northern stronghold centred on their capital, Jorvik. The Danes had split their lands into three *ridings*, North, East and West, this being the Norse word for *third*.

Beyond the common and wood the road suddenly descended into the small valley of Lindrick Dale. They splashed through Anston Brook as it trickled across the road to join the River Ryton to the south.

Peregrine felt anticipation grow, he leaned out of the coach, searching for the first glimpse of his destination. They were close now. Anston Brook lay on the northern edge of the Kiveton estate.

The coach climbed steeply out of Lindrick Dale, past the woods of the Anston Stones quarry and onto an escarpment. The road emerged onto a ridge that gently descended into a small valley. And there, in the bottom separated by Anston Brook, were the two villages of North and South Anston. They were both tiny hamlets of stone cottages, the nearest of them dominated by the spire of Anston Church while, across the other side of the brook, North Anston clung to the opposite valley side.

The road ran straight for several hundred yards then turned right, dropping down into South Anston. Branching to the left was the entrance drive to Kiveton. Unusually, the drive stretched beyond the boundaries of Kiveton Park itself, running along the southerly edge of South Anston and connecting to the main road.

Peregrine's coach turned left onto the driveway, steering between two orderly lines of lime trees. The trees were set twenty-five feet apart and thirty feet back from the edge of the road. They were tall, majestic trees whose sturdy trunks rose from the ground like the legs of giant elephants. They marked the road more effectively than any signpost . Six hundred of them lined the avenue for over a mile and a half leading across the park.

After half a mile, they came to a stone wall leading left and right. Straight ahead, two mighty stone pillars rose into the air, topped with octagonal stones. Hanging between the pillars were two wrought iron gates painted black and topped with gold spikes. In the middle of each gate was the coat of arms of the Duke of Leeds. When closed, the gates formed a depiction of a large black bird, with a fierce beak, its wings outstretched to show its formidable size. It was probably intended to be an eagle, but it's black colour and large beak had earned it the name, the Crow Gate.

To the right, a small road led back down into Anston. To the left, a lane continued southwards and uphill, following the low stone wall. It led to where the hunting dogs were kept, so it had earned the name Dog Kennel Lane.

The coach continued through the Crow Gate, guided unerringly between the double line of lime trees. The heads of deer shot up to look in their direction as the gates clattered shut behind them. It climbed up an incline then topped a small hill and there, before him, was Kiveton Park. It stretched off to the south and south west as far as the eye could see. Open heath was dotted with small spinneys of trees and clumps of wild shrubs. In the near distance the afternoon sun glistened on the water of a large pond. To the north a large wood could be seen and, beyond it, just visible, lifting its head above the treeline, the square, Norman steeple at Todwick. The avenue of limes continued westwards for over a mile, dropping slightly before rising to the horizon where, perched on the edge before the ground tumbled away into the Rother valley, stood Kiveton Hall.

The hall was in a wide, open Queen Anne style, symmetrical around the frontal elevation. The front itself had a Palladian derived pediment mounted on four huge pillars as high as the house giving it the impression of a greek temple. The triangular pediment held the crest of the Duke of Leeds fashioned in the finest stone from the local Castle quarry. Across the front of the house were twenty-two mullioned windows, eleven on each storey, stretching across the entire width. Above all this was a garret storey built into a part tiled and part lead roof with eight evenly spaced windows.

On either side of the main house were the two giant pavilions, built to a similar design but only two thirds the height of the main residence. On each, six sets of large windows looked out onto the gardens.

Peregrine had seen it all before, years ago, but as a child. Now, with more of an understanding of the architecture, symbolism and authority it projected, he saw it again with adult eyes.

He was in awe and more than a little daunted. This is my inheritance, he thought to himself, nervously. It would be an immense undertaking and a huge responsibility.

As the coach way came to an end it met a wall which spanned its entire width. The wall bowed out towards them. In the centre of the wall two large pillars rose with two large gates hung in the middle.

The coach came to a halt and turned in front of the gates. Then it suddenly lurched violently forwards with a loud crack.

It stopped as if it had hit a sudden wall and Peregrine found himself hurled out of his seat.

Unhurt, he opened the door and, with as much dignity as he could muster, climbed out and ceremoniously brushed his clothes.

"Apologies, my lord," said one of the coachmen as he looked under the coach. "The axle appears to have broken."

Peregrine smiled. He wasn't surprised really after the five days of battering the coach had endured. "Well, at least it got us here. We can ask little more. Can it be fixed?"

The coachman shrugged, "I think it will need a completely new axle."

"Well, I won't be needing it for a long time. I'll leave it with you to make the arrangements."

"Aye, my lord," said the coachman.

Peregrine continued through the high gates and into the first of two huge terraces that formed the gardens. He walked up the central path which was thirty feet wide. On both sides of the path was set a line of eight cypress conifers, each a man's height and beyond that two square flag gardens formed from Yew hedges. Peregrine ascended the two sets of stone stairs to the upper terrace. This terrace was even larger than the lower one consisting of four square lawns set with statues in each corner and centrally. Between the square lawns were ornamental flower beds, bare at this time year, but by spring the house gardeners would have planted them up with vivid swathes of colour.

He climbed the final set of stairs and pushed open the door to enter the house. He found himself in the Great Hall. A huge plymouth marble fireplace dominated one wall and, above it, a huge portrait of Charles I. On reflection Peregrine found it strange that a family that had deposed one king should have a portrait of another, previously deposed, king in such pride of place. Whatever the mixed message, it was a fine portrait and it did emphasise the family's connection to royalty, one way or another. Other than the portraits that filled the walls, there were also some fine statues positioned in favourable locations. Hercules, Venus, Paris, Diana and a truly beautiful statue of Lucretia.

A servant entered on some errand and Peregrine called to him. "I am the Earl of Danby. I have just arrived, could you inform Lady Bridget I am here."

The servant bowed, "Of course, my lord. We were informed. Lady Bridget is in the Drawing Room. If you follow me, my lord."

Peregrine followed the man out of the Great Hall and up two flights of stairs to the second floor then through a large, wooden door into a large room. This room was also filled with an abundance of paintings, but also over a dozen chairs and other assorted furniture. His mother, Lady Bridget, was sitting in of the chairs near the fire.

"The Earl of Danby, my Lady," announced the servant, showing Peregrine into the Drawing Room and then closing the door behind.

"Pip!" said his mother without rising from her chair. "So, you decided to join us for Christmas after all?"

Peregrine walked closer to the fire. It was blazing, but the room was so large that its heat was only felt in the nearer half of it. "Aye, I was hoping this would be more suitable for Christmas than Wimbledon. There was only grandfather and me there, anyway."

"Oh, I doubt that," said another, man's voice. For the first time, Peregrine noticed someone else was sat in another chair. He was dressed all in bottle green tunic with black trousers and shiny, knee high boots. His boots shone they were so well polished. He made Peregrine, who still wore the dust of his journey, feel suddenly underdressed. He recognised his sister's new husband, Henry Somerset. "What I mean," said Somerset. "Is that I've never known the Duke to be alone for more than an hour without receiving some visitor or other."

"Yes," admitted Peregrine. "He was... preoccupied."

"It really is irritating. Whenever I've needed to see him on some business or other and I've had to wait, like some naughty schoolboy outside the headmaster's office."

Lady Bridget laughed. She said to Peregrine, "You know Lord Somerset, don't you, Pip?"

"Yes, of course," replied Peregrine. "Is my sister around?"

"She's off somewhere," said Somerset, idly. "I've given up trying to keep track. She has the most innate ability to disappear, usually when she's most needed."

"She's always been the same," replied Lady Bridget. "She has her own mind."

"A headstrong child can be annoying," remarked Somerset. "A headstrong wife can be downright inconvenient! I should know, I'm on my third!"

Peregrine smiled weakly as his mother laughed loudly. He had only been here a few minutes and already they were getting on his nerves.

"I think I'll go to my room. It's been a long journey," he said.

"Of course, dear," said his mother. "I think they've made the Green Bedroom up for you. Do you remember where that is?"

"South west wing?" he replied hesitantly. "First floor?"

"That's right. You can just follow the corridor round, it's easier than going down the stairs."

"I'll find it," conceded Peregrine. "Good evening, mother. Lord Somerset."

"Call me Henry," said Somerset. "We are brothers-in-law now."

Peregrine nodded. "Good evening, Henry," and turned and left.

His mother watched the closed door for a while. "I hope Christmas will allow him to move on from William's funeral."

"They were close, I gather," replied Somerset.

"Perhaps his only real friend," she said worryingly. "Which is a pity, I'm not very good at finding people friends. Only wives and husbands."

"As I can confirm," he said with a smile.

"Yes," she agreed. "Speaking of which... where has that wife of yours got to?"

He shrugged helplessly.

Peregrine started off to find his room. Apart from main part of Kiveton Hall there were two pavilions, one to the north and one to the south. Each pavilion was itself shaped like a square bracket with two outward facing wings. So, the house had four wings, north-east, north-west, south-east and south-west. He followed the corridor to the end of the main house, where it turned a corner into the south pavilion. He then followed it along, past the corridor to the south-east wing and to where it turned another corner into the south-west wing.

Before he could reach the final corner he heard giggling from further down the corridor. As he turned the corner he saw his sister, Mary, approaching, accompanied by one of the young footmen.

"Pip, you're here," she said with some surprise. "I was just checking to see if you were in your room. I think you're in the green one."

"I've just arrived," said Peregrine. He noticed how the footman continued past them, but as he did so he seemed to exchange a glance with Mary. "I spoke to mother and she said I was down here."

"Yes, right on the end, away from everything," she commented hazily. "Probably a good idea actually. I'm expecting Christmas to be dull, dull, dull."

"I'm not looking forward to it," he admitted. "It's never been my favourite time of year... too cold!" He paused then said, "Your husband was wondering what had happened to you."

"He's never happy unless he knows where I am every minute," she said with annoyance.

"I guess that's a good quality in a husband, isn't it?"

"Is it? He's my husband, not my keeper!" Her face darkened. But then she looked at Peregrine and the look vanished. "But, never mind that. It's my problem. Your room's down there on the end." She smiled rather weakly, "Try to make the best of it, anyway. It's been a depressing few weeks for everyone, but, I guess, for you especially. Maybe a change of scenery will do you good. I hope you manage to enjoy yourself. "

"Thanks," he said without much enthusiasm.

12th December 1711

Tom Crowther enjoyed his job. He had started as a stable boy at Kiveton where he worked with the horses. There were lots of horses at Kiveton, all sorts of different sizes and used for all sorts of different jobs. The horses provided the muscle that drove the entire estate from pulling wagons and coaches, to farming, to the fine pedigrees that were used for leisure and hunting. The only missing type of horse at Kiveton were race horses. The Duke did not enjoy gambling of any sort, he considered it to be the pastime of fools. He regarded risk as something that needed to be managed and planned for not as a source of entertainment.

When he had started, Crowther had simply cleaned the stables and fed the horses, but then he had graduated to ensuring the horses were in good condition. After some time he was in charge of the carriage horses that were used to pull the coaches, at that point he had stable boys working for him. Then he took responsibility for more than just the animals, but for the vehicles themselves. This was a wider responsibility, the coaches needed cleaning, repairing, polishing to ensure they were always in prime condition should the family need them.

The coach that had come up from Wimbledon wasn't Crowther's direct responsibility as it didn't belong to Kiveton, but it belonged to Wimbledon House which made it family property. So when it arrived at Kiveton it was assumed that Crowther would adopt it and do everything to ensure it would be ready when it was needed again, presumably to return to Wimbledon. Sadly, that also meant he was responsible for any repairs.

Which is why he found himself standing before a broken

coach in the coach house and wondering what work would be required. The coach was supported up on wooden blocks while the wheelwrights, that worked for Kiveton, had removed the front wheels and then unbolted the front axle. The axle was a long rod with conical spindles on each end.

The wheelwright came over the Crowther holding the axle. It had snapped into two pieces about three quarter of the way along its length. The break formed a sharp, ugly break. The wheelwright held both pieces in his hands.

"It's completely broken, Mr Crowther," he said, holding the two pieces up. "Broken right in two. We may need a new one."

Crowther nodded reluctantly. "That sounds like it will be expensive."

The wheelwright shrugged, "The coach won't go anywhere without it."

Crowther nodded, "Can you mend it?"

He shook his head, "Not me, I do wood, you see. Wheels are made of wood. It's carpentry really."

"Fine," said Crowther with some irritation. "Then how?"

"You would need a blacksmith."

Crowther sighed, the stables didn't really have a lot of use for blacksmiths. Crowther came from the village of Todwick next to the Hall. He was sure there was no blacksmith there. "Where's the nearest? Brookhouse?" he asked.

"There is one there, but there's one in Wales." Wales was the village to the west of Kiveton. "Down to the crossroads, turn right then follow the lane to the bottom."

"Right," said Crowther. He called across to one of the workers on the other side of the coach house. "You there! Get that wagon ready with one of the mares." He turned back to the wheelwright. "I need you to put both pieces of that axle on that wagon. Then get on with the other stuff you've got to do. I'll take it myself."

"Yes, sir," said the wheelwright.

Less than an hour later Crowther drove the wagon out of the stable block. He drove through the black gates between two stone pillars, then turned the wagon left towards the village of Wales. He crossed in front of the large windows of the North Pavillion then followed the black fencing in front of the Hall. To his left, behind the fencing, a huge courtyard led to Kiveton Hall's main entrance, set high at the top of a flight of stone steps. Crowther continued on past the fencing and the windows of the South Pavillion, the track descending down to the junction where it met the main Anston to Wales road. He turned right at the junction, continuing along the road between high hedges. The road undulated through several small hills and troughs. After a few miles cottages began to appear on the side of the road and he knew he had entered Wales village. A road went off to the left, up a small hill where the main part of the village and the church were. The main road curved to the right then straightened and, where it did, another road went right. Crowther turned the wagon and followed the road to the right. It wound gently right and left down the narrow lane past quaint limestone cottages with slate roofs. Eventually, to the right, there was a small hill and then, past it, a small track leading to the right.

Crowther reined the horse up the track which extended for fifty yards before opening out into a large yard. To the left was a small pond while, in front of it, was a large wooden hut with smoke teaming from a metal chimney in the roof. To the right of the yard a small cottage stood. Basic but well cared for. He stopped the wagon in the yard in front of the hut and climbed down. A youngster, probably about twenty, with unruly dark hair emerged from the hut, wiping his hands on a cloth.

"Can I help?" asked Henry Mirfin.

"I hope so," said Crowther. "I'm Thomas Crowther, stable manager at Kiveton Hall. We have a coach with a broken axle that we would like repairing."

"Do you have it with you?" asked Henry.

"Certainly," replied Crowther and extracted both axle parts from the wagon. Henry inspected them. "Do we need a new one?" asked Crowther.

"Maybe," said Henry uncertainly. "I'll ask my Pa. Pa!" he shouted.

A bald man in his fifties came out of the hut. He was tall, thin framed but developing a middle aged belly. He was wearing a long, thick apron. "Yup?" he asked.

"We need a new coach axle if it is possible," explained Crowther.

Robert Mirfin took the pieces from his son's hand and examined them. "This is a coach axle, you say? Like from a wagon?"

"Yes", said Crowther. "From a passenger coach."

Robert scratched his head, "Most wagon axle's we get round here are wood. When they break I usually make a brace to hold them together. But this is entirely metal."

"Can you reproduce it?"

"Well, I could, but that'd be expensive."

"Aye, I thought so..."

"It'd be cheaper if I just fix it."

Crowther brightened, "You can do that?"

"I should think so. It's a fancy axle, but it's just metal at the end of the day. I just need to furnace weld it together."

"Well, that would be good. How long would it take?"

Robert looked at the broken axle again, "Um, I could probably do it tomorrow. I'd like to make sure it's a proper job, not rushed or anything."

"It isn't urgent. As you say, it's better it's done properly than quickly."

"Well, that's fine then. Leave it with me and I'll have Henry bring it back up to the hall day after tomorrow."

Crowther smiled, "Oh, you'll deliver it? That's great. I'll make sure that they are expecting you and there'll be someone there to fit it."

Crowther held out his hand and Robert shook it warmly. Then he clambered back on the wagon, coaxing the horse round to start the journey back to the Hall.

That's that sorted, he thought happily and smiled to himself.

14th December 1711

Elizabeth awoke early and groaned. How she longed for summer when she could awake to bright sunlight and pleasant weather. With the onset of winter, her warm bed had started to exercise an almost irresistible lure every morning. It was an act of will to put her feet to the floor. The splash of icy cold water as she washed was as sharp as a slap in the face. But at least it drove out the last vestiges of sleep. She dressed and went to wake brother Henry who was sleeping on a bed in the kitchen.

He groaned in response to Elizabeth's fervent shaking. With resignation he clambered into his clothes, eyes only half open, and made his way to the wash house. A blind adherence to routine rather than any conscious thought was guiding him round.

Robert was already up. He was having a basic breakfast of bread and hard cheese. The fire in the kitchen was already lit, it gave a welcome warmth.

"I could have lit the fire, Pa," she said.

He huffed, "I've been lighting fires my entire life, why stop now?"

She sat down at the table, broke herself off some bread and nibbled it idly. "Pa, have you made that coach piece for the Hall?"

"Hope so. I'll check it this morning, but it should be ready for Henry to take back."

"I was wondering," she said slowly. "Could I go with him?"

"It doesn't take two. It's big, but there'll be boys up at the hall to help. They need to fix it to their coach, we know nothing about that, I just make the thing."

"Aye, but, well, I don't get to go to the Hall and I'm curious."

He stopped eating and looked at her through narrowed eyes. "Curious? Aye, I can see how you would be. It's a different world up at the Hall. More in common with the world in those books of yours."

"Well yes, quite so," she said, uncomfortable at being assessed so easily. "And I'd quite like to see it. And since Henry's got to go up there..." her voice trailed off.

He thought about it for a second then resigned himself. "I don't see any harm in it," he said with a smile. "You can keep him company."

"Keep who company?" said Henry, coming back into the kitchen.

"Looks like you've got a passenger," said Robert wryly.

After breakfast, Henry went out to the stables to get the wagon ready and, with Robert's help, manhandled the new axle onto it. Henry and Elizabeth jumped on board and, with a flick of the reins Old Sam, their piebald stallion, was effortlessly pulling their wagon out of the yard and onto the lane towards the centre of the village.

The village of Wales, where they lived, was little more than a small hamlet, a cluster of cottages around a crossroads. The village had existed for hundreds of years. It was mentioned in the Domesday Book, six hundred years earlier. In all those centuries it's character had changed little. It was primarily a farming community, but there had always been blacksmiths here.

At the crossroads, the wagon turned left, following the road to South Anston. The morning was thankfully dry, but it was still cold. The road they rode was little more than a track, but the cold had at least hardened the muddy ruts into a passable surface. Small, stone cottages lined the road, their walls several feet thick, their roofs occasionally thatched, but mostly made of grey Yorkshire slate.

Slowly, the wagon left the village entirely and entered open country. After a couple of miles they reached a junction. A road split from the main road and went left and up a steady incline called Red Hill. To the right of this road a low wall marked the boundary of the Kiveton estate. Henry guided Old Sam up the road to the left. They climbed up Red Hill onto the top of a raised escarpment. As they cleared the top of the hill the road levelled out on to the flat. As the wintry clouds cleared, a bright lantern of sunlight suddenly illuminated the fields to each side and there, off to the right of the road, two hundred yards ahead was Kiveton Hall.

The Hall was an imposing presence, rising from the fields around. A powerful rectangle of stone with two huge wings. It rose two storeys high topped with a sloping, part tiled roof. It was the largest building Elizabeth had ever seen. Dwarfing the tiny cottages or little church of Wales. Even challenging the spires of Laughton-en-le-Morthen or Anston which rose like a fingers pointing the way to heaven and could be seen for miles around.

As they proceeded up the road they drove past a huge wing. Revealed behind, was the rest of the building. The wings that had seemed so impressively magnificent just belonged to the South Pavilion. Beyond it was a huge courtyard and, across that, yet another towering pavilion. And between the pavilions, like the back of a giants throne, was the main hall. Even higher, even wider, even larger. An imposing symbol of wealth.

That was the point, thought Elizabeth, just like all the windows. Row after row of crystal panes that formed windows as high as the Mirfin's cottage. A towering wall of glass in an age when most people's windows were small and few. They caught the sun, reflecting dazzling beams of light, making Elizabeth raise her hand to her eyes.

The windows were a statement, she thought, that the people who lived here commanded resources on an unimaginable scale.

The wagon passed the Hall proper and followed the line of the high wall until it reached the open gates of the stable block. Henry guided Old Sam through the gates. The wagon pulled up in the stable yard. Henry jumped down and Elizabeth followed more sedately, her eyes roving over the awesome buildings. Henry started getting the repaired axle off the wagon as two men came over from the coach house. Tom Crowther came over with them.

"Take it over to the coach and see if it will suffice," said Crowther to his men. He turned to Elizabeth who was looking around, gripping herself to hold off the cold. Crowther said to her, "Come with me. We may be some time and there's no need for you to freeze with the rest of us. I'll take you somewhere warm."

"Thank you, it would be very welcome," she said.

He led her to a doorway in the corner nearest the wall of the North Pavilion. He opened it then stood aside for her to enter. Inside was a small, room with wooden floors, a fire roaring by the wall and some wooden furniture.

"You can wait here, if you wish. It's warmer. Take a seat, it's one of the servants garret rooms there won't be anyone coming in to bother you."

Elizabeth smiled and lowered herself into one of the wooden seats by the fire. Crowther smiled back then went back out.

She looked round, it was a largely brown and white room. The walls were whitewashed with a dour plainness. Everything else was a dark brown wood, from the fireplace to drawers along one wall to the very chair she was sat on. The floor was dark, oak floorboards. Everything in the room functional, a servants room.

But she was in Kiveton Hall! She couldn't believe it. She had seen it many times *from the outside,* it was, after all, visible at the top of the hill from her bedroom window. She had often wondered what was in it. What treasures did it contain? And now here she was.

She couldn't help a slight creep of disappointment. Well, yes, here she was alright, but in a room that was less than impressive. Little better than their own cottage. Her eyes strayed to the other door in the room, a sturdy, oak door. Her mind raced off in directions another part of her mind immediately chastised her for following.

Where did that lead to?

What was on the other side?

But *who* was on the other side? Whoever it was they

wouldn't be expecting to find her there. And they wouldn't be too impressed with her excuses.

If there was anyone. There might be no one on the other side. It was a large building, there couldn't be people in every part of it all of the time. After all, there wasn't anyone in this room, most likely there wouldn't be anyone in next room either. No one would know if she just took a look.

She rose from her chair and slowly walked to the door. Nervously, she put her ear to it and listened. There was nothing to be heard. Maybe no one was on the other side. Her hand reached down and gripped the brass door knob. It felt cold and smooth. She looked round nervously, but of course she was alone. Her heart quickened and breathing became a little more difficult. She hesitated, dark doubt creeping round the edges of her mind.

If she opened the door she might regret it. But if she didn't open the door, if she left and rode home with Henry, she would spend the rest of her life wondering what was on the other side.

She made up her mind suddenly, banished her reluctance, turned the door knob and pushed the door open.

Nervously she peered round the door. It was an empty corridor. Dark oak floors and pale, yellow walls. There was no one in it and there was a door at the other end. Elizabeth entered, hurried down the corridor and opened the door.

She entered a huge room, over fifty feet long and over thirty feet wide. Giant windows covered one wall, allowing the sun to blaze in so much that Elizabeth found herself squinting it was so bright. The room was adorned with warm, patterned rugs and generous sofas. There was no one in it.

Slowly, she entered. Her eyes gaped wide, the room was full of fabulous objects beyond imagination. White statues stood on pedestals against the walls, a bust of some Roman gentleman, a tall woman draped in fine cloth carrying a hooked sceptre and wearing a crown with a snakes head. There was a statue of a beautiful woman, completely naked standing in a huge sea shell and, next to her, a smaller, angelic figure with a bow and arrow. They looked oddly familiar, from her book on roman mythology that she kept at home. Venus and Cupid perhaps?

But it was the fabulous paintings that really caught her attention. The walls were covered with them, different subjects and different sizes, any one of them would have been a priceless treasure in a normal house.

The ones that drew her attention were the landscapes, exotic locations that she had only read descriptions about were here brought to vivid life with vibrant colours. Four in particular all seemed to be different views of the same place. People wandering idly through a huge square surrounded by pillared buildings, the dome of a magnificent cathedral and, standing over them all, a huge Italian tower like a mighty spear piercing heaven.

Her eyes would not stop staring, hungrily absorbing every detail.

Then sudden panic. She shouldn't be here. What if she was discovered? What would she say? She should go back quickly. She turned to make her way back through the door...then froze.

A blonde haired woman stood behind her, watching her. "And what do you think you are doing?" asked the woman.

"I..uh..I was..." stuttered Elizabeth, her mind racing through possible things to say and discarding them all as unsuitable.

"Stealing?" suggested the woman, levelly.

"No!" exclaimed Elizabeth in shock. "No, no, definitely not. I was...um," she sighed. "curious."

"How did you get in here?"

"Through that door," she pointed. "We brought a wheel, or something, to the stables. I was keeping warm in the servants room and I became...curious."

"Wheel? You mean you've repaired Peregrine's coach?" she asked.

"My father and brother have. I just, sort of, came along..." Elizabeth was painfully aware how lame it all sounded as her voice helplessly trailed off.

The woman's eyes narrowed as she examined Elizabeth closely. "You are the blacksmith's daughter?" she asked.

"Yes. I didn't mean any harm. Honest!" Elizabeth sighed, "I shouldn't have come in here, but I just wanted to see what it looked like. I'm sorry."

The woman smiled, much to Elizabeth's relief. "Well, never mind. No harm done, is there. Curiosity is a good thing. We just have to be careful, otherwise, if something goes missing a lot of awkward questions get asked."

"Of course," said Elizabeth. "I've very sorry. I'll be on my way..."

The woman ignored Elizabeth, looking past her at the set of paintings Elizabeth had been looking at. "You like Venice?" she asked.

"Um, oh, is it Venice? I didn't know. I just thought it looked like a beautiful place."

"Yes, Venice," said the woman gently, turning to look at Elizabeth again. "St Marks Square. You are familiar with it?"

"Oh no," said Elizabeth with a laugh. "But I do have a book about a voyage round Italy and I just thought it looked, sort of, familiar."

At that point the door burst open and a rather exasperated Crowther came through. "There you are!" he exclaimed with relief. "You were meant to stay in the room I put you in!" He turned to the blonde woman, "I'm so sorry, Lady Mary."

Mary held her hand up to stop Crowther. "No, no, I asked her to come in here and look at the Vanvitelli's." she lied.

Crowther spluttered to a halt. "You asked her..."

"Yes, she says she likes Venice."

Crowther didn't look convinced, "Did she indeed...well, the coach has been fixed so her brother is waiting to leave."

"Of course," said Elizabeth hurriedly as she gathered herself to leave. Then she stopped and turned to Lady Mary, "Thank you for showing me the pictures, my lady."

"They are there to be admired," said Mary, absently. As Elizabeth turned to leave, Mary said "Actually... we have lots of other things, if you are interested?"

"Interested? Yes, I would be very..."

"Well, how about if you come up here on Saturday, say one o'clock, and I'll organise a little tour?"

"That would be...wonderful," gushed Elizabeth with a grin.

"Well, that's settled then. Saturday it is then. And we'll see if we have anything else that might impress you."

Crowther opened the door and guided Elizabeth through it with his arm. He cast a suspicious glance at Mary as he left.

Mary stood there, smiling to herself. Pip could use a little diversion, she thought. Something to get his mind off William's funeral. Something to cheer him up. They both like Italy. And she is pretty, in a sort of rustic, country girl sort of way. Yes, she might do nicely.

16ᵗʰ December 1711

Peregrine hesitated as he entered the Garden Room, he was through the door before he saw his mother, sister and her husband we already there. He paused, inclined to turn around and leave before he was noticed.

"Ah, Pip dear," came his mother's voice. His heart sank. Too late, he had been seen. "Come and join us."

The Garden Room faced east with two huge windows offering unrestricted views of the grounds. The early morning sun bathed the room. Through the windows stretched the large parterre of the upper terrace. Dew twinkled on the carefully manicured low hedges where, beneath the bare soil, bulbs eagerly awaited the coming spring. Beyond the terraces, the Long Drive stretched, arrow-like between twin lines of lime trees, towards the distant spire of Anston church where it met the main road. Surrounding it all was a misty parkland of grassy plains and gentle copses in the bright morning sunlight. The edges of the park were so far away, they mingled with the distant rolling hills towards Thorpe Salvin and beyond.

It looked welcoming and warm, but Peregrine knew at this time of year the air would carry a bite that heralded the onset of winter. Still, he thought, it would be good to get out.

He lowered himself down into a chair, maintaining an empty place between himself and his mother, who sat at the head of the table, and his sister and brother-in-law who sat across from him. A servant poured some tea into a cup for him. He added some sugar and sipped it quietly.

His mother, Lady Bridget, said "how are you settling in, Pip? Managing to find everything? You haven't been here for quite a while, but I expect you remember where things are."

"I have found most things. Although there have been some changes from what I recall. It seems much more complete than I remember when it was first built."

"Well, it takes time to fill a house this size. There are still lots of rooms I don't know what to do with."

"Like the chapel," said his sister, Lady Mary, with a mischievous grin in Peregrine's direction.

"No," replied his mother with irritation. "Well, not in the way you mean. Obviously, I know what to do with the chapel...and it is on the list. It's just some way down the list because there are other rooms I haven't decided what to do with and they take my attention. Besides, the chapel is such a large room and such a convenient place to store things until I find a place for them."

Peregrine looked around the Garden Room. The floor was covered in italian marble as white as milk with thin veins of grey and orange. The walls were hung with a pale green wallpaper painted with depictions of a variety of flowers in bloom. It created the impression of summer even at that time of year.

"You've done well with this room," he admitted.

Lady Bridget looked around, "I was in two minds about the wallpaper, but I think it works well."

Henry Somerset, Mary's husband, agreed, "It is a delight, madam. And so..." he searched for the word. "Revolutionary."

"Yes," said Mary. "Wallpaper is usually for the inside of cupboards."

"Just so," replied her husband. "Your mother sets a new fashion."

Bridget smiled, "Why thank you, Henry. It is nice to know someone appreciates my taste."

"Well, I like it," agreed Peregrine as he helped himself to some fruit, bread and cheese. "It is a garden room, after all. It makes sense that the inside should resemble the outside"

"Quite," said Bridget, satisfied she had been justified. She looked at Peregrine, "And what have you planned to do today?"

"I haven't given it much thought," he admitted.

"Well, I have decided to go hunting," announced Somerset.

"You did that yesterday," complained his wife.

"Aye, but I saw a particularly large stag in Clumber that managed to elude me. If I don't get it I just know it will bother me."

"Clumber?" said Peregrine. "I thought that was the Queen's hunting park?"

Somerset grinned in a self-satisfied manner. "It was. You see, three or four years ago the Queen asked John Holles, the Duke of Newcastle, to enclose Clumber for a hunting estate and to manage it on her behalf. Which he did. For his trouble he was awarded a thousand pounds a year, but he was also allowed to leave ownership of Clumber to his descendants." Somerset paused for effect, taking a bite of an apple. "Well, the poor man only went and died earlier this year! And he had no heir, just a daughter that he'd already married off. Clumber ended up with his nephew, my good friend Thomas Pelham, younger than yourself actually, Peregrine, but a really excellent chap. Anyway, I think he's in some infernal legal dispute with his aunt, that daughter I mentioned, who probably can't understand why it was left to Thomas. But, never mind that, in the meantime Thomas gets to hunt in it and, as his friend, so do I." He looked at Peregrine, "And you too, if you want to come along?"

"Not just now," declined Peregrine. "But thanks for the offer." Spending the day with Somerset wasn't Peregrine's idea of good use of time. He would rather be on his own.

"You should go, Pip," said his mother. "You're looking quite melancholy and I'm sure lounging around the house isn't helping. Men need to get out and kill things to get the blood back in their cheeks. It's only natural."

"I'm not really in the mood," replied Peregrine.

"There are other ways to put blood back in a man's cheeks," said Lady Bridget thoughtfully. "I received a letter from the Earl of Oxford, his daughter is looking for a husband."

Peregrine groaned. Mary interjected, "Isn't it a bit early for that, mother? Pip's still young he needs to enjoy himself first."

"Enjoy himself? He's just spent two years touring the continent. We all like enjoying ourselves, but we also have to keep our thoughts on the real world. The Earl of Oxford is influential, it's a good family..."

"I didn't know you were proposing I marry the Earl of Oxford," said Peregrine sarcastically.

"Don't be flippant, dear," said his mother condescendingly. "As Henry's story about the Duke of Newcastle shows, we have to be prepared for the future. William understood this..."

Peregrine suddenly rose from the table. "I'll speak to you all later," he said and walked out.

"What have I said?" asked his mother desperately. "It's all true. There's no getting round it."

Mary sighed. "Just leave him alone for now, mother. I'll talk to him later."

It wasn't until much later in the afternoon that Mary managed to find Peregrine. He was in the Saloon, the same room she had met Elizabeth.

He was looking at the four views of Venice, remembering when he was there just a few months previously with William. Life had seemed so wonderful then. So straight forward. They were young, they were wealthy and their futures stretching ahead were bright and untroubled. William's dark, good looks

and, perhaps that extra bit of maturity, had proved an irresistible draw for the women they met on the journey. Peregrine
had gone along with it, cruising effortlessly in William's wake.
People just seemed to want to be close to the Earl of Danby
and, when it became too crowded for them all, well, there was
always the younger brother, waiting in the wings for the left-
overs. The consolation prize, certainly, but a close enough second none-the-less. Peregrine realised now, that they had really
wanted to bask in William's glow and, compared to that, he
himself was just a pale reflection. But what becomes of the
sun's reflection when the sun itself has gone?

"Thinking about Venice?" asked Mary from behind him.

He nodded, "And other things."

"Marriage, perhaps?" she laughed. "I did warn you what
mother was like."

"I feel like I'm trapped in someone else's life," he complained. "It should be William getting set up with the Earl of
Oxford's daughter!"

"Look on the bright side, she may be really nice."

"And if she isn't? Will she take no for an answer? Will the
Earl of Oxford? Will mother?"

"It isn't the end of the world, Pip. It's just a marriage. If
someone else arranges it they only have themselves to blame if
it doesn't work out."

"But it will be too late by then. Marriage is for life, there has
to be more to it than this!"

"Well, there's always room for...extra-curricular activities,"
she said with a smile.

Peregrine felt he had lost her point "What do you mean?" he
asked.

"Never mind," she said dismissively with a wave of her
hand. "I have a favour to ask."

"Oh?" he said warily.

"Now, don't be like that. You may enjoy it." she sidled over
to statue of cupid, looking at it with mock innocence. "There's
someone coming visiting the house on Saturday for a tour.

You know I'm hopeless at that sort of thing, they're all just ornaments and nice coloured pictures to me. I need someone to show them around, answer their questions, impress them with knowledge..." She looked at him directly, "I thought you might be better suited to it than me. God knows, you can't be worse."

"How many people?" he asked with a frown.

"Just the one. Don't worry, she won't be any trouble, she just wants to look around really."

"She? This isn't something mother's set up is it?"

Mary laughed, "Oh, no. Mother knows nothing. She isn't the daughter of some lord or other...quite the opposite actually. She's just someone from the village who said she was interested in seeing the house. You can do that, can't you, Pip?"

"I suppose so..." he said hesitantly.

She grinned, "Well, that's settled then. One o'clock on Saturday. I'll introduce you." She came over until she was standing very close then spoke in a quite voice. "And, Pip, don't tell anyone about this, especially not mother. It can be our little secret." She smiled up at him.

He sighed, he didn't understand the need for all the secrecy and a little voice in his head told him Mary wasn't to be trusted. But he couldn't see an obvious problem. "Alright, that's fine."

"Wonderful," she said happily and walked away leaving Peregrine more than a little bemused.

Chapter Three

I t had been a busy morning at the Mirfin's cottage. Elizabeth had got up early, done all the jobs she usually did, as quickly as possible and then started on the real work of the day...getting ready to go out.

She had washed thoroughly and spent far longer than usual doing it. Then washed her hair and got all her best clothes out ready and laid them on the bed. She had decided to wear her very best dress, the dark blue one. Not that she had a lot of choice, but her other one, her green one, was looking a little faded these days.

She sat before the mirror in the kitchen while her sister, Susanna, brushed her hair. Elizabeth's hair was black, naturally thick and fell to below her shoulders. But, being long, it tended to knot. Normally, that didn't matter, but not today.

Susanna switched to a comb and pulled at a stubborn knot. "This is the last one, I think," she said. "Then I'll brush it through again. It looks wonderful, all shiny."

"Not bad," replied Elizabeth sceptically. "It's getting there."

"What a faff!" said Henry standing at the entrance to the kitchen. "I could have dressed ten times by now."

"Some of us prefer not to go around looking like an unmade bed," replied Elizabeth irritably.

"Men!" exclaimed Susanna. "They just have no idea."

"You didn't go to this much trouble when you went up to the Hall last time," said Henry.

"She didn't know she was going to meet someone important then, did she?" explained Susanna. "Today she *knows* she's seeing Lady Mary."

"Lady Mary," scoffed Henry. "All this trouble and you're not even meeting a man!"

Susanna stopped combing hair, realising that she would have to explain a few basic truths to her brother. "Looking good is *lot* more important when you're meeting another woman."

He frowned,"How do you figure that out?"

"Because women always judge you against themselves, of course. They always size you up to decide which one of you looks the best. They always know how much effort is involved and can tell straight away when you've been slack. But men are easy, a smile, a bit of leg and low top and they're happy."

"Uh, that's not true," he said not very convincingly. "Anyway, what do you know about it? You've only ever been to school and church."

"A woman knows these things," replied the fourteen year old mysteriously.

"Well, I suppose you'll be wanting me to take you up there in the wagon?"

"Oh, yes please, Henry, if you could," said Elizabeth. "I don't want to mess myself up and to have done all this for nothing."

"Alright, I'll get the wagon ready then." He went out, mumbling to himself.

"And thanks for helping, Sis" said Elizabeth to Susanna. "It's good to have another woman checking me over to make sure I look alright. Ask a man how you look and you can never trust what they tell you."

"That's so true. Now let me just get that last knot and then I think you're all set."

Later, Elizabeth donned a white coif, pushing her hair neatly underneath then grabbed a warm shawl and went out into the yard. She kissed Pa and Susanna bye, clambered aboard the wagon, then Henry shook the reins and Old Sam obediently started forwards, pulling the wagon behind. As they passed the lane that led to Wales church Elizabeth gave a silent thanks to God that it wasn't raining or she would have arrived at the Hall looking like she had just received a ducking in the forge pond! As it was, the wagon made good time and pulled gently into the stable yard at Kiveton Hall.

Elizabeth climbed down. "I suppose you'll want a lift back. How long will you be?" asked Henry from where he remained on the wagon.

She shrugged, "I don't know. Could you give me an hour or two?"

At that point the door to the house that Elizabeth had previously gone through opened and Lady Mary stood there. "He can come in and wait," she said. "Where you waited before. The fire's lit in here."

"Alright," said Henry and climbed down from the wagon. He tied Old Sam up and then went over, wearing his best smile.

"Thanks again, my lady, for offering to show me the house," said Elizabeth uncertainly. She steeled herself, but she couldn't help it, she felt very uncomfortable.

"Of course," said Mary. "Please, come in."

Henry didn't seem to be uncomfortable at all, but went straight inside as if he was just walking into his own cottage.

I wish I had half his nerve, thought Elizabeth as she followed her brother into the same servant room that she had been in before. As before, the fire was roaring merrily in the fireplace. Henry was already standing there with his back to it as if he owned the place!

Elizabeth felt so far out of her depth as far as etiquette went that she didn't know whether he was doing the right thing or whether he was showing herself up in some outrageous fashion. She looked at Mary for her reaction, but she seemed not to care less. Which was reassuring in a way.

"Make yourself at home," said Mary. "We'll come back here

when we have finished. It shouldn't take too long, but you never know..."

"That's fine," said Henry with a smile. "Don't worry about me. You have a good time."

"Yes, well, I'm sure she will," said Mary and ushered Elizabeth through the other door and then down the corridor into the Saloon.

Elizabeth swore she had never been so relieved to leave a room. Not knowing what her brother was going to say next had been playing havoc with her already wrought nerves.

As they entered the Saloon, Elizabeth found there was a man waiting for them. He was tall with narrow shoulders. He had a round face with a large, sharp, angular nose. His mouth was small, but with full lips and his chin had a large dimple. His hair was blonde and straight which he wore long. Most of his hair was pulled back into a ponytail, but strands on the side fell loosely and casually down his neck. He had large, round eyes that seemed to have a haunted look about them.

"This is my brother, Lord Osborne, the Earl of Danby," said Mary. "He'll be showing you around. He knows a lot more about things than I do."

An Earl? Oh my God, thought Elizabeth, her heart was racing. Not sure what she should be doing she curtsied as best she could.

"I'm so sorry," continued Mary. "But I don't think I know your name."

"Elizabeth, Elizabeth Mirfin, my Lady," she stuttered.

"Elizabeth," mused Lady Mary. "That's a nice name."

"Well," said Peregrine. "Welcome to Kiveton, Elizabeth. Have you been here before?"

"Yes, once, just this room," she blurted. "My lord."

"Fine. And don't feel you have to end every sentence with *my lord*. It's something the servants do. It isn't necessary for you."

"Alright," she said with relief and smiled.

She has a nice smile, thought Peregrine idly.

"Well," said Mary. "I can see you two are getting along so I'll leave you to it." She turned to Elizabeth. "Have a nice time."

"Thanks," Elizabeth replied clumsily.

Mary smiled and walked off through another door into another part of the house.

Peregrine looked at Elizabeth, wondering where he should start. What he should say.

Then Elizabeth saved him and broke the silence before it became embarrassing. "When I was here before I just wandered around trying to look at everything. I've never seen a room like it, full of statues and paintings. They are so beautiful."

"This is the Saloon," he said. "A living room. Guests are brought in here to relax. The statues and paintings are intended as talking points."

"Talking points?" she asked. "I don't understand."

"You're meant to discuss them. They're there to encourage conversation."

"A good room for us to start in, then," she said.

"Yes, a good choice," he admitted. He looked at her closely. She was well-dressed in blue with a white coif covering her hair, but there was something about her clothing that seemed...plain. He couldn't quite determine what it was. He was accustomed to the clothes that the women in his family wore, which were so fine that simply wearing them was enough. But Elizabeth's appearance looked like it had required far more effort. "I hope you don't mind me asking this," he said. "But, who are you? How do you know my sister? How did you come to be here?" He paused, "I'm sorry for being so abrupt, but she has told me nothing."

"I see," she said sadly. "You mean she's just dropped you in it?"

He smiled, "Crude, but succinct. So?"

She sighed. "I sneaked in here because I wanted to see what it looked like...and Lady Mary caught me. But then she asked me if I would like her to show me around. Well, I agreed because I really would like to. That's not a lie. I am interested."

"And where do you come from, Elizabeth?"

Her eyes dropped to the floor. "My father is the blacksmith in the village. He repaired a coach from here. When we brought it back I couldn't resist taking a look...."

"Alright, that makes sense. I can understand that."

"I expected your sister to show me around. That's what she said...or implied. I'm sorry, you don't have to if you don't want to. It's been a big misunderstanding. I'll go..."

She turned to walk towards the door, but he grabbed her arm and stopped her. "I didn't say I didn't want to. How come you're so interested?"

"I suppose it's because I have some books at home..."

"Really? You can read?"

"Yes, I can read!" she said indignantly then stopped herself. "Sorry. But yes I have some books. One is about Roman mythology. And I have two others about Italy..."

"Italy?"

"Yes. It's a journal...about the wonders that can be seen on a Grand Tour..."

"*I've* just returned from a Grand Tour of Italy," he said with amazement.

"You've been to Italy?" she asked incredulously.

"Yes, I spent nearly two years there..."

"Two years," she repeated. "You must have been to Rome?"

"Yes, we spent weeks in Rome," he said.

"Did you see the Colosseum?" She asked slowly, as if afraid to do so.

"Of course," he grinned. "We went in it. We stood where the gladiators had stood. We sat in the same seats spectators had sat in centuries ago and watched the games in the arena."

"It exists," she said dreamily. "Sometimes, I wondered if it was all just a story in a book. That it didn't exist at all."

"Yes, it is real," he said earnestly. "We saw lots of places like that."

"You have been to the Forum Romanum?" she asked.

"Well, yes. That leads to the Colosseum. But also the Pantheon, the Circus Maximus, the Arch of Constantine..."

"And they are all ruins?"

"They are over fourteen centuries old! Still, they have a power simply because they are that old. I sat and wondered what those ancient stones had seen."

"If only they could speak," she said quietly.

"Yes, quite," he said, for some reason it was as if he had noticed her for the first time. "That's exactly what I thought."

"You've seen things I can only imagine," she said. "Places I have read about in my books. You have visited them. You made them real."

"They are real," he insisted.

"Not for me. For me, they exist only here." She tapped her temple with her finger. "In my imagination."

"And now, for me too. Just memories." He sighed. "They seem a long time ago, and it wasn't even that long."

She went over to the four fabulous views of St Marks square that filled one wall. "And Venice? You went there too?"

"Yes," he said. "That's the Doge's Palace," he said pointing out a building mounted on giant pillars and a large set of stone steps guarded by mighty statues. "And that is St Marks Basilica, a large cathedral. Those four giant horses above the entrance were looted from Constantinople during a war."

"Constant...in...ople," she said slowly. "Where is that?"

"The capital of the Ottoman Empire," he explained, to which she looked blank. "It used to be called Byzantium. The capital of the Eastern Roman Empire. Beyond Greece."

Her eyes brightened, "Greece I have heard of. Beyond that, you say. That must be a very long way away."

He smiled gently, "Yes, it is, I suppose. I have never been." He turned round, "And do you recognise the statues in this room?"

"Some. Venus and Cupid perhaps?"

"Yes, that's right. "

She looked at the statue of Venus. Its smooth, gentle form captured and frozen in white marble. Venus was turning her neck slightly and had a very human expression. "It's beautiful," she said.

"Well, she is the goddess of love," he replied. "She is meant to be captivating. And the roman emperor is Nero."

She looked at the roman bust. A man with curly hair and beard with thick neck and fat face turning his face to the left as if to look behind. It was rendered so lifelike that she nearly expected it to speak.

"A king of Italy?" she asked.

"An emperor, the kings of Rome controlled all the countries of the Mediterranean in those days."

"Like a Pope?" she asked.

"Before Popes existed," he replied.

She was taken aback. The church in Wales was the oldest building she had ever seen, it was hundreds of years old. But that was the English church. The Popes in Rome were the heads of the *old* church, the Roman church, which was even older. Here was the depiction of someone before even those times.

Peregrine didn't notice her consternation, he was lost in his own thoughts. "He was the emperor after Claudius, I believe. His mother tried to control him," he said distantly, his eyes focussed straight ahead. "He recited the *Sack Of Ilium* while Rome burned."

"Ilium?" she asked, feeling like she understood very little.

The question drew him back from his reverie. "Uh, yes, Ilium. The roman name for Troy, as in Homer's *Iliad*." He looked at her helpless expression and realised he was explaining nothing. He smiled, "Here is the short version. Troy was an ancient city even older than Rome. Paris, a prince of Troy, goes to Mycenae in Greece. He falls in love with Helen, the queen of Mycenae and brings her back to Troy. The king of Mycenae wages a war to get her back and, at the end, Troy is burned." He pointed to a statue of a well-built man, standing at ease, completely naked apart from a helmet on his curly hair. "And here is Paris himself," he announced. "And next to him, of course, Helen of Troy." He indicated a white alabaster statue of a young woman dressed in a long, Grecian robe which hung loosely from her shoulders apart from a patterned band below her chest. Her gaze was cast shyly downwards. As always, Peregrine thought her flawless, milky white features came very close to perfection. "The face that launched a thousand ships, " he murmured.

"I like her clothes," said Elizabeth. "Do all the things here have stories?" she asked. "Like the one about Ilium?"

"I suppose they do," he said thoughtfully. "Most of them, anyway. Some are just paintings of horses."

"But even a horse must have a story. Enough to make someone want to paint it."

"Yes, I suppose so."

"And what is her story?" asked Elizabeth looking at the statue of a tall woman carrying a hooked stick. She wore a headdress with a snake's head emerging from the forehead.

"Cleopatra, the last queen of Egypt. Egypt had a history stretching back six thousand years, but eventually it was incorporated into the Roman Empire. She was a consort of Roman Emperors Julius Caesar and Mark Anthony."

"It must be wonderful to live your life surrounded by such beautiful things," said Elizabeth breathlessly. "Surrounded by stories."

He was gazing at the Cleopatra statue intently. He had always thought that the expression could have been better, but now he looked at it he realised that was a minor imperfection. The turn of the head and the detail in her drapery made it a thing of beauty. "Yes, they are beautiful," he agreed. "I had forgotten just how beautiful they were."

She walked over to look at a picture of a man, his hands tethered above his head, a cloth tied loosely around his waist and an arrow piercing his side. But his gaze was cast upward, not in pain, but in hope. Beside it was a similar portrait of the same man, but this time his hands were tied behind him. It was more grainy in its composition and seemed to show more pain than the first painting.

"Is that Jesus?" she asked.

"Saint Sebastian," he said. "A martyr. He died tied to a tree. I suppose it does hark back to the death of Christ. One is by Guido Reni, the other by Titian. They are both together for comparison because they are the same subject. They are a hundred years old. I've always thought the colours and light are very good."

"It's as if I am there," said Elizabeth.

Elizabeth was even more impressed with the Poussin landscapes. Their accurate depictions of tree filled glades really did make her feel like she could step into them. Although she was less impressed with the Rubens family portrait although she loved the vivid colours of the dresses.

They continued through into the Vestibule, a smaller room containing a pair of paintings depicting views of Rome.

Then into the Drawing Room. A room full of comfortable furniture and light, pastel shades. The pictures here were gentle scenes of waterfalls and landscapes.

Then into the Great Hall. It was a double height room, the walls adorned with paintings. So many that Peregrine had to admit he didn't know them all. Many were notable people. He reeled off the ones he knew, the *Earl of Strafford* by Van Dyck, *Alderman Hewet* by Holbein, the *Earl of Arundal*, the *Duke of Newburgh*. Two by Titian, one of himself and the other of Lot and his daughters. A gruesome picture of David with Goliath's head.

In pride of place, King Charles I on a white horse, entering victoriously through a giant arch.

"It's by Van Dyck," said Peregrine, but the name meant nothing to Elizabeth.

But the Kings's name did, "King Charles, who was beheaded by the puritans," said Elizabeth, glad to be on a subject she knew something about. "They banned Christmas."

"Well, yes," said Peregrine sceptically. "Not such a bad idea actually."

"You sound like my father," she said with a smile. "He always says he doesn't like Christmas, but he's always the one putting the holly up."

Peregrine smiled warmly, "He sounds like a fine fellow."

"Oh, we're simple folk really. Nothing as grand as this," she flung her arms up at the grandeur on display.

"It's all just for show," said Peregrine sadly.

"What do you mean? You live in a palace of treasures."

"I don't live here," he said simply.

"You don't...but I thought...you're an Earl."

"Yes, but I don't know where I live. As for being an Earl, I am now, but only because my brother died recently. "

"I'm so sorry," she said sincerely. He looked at her and realised she really meant it. She wasn't just saying it, like everyone else who had said it to him recently, because it would be bad form not to or because it really messed up their plans for the future. She said it because she was genuinely sorry to hear it. "This is the Duke's house, though?"

"Oh yes. One of them. He built it to impress people, but he lives in Wimbledon."

"He's your father?"

"Grandfather. My father doesn't really live here either, he's usually in London. Mother's here more than anyone, but even she spends a lot of time at North Mymms, where I was born."

"And Lady Mary?"

"Visiting for Christmas," he declared.

"So, where do you live?"

He paused, not quite sure what the answer was. "Nowhere," he finally admitted. "I don't seem to fit in anywhere."

"Then it seems to me you should take this place because no one else seems to care!"

If only it were that simple, he thought. But it was a nice idea.

"Elizabeth, come with me and I'll show you something special."

She followed him out through a huge door and into a dark oak panelled hallway. There, before her, was a huge staircase, as wide as a bedroom in their cottage! It rose between two decorative wooden pillars like giant chess pieces. It curved gently upwards, hugging the wall, somehow suspended in the air without obvious support. The entire staircase was made completely from oak, stained a rich, dark colour. The bannisters, that edged it were as thick as a man's arm mounted on ornate, intricately carved balusters. A deep red carpet traced every stair, cascading down them in a sanguinary flood.

"Come on," he said and beckoned her up the stairs. She followed hesitantly. The carpet had a deep pile under her feet. When she considered how much she had spent on a rug back home, the cost of this carpet alone made her head spin.

Her eyes drifted upwards and her mouth dropped open. Above the staircase, the entire ceiling was a gigantic mural. A painting the size of a small house. A cloudscape of soft, woollen clouds against a pale, blue sky. And reclining, standing, lounging or even flying on and around those gentle cushions were a dizzying array of characters. Some armoured, some naked, some draped in coloured robes. Musicians, deities, nymphs, angels and soldiers. Perhaps thirty or forty different entities. In the middle, the centre of everyone's attention, stood a naked young girl being dressed, crowned and offered an assortment of offerings by the surrounding characters. Looking on, in the middle distance, sat two male god figures, coronas bristling around their heads.

"The Creation of Pandora," said Peregrine with undisguised satisfaction. "Isn't it magnificent?"

Elizabeth was speechless. "It is a masterpiece," she mumbled.

"In Greek mythology, Pandora was the first woman created by the gods. The painting illustrates that moment of creation."

"Like Eve in the Bible?" she asked.

"Yes, just so. In the Greek version Pandora ultimately releases evil into the world."

"That's typical," said Elizabeth with a smile. "Blame it on a woman!"

Peregrine grinned. "But she also releases Hope."

"Well, that's true. There's always that."

At the top of the stairs he led her through another door into a huge dining room. At the centre of the room sat a large banquet table made of Egyptian marble on a wooden frame. On one wall was a large double hearth beneath a purple marble chimney piece. Pastoral tapestries of lakes and woods hung on the walls and large windows looked out onto the garden.

What took her gaze, though, was a scene of a huge dining table showing a wedding feast with dozens of guests. Every guest was unique and had their individual characters. The main figure sat in prime position with a series of wine pots.

"It's *The Marriage at Cana*," explained Peregrine. "It comes from the Bible story where Jesus turns water into wine. A suitable subject for the Dining Room, I think." He led her over to a large painting on the wall. "This is the four continents of the World. Europe, Asia, Africa and America."

She looked at the portrait of four heavily bearded men apparently camping under a twilight sky. "But they are people," she said.

"They are personifications of the four continents. They are represented as four men."

"And four women."

"Ah, the women represent the great rivers of those continents. The Danube, the Ganges, the Nile and the Rio De La Plata."

"I've never heard of any of those rivers," she admitted. "But I like the big cat and the lizard," she said pointing to a snarling tiger and a crocodile.

He showed her another painting, one of his personal favourites. The Four Evangelists by Titian which was heavy and inexpressive, but had a good diffusion of light.

"I suppose we should get back," he said. "I've enjoyed showing you around."

They came back down the stairs and started making their way back to where Henry would be waiting.

"Thank you so much for showing me round. It's been...well...beyond description really." She looked around, "I suppose this place will look even more magical at Christmas."

"I'm dreading it," he admitted.

She stopped suddenly and looked at him. "Why's that?"

He shrugged, "I suppose it's my first Christmas without my brother."

"But you have your family here."

He laughed humourlessly. "As if things weren't bad enough. I'm not sure I want to spend any time with my family any more."

In silence, they walked back to the Saloon and the door leading back to the corridor where Henry waited.

On impulse, Elizabeth suddenly turned to face Peregrine. "Look, I have an idea. You've shown me around today, it seems only right to return the favour. Well, in a way. I mean, a tour of our house wouldn't take longer than two minutes, but we have roaring log in the fire, a lot of holly, lots of food, too much to drink and, well, we usually have a good time. You would be welcome to join us...." She stopped, looking suddenly embarrassed. "Listen to me? How silly am I? Inviting an Earl over for Christmas. Please, just forget I said anything."

"No," said Peregrine suddenly. "I would love to."

"You would?" gasped Elizabeth. Then she smiled warmly, "Well, that's fine then. Say, three o'clock in the afternoon on Christmas Day?"

"I'll be there," he said with a grin.

"Great," said Elizabeth and turned to leave. "I'll see you then." She turned and went out through the door where Henry was waiting.

Peregrine looked at the closed door. He felt a strange sense of loss as if someone had just blown out a candle or opened a door to the cold. How odd, he thought, how very odd. But he smiled and realised, for the first time, he was looking forward to Christmas.

24th December 1711

In the following days Elizabeth tried to find the right time to tell her father that they were having a guest for Christmas, but somehow the time never seemed to be quite right. Either, he was busy, or she was busy, or it was a moment of quiet and she didn't feel like disturbing it. She would always decide to just leave it to the next day. There would be plenty of time. And then, before she knew it, it was Christmas Eve and time had run out and there were no more days left. She had to mention it today.

That morning they all went down into Wales Wood to finish off getting the final stuff for Christmas. Tomorrow would be First Night, in theory the start of twelve nights of eating, drinking and generally frivolous behaviour. As far as work went, it was a very quiet time of year. On the farms the crops had been harvested months ago, the fields had all been burned, tidied or ploughed over. There wouldn't be any more setting or scattering of seed until the soil warmed up in spring. The blacksmith trade wasn't especially seasonal, but there was a contagious effect, as the farms wound down the smithy work they might have asked for was put off until next year. There was general lack of urgency that spread throughout the entire village. It was a time for closing the door, setting a hot fire, putting on your warmest clothes and having lots to eat. A time to hanker down and take some time to take it easy.

Which was all well and good, except that meant there was a lot of preparation to do beforehand. Which is why the Mirfin's went down to Wales Wood. The wood lay to the west of Wales village, a stretch of wild woodland that occupied the small valley where the River Rother ran northwards towards the small town of Rotherham. When it came to decorating the house people looked for bright colours, but in midwinter, most plants were dormant and often bare of leaves let alone flowers. But there were a few exceptions. Ivy was abundant and retained its verdant green leaves all year. Holly was the same, but also had the added attraction of producing bright red berries in winter. Ivy could be just picked off the ground. Holly grew as a tree and had to be picked with care because it's leaves and could be sharp. Mistletoe was a different matter. It was also evergreen, but had small, white pearl like berries at Christmas. It was semi-parasitic, growing on the branches of lime, poplar and hawthorn where it took nutrients from its host tree. So gathering it usually involved a climb. So, that was Henry's job, although Susanna was keen to have a go Robert told her to leave it to her brother.

It didn't take too long to gather more than enough then they loaded it onto the wagon and Old Sam faithfully wheeled it all back home. Once there, they set about decorating the kitchen and living room with various combinations of foliage. It took longer than expected. Most of it needed cleaning to remove insects and webs for a start. Then everyone took bits and put them up around the room. There would then follow a period where the others would criticise, a discussion would occur, then everyone adjusted everyone else's efforts until a consensus was agreed.

Elizabeth stood back and assessed the result. It was good to have a change of colour in the house. It seemed to make the room more cozy and welcoming. Yes, it would do.

Then it was time to start preparing vegetables. They would be peeled and cut then stored overnight so they could be cooked tomorrow. Elizabeth and Susanna sat opposite each other at the kitchen table, knives in hand, peeling and cutting. Their father, Robert, sat at the other end of the table preparing the turkey they would cook. It involved plucking and then removing the guts, replacing them with stuffing they have prepared earlier. He had already removed the head and feet with an axe in the yard outside. Elizabeth had insisted he do that outside instead of in the kitchen. If she could have she would insisted he did it all outside so she didn't have to watch. But it was cold out and she couldn't really ask him to do that.

"Stop being squeamish," said Robert. "My father used to ring…"

"Yes, that'll be enough of that, thank you," interrupted Elizabeth. "I'd rather not know any of the grisly details. It puts me right off! If I think too much about it I'll end up not eating it at all."

"Yes, me too, Pa," agreed Susanna. "It's gruesome!"

Robert shook his head, "I don't know what's up with you two. Your Ma wanted you to be little ladies and now look what's happened? I don't know what sort of wives you're going to make some poor chap."

"Very good ones," said Susanna.

Robert gave a humph. "I don't mind, Pa," said Henry enthusiastically. "I like to see how it's done."

"See," said Robert proudly. "That's my boy!"

It was much later, when they were all sat round the table having something to eat, that Elizabeth thought to herself it's now or never.

"Pa," she said hesitantly, while concentrating on moving food around her plate. "You know when we come back from church tomorrow we'll be having lunch."

"That's the idea," replied Robert.

"Well, I've...sort of...invited someone to join us."

"Really? First I've heard of it."

"Well, he said he wasn't looking forward to Christmas lunch and I said, if he felt that way, he would be more than welcome to join us."

Robert stopped eating and looked at Elizabeth. "He? Who's is this *he*?"

"Lord Osborne," she replied sheepishly.

Henry laughed, "Lord Osborne! Be serious, no Lord is going to join us for Christmas!"

Robert waved him to be quiet. Robert was serious, "The Duke?"

"No!" said Elizabeth. "His grandson. He showed me round the Hall and that's when I asked him. I mean, he invited me to their house so I invited him to ours..." her voice trailed off.

"And he agreed?"

"Yes, yes, it's all arranged. I told him to join us tomorrow afternoon and he said he would."

"He was having a joke with you," said Henry with a grin. "Can you imagine what they're having for Christmas up at the Hall? And this Lord is going to give all that up and come down here to our cottage to share our turkey? Nah, he was having a laugh."

"He wasn't, he was serious," replied Elizabeth, defensively.

Robert sighed, "It does seem unlikely. It's not happened before, but then no one from this family has ever gone on a tour of the Hall before now. So, may be...."

"Well, I trust him," said Elizabeth. "He seemed honest. If he had changed his mind he would have let us know by now. He's only at the top of the hill, for Goodness sake! No, I think if he says he'll be here then...he'll be here!"

"Does that mean Christmas lunch is cancelled?" asked Susanna. "If we have to entertain a lord it won't be like normal."

"Not at all," said Elizabeth with determination. "Everything goes ahead as planned. There's just an extra person, that's all."

"That's all?" laughed Henry. "The Duke of Leeds pays us a visit and we just carry on as if it's nothing."

"He isn't the Duke of Leeds!" said Elizabeth with irritation. "He's his grandson. The Earl of something or other..."

"Oh, that's fine then," said Henry sarcastically. "If it's just an Earl!"

"Look! *I* invited *him*. *He* is visiting *us*. Not the other way round. This is on our terms, not his. We do Christmas as usual and he can join us....or not....it's up to him."

"Well, it seems to me that it's all set then," said Robert gently. "We carry on as normal except we set another place at the table and then we see what happens. You're right, he might be an Earl of something, but in this house, I am the master and he's eating at my table. And... uh... since he's a friend of yours, he's very welcome."

"Thanks, Pa," said Elizabeth with feeling.

Susanna sighed dreamily, "A Earl coming here. I bet he's really handsome."

"I still think he won't turn up," said Henry, which just

earned him angry looks from both girls.

25th December 1711

Elizabeth hadn't slept all night. Her mind kept turning over and over. Running through scenarios for Peregrine's visit, discovering possible problems, struggling for solutions and then starting all over again. She tossed and turned endlessly through the long winter night. Eventually, she decided she would feel better if she got up rather than enduring the fruitless ordeal of trying to sleep.

She had a wash and dressed then went into the kitchen. A quick look round to make sure everything was just right. She decided it wasn't and started tidying the room. Sometime later the others started drifting in, helping themselves to breakfast, making crumbs, moving chairs, leaving things generally out of place again. By the time everyone was ready to go to church, Elizabeth decided she just needed to tidy round once again before they left.

It was a cold, dry morning as they left the cottage then walked up the lane to the crossroads. The air was crisp. Their breath steamed out ahead, but the brisk walk soon warmed them with a welcome invigoration.

Elizabeth found herself smiling as her heart started to quicken. Lord Osborne was coming over for Christmas. No one else in the village could say that! No one else had ever said that. It was exciting. It was different. *He* was different. He was as far removed from the farm lads and bakers boys in the village as it was possible to be. And he was coming to visit...

There was a sudden panic as she thought, I *need to tidy the kitchen when I get back.*

They followed the lane up and small incline to the crossroads in the village. Right led to Wales Wood and the river, left to Kiveton and then Anston. They turned left and then immediately right, continuing up the hill. This was Wales proper, the main part of the village. A series of white limestone cottages with thatched and tiled roofs lined both sides of the narrow lane, their chimneys puffing black smoke into the winter sky. The road rose more steeply on this side of the crossroads, rising up to the broad escarpment upon which the village was situated. The road passed between two walls and then, on the left, amongst a patch of green grass was Wales church. A small church with square, Norman bell tower. A small path led up to an old arched door. People were making their way down from higher up in the village, up the church path and into the church.

There were several shouts of Merry Christmas from the crowd. The Mirfins, especially Robert, greeted many of the people they met in the same way. Most of the people they saw had lived their entire lives in Wales. Robert himself had been born in Laughton-en-le-Morthen to the north, but had moved to Wales when he married. All his children had lived all their lives there.

They entered the church and assumed seats in the wooden pews. The service was a happy, light, jovial affair with a sermon and some hymns for people to join in. Elizabeth couldn't get her mind on it really, it kept drifting back to the forthcoming lunch and their new visitor. Everything may be ready, it still needed cooking. She kept thinking why was she wasting time here when there was so much to do.

Calm down, she told herself. *There really isn't that much to do and, anyway, it's no more than any other Christmas Days and they worked out fine.*

Either way, she was relieved when the service was finally over and they could file out of the church. She found it slightly irritating the way her father seemed to stop and pass the time with everyone he met. Did he really need to speak to absolutely everyone?

But then they were walking down Church Lane again, back across the crossroads and back down the lane on the other side home. Everyone seemed happy. Susanna was still singing the hymns and asking Henry if he thought she sang well.

"Hardly," he laughed. "You were so out of tune I thought you were singing a different song to the rest of us."

"I was not!" she said and gave him a playful thump on the arm.

Even Robert seemed happy, quietly puffing on his pipe as he walked. The smell of the tobacco wafted across to Elizabeth. She loved the smell, but could never imagine what possessed people to breathe in all that smoke. It must be like standing with your head over a fire.

Soon they were back home, hurrying through the door into the welcoming warmth of the hot fire. The Yule log they had collected yesterday was still burning merrily. By rights they should have lit it using an ember from the log they burned last year, but that never seemed to work out somehow. They should also choose a log that would burn throughout the Christmas season, but that didn't happen usually either. With luck they would get three or four days out of it. It didn't matter, it was great while it lasted.

Elizabeth and Susanna got straight on cooking lunch. This mainly involved roasting the turkey and cooking lots of different root vegetables such as carrots, parsnips and beans. There was a rich onion gravy to go with it and a sweet sauce made from local berries.

By mid-afternoon, everything was ready. The table was set and, after a final check, everyone assumed their seats and then waited rather awkwardly.

"I guess we are one short," commented Robert with a smile. "We'll wait a while."

"I'm sure he'll turn up," said Elizabeth unconvincingly.

After several anxious minutes they heard the sound of horses hooves in the yard. Her heart missed a beat. Everyone's heads turned to the window, but Henry was the one who got up and looked out.

"He's here!" announced Henry. He rushed to the door, opened it and ran out into the yard.

Susanna rose from her seat, but then realised she didn't

know why and just stood there, waiting. Elizabeth and Robert remained sitting. Elizabeth daren't stand up, that would risk losing the fragile control she had on her nerves. The tension rose as they heard voices outside and horses hooves being led to the stable.

Henry's showing him where to put his horse, thought Elizabeth.

Then the door burst open with a blast of cold air and Henry burst in with a huge grin on his face. Peregrine came in behind him. He wore a long, grey cloak. His long, blonde hair was, as usual, tied firmly back into a ponytail.

"Good afternoon," he said. His voice was very casual, not nervous at all.

The same couldn't be said for Elizabeth, who couldn't make her mind up what she aught to be doing at this point.

Should I shake his hand? Curtsy? Or just sit where I am?

Eventually, her mind was made up when she saw her father getting to his feet. She rose at the same time.

"Please, don't get up," said Peregrine as he unfastened his cloak. The clothes he wore were very simple and functional. Not dissimilar to clothes anyone in the village might wear. Elizabeth hadn't known what to expect, but it was a relief that he hadn't turned up in something elaborate and expensive. Peregrine went over to Elizabeth, took hold of her right hand, which was as limp as a dish cloth, and then bent down and gently kissed the fingers. "Elizabeth," he said as he straightened. "Thanks for inviting me here today."

He turned to Susanna who was just standing and staring. "And what would your name be?" he asked.

"Susanna," she said automatically, without taking her eyes from him.

He kissed her hand, "It is a pleasure to make your acquaintance, Susanna."

He went over to Robert and offered his hand. "Sir, you do me a great honour today and I am grateful. Your daughter invited me here, but I know that was without your knowledge or permission. I hope you will allow me to earn the right to sit at your table this Christmas Day?"

"Aye, of course," said Robert. "You are very welcome." He took Peregrine's hand and shook it firmly.

Peregrine took two bottles out from inside his cloak. The first he handed to Robert. "This is for you, sir, by way of thanks for entertaining me today. It's brandy, French brandy."

"Many thanks," replied Robert looking at the bottle intensely. "I don't think I've ever had..."

"Ah, then you should start slowly," said Peregrine. "Sip a small portion of it with your pipe tobacco. You'll find they go very well together." He put the other bottle in the middle of the table. "This one is for general consumption. A bottle of sack from Jerez de la Frontera. Again, small portions, but it is sweeter and should appeal to a wider audience."

"Shereth?" asked Elizabeth. "Where's that?"

"Spain," said Peregrine. "South West Spain. Near Cadiz."

Elizabeth felt that wasn't really helping. "You have been there?"

"No," he said with a smile. "I just drink their liquor."

"Are you really an Earl?" blurted out Susanna suddenly.

"Susanna!" said Elizabeth in embarrassment.

Peregrine just chuckled, "So people tell me. But I am also just a man and, on this day especially, I would very much like to be just that."

"But what do we call you?" asked Henry.

"Ah yes, my name. Peregrine. Peregrine Hyde Osborne. I know...it's a mouthful. Most likely my mother's invention, Hyde being her maiden name. To be honest, I never much cared for it. My family call me Pip, which I don't care for either - always sounds like a child's name to me. My brother always called me Pen and I would really like for you to call me that too."

Elizabeth went over to him and reached out her arm. "Can I take your cloak, Pen?"

"Of course. Thank you." He hurriedly took it off and handed it over to her.

"Well, take a seat and we'll get dishing up. Pa, will you carve the turkey, please?"

"Certainly," said Robert and they all took their seats.

They ate from pewter plates using mainly one or two knives then used some bread or a spoon to lap up the gravy. The meal was mainly slices of turkey that Robert carved from a bird that had been freshly roasted. Added to it was a selection of boiled vegetables.

"I imagine it's not quite what you are used to," said Elizabeth a she finished dishing up and sat down to eat.

"It's good, hearty fare and very welcome on such a cold day," said Peregrine happily. "Besides, I find these days that the substance of the meal is of much less significance than the people and places I eat it with." His eyes drifted away, "Recently, I sat with my brother high on cliffs overlooking Genoa, watching the sun set over the Ligurian Sea. We ate some bread, dipped in olive oil, a little salt and a cup of beer. Yet, it was one of the most memorable meals I have ever had." He looked at Elizabeth and smiled, "As I am sure this will be."

Before Elizabeth could answer Susanna said, "Where's Genoa?"

"Northern Italy," replied Peregrine taking a mouthful of food.

"Where's Italy?" came the reply.

Peregrine paused eating for a second. Then, when he had cleared his mouth, he said, "This is England, yes?" Susanna nodded. *Everyone knows that* she thought. "If we ride south for," he paused in thought, "perhaps seven or eights days, then we come to a narrow sea. If we cross the sea on the other side we are no longer in England, we are in France."

"Where my brandy comes from," said Robert with a grin, pointing to the brandy bottle.

"Indeed," continued Peregrine. "If we ride south through France eventually we come to another sea, the Ligurian Sea. Then, if we turn left and follow the coast eastwards, we eventually leave France and enter the Kingdom of Sardinia which is in Italy. And shortly after that we see the city of Genoa."

"I see," said Susanna. "I didn't know," she said slightly shamefully.

"No, of course not." replied Peregrine gently. "How could you know if no one has ever told you? Well, now you know." He resumed eating.

"Is Genoa a beautiful city?" asked Elizabeth dreamily.

"It used to be," he replied. A hundred years ago it attracted great artists like Rubens, Caravaggio and Van Dyck. But since then it has declined somewhat and it was burned by the French twenty-five years ago. But some things cannot change, the cliffs, the sea and the mountains behind it remain magical."

"They have mountains?" asked Elizabeth who had only ever seen the rolling hills around where she lived.

"Certainly. The Maritime Alps," said Peregrine. "Where Europe's mightiest mountain range meets the sea."

"When I grow up I'm going to go to Genoa," announced Susanna.

Henry laughed, "You'll be lucky to get as far as Chesterfield."

"I will not!" she said and threw a piece of carrot in his general direction.

"Now, now," said Elizabeth. "What will his lord...I mean, Pen...think of us."

"Well, I'll tell you something," said Peregrine to Susanna. "Over a hundred years ago a man lived in Genoa who dreamed of crossing the Atlantic Ocean. That's a sea so large it could swallow the whole of England many times over. People said he was mad, they said it couldn't be done. But he didn't listen to them. He took his ship and tried to sail across that ocean, even though he had no idea what he would find or even if there *was* another side. But he succeeded. He did reach the other side. And he discovered The New World. So, you hold onto those dreams of yours, Miss Susanna, because despite what anyone might tell you, no one knows where they might take you."

"Have you ever been to the New World, Pen?" asked Elizabeth.

"No, to be honest it lacks any appeal for me," said Peregrine. "Virginia is a wild frontier. I'm afraid I prefer my creature comforts."

"When I was a younger," said Robert. "My brother William and me took a trip to see the sea."

"Really?" said Elizabeth. "I never knew you had seen the sea."

"Well, I must have forgotten," he said. "Anyway, we rode out to Lincoln and then from there out eastwards until we reached the coast. There was a huge plain of sand, waves rolling onto it and beyond that...water. Water as far as you could see. More water than you would ever imagine." He sighed, "But, as you say lad, I was glad to get home. We'd slept with the horses and got rained on more than once," he said with fond laugh. "Aye, there's a lot to be said for the comforts of home."

"I'd like to see the sea," said Elizabeth. "It must be an amazing sight."

"I don't think I can imagine that much water," admitted Henry. "I've only ever seen the river and few fishing ponds."

"Me neither," agreed Susanna.

But Peregrine was struck by something else Robert had said. "You say you have a brother called William?"

Robert nodded slowly, "Did have. Five years younger than me. He died last year."

"My brother, William, died a few months ago," said Peregrine.

Robert shrugged, "It happens. We lost Mary, the children's mother, and my eldest daughter eight years ago. Youngest daughter three years after that. Nothing you can do about it. Just have to pull yourself together and get on with it."

Elizabeth asked, "Was your brother older or younger than you, Pen?"

"Older, by fifteen months."

"It must have been good to have an older brother," said Henry. "I've never had one, just blinking sisters."

"And after all we've done for that boy too!" said Elizabeth

with mock indignation.

"Yes," said Susanna. "We just aren't appreciated."

Everyone joined in a round of laughter. Peregrine realised that it was the first time he had laughed in a very long time.

The afternoon progressed well. They finished the main meal with more than a small helping of the sack that Peregrine had brought. As they did even more laughter ensued, often without really knowing what they were laughing at.

They tidied away the plates and then bowls were issued and then an even larger bowl was brought to the table and placed in the centre.

"Ah, great," said Henry. "This is my favourite."

The lid was taken off and a steaming pudding was tipped out, upside down, onto another plate.

"Plum Pudding," said Susanna getting her bowl ready to receive her share.

"What's Plum Pudding?" said Peregrine. "I've never heard of it."

"It's what they're all eating in London," said Elizabeth.

"Really? Well, it's a new one on me."

"Well, it's nice to know we can manage to stay ahead of Kiveton Hall on some things," said Elizabeth with satisfaction.

"Here's an idea," said Robert and poured some of his brandy bottle over the pudding then, using a light from his pipe, he lit it. The pudding burned with a mellow, blue flame. They all started cheering. The flame burned for a few seconds before slowly fading then Elizabeth dished the pudding out into everyone's bowls.

"There's no plums in it," said Peregrine.

"That's what I said," declared Henry. "But it's still great." They all agreed.

It was many hours later, after they had eaten and sat round the fire telling stories and generally enjoying each others company, that Peregrine made his way out to the stable. It was a bitterly cold night, although the sky was full of clouds. Wisps of snow were drifting down to settle in the yard. With Henry's help he got his horse ready and, with some difficulty, considering how much sack he had drunk, managed to get into the saddle. The rest of the family stood in the doorway watching him leave.

"Be careful making your way home," shouted Elizabeth. "It's starting to snow. Go slowly."

"Merry Christmas," he shouted as his horse started off. "Thanks for a great day!"

"Merry Christmas, lad!" shouted Robert after him.

"Is he really an Earl?" asked Susanna when they were back in the kitchen. "He doesn't act like one."

No, thought Elizabeth to herself, but he is. Whether he likes it or not.

Chapter Four

T he snow came down heavily overnight. Thick flakes fell in sheets, carpeting the ground to knee height.

Peregrine rose late and winced, his head was hurting from too much sack. He looked out of his bedroom window. The grassy slope that ran down to the main road was a smooth expanse of fresh snow. The skeletal outlines of trees stood firm, their dark bones vivid against the bright background. Hedges and shrubs bowed their heads in submission to the winter. Snow flakes, so light and fragile that they lasted only seconds if caught in the hand or could drift on the merest breeze, now used their combined weight to bend the insubordinate branches to their cold will.

Peregrine wiped the condensation from the glass of his window and shivered. On some of the panes a sheen of ice split the morning light into an array of prismatic colours.

It isn't a day for going out, he thought to himself. More of a day for recovering.

He clambered into some clothes. They were freezing cold which immediately made him wish he hadn't bothered. But he lived in hope they would warm up eventually. He opened his bedroom door and went downstairs.

It was mid-morning so breakfast was out of the question, and he just couldn't face it anyway. Instead he made his way to the Drawing Room only to find that the rest of his family had made it there before him. His mother was sitting by a fire that was roaring away in the grate like a demon. His brother-in-law, Henry Somerset, was lounging in a chair holding his head in one hand. There was no sign of his wife.

There were two other people in the room. One was his Aunt Bridget and her husband, Philip Bisse. He was large, fat, bald man in his mid forties with a penchant for flowery costumes. Peregrine had always found him to be a humourless fellow. He was the Bishop of Saint Davids in Wales. He had been in charge of proceedings at Williams funeral.

Peregrine lowered himself gently into a chair and managed to attract the attention of a passing servant. "Could I have some tea, please, with honey," he asked.

"You look like I feel," said Somerset from the seat opposite, cradling his head. "I think I may have over indulged on the old vino last night."

"Well, it is Christmas," said Peregrine.

"Yes indeed," he replied. "I'm always a firm supporter of tradition, but I'm afraid I am paying the price."

"You're faring better than your wife," said Aunt Bridget. "Poor Mary won't even leave her bed this morning. The poor love."

"A bit under the weather this morning," explained Somerset to Peregrine as an aside.

"I have very little sympathy," said Philip Bisse bombastically. "I have always been a man who knows his limits and advise others to know theirs."

"Quite right, dear," said his wife. "We have seen many Christmases and have never suffered as a result."

"Yes. Know your limits. So far and no further," advocated her husband.

"I know my limits," said Somerset wearily. "I just chose to exceed them."

Peregrine's mother said, "Anyway, Pip, where did you get to last night? You disappeared after we got back from the church and no one knew where you were. Someone said you went riding."

"I went to see some friends," he replied.

"Friends?" said his mother sceptically. "I didn't know you knew anyone here. As soon as you reached schooling age you went to the continent, how could you know anyone?"

"I didn't say they were old friends," said Peregrine.

"New friends, then? You've made some friends? Well, that's good. If a little... unexpected."

Peregrine smiled. Doing things his mother didn't expect made him feel good. It proved she didn't know everything about him.

"The ability to make new friends will be useful to you in future," said Aunt Bridget.

"Provided they are the *right* sort of friends," added his mother, still looking straight at him with her penetrating gaze. He did his best to ignore her.

"And speaking of making new friends is there any sign of a possible match for him?" said Aunt Bridget to Peregrine's mother.

"I have heard from the Earl of Oxford," replied his mother. "His daughter is available."

"Ah good. It doesn't do to hesitate on these things, I mean how old is Pip now? Nineteen?"

"Twenty," replied Peregrine's mother.

"Well, there you are you see, time moving relentlessly on. Look at my first husband, Charlie, 1st Earl of Plymouth, died when he was twenty-three. I'd only just married him. Not enough time for children, so no heir. It was a dreadful mess. I had to fight tooth and nail to keep a roof over my head and the clothes on my back. I wouldn't wish it on my worst enemy."

"I remember it, dear. We were terribly worried about you. So, there you are, Pip, I'm doing it all for you."

Bishop Bisse decided to add his two pennyworth. "If you take my advice, lad, you'll get married quickly and get to work straight away on having a few young 'uns...."

"Really, Philip, do you have to be so coarse," commented Aunt Bridget.

"I say it as it is," replied Bisse. "That's my way, call a spade a spade and then everyone knows where they stand. You see, lad, once you have an heir or two in the bag the pressure is off. You can relax, do a bit of fishing, riding or whatever takes your fancy knowing you've done your bit."

Aunt Bridget added, "But until he's settled down it's all so... uncertain. If anything should happen to him...well, let's not even think about it."

"And it's the same for the Earl of Oxford," said Peregrine's mother. "He's got a loose daughter he needs to get pupping as soon as possible. It's worse trying to match daughters than find a match for sons."

"Oh, I can imagine. It's so competitive."

"I did well with my girls really."

Somerset waved his hand regally, "Why thank you, madam. I do consider myself a bit of a catch."

Peregrine's mother slapped Somerset playfully on the shoulder. "Yes, Henry, I was happy to find you in the net. And young Bridget is married to the Reverend William Williams in Chichester. I was lining William up with the Earl of Oxford's girl until..." She looked across at Pergrine and, for a moment, sympathy flashed across her face until she regained her composure. "Well, until William didn't return from his Grand Tour. Then I had to put Pip forward as a possibility."

"And Oxford is happy with the prospect?"

"So far. It's early days. I'm hopeful."

Peregrine quickly finished off his tea. "If you'll excuse me. I'm suddenly feeling a little under the weather too. I think I'll go back to bed."

"Alright, dear," said Aunt Bridget. "Have a sleep and we'll see you later."

Peregrine walked slowly out of the room, he resisted an urge to run.

His mother watched him go. *I wonder who his new friends are.*

That might need nipping in the bud. And I really should write to
the Earl of Oxford as soon as possible after Christmas.

29th December 1711

The weather did not improve over the next few days. It snowed
intermittently and the freeze continued unabated. In Kiveton
the fires in all the rooms that were in use were kept roaring,
heating the large spaces without effort. Hot drinks were continuously available and food was in abundance. Selections of
cold meats and sweet cakes and puddings were out all the time
and could be eaten as and when the urge took. But the family met in the evenings more formally for soups and roasted
meats.

In between meals Peregrine kept to himself as much as
possible. The various other members of the family seemed to
spend the major part of their conversation discussing other
people that he only vaguely knew. Quite often the comments
were less than complimentary. Peregrine felt sure that a lot
of the statements his mother or Aunt Bridget made they
wouldn't dare to say to the people concerned. The combination
of gossip, tittle tattle, unsubstantiated jibes and thinly dis-
guised one-upmanship began to wear on him after a while and
he felt it better to steer clear.

So, it was with some surprise that there was a knock on his
bedroom door one morning. He had been sitting reading a
book he had taken from the library. He opened the door and in
breezed his sister, Mary.

"Come on, we're all going out and you can join us."

"Where? We are snowed in. And it's freezing."

"Out! Out of this prison to get some fresh air and some blood
pumping. Henry's had this idea and we're going to go skating
on the lake."

Peregrine laughed, "Skating? I can't skate."

"Now, now," she scolded him. "There's no such thing as
can't, you just haven't tried yet. We're all going - and that in-

cludes you. Grab some warm clothing."

He picked up his warmest coat, a scarf then found some gloves in a drawer and took them with him. Then, Mary pushed him out of his room, along the corridor and down the stairs to the lower floor. There, a crowd was gathered before the South Pavilion door that led outside. There was his mother, Lady Bridget, then Aunt Bridget and Philip Bisse and finally Henry Somerset. There were also as many servants carrying, amongst other things, boxes full of skates. Lady Bridget and Aunt Bridget both wore grey ankle length coats with fur lined hoods. Bisse was dressed in floppy, wide pantaloons that came to just below his knee. Below that he wore thick, leather boots. He sported a wide brimmed hat and a ruff round his neck. Somerset was dressed similarly, except that his coat was the brightest red while his hat was holly green with a single, long, goose feather for decoration. Compared to Somerset's colours Bisse looked drab.

Peregrine's sister placed a warm, woollen hat on Peregrine's head. "You'll need that," she announced as she put on a coat not dissimilar to that worn by the other lady's, except Mary's was bright blue. Even the fur round the hood seemed to have a slight touch of blue to it.

A servant opened the door and they were greeted to a blast of arctic air that made them all shiver involuntarily.

I have a feeling that I'll be glad when this is over, thought Peregrine to himself.

Somerset had got a walking stick from somewhere and now brandished it like a sceptre, pointing the way out into the snow. "And off we go!" he shouted and charged out, challenging everyone else to follow. Which, somewhat reluctantly, they did.

The South Pavillion of Kiveton Hall was a large building in it's own right. Two storeys high with garret rooms in the roof, it had two wings of it's own. The south-west wing where Peregrine's rooms were, and the south-east wing where the Pavilion attached to the side of the main house. They emerged into the large courtyard that lay to the south of the Pavilion. It was a large, open space edged with limestone walls on the east and west. Directly ahead of them an iron fence marked the transition from the courtyard to the South Lawn. Both were now a foot deep in snow and, without the fence it would be impossible to discern where one ended and the other began.

Led by Somerset they trudged on, kicking snow aside and forcing their way through. Peregrine looked back and somehow regretted how the smooth vista of snow was now defiled by the channel they had carved roughly through it's pristine surface. It would not recover, once blighted by the mark of their crossing even fresh snow could not hide the ragged scar they had wrought. It seemed sad. As if, in their haste they had stained perfection and now it was beyond their ability to enact a repair.

The South Lawn was a thousand feet long, set on a hill gently sloping down to where a set of four gates marked the exit. The Lawn was also two hundred feet across. On it's eastern side a double line of conifers marked it's boundary. Mighty trees, impervious to the winter cold, their evergreen branches briefly held the snow before letting it fall in resounding cascades of ice. On the west side was the stone wall marking the extent of the park, half submerged now in windswept drifts of snow.

As they proceeded down the South Lawn, to their left they could see the wall of the Kitchen Garden, where the fresh produce that sustained the hall was grown. At the corners of the Kitchen Garden were set square towers where the gardeners frequently sought respite from rain or could keep a look out for birds taking crops. The Garden was eerily silent and derelict at this time of year.

Half way down the South Lawn they turned left, between a gap in the double line of conifers and onto an east running, straight road through the park. This was Lodge Hill Avenue, a straight road marked by double lines of lime trees on both sides stretching for nearly four thousand feet to Dog Kennel

Lane.

Thankfully, the snow was not as deep on Lodge Hill Avenue and their progress was swifter. To their left was the wall of the Kitchen Garden while to the right the raised beds that, come spring, would be a blaze of colour, but now slept beneath a snowy blanket.

A thousand feet down Lodge Hill Avenue and the wall stopped. Beyond the lines of lime trees on each side now was the open parkland. A featureless expanse of white, unbroken snow where the occasional tree broke through defiantly. They continued a further thousand feet and then the tree line stopped briefly before continuing a few yards further down as a single line of limes. To the left and right of them a frozen lake lay silently, it's grey surface scratched and scraped by the animals that had braved it. A cold mist hugged the surface through which a flock of ducks and a few swans could be seen bravely sitting huddled on the ice.

A small beck ran through the estate here from north to south. The beck had been dammed a little to the south which had created the small, thin lake, Lodge Hill Pond, that the Lodge Hill Avenue straddled. The pond was a source of water for the corn mill that was situated a few yards away on the opposite side. The Avenue crossed the lake on a flat bridge.

They didn't cross, instead they left the road, following the bank north to where the lake widened. Somerset decided that this spot would be perfect for skating. Everyone else looked rather suspiciously at the lake ice wondering whether it was firm enough to hold their weight.

Somerset had no such trepidation. Wasting no time he donned his skates and made his way out onto the ice.

"Careful, Henry," said Lady Bridget. She turned to her daughter, "Are you not concerned, dear?"

Mary wasn't watching Somerset, she was busy putting on some skates of her own. "No, fortune always favours him. He'll be fine."

"It's a thin line between bravery and recklessness," murmured Lady Bridget.

"And thin ice between delight and misadventure," said her sister-in-law.

But by then Somerset was skating boldly over the ice without apparent difficulty. He waved back as he gathered greater speed.

Bisse wasn't convinced. "It is one thing for the ice to hold a thin rake like Henry, but I have a more manly, stouter frame. I fear I may stress the ice more intensely."

Mary made her way down the edge of the ice, then stepped onto it and pushed off. She floated serenely onto the ice as her husband came speeding past.

"Show off!" she shouted

"Always!" he shouted back as he turned suddenly, dug in his skates and stopped abruptly in a cloud of snow.

Lady Bridget and Aunt Bridget were holding onto each other for support as they made their way onto the ice. With great care they slowly skated away from the shore and began to relax.

With resignation Peregrine put on a pair of skates that seemed to fit him reasonably well, although it still felt as if he had tied a brick onto each foot. Carefully, he made his way to the ice.

His sister Mary skated slowly over, stopping near him. "It'll take a while to get used to it," she said. "But it's worth it."

Peregrine was holding onto a thick branch from an over hanging tree as if his existence depended on it. He certainly believed that his balance depended on it. It felt so slippery under foot that he felt if he moved his weight one inch in any direction his feet would fly out from under him like two unleashed greyhounds.

His mother and Aunt Bridget were doing significantly better. They slowly perambulated around the ice, never far from each other, but with a quiet confidence that put Peregrine to shame.

But Peregrine did feel he was getting more confident. The

more time he spent trying to stay upright the more he seemed to get used to it. After several minutes he let go of the branch he was holding and stood there, like a statue, too wary to move, but at least he was stable. Until he tried moving his feet and then instability overwhelmed him and he clutched back on to the branch again.

"Well, you nearly managed it," laughed Mary. "Try again."

So he did, with mixed results. But slowly, after several abortive attempts, he did manage to wean himself off the branch and slide out onto open ice. Just as he was beginning to think he had got the hang of it, his feet slid away from him and he found himself sitting painfully on the ice. He turned onto his knees and then slowly, one foot at a time managed to get back onto his feet.

Mary clapped,"We all fall over many times at the start. You're doing well."

As time passed, Peregrine improved more and more until he could relax and start to enjoy the experience. Although, he concluded that, as experiences go, it was fairly limited. The area of the lake they could explore was small and, being flat, it did not have very much variety. After about half an hour he began to tire of it and started to make his way back to shore. His mother and Aunt were already removing the skates and giggling happily. Mary followed Peregrine off the ice and started removing her skates.

Somerset seemed quite reluctant to leave. He had mastered skating on one leg now and was showing off even more of his elaborate skills. But, eventually, he also came ashore. They all put their skates back in the boxes and then chatted happily about what a great time they had had. Slowly they started retracing their steps up Lodge Hill Avenue and the South Lawn towards the South Pavilion.

"So I was right, wasn't I?" asked Mary as they walked back.

"About what?" asked Peregrine.

"It was good to get out and get some fresh air rather than spend another day in that prison."

"Yes, you were right," admitted Peregrine reluctantly.

She moved closer to him so the others couldn't hear and lowered her voice. "And was I right about the other thing, too?"

"What other thing?"

"When I left you alone with the blacksmith's daughter. Was I right to do that?"

Peregrine sighed, "Yes, you were right to do that too."

Mary laughed. "You see. Big Sister knows best! When you disappeared on Christmas Day no one knew where you had gone, but I knew." She came even closer and whispered consiprationally, "Don't worry, I've said nothing. Let them keep guessing. Me and you, Pip, we're on the same side. Us against them." She winked at him.

31st December 1711

Two days later the temperature had risen and the snow had gone. It was still cold, especially in the winds that tended to blow up the hill on which the Hall was situated. But Peregrine was determined to go out. He felt a desperate urge to ride down into the village and see what was happening. How everyone had got on with the snow. Part of him wondered, rather illogically, if they still remembered him. Perhaps they regarded Christmas Day as just a single event they didn't expect to be repeated. Maybe they didn't even *want* it to be repeated. They had seemed friendly, but they hadn't invited him again. If he went there now he would be arriving unannounced and uninvited. Perhaps unwelcome.

He had to find out. One way or the other, he had to know where he stood.

So, that morning he went to the stable block and saddled up his favourite horse, Theseus, and rode down the road towards Wales. He reached the crossroads in Wales and turned right down the lane to the blacksmiths. About halfway down he encountered a crowd of people in the road milling around which forced him to stop. He was wondering how best to make his way through when he heard a voice shouting to him.

"Pen!, Pen!" He looked down and Henry Mirfin was standing just ahead of the horses flank. "I didn't know you were coming down for this."

"For what?" shouted Peregrine back.

"Football, we're having a game of football. I'll lead your horse through to the field where we're going to play." Henry took Theseus by the reins and led him through the crowd, up a lane that led off to the right. The crowd thinned noticeably but Peregrine noticed for the first time that they were all moving in one direction. The same direction they were now moving. The lane they were now on turned abruptly round a corner to the left and then, on the left was a large open field. Henry tied Theseus up to some fencing on the side and Peregrine dismounted.

"Good to see you," said Henry. "We need all the men we can get."

"I've never played football," admitted Peregrine.

Henry laughed, "Well, there's nothing to it really. There's two teams, us from Wales and those lot from Todwick...You're not here to play for them, are you?" suddenly suspicious.

"No, don't worry, I didn't even know it was happening."

"Ah good, we can recruit you then. I think they've probably still got a bigger team, but never mind."

"And how's it played?"

"Oh aye. Well, you see that hedge at the far end? That's their goal. And this hedge here is our goal. There's two teams and a ball. We have to put the ball in their goal and they'll try to put the ball in ours."

"And how do we do that?"

Henry gave an evil smile, "Anyway we can. Carry it, throw it, kick it, whatever you want. Only one rule, no fighting unless you're trying to get the ball. Clear?"

"I think so," he said. "How long are we playing?"

"Till midday. Someone's keeping watch on the shadow the stick's throwing and they'll let us know."

"Alright, I'll follow you." Peregrine was beginning to wonder what he had let himself in for, but at least he had an answer to one of his questions. Henry definitely remembered him.

The two teams filed out into roughly the middle of the field and waited. A man came out to them holding a ball. To Peregrine the ball looked more like a pigs bladder filled with water, which was probably what it was. The men stopped milling around aimlessly and suddenly focused intently on the man with ball. Then the man threw the ball high into the air. All eyes followed it, trying to predict where it would land.

It landed amongst a group of Todwick men. Eager hands grappled the air and caught it. It disappeared into the crowd, lost in a writhing mass of menfolk. As one the mass surged forwards with their prize towards the Wales goal. In response, Henry and the men around him shouted a war cry and charged forward to intercept them. Peregrine was pushed forward with them, hopelessly lost in the tumult and the running bodies around him. He ran with the crowd, determined not to fall and risk being trampled.

In seconds, the two sides clashed. Hands grabbed arms and heads, legs braced to force the opposing team and the invisible ball in the direction of the opponents goal. The game quickly descended into a writhing scrum as the two sides, now locked together, pushed with all their might to force the others to give ground.

Peregrine joined in with his teammates, pushing with all his might in the direction of the opponents goal. He felt the muscles on his arms and legs aching with the exertion. For many minutes the two teams faced each other, neither forcing the other to budge much at all. Then the scrum moved back as the Todwick team found new strength. Peregrine felt himself being pushed back against his best efforts. Then suddenly, the men around him seemed to harden their resolve and, with angry shouts, the advance was halted and pushed back the other way.

So it continued for a good while. The scrum flowed first in

one direction only to run out of steam and be halted and be pushed back again. Then this would repeat in the other direction until this advance in its turn was repulsed.

During all this time Peregrine was totally unaware where the ball actually was. All he concentrated on was pushing back against the advancing Todwick men. He didn't know which side even had possession of the ball. For all he knew the ball could have burst at the start of the game, but everyone was so unaware that the game had proceeded without it.

Then suddenly, in one of the endless advances of the Todwick men, Peregrine found that his aching body was struggling to slow their progress. Somehow, he felt that his team mates around him were struggling then, before he knew what was happening, some just seemed to give up and the defensive line began to crumble. As some men stopped resisting the other side sensed victory and redoubled their efforts. In seconds, the Wales line broke and the Todwick team tore through. Wales men fell to the floor and the advancing wall of manhood trampled over them with little regard for their safety. Peregrine felt himself picked up and thrown aside as the oncoming tide of muscle became irresistible. He was left on the floor, discarded, just in time to turn and see the Todwick team race victoriously towards the Wales goal and plant the ball in it.

A loud cheer rose up from their ranks as they leapt into the air with joyous abandon. Like his team mates, Peregrine felt the dark despair of ignominious defeat.

The two teams reformed in the centre of the field. The retrieved ball was thrown once more into the air and, once more, the two teams butted against each other like two angry male rams. They groaned and shouted, pushed and strained until their very sinews screamed for release. The action ebbed and flowed from goal to goal like the tide on a beach until, finally, it was the Todwick side that broke and the Wales side smashed through to score an equalising goal.

Peregrine yelled out with elation and leapt into the air. As he turned, Henry was behind him, yelling so hard he was nearly weeping. They hugged each other in celebration, jumping up and down together, drunk with their victory.

Then, once again, the teams reformed, the ball was thrown and the struggle resumed. Weary muscles once more took up the strain, men cried out with the pain of the exertion, but they refused to submit. The two teams were locked together, braced like two evenly matched arms wrestling over a table top. The stress plain to read on every taught muscle, but each refusing to yield.

There could not be much longer to go. They just needed to hold out a little longer. It would soon be midday and the game would end as a draw. Hold, hold, hold firm. Then Peregrine felt the Todwick line give, ever so slightly, the merest inch, a small sign of weakness. He pushed with everything he had and, then from somewhere, strength he did not even know he had. Slowly, the Todwick line began to fail. Inch by torturous inch it was forced back and back towards their goal. Their attempts to marshal their reserves proved ineffectual and they found themselves backing more and more. Then a tipping point was reached and, with yells of anger, their line broke and men of Wales stormed through to go into the lead.

With midday almost upon them the decision was taken to end the game with a victory to Wales. This led to even more cheers from the winning team and dogged resignation from the losers.

Peregrine found that men he did not know came up to him and clasped his hand warmly, beaming their warm celebratory smiles and slapping him on the back in comradely fashion. It was an infectious moment. He caught their happiness and enthusiasm and grinned so hard his face began to ache as much as the rest of his body.

Henry caught up with him and hugged him. "We did it! I can't believe it. We don't usually, they're a very tough team to beat."

Peregrine laughed, "I am absolutely worn out."

"Aye, me too," Henry laughed back. "And look at the state of you!"

Peregrine looked down at the mud caked on his clothes and hands. Henry was in a similar condition. They looked at each other with broad smiles.

"I didn't think we were going to manage that last time," said Peregrine. "I was completely exhausted."

"Me too. I was way beyond exhausted. I guess they were too."

"I was giving up and then I felt them begin to waver and knew I had to push even harder. When their resistance broke, well, I was so elated."

"Aye, it's a great feeling," agreed Henry. "But a dirty business. We had best get back and clean up."

They picked up Theseus and made their way back along the lane with the rest of the crowd that was now dissipating. Most people turned left, up into the main part of the village, but they turned right, down towards the blacksmiths yard. Peregrine unsaddled Theseus and then led him into the warm stable with Old Sam where he began to eat some hay.

Elizabeth and Susanna were waiting for them when they emerged from the stable. They looked Peregrine and Henry up and down in appraisal. "Look at the condition of you two," said Elizabeth with a smile. "I hope you enjoyed yourselves rolling around in the mud. Now, get those clothes off."

"I hate this bit," muttered Henry as he began to undress.

Peregrine felt the icy wind blowing through the yard and thought better of it. "Look, Elizabeth, I'll be fine. I'll..."

"Off!" she said sternly.

Peregrine looked around uncertainly for any support, but found none. Resignedly he took off his coat and put it to one side and then began to unbutton his muddy clothes. With every item of clothing he discarded he felt the temperature drop a little further. Eventually, he and Henry stood, holding themselves for warmth and dressed only in their loose undergarments.

Susanna smirked as she collected up their clothes and took

them into the wash house for cleaning. She returned carrying a bucket of cold water.

"You can go first, Henry," said Elizabeth.

Without a word Henry made his way over to the bucket and picked it up in both hands. He was shivering with the cold, and the look on his face was a picture of trepidation. Suddenly, he raised the bucket above his head and turned it over, drenching himself in freezing cold water. He yelled out as if in pain. Then he handed the bucket back to Susanna.

"Inside and get warm," instructed Elizabeth as Henry made his way through the kitchen door, his teeth chattering like a couple of rattles. Susanna came back with another bucket of water and put it down on the floor. Elizabeth turned to Peregrine, "You're next."

An spark of rebellion flickered through his mind, but he saw the look on Elizabeth's face and quenched it. Resignedly he went over and picked up the bucket. It was heavy and took both hands with determined effort. He looked at the cold water, it looked so harmless, but he had to steel his will to raise it over his head.

Just do it and get it over with, he scolded himself and turned the bucket over.

It was as if a curtain of ice descended on him. His senses were so heightened that he felt it's steady progress down his body even though it took a fleeting moment. He drew breath instinctively in a flash of panic.

And then it was over and he stood there, soaked, his every muscle involuntarily twitching with the cold. His teeth chattering like some voiceless madman.

"Get inside quickly," said Elizabeth, pushing him through the door into the warm kitchen.

The heat from the fire was as welcome as a hot blanket, it's embrace wrapped around him and calmed his jittering muscles like a soothing balm. His skin tingled and felt fresh, clean and invigorated. Henry stood next to him, smiling as they bathed in the fire's welcome radiance.

Elizabeth came into the kitchen from the living room holding a pile of clothing. "I'll clean your clothes for when we see you next," she said to Peregrine. "I've had a look and here's a selection of Pa and Henry's clothes that might fit you. You can bring them back with you next time."

"Thank you," said Peregrine. "You're very generous."

"Not at all," said Elizabeth. "I expect you to bring them back or we'll start wearing yours - and yours are better." She smiled.

He laughed in agreement. So he was welcome here. They did want him to come back.

Not for the first time he noticed that when she smiled at him, part of him didn't want her to stop. It was a warm, friendly smile, but there was something else about it. Her brown eyes looked at him and didn't immediately look away. She held his gaze for a moment longer than was otherwise necessary. He thought he saw something in her eyes that he wasn't used to seeing in people. She seemed interested in him. Almost intrigued by him. For someone like Peregrine, who had lived his life largely unnoticed by everyone except his brother William, it was an unfamiliar experience. But not an unpleasant one.

In return he found himself starting to notice things about Elizabeth that seemed to have previously eluded him. That she was roughly his age, perhaps a little older. That she had a habit of tucking her hand in a pocket under her apron. The way her petticoats rustled when she walked. The way that two strands of her black hair had come undone and now dangled loosely around her neck.

"Hot broth," she said suddenly, breaking his line of thought. She placed a bowl of hot broth on the table. "Get it while it's hot. I don't want you two catching cold." She turned back to get another.

Henry and Peregrine dressed hurriedly and then assumed their seats at the table. Elizabeth gave Henry the next bowl and they began to eat. It was warming, driving the final vestiges of the waters chill from their bones and it filled a gap in their stomachs.

She sat down in the seat next to Peregrine, even though she had no bowl of broth herself. "We had ours just before you arrived back from the match," she explained.

Peregrine found himself very aware of how close to him she was sitting. She didn't need to, there were plenty of seats further away, and she didn't really have any reason to sit at the table at all, but she had chosen to sit next to him. She had done it casually, as she might sit innocently next to anyone, nothing could be read into it. But, nevertheless, Peregrine found it was a fraction too close to be as casual as it seemed. The hairs on the side of his body next to her seemed to rise of their own accord quite outside of his control. To his surprise, he found he was quite enjoying the proximity.

"So how was the match?" she asked. "I didn't know you were going to be playing, Pen."

"Neither did he!" laughed Henry. "We needed as many men as we could get and Pen just happened to be passing. So I grabbed him."

"Have you played it before?"

"Not at all," admitted Peregrine. "I've not heard of it. It's more of a physical than a skill game, isn't it?"

"More like brute force really," she said. "That's why I was surprised when I saw that you'd been playing. You strike me as a bit too refined for it. Not a ruffian like our Henry."

"Hold on, what do you mean by that?" said Henry with a laugh.

"Let's be honest. A blacksmith is better suited to it than a gentleman like Pen here."

"It helps if you've got a bit of muscle," admitted Henry. "And spending your day thumping metal with a lump hammer will build plenty of that."

Peregrine interjected, "While that's true, I found it a rewarding experience. Quite elating really. Justifying any exertions."

She looked at him quizzically, "See, you don't even speak like they do."

"Leave him be! So he uses big words," said Henry. "He can hold his own in a scrum and that's what matters."

"I meant it as a good thing," said Elizabeth with irritation. "What ever made you agree to do it?"

"I hadn't done it before," explained Peregrine simply. "The other day my sister asked me to go skating. I had never done that before either. At first I was reluctant, but I agreed. To my surprise I quite enjoyed myself. So, when the opportunity arose to try something else I hadn't done before I just thought, well, why not? I might enjoy that too."

"And you did, too, didn't you, Pen?" said Henry with a grin. "And It's valuable exercise too," he added.

"Exercise it may be," scoffed Elizabeth. "Valuable? I doubt it. Still, if you enjoyed yourselves I suppose it's harmless enough."

"I don't know about harmless," said Peregrine. "To be honest, at times I thought it was downright dangerous."

Henry and Peregrine laughed, thinking back to the challenges of the day.

Elizabeth reached across and gathered up their empty bowls. As she did so, momentarily her leg brushed Peregrine's. It was only briefest, the lightest of touches, but just the idea that her thigh was so close to his seemed suddenly exciting. And then it was gone as Elizabeth got up to take the bowls for washing. Oddly, if he thought hard he could still remember what it felt like. He clung onto that memory, afraid he might forget how it felt.

"Do you play football often?" Peregrine asked.

"Nah, some mates might get together for a game occasionally, but a village on village match is rare." replied Henry. "It has to be when no one's working, you see. Like now. Although, someone from Todwick told me they went for a spell where they played Anston every Sunday afternoon. But I don't think they do now."

"You always play Todwick?"

"Not always. Sometimes Anston, Harthill, Woodhall, Aston, Beighton. Who ever can get a team together. Why? You want to play next time?"

Peregrine nodded, "Yes, I think so."

Henry smiled, "Good. Hey, do you want some beer? I'm going to get some."

"Yes, beer would be good." Henry went off to get it leaving Peregrine alone.

Elizabeth returned with two bowls now cleaned. "So, Pen, what brings you down here?" she asked as she started putting the bowls away.

"The football game," he replied uncertainly.

"No, what I mean is, what brought you to Wales so that Henry could grab you for the football? You didn't know about it before you got here."

"I, uh, was tired of being in the house and just wanted to get out. You're the only people I know here so I thought I'd come down and see what you were doing."

"So you *were* coming to see us then? Not just out riding?" She turned round and looked at him with an unwavering gaze.

"Yes," he said returning her look. Then quietly he said, "I was coming to see you."

Elizabeth opened her mouth to say something, but before she could speak Henry came back in. "Here we are," he announced, putting two cups of frothy beer on the table. "Wales' finest! Well, it's probably brewed in an abbey somewhere - where ever Bob Pinder gets it from. But it's still the best beer in Wales."

Elizabeth laughed, "It's the *only* beer in Wales."

"Well, there you are then. I'm right."

The beer was dark brown with a frothy head. It had a slightly bitter, almost nutty taste, but it was refreshing. Peregrine took a good gulp and decided he could get used to it rather quickly.

"It's very good," he said.

Henry smiled. "Aye, but be careful. It creeps up on you. You might find yourself falling over after five or six pints. Don't worry I'll throw you over your horse and I'm sure he can find his way back."

They laughed. "He's certainly a fine horse," said Elizabeth.

Peregrine nodded. "Yes, he saw me home safe before so I've decided to stick with him. He's called Theseus."

"Unusual name," said Elizabeth. "The hero who slew the Minotaur "

Peregrine looked at her and grinned, "Yes, you're right. You never fail to surprise me. He follows the thread and finds his way home out of the labyrinth. So I have faith that the horse with that name can find his way home too."

"He follows the thread Ariadne gave him...to guide him to safety," she continued.

"Yes. So, in a sense, she saves him."

"And she falls in love with him."

"Yes," he replied.

"But he betrays her."

"Yes, well, it's a story. Best not to read too much into it," replied Peregrine, for some reason feeling uncomfortable.

Henry laughed, "Elizabeth, you were so lucky to meet Pen, you know."

"Was I?" she said unsteadily. "Why?"

"He's the only one round here that actually knows the stories in your books better than you do. Me and Pa listen, but, to be honest, we're more suited to talking about making the new fence round the church or how Mr Stacey's horse needs new shoes. You know, everyday stuff. It's good that you've got someone to talk to about dreamy things and faraway places."

"I suppose it is," she said slowly looking at Peregrine.

"Do you like horses, Elizabeth?" he asked suddenly, on impulse.

"I can ride. I used to ride our horse, Sam, but I don't any more. He's getting too old. We just let him rest unless he has to take the wagon somewhere."

"I was thinking of taking Theseus out for a ride at the weekend. Somewhere further afield, explore a bit. But I don't know the area so I was wondering if you wanted to come along so I don't get lost."

"I'd like to but, as I say, Sam's too old and I don't ride him any more."

"That is no problem. We have lots of horses up at the Hall. If you want I can bring you a horse."

She looked at him for a while, trying to weigh things up then said, "Yes, That would be great. Which day? Sunday would be best for me, after church."

"Then Sunday it is," he replied with a grin. "I'll look forward to it."

Henry grinned. "Good!" he declared. "She needs to get out more. I don't suppose there's any chance of you taking my other sister out with you as well?"

At that point Elizabeth hit him with the dish cloth.

Before anything else could happen the door opened and Robert Mirfin came in with Susanna. "Oh, Pen's here," exclaimed Susanna. "That's a surprise."

"He joined in the game," explained Henry. "Which we won."

"And how was Uncle Jack?" asked Elizabeth.

"Same as usual," said Robert.

"They're doing New Years tonight at Uncle Jacks," said Susanna. "They're staying up to midnight to see the New Year in."

"Silly idea," grumbled Robert. "I told him, New Years on March 25th, always has been and always will be. They can't go changing things like that, people will be one year older three months early."

"A lot of people seem to be switching to the new New Year now," said Elizabeth. "It's all the rage."

"We could have new New Year and old New Year too three months later," said Susanna with a grin.

"Definitely not! It's madness, madness. How's a man meant to get his mind round that sort of thing. Whatever next? Two birthdays for everyone, two Christmases, three Easters."

"Two birthdays? That would a great idea," said Susanna.

"No, no, not in this house. Not while I'm still breathing," grumbled Robert getting his pipe out to soothe himself with a smoke.

"Are you having New Year tonight, Pen," asked Susanna.

He shook his head. "No, we're sticking to March, I believe. For now anyway. For what it's worth, I wouldn't really want to have New Year right in the middle of Christmas. We're only at, what, Seventh Night. Better to leave New Year where it is as a separate celebration."

"Couldn't have said it better myself," said Robert. "Blinking new ideas. I wasn't that keen on bringing Christmas back in the first place."

Henry put a beer down in front of Robert. "Have a beer and try and get in the Christmas spirit."

"Cheers, that's very welcome," said his father.

Peregrine stayed for the next few hours until darkness had fallen. After a brief meal and several more beers he thought he should start making his way back. Finishing off his last beer he rose to his feet and gathered together his things. He went out to the stables and saddled up Theseus then led him out into the yard and tied him up. Then he went back into the kitchen.

"I'm ready to get off back now," he said. "It was good to see you all again. Let me know when the next match is, Henry."

"Will do. Though it'll not be for a while," said Henry.

"Aye, see you again," said Robert, quietly smoking his pipe.

"Bye, Pen," added Susanna happily.

Elizabeth came over and walked with him to the door. "You're still thinking of going out riding on Sunday?" she asked.

"If you still want to," he replied. She was standing quite close to him, as she spoke she was looking directly up at him. Her gaze never drifted. "I mean I don't want to force..."

"I still want to," she said quickly. "If you want to..."

"Oh yes," he said just as quickly. "I'm looking forward to it."

"Well, I'll see you on Sunday then."

And then Susanna laughed. "Oh no, oh no. You're caught."

They were both stood in the doorway and they both looked at her wondering what she was talking about.

Susanna pointed above their heads. "You have to do it. You've been caught."

Peregrine and Elizabeth looked up, hanging in the doorway above their heads was a sprig of mistletoe. Elizabeth's heart sank, "Oh no, no."

"Oh yes," insisted Susanna with a laugh. "You've got to. It's tradition and you've been caught."

Elizabeth looked up at Peregrine who was looking back levelly. "It looks like we may have to," she said shyly.

"Well, I don't want to stand in the way of tradition," he said. His hands held her waist and, with slight pressure, he pulled her towards him. Her upraised face met his and his lips brushed hers lightly in a gentle kiss.

As he pulled away Elizabeth suddenly realised her eyes were shut and opened them quickly. His face was still very close. She realised her heart was racing. His hands were still resting on her waist and she didn't mind at all.

"Well, I'll see you on Sunday," he said gently.

"Uh, yes, Sunday," she managed. She seemed to be having difficulty putting words together.

Peregrine turned to Susanna with a grin, "And you are a trouble maker!"

"I know," said Susanna, almost jumping with delight.

"Goodnight everyone," he said with a laugh and left.

Elizabeth stood there for a moment, her index finger stroking her lips where he had kissed her.

Chapter Five

Peregrine woke early that morning. He literally leapt out of bed and quickly threw back the curtains with unbridled enthusiasm. It was a bright, sunny, morning. Undoubtedly, it was cold. Frost clung to the grass of the South Lawn and a little fog lingered round the double row of sentinel conifers that lined the lawn to the left. But it wasn't raining, and it wasn't snowing. It was a fine day for wrapping up warm and going out. With the right company, of course. And today he was going out riding with Elizabeth.

He felt a sudden racing in his heart as he thought that. It had been a desperately slow few days waiting for Sunday to come round. Time had ticked by at a glacial pace as he tried to conjure new ways to waste it. Every moment had seemed like an obstacle. He had just wanted to quicken the clocks, move them on to Sunday and skip the intervening period. He had wanted to cut those irritating two days from his life, throw them away and get on with the important things. But time would not heed him. It would not fly by a second faster. Worse, it slowed until the minutes hung like leaden weights that he dragged with difficulty from hour to hour. In contrast, his mind leapt around like a caged bird, battering itself against the wires of its cage in a desperate, fruitless, effort to escape. If he tried to read, then he found his thoughts soon wandering back to Elizabeth until he could not recall what he had read. If he ate he could not remember what he had eaten. If he walked in the gardens it seemed so vacant, empty and pointless...because Elizabeth was not there to share them. How he had wished those two days would hurry and end.

And now they had ended. He felt like a prisoner on the day he would be released from captivity. He dressed with haste and virtually flew down the stairs into the Garden Room. His mother, Aunt Bridge and Philip Bisse were already there having breakfast. There was no sign of his sister or her husband.

Light was streaming through the large windows with blinding intensity. His mother kept holding up her hand to shield her eyes. Servants were running around, placing a selection fruits, cheeses, cold meats and bread on the table for the family to help themselves.

Peregrine breezed over to the table and quickly seated himself. He grabbed a small plate and started filling it with bread, cheese and fruit. He asked a passing servant for some tea and began eating ravenously.

"Good morning, Pip," said his mother formally. The others intoned a similar greeting with little enthusiasm.

"Good morning, everyone!" replied Peregrine happily. "What a fabulous morning."

"Is it?" said Aunt Bridget. "It's a cold one as usual. That's the thing about Christmas, it's the longest of holidays at just the point in the year when you can't go out."

"It's the time to celebrate the birth of Our Lord," said Bishop Bisse. "A time of great joy for all mankind."

"Um," murmured Aunt Bridget. "Well, I pity the poor babe having to be born in the middle of winter. You would think Mary would have timed it so as to give birth to the poor darling when it was warmer."

"I don't think she chose it, dear," replied Bisse condescendingly. "God himself chose the date for the conception."

"It's always the case. The poor women never get to chose the date, it's just nine months after the men's sap has risen."

"You sail close to blasphemy, my dear," admonished Bisse. "Besides, the birth had to coincide with the arrival of star of Bethlehem in late December. It's all perfectly planned, as you might expect."

"Well, he could have made the star arrive later, say in June. He is God after all."

"I don't think anyone knows," said Peregrine suddenly.

"Knows what, dear?" asked Aunt Bridget.

"On what date Jesus was born," said Peregrine idly.

"I think you'll find that the Bible is our reference in this matter," said Bisse haughtily.

"The Bible is silent on this," replied Peregrine. "It doesn't give the date or even the year for that matter. It's been left to people to make it up. I think the first reference to it being in late December is in a Roman almanac from the 4th Century."

"Humph," said Bisse.

"Well, whoever decided it," said his wife. "I wish they would have decided to put it in summer."

"People can't just decide to pick a different date because it's warmer," said Bisse with uncharacteristic irritation. "This is the most significant event in human history, we cannot just change it on a whim."

"But if they don't know when it is," she said. "Then they are just picking any old date and I'm just saying they could pick one that was at a more comfortable time of year."

"But they *do* know," said Bisse. "Theologians and wise men have studied this issue in depth for centuries and, after painstaking analysis, they have determined the precise date."

"Well, then there's the question of calendars," said Peregrine as he chomped on an apple. "Our Christmas Day isn't on the same day as it is in other places."

"What are you talking about, dear?" asked Aunt Bridget.

"We use a Roman calendar, but most countries in Europe use a Papal calendar that's eleven days different to ours. So even when we agree on a date we can't agree on which day that lands on."

"That can't be true," she said with a laugh.

"Actually, he's right," admitted Bisse. "The Papists use a different calendar. There are rumours of us having to adopt it one day. But I don't think we should. We are English after all, we plot our own course, we don't have to bend the knee to these continentals. I hate foreigners. And Papists. And I hate Papist foreigners most of all."

Peregrine smiled to himself. "I thought the Church advocated we should love our neighbours?"

"Neighbours yes. Papists and foreigners, definitely not!"

His mother noticed his smile. She said, "You're enjoying yourself."

Peregrine looked up. "Me? No, not me. How could I do that?"

"Oh, yes you are," she replied. "I recognise the signs from when you were a boy. You're...happy."

Peregrine laughed. "God forbid," he replied. And then to Bisse, "Sorry, Bishop."

Lady Bridget studied him closely. "Yes, definitely happy."

Aunt Bridget said, "Well good luck to you, Pip. Staying happy in this climate is a major undertaking. Don't you think Christmas goes on far too long? What are we up to now? Tenth Night? I would have been glad to stop about Third or Fourth. "

Her husband didn't answer, but instead turned to Peregrine's mother. "It's been a pleasure staying here, Lady Bridget, but I must admit, I'll be glad to get back to Pembrokeshire," said Bisse absently. "See how things have managed while I was away."

Peregrine's sister entered and assumed a seat near Peregrine and started assembling an assortment of fruit.

"Its been a pleasure having you to stay, Philip," said Peregrine's mother to Bisse and then to Mary. "Have you noticed that Pip's looking a lot brighter today, Mary?"

Mary stopped peeling an orange and looked at Peregrine. "Oh yes, I see what you mean. He's looking all chirpy."

"Any idea what would be causing that, Mary?" asked her mother.

"Not the slightest," she said, smiling at Peregrine. "I suppose we could try asking him."

"Something tells me he wouldn't be very forthcoming," said his mother suspiciously.

Peregrine drank his tea off and rose from his seat. "Well, it's been good listening to you talk about me, but I really must be going now. Things to do, you know." With a sharp nod to his mother, aunt and sister he left the room.

"He's a strange one," said Aunt Bridget after he was gone. "I'm not sure I can quite work him out."

Peregrine went up his room and donned a warm coat, scarf and gloves then made his way out to the stables. Once there he instructed two boys to saddle two horses. He selected Theseus for his own horse, for Elizabeth he chose a young mare called Cyrene. He climbed onto Theseus and then took Cyrene by the reins and led her out of the stable yard and down the road. They walked slowly down Red Hill then, at the junction, turned right towards Wales. Once in the village, at the crossroads, Peregrine turned right and then down towards the blacksmiths cottage.

The two horses clattered into the yard and Peregrine dismounted and tied them up. He went to the door and hesitated for a few moments then knocked. It opened almost immediately.

Elizabeth smiled warmly, "Good morning. You managed to get another horse then?" she said looking past him.

"Of course," he said. Moving back out into the yard to where the horses were tethered. Elizabeth patted Cyrene gently on the neck. "Her name is Cyrene."

"Another figure from Greek myth?"

"I believe so, if an obscure one. I think the god Apollo fell in love with her when he saw her wrestle a lion."

Elizabeth stroked the horse, "This one doesn't look like she'll be doing anything like that. She looks very gentle." She turned to him, "Thanks for doing this, Pen. I didn't realise how much I missed it."

"You don't need to thank me. I should thank you for coming along."

"Shall we get going. Where were you planning to go?"

"Down through Wales Wood and then along the river?"

"Sounds good to me," she agreed enthusiastically. "Oh, and before we go any further I've an admission to make."

"Really?" he said lightly. "And what would that be?"

"You may be used to fine ladies who ride around elegantly in side saddle fashion. I'm afraid I learned to ride like a man." She looked at him, wondering what his reaction would be.

"Good," he replied nonchalantly. "I ride like a man too. But don't you find your petticoats get in the way?"

"Ah, I put a split in these petticoats so they're better suited for riding. I know, it's indecent..." she said sheepishly.

"Indecent," he agreed. "But very practical. Shall we get going?"

She smiled with relief. "Aye, let's be away."

They climbed into the saddle then made sure they were comfortable. Robert, Henry and Susanna had come to the door to see them off.

"Enjoy yourselves," shouted Susanna, waving enthusiastically.

"Yes, have a great time!" shouted Henry.

They shouted back thanks and then with broad smiles on their faces, they guided their horses slowly out of the yard.

Robert, Henry and Susanna watched them go.

"Don't they make a lovely couple," said Susanna.

"Maybe," agreed Robert. "But that's two worlds that should never have touched." He sighed, "I hope she knows what she's doing - but I doubt it."

They rode up the crossroads and turned right, then along the road for another six hundred yards. The road rose up a steady incline to the brow of the hill. Once over the brow the road fell away sharply. Ahead of them the road ran straight down the incline to another crossroads where it met the main road to Rotherham.

They paused momentarily to take in the view. Beyond the crossroads stretched the endless canopy of Wales Wood. It spread down into the valley where it met the River Rother running directly across their path. On the other side of the river the far bank rose up to a rolling, wooded hill where the village of Beighton sat. Beyond Beighton the ground sank into another dale before rising once again up to Ridgeway Moor which sat like a dark shadow on the horizon. Beyond Ridgeway was Derbyshire.

As they proceeded down the hill towards the Rotherham Road crossroads Peregrine asked, "How far have you been over there?"

"I've never really been across the river," she admitted. "The nearest bridge is downstream at Woodhouse where the road goes up the hill to Handsworth. I've crossed the bridge, but there isn't really any reason to go further."

"You've never been curious?"

"Perhaps," she admitted. "But if you're on foot it's quite a walk to satisfy that curiosity. Although, beyond Handsworth is Darnall and beyond that is Sheffield. Now I have been curious about Sheffield. It's on the River Don, that's a major river, not like this one. And it's where they make the knives. They must be great craftsman. Pa can make many things in iron and steel, but only the crudest of knives."

"I've never been there either," admitted Peregrine. "But, you're right Sheffield is renowned throughout the country for making knives. Has your father always been a blacksmith?"

"Always. And his father. And his father before him. And Henry will be too. It's kind of a Mirfin tradition. There's a story Pa was told by his father that there's a record of a John Mirfin in Slade Hooton in 1379 and guess what - he was a blacksmith. So, we've been doing it for quite a while."

"Slade Hooton? That's beyond Laughton, right?"

"Aye, Laughton's on one side of a valley, Hooton's on the other. Brookhouse is in the bottom. My grandpa lived in Brookhouse, Uncle Jack still does. Pa was baptised at Laughton

Church."

They led the horses across the Rotherham Road crossroads and then down the road on the other side into Wales Wood.

"If your family was from Laughton, how come you're now in Wales?"

"Because of love," she said, looking across to see his reaction. "Pa fell in love with his own cousin and she lived in Todwick. So he looked for work near her. They married and ended up in Wales."

"Who ever loved that loved not at first sight."

"Pardon?"

"Shakespeare," he said. "Or is it Marlowe. I forget. Probably both."

"I've never heard of them."

"Then that is something I must remedy. I'll get you a book."

"Oh, I couldn't possibly ask..."

"Shh," he held up his hand. "You're not asking. I'm giving it to you. Which reminds me, I have a surprise for you."

"Really? What?"

"Well, if I told you it wouldn't be very much of a surprise, would it? You'll have to wait."

The road they were following ran straight for the first stretch. On either side, the towering ash, birch and beech trees of Wales Wood grew as thick hedges. Eventually, the road turned to the left for two hundred yards and then it emerged from the wood on to the grassy banks of the River Rother.

The Rother ran in a ragged line south to north, ultimately joining the larger Don at Rotherham. It was generally a small river but, still, it was several yards across and it ran deep. It was a difficult river to ford without a bridge. They turned the horses northwards along the river bank, following a well worn path.

"So, when do I get this surprise?" she asked.

"I haven't decided. You'll have to be patient."

"I do believe you are a tease."

"I shouldn't have said anything."

"No, you shouldn't." She laughed. He realised he liked to see her laugh. So he laughed too.

She shook the reins and her horse broke into a trot. So Peregrine did likewise with Theseus. They followed the Rother's bank along. It opened out onto a flood plain with grasslands and marshes on both side. They continued downstream. After a mile or so they slowed to a walk.

"So, what do you have to say for yourself, Lord Osborne?" she asked as their horses drew side by side.

"Concerning what?"

"I keep asking myself why the grandson of the Duke of Leeds is out riding with me. I'm just the village blacksmith's daughter."

"I like you. And you're not *just* the blacksmith's daughter. You also know who Theseus is. You know about Rome, Florence and Venice. You crept into Kiveton because you wanted to see what was inside. All this means I have more in common with you than any of the people currently living there. But tell me, why is someone like you out riding with me?"

She smiled. "You intrigue me, Pen. To say the least you are not like the men I usually meet."

"Because my family is wealthy," he said, sounding disappointed

"No, not quite. Even though your family is wealthy, you choose not to be with them. You're searching for something. Something that your family, despite all their money, is unable to provide."

Peregrine turned away, suddenly feeling uncomfortable. He wasn't sure whether Elizabeth was proving a little too perceptive or he was a little too transparent. But, either way, he felt suddenly exposed in a way he was not accustomed too.

"Ah, there's the Mill," he said.

Ahead, they had reached the point in the river where the road from Worksop to Sheffield crossed the Rother. The old, grey stones of the medieval bridge stood impassive to the passing of time and traffic. Withstanding one and effortlessly conveying the other. The river flowed ceaselessly through its arches as it had for centuries. In front of the bridge was the old Woodhouse Mill. It was no longer a wooden house, the mill had, presumably, been rebuilt at some time in stone. But its purpose remained the same and the huge, wooden water wheel on its side turned relentlessly in the flowing water to grind the corn for tomorrows bread.

They dismounted, tied up their horses and then sat together on the low wall that ran out from the Mill and along the bank.

"Perhaps now is a good time," said Peregrine. He held a square parcel in his hand that he taken from his saddle bag. He handed it to her. It was a leather bound book with no title on it. Carefully, she opened it. The first two pages were coloured drawings of the Colosseum in Rome. Beautifully drawn, the left side showed how it was today while the one on the right was a depiction of how it may have looked during its heyday. The next page was the inside of the Colosseum with the same pair of pictures showing then and now. Then the Great Square, the Forum of Caesar, the Temple of Saturn and many others.

She touched it gently, with reverence, "It's beautiful," she said quietly

"It was my brothers. He drew them when we were in Rome. He enjoyed sketching. Rome inspired him. I'd like you to have them."

She closed the book suddenly, "No, I can't. It's too much."

"He would have liked you to have them," he insisted.

"I didn't even know him," she said. Immediately, she regretted the harsh tone she had used, but Peregrine didn't seem to notice.

"He loved Rome so he drew it. Then he died and I asked myself why did he bother. Why did we go all that way, for all those months, for him just to die before we got home. And then I met you, someone who loves Rome too, but has never seen it and, most likely, never will. And it all began to make some sort of sense. Maybe, he drew it so you could see it. Maybe, he captured what he saw so that you could see through his eyes. So, you see, it's like they were always intended for you."

She frowned and gently touched the cover. "I can't accept this, Pen," she said softly. "This is something for you to remember your brother with. It's all you have left of him, I can't take that from you. And, anyway, I would feel too obligated to you. It would be like I was forever in your debt. I can't promise to ever give you anything as valuable as this."

Peregrine was sat, staring into the flowing water of the river. "Alright," he said gently. "Not a gift then. I'll let you borrow it. Could you keep hold of it for me? And when you feel you know you won't be seeing me again you can give it back. How's that?"

She smiled and clasped it to her chest. "Alright, Pen. I'll look after it for you. It will be a pleasure."

"Good," he said absently. He stood up and picked up a stone from the floor and threw it into the river where it made a soft splash and then was lost. "You were right about me before."

"Regarding what?"

"About me searching for something."

She didn't trust herself to reply. She thought, *Let me guess, you've been searching for someone like me? Is this part of his act? Is he that predictable?*

Eventually she said, "And what would that be?". A sceptical undertone crept into her voice unintentionally.

"I don't know really," he admitted as he threw another stone into the river. "Will and I were born in North Mymms, mother's family home. Mother was a distant figure, we always had to look our best when she visited, all neat, clean and well-groomed. Like a visit from royalty. We were raised by a procession of nannies, some we liked, some we hated. None of them lasted very long. Father was even more remote. He only visited mother when he wanted money, he certainly didn't waste his time with us. When we were seven or eight we moved here, to grandfather's brand new family seat. Except there wasn't really a family to sit in it," he laughed humourlessly at his joke and threw another stone. "Grandfather built the place, but had fallen out with father by then so they avoided each other. Grandfather lived in Wimbleon and London, father lived...well, somewhere else."

She got up and came to stand beside him. "But you told me you didn't live here."

"My grandparents real concern was, and is, the succession. When grandfather dies who is going to take over the family business. They wanted it to be my uncle, Edward, but he died. So they looked to my father but, despite their efforts, he has never showed the slightest interest in anything apart from spending other people's money and the Navy. So, they looked to my brother Will...and me. As soon as they could, they took us under their wing, moved us to London then abroad. Educated us with the finest tutors, sent us on expensive holidays. We experienced a great deal, but we never actually *lived* anywhere for very long. But that didn't seem to matter, because Will was always there. I wasn't alone. Until now."

"And so you came back here?"

"I couldn't think of anywhere else. I couldn't carry on moving around from place to place. I feel like I need to *belong* somewhere." He stopped and looked at her deeply, "And that's what you have. Something that is denied to me."

She laughed, "What could I possibly have that you could not acquire if you wanted it?"

"You belong here," he said simply.

"You overrate it, I think. Like I said, I've never been across this river, but you have seen Rome and Venice!"

"But if, one day, you went to these places and saw them, you would still, eventually, come home. It's as if part of your soul is rooted in these fields and villages. While you were there, something deep inside, would always ache and yearn...for home."

Her eyes narrowed as she looked at him. "I think you also feel this yearning for home," she said. "It's just that you have forgotten where that is. And that's what you are searching for."

"Yes," he said quietly. "But, in my case, it cannot be found. It must be made."

She suddenly felt an overwhelming sympathy for him. He wasn't an Earl any more, he was just someone lost in the dark, chasing every little light and hoping one of them was the way out. Before she knew what she was doing she had put her arms around him and was hugging him. She felt his arms wrap around her, hugging her so firmly. It felt so safe, so secure.

He felt her face against his, smooth and soft. A strand of her hair brushed his face like a ghost's caress. When he breathed in he could smell her, clean and unfamiliar. He felt her body against his, warm, soft and very close.

Then she pulled away, slowly, hesitantly, but firmly. She looked slightly embarrassed. She made a show of straightening her petticoats and pushing her hair back under her cap. "I suppose, we should start getting back," she said, avoiding looking at him.

He couldn't stop looking at her. He consumed every detail. He tried to desperately commit the image, the smell, the feel of her in his arms to memory.

"If that is what you want," he said solemnly.

She stopped and looked at him. "It gets dark early this time of year. That's all."

He clung to the last two words. She said that was all. The dark was the only reason for leaving, not him. She wasn't upset. He fought an overwhelming urge to apologise because he wasn't sure what it was for.

She seemed to sense his insecurity and smiled. His fears melted. "Come on, let's get back," she said. She picked up the William's book of drawings then they both climbed onto their horses and started back the way they had come.

Elizabeth turned to him with a grin. "Race you back!" she shouted and kicked Cyrene's sides causing the horse to gallop away.

"We'll see about that!" he yelled back and set Theseus galloping after them.

Theseus seemed like a hurtling mountain of muscle underneath him as they raced along. The air bit his face making his

eyes weep with the cold and run in rivulets along his grinning cheeks. The sense of speed and strength was exhilarating.
Soon he caught Elizabeth up and he gently tugged the reins to
slow Theseus' headlong race so that both horses ran together,
synchronised, along the river bank.

All too soon they reached the point where the road forked
left and up into the wood and they reined their steeds to a
halt, patting them gently on their necks in congratulation.
Horses and people panted happily, their breath condensing
into steaming clouds in the cooling air.

"You were right," said Peregrine. "You *do* ride like a man!"

"If you wanted a gentle ride with the ladies you should have
stayed in your hall, your Lordship," she shouted back with a
grin.

"You're more of a lady than they will ever be," he said.

After letting the horses rest a while they began the climb
up the hill through Wales Wood, then across the Rotherham
Road.

"And Rotherham? Have you ever been there?" asked Peregrine as they crossed the road and continued up the hill.

"Certainly not," she said. "And wouldn't want to. It's a rough
place, full of thieves and gambling."

He smiled. "One hundred and fifty years ago it was a fashionable college town."

"Really? Rotherham? Are you joking with me?"

He laughed, "No, not at all. It's true. It was a rival of Oxford
and Cambridge. But when the college was dissolved the town
fell on to less prosperous times."

She looked at him, "You know, I learn a great deal from talking to you. I'm just not sure I can remember it all."

"You once told me you had an insatiable curiosity. I merely
try to satisfy it as best I can."

"Yes," she admitted. "My curiosity about Kiveton Hall got
me into trouble."

"I am so very, very glad it did," he said honestly.

They crossed the brow of the hill then rode down to the

crossroads into Wales, turning left down the familiar lane home. A few moments later and they drew into the yard and dismounted. She took William's sketch book from her saddle bag and held it tightly under her arm.

"I would like to see you again..." he said rather dumbly.

She laughed. "Well, of course you'll see me again. Don't forget you still have those clothes you borrowed after the football match. You need to bring those back."

"Oh yes, I forgot."

"So, night after next is Twelfth Night. Are you busy?"

"Uh, no. "

"Well, come down here in the evening. We'll be having something to eat, a few drinks...Henry, Susanna and Pa will be here."

He smiled, "That sounds great."

"That's settled then," she said. She went over to him, carrying the sketch book in one hand. She reached up with her other hand behind his neck, then pulled his head down to hers and kissed him. His arms went automatically around her waist, tightening gently as he kissed her back. They drew apart but this time she held his gaze. "I'll see you night after next then," she said. With that she turned, opened the door and went inside.

He stood in the yard for a few seconds, thinking back over what had just happened. Then he started singing, far too loud and without much tune. He virtually jumped onto Theseus' back, his feet felt so light. Grabbing Cyrene's reins, and still singing, he began the ride back.

As Elizabeth entered the kitchen, three faces turned in her direction with quizzical looks. It caused her to pause momentarily, take a sigh and gather her composure.

"Well?" asked Susanna.

"Well what?" she replied entering the room as nonchalantly as she could.

"How did you get on?"

"Fine. We always get on fine."

"Yes, but did he...you know?"

"Shh, girl," said Henry with irritation. "Pen's a decent sort he wouldn't...." then he looked hopefully at Elizabeth. "Would he?"

Elizabeth laughed, "What's wrong with you two? We went for a ride down the river to Woodhouse. That was it. It was good to ride again. I've missed it."

"Did he woo you?" asked Susanna.

Elizabeth frowned in thought, "I'm not sure Pen would know what that meant. And I'm not sure I would know whether he was or not."

Robert puffed on his pipe, "Well, sounds like you enjoyed yourself."

"Yes, I did. I've invited him to join us for Twelfth Night."

"Oh great!" cheered Susanna. "Pen's coming to the Mallander's barn?"

Elizabeth looked guilty, "I actually haven't told him about that bit. I just invited him here."

Henry laughed, "I'm sure he knows about Twelfth Night. It's the same everywhere."

"They didn't have it when I was a lad," rumbled Robert.

"I'm glad they do now, " said Susanna. "It's fun."

Elizabeth shrugged. "Well, we will see. I've got to get changed out of these riding coats."

With that she went upstairs. Susanna and Henry looked at each other and shared a grin.

5th January 1711

"Ah, Twelfth Night!" exclaimed Peregrine's mother between sips of tea. "I've been looking forward to this all Christmas."

Only four of them now sat round the table in the Garden Room having breakfast. Apart from Peregrine there was also Mary and her husband, Somerset.

Peregrine was thankful that Aunt Bridget and her husband had headed back to Pembrokeshire for their Twelfth Night celebrations. His fervent hope was that he wouldn't have to endure Aunt Bridget and the Reverend Bisse's company again for several months or years.

"Yes," agreed Somerset enthusiastically. "It really is the absolute pinnacle of Christmas."

"Who are you going as, Pip?" Lady Bridget asked Peregrine.

He frowned, "Going as? To what?"

His mother sighed, "I swear I don't know where your mind is half the time, Pip. It's Twelfth Night. We are all going to Welbeck for the festivities. There are going to be several sets of musicians, acrobats, clowns, lots of feasting, of course, and lots drinks. Apparently they have secured some Dom Pérignon wines from France."

"And they are performing a play," said Somerset. "Shakespeare's Twelfth Night. Very appropriate, don't you think?"

"That's the theme," said his sister Mary. "We're going as characters from the play. I'm going as Cesario."

"You're going as a man?" asked Peregrine.

"Yes, that's the theme of the play, isn't it? Viola pretends to be the man, Cesario, then gets mistaken for her twin brother, Sebastian...Or does he get mistaken for her? Anyway, I'm going as Cesario – who's a woman dressed as a man. Makes sense, doesn't it?"

"I suppose so," he agreed.

"And I am to be Sir Toby Belch," announced Somerset.

Peregrine grinned, "Yes, somehow I can see you doing it very well."

Somerset grinned back and nodded in acknowledgement.

"So you have to say who you're going as, Pip" insisted Lady Bridget.

"I see him as Duke Orsino," mused Mary with a wry smile.

"No, I'm not going with you," he said. "I'm doing something else. I have a previous engagement."

Lady Bridget scoffed, "A previous eng...how can you have a previous engagement on Twelfth Night? Nonsense! Choose a character and get ready."

"No, it's true. I am expected somewhere else."

She looked at him as if she might be able to penetrate his mind and discern the workings of it. Understanding dawned, "These mysterious new friends of yours, no doubt?"

"Indeed," he said simply and took a sip of his own tea.

"I don't remember you telling me exactly who these friends were."

"No, well, you wouldn't," he replied. He left it at that, but it only served to intensify her scrutiny.

Mary came to his assistance, "I think it's far more intriguing if they remain mysterious. I mean, if you told us you were just getting drunk with one of the stable boys it would be such a disappointment."

"I suppose so," said Lady Bridget, but she didn't sound completely convinced.

"I agree," said Somerset. "What a bore life would be if we knew everything that was happening around us. There would be no zest to it!"

Mary took Somerset's hand and kissed it gently. "You are so sweet, my love," she said, giving a glance sideways at Peregrine. "Well, whatever you are doing, Pip, have a good Twelfth."

"Here, here!" agreed Somerset.

Peregrine's mother stayed silent.

Peregrine couldn't wait for the day to end. He could concentrate on nothing because his mind kept returning to the forthcoming evening. Finally, darkness fell and, after a couple of hours, it was time to go. Saddling Theseus as usual he raced out of the stable yard gates and down the road. It was only a matter of minutes later that Theseus was clomping into the blacksmith's yard. He unsaddled the horse then led it through into the small stable where Old Sam was already idly chewing hay. He made sure the horse was settled then, with a small bag under his arm, he set off to the cottage.

Hurriedly he knocked on the door. When it opened he felt his jaw drop open. There before him was a vision from a Greek myth. Elizabeth was dressed in a white, cotton dress draped loosely all the way down to her ankles. It stopped below her arms where two straps arched over the shoulders, leaving the arms, shoulders and neck uncovered. It was hemmed at the base with a dark green pattern and a similar dark green band ran round just below the bust line, drawing the fabric in and giving the garment shape. Her long, black, hair cascaded down over her naked shoulders and around her head she wore a bronze tiara-like band.

"I think I may have the wrong house..." he said helplessly.

She grinned, "Come on in, Pen," and stepped aside to let him enter. "What do you think of my costume? I'm Helen of Troy."

He hadn't been able to take his eyes away from her yet. "I don't know what to say. You are a living goddess."

"And what do you think of mine, Pen," came Susanna's voice. She was dressed in a similar way to Elizabeth, but her dress only came down to the knee and it hung off one shoulder leaving the other bare.

"You are both like two heavenly angels."

"Thanks, you say the nicest things," said Susanna.

"She's meant to be Artemis, Goddess of the Moon," explained Elizabeth.

"I brought back the clothes I borrowed," he said putting down the bag.

"We have some new clothes for you," she said, almost with a laugh.

Susanna came over and handed him a pile of folded cotton. "This is your costume, Pen,"

"Oh, now hold on. What's all this about?"

"We're all going to Mallander's Barn for Twelfth Night," said Susanna excitedly.

"Twelfth Night, of course." He turned to Elizabeth, "I don't remember you mentioning this when you invited me"

"It slipped my mind," she replied innocently.

"Aye, I can imagine," he said and examined his costume. "And who am I meant to be?"

"Paris," she said. "They're all inspired from the statues you showed me."

"As I remember the statue of Paris is wearing considerably less than this, so I'm glad you didn't copy it faithfully."

"I thought about it," she said with a smile. "But, then it is winter, so I changed my mind."

"Thanks. You won't believe how grateful I am you had second thoughts."

Silence fell as Henry walked in from the living room. He was wearing an old set of clothes, all frayed and full of holes. He had a straw hat on his head. There was straw sticking out from under his hat, from the ends of his sleeves, from his trouser legs and various holes in his jacket.

"Ooh, it's a Scarecrow!" said Susanna with a laugh.

"Ah, Pen's here," said Henry. "Great stuff. Get your costume on."

Peregrine sighed and went into the living room away from prying eyes and put on his costume. It was basically a white cotton sheet, similar to the others, but the shoulders were completely covered, the head going through a small hole for the neck. It went half way down his calves and was hemmed with the same dark green pattern as Elizabeth's. A green belt went around the waist.

Hesitantly, he went back into the kitchen to be greeted by sounds of appreciation from everyone. Elizabeth came over, standing very close she started pulling his clothes around, folding the material on one shoulder and lifting it slightly on one side. Standing back she examined him in appreciation.

"That's better," she announced. "You're more like what I imagined now."

"How did you make these costumes?" he asked. "They are incredible."

"Oh, just some old shifts and some sewing," she said dismissively. "They aren't very warm though, so we'll have to wear coats too for walking up there."

"Is your father coming?"

Elizabeth laughed, "He's already there, it's only us that are dressing up and waiting for you. He's probably drunk half the beer by now."

Henry was getting his coat, "Then let's waste no more time."

They all grabbed coats and then made their way out into the cold winters night. Thankfully it was a full moon and the pale beams provided ample illumination for them as they made their way up the road and then crossed the cross roads. They continued up past the church and, then a little after that they turned through a gap between the cottages and there before them was a large barn. People were entering through a small open door. They did likewise and were soon inside the Mallander's Barn.

A large fire was roaring in a stone pit on the far side keeping the large room warm. Food and drink was spread out on some tables near by. People dressed in various strange costumes were milling around helping themselves to sweet and savoury snacks. Some people had gone to great deal of trouble to create their costumes, others had not dressed up at all. It all seemed very relaxed.

Susanna took off her coat and threw it in the corner. She skipped around looking, for all the world, like a Greek nymph and shouted "Let's go and get some cake, It doesn't look like they've found the King yet."

Henry threw his coat on top of Susanna's and ran off after her.

Peregrine and Elizabeth took off their coats and put them on top of the others. As Elizabeth took off her coat and revealed her Grecian costume he found he couldn't look anywhere else.

She noticed him looking, "Do I look alright?"

He sighed hopelessly, "I was just thinking I will never be able to look at the statue of Helen again without seeing it for what it is - a poor attempt to emulate your incomparable perfection."

"Yes right?" she said sarcastically. Then she noticed he was actually serious. Her tone softened, "Susanna was right. You do say the nicest things."

She came closer to him and put her arm around his waist. His arm slid gently around her. She felt so small, so delicate. He realised that he would be perfectly happy to live out his entire life standing in this spot, holding her close.

"Let's get some cake," she said. He didn't respond, he felt that any words would only desecrate a fragile moment. "Twelfth Cake," she said when he didn't respond. "They haven't found the King yet."

"What ever you say," he said dreamily. "Where ever you want to go, I want to go too."

She looked at him with a smile, "Yes, well, then let's get some cake."

They went over to where the table a food was laid out. Two huge fruit cakes were in the centre. They had both been cut into lots of pieces and people were helping themselves to one piece each.

"There's a Kings Cake and a Queens Cake," she said to him. "Men take a piece of the Kings Cake and women take a piece of the Queens Cake. If you find a bean in your piece you can be King for the night. I think they've already found the Queen though."

Susanna came over, a half eaten piece of cake in her hand. "Aye, they've found the Queen. It's Mary Parkin. Some Queen she'll be, she's only about twelve!"

"Now, now," said Elizabeth. "Fairs fair, if she found the bean then she's the Queen."

Against the far wall of the barn there were two large chairs set next to each other. A young girl was being dressed in a red cape and a wooden crown was placed on her head. She sat down on one of the chairs and a cheer went up.

Peregrine and Elizabeth got a piece of their respective cakes. Peregrine ate a chunk of his. It was rich and full of dried fruit, it tasted delicious.

"Maybe someone's eaten the bean in the King Cake," he suggested.

Before Elizabeth could answer there was a loud cheer from

the other end of the table.

"It's Henry!" shouted Susanna. "Henry's the King."

They all laughed as Henry, dressed as a scarecrow, was led to the chairs at the far end of the barn. He seemed to be enjoying his new found importance. He donned his red cape with a theatrical sweep and then bowed to receive his wooden crown. Then he turned and assumed his throne, sitting next to his Queen, Mary Parkin.

Peregrine and Elizabeth made their way over to some large bowls further down the table. "Punch," explained Elizabeth. They helped themselves to two cups of it. It was hot and fruity, but also had a hint of some spirit.

"I'm definitely having some punch," announced Susanna, filling her own cup.

"Fine, but be careful how much you have," warned Elizabeth.

At the other end of the room Henry rose to his feet to make his first pronouncement. Making the most of his part, he shouted at the top of his voice, "Hear Ye! Hear Ye! Let the dancing begin!"

A band that Peregrine hadn't noticed before seemed to condense out of nowhere consisting of several string and wind instruments and a drum. Straight away they began playing. Not a song that he recognised, but that didn't seem to matter as lots of people moved into the centre of the barn and started dancing. There seemed to be no order or precision to their dancing, they did what ever they wanted. So there was much jumping, twisting, kicking of legs and waving of arms. It was a chaotic rabble, not the very ordered affair that Peregrine had seen in parties he had seen elsewhere.

"Let's dance, please!" begged Susanna.

Peregrine shrugged, "That's not what I would call dancing, but...oh, what the heck, let's do it anyway!"

He guided the two girls into the centre of the barn and they began moving, gyrating and jumping around in time to the music. Peregrine joined in, initially reluctantly, but slowly he found himself quite enjoying it. He looked at the wide grins on the girls faces and found himself grinning too.

After several minutes, hot and quite exhausted, they made their way for refreshment. They helped themselves to more punch and some of the simple delicacies available.

They were about to resume dancing when the music stopped. Henry, King of the Bean, made a pronouncement. He selected a young fellow by the name of Robert Wainwright to choose some others and together sing a series of Christmas songs. Peregrine recognised a couple of the songs, barely, the renditions beings neither tuneful or faithful to the original melodies. But none of that seemed to matter, the fact that the lads sung at all was enough and the crowd cheered uproariously.

The King of the Bean then declared more dancing and drinking and the music began again. He selected a young fellow by the name of Robert Wainwright to choose some others and together sing a series of Christmas songs. Peregrine recognised a couple of the songs, barely, the renditions beings neither tuneful or faithful to the original melodies. But none of that mattered, the fact that the lads sung at all was enough and the crowd cheered uproariously.

The King of the Bean then declared more dancing and drinking and the music began again. And so the night progressed. Every so often the King would call a halt and make a pronouncement, often selecting individuals to juggle, recite poetry or sing a song. Often it was done poorly, but the participants received the tumultuous applause of victorious heroes. Sometimes people were asked to extract apples from a bowl of water without using their hands or a group might be asked to pass a ball to each other, again, without using their hands. There were group games where a wrapped parcel was passed amongst them while music played and when it stopped whoever was holding would remove a layer of wrapping until finally someone uncovered the prize. Or a game of chairs where a group danced while music played and, when it

stopped, they tried to find a seat. At each turn a seat was removed and so one was left unseated and taken out of the game.

And finally, as the hour grew late, and people began to tire,
the King rose to make another pronouncement. "Hear Ye! Hear
Ye! And now I call on Paris of Troy to recite some lines for my
entertainment."

With a shock Peregrine realised that *he* was Paris of Troy.
He nearly dropped his drink and looked round. Everyone was
looking in his direction, cheering him on. Henry was clapping
and grinning like a drunken buffoon. Susanna had a wide grin
and was clapping enthusiastically. Elizabeth was looking at
him and smiling expectantly.

A silence fell as the crowd waited. He realised there was
probably no getting out of it.

He cleared his throat. There was only one thing that came
to mind really, so he started reciting as much of it as he could
recall.

"All the world's a stage, and all the men and women merely
players. They have their exits and their entrances and one man
in his time plays many parts."

Surprisingly, he noticed he seemed to have their attention.
They were quiet, waiting for him to say something else.

So he continued, "At first the infant, mewling and puking in
the nurse's arms. And then the whining school-boy, with his
satchel and shining morning face, creeping like a snail, unwill-
ingly to school. And then the lover,sighing like a furnace, with
a woeful ballad. Then a soldier, full of strange oaths, seeking
the bubble reputation even in the cannon's mouth. And then
the justice, with fair round belly with good capon lined, with
eyes severe and beard of formal cut, full of wise saws and
modern instances." He paused and looked round the expectant
crowd, "But then the scene shifts into the lean and slippered
Pantaloon, with spectacles on nose and pouch on side, his big
manly voice turning again toward childish treble, pipes and
whistles in his sound. To the last scene of all. Without teeth,
without eyes, without taste, without everything. "

He stopped as his memory failed. Slowly, people around began clapping and then cheering their approval. He found himself grinning and gave a polite bow of appreciation to his audience.

"Another," shouted Henry. "Tell me another, Paris. If you can!"

Peregrine found himself warming to the attention. More confident now, he took hold of Elizabeth's hand. Since he was meant to be Paris, he said "Was this the face that launched a thousand ships, and burnt the topless towers of Ilium? Thou art fairer than the evening air. Clad in the beauty of a thousand stars. Brighter art thou than flaming Jupiter. More lovely than the monarch of the sky. And none but thee shall be my paramour!"

The crowd erupted into cheering and applause and he bowed graciously while Elizabeth curtsied to the crowd.

Henry held up his cup of punch in salute and shouted, "Well done, Paris! Now, on with the dancing and the music!" And the band resumed playing.

Still holding each other's hands, Elizabeth and Peregrine went over to the table and poured out some more punch.

"I need a stiff drink after that," he admitted.

She turned to him. "You certainly have a way with words," she admitted.

"Not my words, I'm afraid. Marlowe's. But I meant them all, you do look glorious."

She took a sip of punch, looking at him over her cup. "I will have to be very careful with you, Pen. You have a way about you that could turn a girls head."

"My head is already turned. You have dazzled me."

Before she could reply she was interrupted as Susanna came over. "I'm feeling dizzy," she declared. "All this dancing and punch is starting to make the world spin."

"It's getting late," said Peregrine. "People are starting to head off home. We should think about doing the same."

"Aye," agreed Elizabeth and then to Susanna. "I think you've had enough merry making for one night."

"What about Henry?" asked Peregrine.

"Oh, he can make his own way. The King can't leave until the end." She looked across to where Mary Parkin, the Queen of the Bean, was dancing with Henry. She seemed to be having the time of her life. She kept dancing closer to him, causing him to pull away to which she would then dance closer again. "His Queen seems to be quite smitten with him." commented Elizabeth, stifling a laugh.

"She's two years younger than me!" said Susanna in astonishment.

Elizabeth shrugged, "I guess she likes an older man! It's been a night for surprising matches." She cast a glance at Peregrine.

Susanna stumbled, "Oh, my head!". Peregrine reached over and steadied her then he put his arm around her and held her while Elizabeth fetched their coats. When Elizabeth returned they put on their coats then, with one arm still around Susanna's shoulders, Peregrine held out his other hand for Elizabeth.

Her hand slipped inside his and together all three set off for home.

Chapter Six

Peregrine was lazing on the banks of a river. He laid back on a soft cushion of grass and gazed, contentedly upwards. It was early Summer and the sun was blazing down from a cloudless sky. He felt its soft warmth against him, like sleeping in front of a roaring winter fire. Elizabeth leaned across him and kissed him gently. He heard himself moan.

"See, I think that's worked," said Susanna's voice.

"Well, at least he looks more alive now," came Elizabeth's reply.

He frowned. Then he opened his eyes. Elizabeth and Susanna were stood over him, looking down intently.

"Am I in Heaven?" he asked quietly.

"Far from it, I'm afraid," replied Elizabeth. "Although for most of the morning you've been doing a good impression of someone bound for it."

"Elizabeth woke you with a kiss," said Susanna excitedly. "I told her to try it."

"If that hadn't worked, I was going to move on to a cup of cold water."

He raised his head and immediately regretted it as blood thumped painfully through his temples. "God's Teeth, that punch is well named." He was in the kitchen of the Mirfin's cottage, laying on a single bed in front of the hot fire. It was very comfortable and relaxingly warm. When he compared it to waking up in his cold room in Kiveton on winter mornings this was much preferable. He fell back and sighed. "No, I think I was right. I am in Heaven. Anyway, how come you two seem so robust?"

"The secret is to drink lots of water," said Elizabeth. "I had four cups of it when we got back."

"I was sick," said Susanna sheepishly. "But Elizabeth says that got rid of most of it so I felt fine this morning."

"I don't remember any of that," he admitted.

"I'm not surprised," said Elizabeth. "We came through the door and, the next minute, you flopped down, snoring, on Henry's bed."

"Well, I slept very well. I had a wonderful drea...hold on, I have no clothes on!"

Elizabeth smirked, "Yes, well, we thought you might be more comfortable. Besides, they weren't your clothes, they were the ones we gave you. If you remember, Paris."

"Oh yes. Well thanks. " He paused then said, "What do you mean by we?"

"Well, she couldn't do it by herself," said Susanna with a grin.

"Great. You know, this is a very hospitable household...if you don't mind being stripped naked while you're sleeping!"

"Relax," said Elizabeth. "We've both seen men naked before, you know. We live with a brother and a father. You're no different to them. You've nothing to hide..."

"Well, very little anyway," said Susanna and they both laughed.

"Oh, thank you very much, ladies," he said with a smile. "What's happened to Henry and your father anyway?"

"They never came back," said Elizabeth. "Probably sleeping it off on the floor of the barn if I know them."

"Men, eh," sighed Susanna. "They just can't take their drink." and they both laughed again.

"I'm so pleased we're such a huge source of amusement for

you," said Peregrine, wearily as he got up slowly and sat on the side of the bed, wrapped in a bed sheet. He held his head in both hands. "Thank goodness Christmas is over for another year. I don't think I have the stamina for it."

Elizabeth gave him a cup of hot water with honey in it. He took a sip, it didn't taste too bad. "Do you have any tea?"

She put her hand to her chin thoughtfully, "Tea? I do believe the kitchens have just run out, my lord. I'll send one of the boys off to China for some."

He smiled and nodded, "Yes, yes, very funny. This will do nicely."

"It has willow bark in it. It's better for you than the foreign stuff. And cheaper."

To his surprise, by the time he had finished it he was beginning to feel better. Wrapped in a bed sheet to shield his modesty he made his way into the living room where his clothes were piled up. Quickly, he dressed and then headed back into the kitchen and sat down at the table.

"What hour is it?" he asked innocently. "I have absolutely no idea."

"It's past midday," said Susanna.

"I've been asleep all morning!" he exclaimed with shock. "I didn't realise I'd had that much to drink."

"Maybe you were just tired?"

"I was having a very good sleep. Maybe that is it – I was just having the best sleep I've had in a long time." In fact, when he thought about it, it was the most restful sleep he had had since...well, since William got ill, three months ago.

He looked around at the two sisters busying themselves with their chores, at the hot fire burning in the hearth, at the simple, unpretentious, wooden furniture. It was a world where meat was so expensive it was an occasional extravagance. Where tea was a luxury beyond your wildest imagination. Where everything but the most basic of essentials were beyond your reach. And yet, there was something here that was missing in the splendid, vaulted palaces and sprawling estates of the Osborne family. A common bond of shared experiences and simple pleasures. They were a group of people that cared and looked after each other, not for personal advantage, but because they were a family.

Family meant a very different thing to the Osbornes. It stood for something. A proud history, of bloodlines and alliances, of commitments and responsibilities. A family rooted so firmly in the past it had become obsessed with managing its future. To them, the future *was* the past. The difference was just a matter of time and perspective.

"A penny for them?" said Elizabeth as she slid into the seat next to him.

"Sorry? What?"

"For your thoughts. You seemed miles away."

"I was just thinking how different your life is from the one I live."

"Oh goodness, yes! A couple of the statues in your house are enough to buy this entire village."

"For what is a man profited, if he shall gain the whole world...and lose his soul?" said Peregrine solemnly.

"That's from the Bible," said Susanna with satisfaction, and then with some doubt, "Isn't it?"

"Yes. Matthew chapter sixteen, verse, uh, twenty something."

Elizabeth took hold of his hand, "Well, don't you worry, Pen, you won't be losing your soul if I have any say in the matter. And I intend to."

He gripped her hand tightly and smiled.

"You seem to know everything, Pen," said Susanna sitting in a place opposite him.

"Aye, well, I didn't know that willow bark tea cured a headache so I guess I don't know everything. I feel a lot better, thanks."

The door opened and in came Henry and his father.

"About time!" said Elizabeth. "Where have you two been all night? As if we didn't know."

"I wasn't feeling too well this morning," said Robert, warming himself next to the fire. "There must have been something wrong with the beer I was drinking last night."

"Aye, like too much of it. And what's your excuse?" she asked Henry.

"Alright, I admit it, I was fairly drunk last night. But then, I was the King, it's expected, I didn't want to do it half-heartedly. I was thinking of the family reputation."

"Of course you were," she replied sarcastically.

"And besides, I've had that Mary Parkin following me round all morning. It took me ages to throw her off."

Elizabeth laughed, "Yes, I noticed you've made quite an impression on young Mary."

"Aye, young is the word. She needs someone her own age."

"Perhaps she prefers a more mature man."

"Aye, well she can go and latch on to a different mature man," he complained. Then he seemed to notice Peregrine for the first time. "I thought you would have gone home by now?"

"I borrowed your bed last night," said Peregrine. "And actually, I've only just got out of it now."

"Well," laughed Henry, "If you can't sleep in someone else's bed on Twelfth Night then when can you!"

"Henry Mirfin! What are you trying to say?" said Elizabeth with mock anger.

"Nothing, nothing. The best I managed was a piece of floor in the barn." He stretched and winced. "And my back is killing me."

"I can recommend the willow bark tea," said Peregrine.

"Sounds great. I'm going to have a lay down on Pa's bed." Henry walked painfully over to the stairs.

"I'll make some and bring it up to you," said Susanna.

"And I'm going in the living room for a smoke," said Robert. "Now Christmas is over maybe we can get back to normal round here." He left the room.

When Susanna had gone upstairs taking the tea to Henry, Elizabeth turned to Peregrine. "You said some things last night when you were pretending to be Paris and I was Helen. I wondered, how do you feel in the cold light of day? Were they just something to say in the heat of the moment? I mean, I understand. You were under pressure and all that and you'd had a lot to drink and it was Twelfth Night. It's easy to get carried away...."

He placed a finger gently on her lips and she stopped.

"I meant every single word then and I stand by every single word now."

She sighed "But you can't.... I mean look at us. Look who you are and look who I am!"

"I know," he said simply. "I am extremely fortunate."

Her brown eyes looked into his. "Will you be serious for a moment."

"I am being serious. I am spellbound."

"You are also the Earl of...uh"

"Danby."

"Yes, quite! There is no future for us. You live at the top of the hill in Kiveton Hall and I live at the bottom in the blacksmith's cottage."

"It's just a hill."

"No, it's more than that. It's a meta...what's the word?"

"Metaphor," he said with a smile. "You see, I love the way you know words like that."

"Yes, well, I read a lot. Actually, you're the only person I know I can say them to."

"You see. We were destined for each other."

She shook her head helplessly. "I am trying to be sensible here. Think what your family would say?"

"I have no interest, what-so-ever, in what my family think."

"Well, you should. They own everything around here. That means the livelihoods of everyone in this village and Todwick, Anston, Harthill and who knows what else."

"They don't own me."

"Well, I'd like to be there when you try and tell them that!"

"I hope you will be."

She sighed in exasperation, "It's just...the world is very large and we are very small. I'm just not sure what we want matters very much."

"It matters to me. I hope, in time, it might matter to you."

She looked at him earnestly. "You're the Earl of Danby, you can do better..."

"They don't come any better."

Susanna came down the stairs. "Well, that's him back in bed, he wasn't up long. I wouldn't be surprised to find Pa asleep too."

"And shouldn't you be getting back while it's still light, Pen?" said Elizabeth.

"If I must."

"I was just thinking that your family will be wondering what has happened to you."

"I doubt it. They've probably stayed over at Welbeck anyway."

"Welbeck?" exclaimed Susanna. "Welbeck Abbey?"

"Yes, they went there for the Earl of Portland's Twelfth Night event, I believe. Mother wanted me to go, but I declined."

"You were invited to the Earl of Portland's Twelfth Night at Welbeck Abbey," said Susanna in disbelief. "And you turned it down? It would have been absolutely out of this world."

Peregrine shrugged, "Nothing at Welbeck Abbey could live up to last night."

Susanna sighed, "In Mallander's Barn? I enjoyed it too, but, Welbeck Abbey, that would be something else."

"I danced with Artemis and Helen of Troy. Could Welbeck match that?"

She sighed, "Well no, but maybe you could have tried it to see."

"Anyway," interrupted Elizabeth. "You had better check your horse. He's been in our stable with Old Sam all night."

Peregrine nodded and pulled on his coat. He went over to Susanna and, much to her surprise, gave her a big hug. "Thanks for everything. I'll see you again," he said.

"Oh, yes, see you again, Pen," she stuttered.

Elizabeth went out to the stable with Peregrine. Theseus was nibbling hay in a typical, unconcerned fashion as they entered. Peregrine saddled him up as quickly as he could.

He turned to Elizabeth. "When can I see you again."

"Well, today's Wednesday, what about Friday?"

"Alright."

"Horse riding again?"

He nodded, "Alright. In the morning. We'll take them over to Laughton Common."

"Sounds fine," she agreed.

"So I won't see you tomorrow then?" he said, moving closer.

"You were here yesterday, all last night and today too. Any more and you may as well move in."

"Now there's an idea – do you have the room?" He took a step closer until they were only inches apart.

"Only in here with the horses."

"Sounds ideal."

"Weren't you meant to be leaving?"

"I'm having problems finding any motivation. Everything I want is here and nothing I want is there."

"I'm seeing you again on the day after tomorrow."

"That means I have to survive tomorrow without seeing you."

"Well, please survive it. Otherwise I'll have no one to ride with on Friday."

"There's only one way to survive that long."

"And what is that?"

"If I have something to remember you by..."

His face moved closer until their lips touched in a soft caress. His arms closed around her, pulling her body closer to his. Her lips parted slightly and their tongues touched, stroking each other with delicate intimacy. Just the idea of being so close to such an intimate part of her sent his senses spinning. How long it lasted, he could not say, his mind lost all track of time. But, eventually, they pulled slowly apart.

She looked up at him with a look that made it very difficult indeed for him to consider leaving. "Will that sustain you for a day?" she asked.

"No," he said sadly. "But I will endure it and count off every tedious second until Friday."

"I'll see you on Friday, then."

He grabbed Theseus' reins and led him outside. He climbed into the saddle. "Till Friday, then," he said and waved. Then, with a shake of the reins, he directed Theseus out onto the lane.

8th January 1712

It was another bright, cold morning. The sun projected a pale heat into the stable yard at Kiveton. Facing westwards it was the last place to feel the days warmth, the long shadows of the stables themselves merged with those of the North Pavilion to create a dark, unwelcoming space. Even now, in mid-morning, the last vestiges of night's frost clung on to the ground and crunched beneath the turning carriage wheels.

Henry Somerset stood patiently waiting for his carriage. As it drew close, the coachman pulled back hard on the reins as the two horses drawing it stomped rebelliously and snorted in the cold air. Finally, they settled down, resigned to wait patiently.

Somerset was dressed in mauve jacket and hose with long, thigh length, black leather boots. The outfit was edged in white lace. A cavalier hat complete with a long, purple ostrich feather was perched jauntily on his head

He turned to his waiting wife, his dark, handsome features belying the crisp morning and radiating their own warmth. "You still expect to stay here another few days?" he asked.

"Well, I'm not allowed on your hunting trip so I may as well."

"Now, now, my dear. As I have explained, it isn't just a *hunting trip*, as you call it. It's a meeting of Her Majesty's Body

Guard. Wives are not allowed. If I play my cards right then, the word is, they intend to make me a captain later this year. Who knows where that could lead? I may be a Knight of the Garter by Christmas. Imagine that!"

"That's wonderful," said Mary without much enthusiasm. "I thought you were already a member of the Brotherly Circle? Isn't that enough?"

"You mean the Brothers Club! And, yes, that was a great honour. But this would be Captain of the Honourable Band of Gentlemen Pensioners. A much greater honour, if I can pull it off."

"I suppose I'll see even less of you if all this happens?"

"Don't be like that, my dear, think of the prestige! I am determined to entertain the Queen again, just like we did ten years ago at Badminton. Think of that!"

Mary didn't look too impressed. "I suppose so. But surely there is a limit to how many honours you can accumulate in a lifetime?"

He laughed. "Dear Mary, sometimes you do say the most outrageous things! Look, I shall meet up with you at Badminton in two weeks. Fare you well." He climbed aboard his carriage, closed the door and tapped on the roof to indicate his readiness and then he was away.

"Farewell," she murmured sadly as she waved to the departing carriage.

Tom Crowther was crossing the stable yard at just that moment. When he saw Mary he paused momentarily and stood looking in her direction. She noticed. As she turned to go back in, a mercurial smile briefly flashed across her face.

She entered through a door in the north-east wing and entered one of the servant halls. The entire North Pavilion was largely reserved for kitchens, store rooms and staff quarters. She went up the stairs onto one of the upper floors then turned left, making her way into the main part of the house. She emerged into the West Gallery which overlooked the courtyard facing the Todwick road. It provided a good view of the expansive courtyard below and the road beyond the gates. On a clear day like today it was possible to see for miles, over the wooded valley of the Rother and beyond to distant Sheffield and the Derbyshire dales.

To her surprise Mary found her mother admiring the view, staring intently through the large expanses of glass.

Lady Bridget saw Mary and beckoned her over anxiously. "Look, Mary, down there on the road."

Mary saw two horse riders slowly making their way along the road in front of the house towards Todwick. "At what?" she asked.

"Isn't that Pip?" asked her mother.

Mary looked again. "Perhaps, I'm not sure, it is some way off."

"I think it is," replied Lady Bridget decisively. "I was informed that he took his horse out this morning."

"Informed? By who?"

"I asked Crowther to let me know about Pip's comings and goings. I'm concerned about him. The more intriguing question is - who is that with him?"

"I really wouldn't know," said Mary innocently.

"Perhaps one of his mysterious friends?"

"Well, assuming it is Pip, then I suppose it's a possibility...."

"Oh yes. And there's something else very interesting about Pip's companion. It's a woman."

"Are you sure? It is far away and, besides, they are both riding astride their horses."

"But she is wearing stays," declared Lady Bridget triumphantly.

Mary said nothing at first and then, "Well, even if it is Pip, what of it? He's young. He's a bachelor. Let him enjoy himself."

Lady Bridget turned from the window as the riders became obscured behind the North Pavilion. "Innocent fun is all well and good provided it remains just that. Innocent. But should it become serious...Then we have a problem. Pip strikes me as a very impressionable sort. Easily diverted. Even led astray. He is the heir to the Dukedom. I don't want him to stray too far."

"I'm sure Pip is well aware of his obligations," said Mary defensively.

"Let us hope so," said Lady Bridget.

Elizabeth and Peregrine had no choice but to ride their horses in front of Kiveton Hall, the alternative would have been to leave the road entirely and make their way across country. There was the risk of discovery, but Peregrine was past caring any more.

As they drew nearer to the Hall, Elizabeth felt her self confidence draining away. The Hall seemed to crouch on the horizon watching them approach. The South Pavilion's two wings appeared to reach out to them in a mocking embrace. Its plethora of giant windows could hide so many eyes. They could observe her. Dissect her. Seek out and expose every pitiful flaw.

It seemed to take forever for the horses to reach the Hall itself. The road ran along the boundary wall and, beyond it, she could see the endless green carpet of the South Lawn. So large it seemed to consume a space larger than Wales village itself.

Who was she to challenge the people who owned this? Who was she to risk their wrath? As the Hall grew larger, her self esteem shrank accordingly.

It calmed her to some extent that Peregrine seemed completely unperturbed by the Hall. He nonchalantly pointed out the windows of the south-west wing which were his rooms. He indicated nuances in the architecture and elements of design as if conducting a tour.

Their horses passed the South Pavilion's courtyard and then the even larger main entrance courtyard behind which the main building rose three storeys into the air. A huge wall of carefully sculptured brick, stone and glass.

She dare not look. Afraid of who or what she might see. She kept her gaze focussed on the road ahead, wishing the horses on as quickly as possible.

Just as slowly, they passed the nearer windows of the North

Pavilion and then the long outer wall of the stable block. Finally, the wall ended and the trees of the park took their place. More natural, more familiar and less imposing.

"Your house is very...impressive," she said when she felt she had regained enough of her composure to allow her to speak.

"Oh, it isn't my house," he replied in a very off-hand way. "It belongs to my grandfather. The rest of us just occupy it occasionally. Mother mainly. "

"It's a large house for one person. Or even two or three."

"Yes, well its main purpose is to entertain and impress visitors. And visitors need somewhere to stay so it has the capacity to handle large numbers of them."

"Our little cottage must seem very small to you."

He looked across at her with a beaming smile. "You know I would rather be in your cottage any day."

"I never know when you're being serious," she admitted.

"Then be assured. I am serious." He reached across and held her hand reassuringly.

They continued up the road through Todwick village. Todwick was a series of small cottages clinging to the undulating road. Then, where the road levelled out, set back amongst a large green field was the church. They continued past. A road forked to the left, but they rode past and over a hill until they finally approached the crossroads where the Worksop to Sheffield road ran east to west. The road marked the northern boundary of the Kiveton estate. Over the road, to the west was the neighbouring estate of Todwick Grange.

They crossed the Sheffield road and continued on the other side. The road went between fields on each side for a mile and then completely opened out into a large, open area of grassland, Laughton Common. They left the road, letting the horses gallop freely across the open area.

Cattle were grazing idly in dispersed herds and looked up curiously as the horses charged by. The common was dissected by the main road from Dinnington, it ran across their path. They drew their horses to a stop before the road. Half way along the road there was a junction and a road that ran north, up a gentle slope. On the top of the hill a towering limestone spire protruded from a small spinney of trees and rose into the blue sky.

"The church at Laughton-en-le-Morthen," said Elizabeth, indicating the spire. "That's where the Mirfin's come from. Pa was baptised in that church."

"Now that is an impressive building. You can see that spire from miles around."

"Pa reckons from the tower you can see Lincoln."

"Another impressive building. Have you ever been to Lincoln?"

She shook her head. "I must seem to have been nowhere to you."

"Not at all. I haven't been to Lincoln either. Though I've seen pictures. One day we will have to go."

She laughed, "Oh aye, just go to Lincoln – just like that!"

"Why not?"

"Well, for a start it must be thirty miles away, at least."

"A days journey."

"And where would we stay when we get there?"

"In a coaching inn like I did when I travelled up from Wimbledon. I can afford it."

She paused in thought then said, "How can you afford it? You don't seem to work at all."

"I have an allowance from grandfather's estate," he explained.

"Do you mean you are employed by him?"

"That's one way of looking at it."

They continued walking the horses up the slope to Laughton and Elizabeth fell silent. *You say they don't own you,* she thought to herself. *But I'm sure they feel that you owe them something. He who pays the piper calls the tune.*

"Is Lincoln on the sea?" she asked.

"No, but it's nearer to the coast than we are. Why?"

"I would like to see the sea. Just once. I can't imagine that much water – it must be an amazing sight."

"It is," he agreed. "Even the air seems somehow fresher. And, of course, you can go swimming."

"I can't swim."

"You'll learn. It's just a question of confidence and trust. There's so much I'd like to show you. Things I've done before, but I want to do them again and share them with you."

"Please don't do that."

"What?"

"Tantalise me with promises I'm not sure will ever happen."

"Why won't they happen?"

"There's a lot of things that can go wrong between here and there and I'd just rather avoid the disappointment."

"I understand. But that's what you have given me."

"What?"

"Hope," he said simply. " I had lost that, but you have given it me back."

She said nothing, but found herself smiling fondly to herself. He had a certain vulnerability and innocence that she found quite captivating. For someone who knew so much he had an endearing childlike naivete.

They topped the hill and entered Laughton. The white stone cottages on each side of the road shone in the sun. At the crossroads in the centre of the village to the left, the church stood like a mighty heavenly monument. Ahead, the road descended down into a valley before rising again on the other side of a trickling brook. At the top of the opposite ridge a small hamlet of cottages clustered round a manor house. In the bottom of the valley some more cottages snuggled along the banks of the brook. To the left of the track, someone had created a basic bench from three pieces of wood. A place to sit and take in the view. They dismounted, tied up their horses who immediately lowered their heads and began eating. Elizabeth sat on the bench, it was certainly a good point to pause. He came and sat next to her, his arm went around her waist and she reciprocated by putting her arm around him. Together they looked down into the small dale.

"That's Slade Hooton opposite," Elizabeth said pointing to the cottages opposite. "And that's Brookhouse down in the bottom. Pa's brother, Uncle Jack, lives in Brookhouse."

"It's an idyllic little valley," he replied.

"The Mirfins have been blacksmiths and landowners here for centuries. The family seat was at Thurcroft Hall, on the other side of Brookhouse. Another arm of the family now live at Slade Hooton Hall. They own most of the land round Hooton. That's their new manor house over there, built around the same time as Kiveton." She paused. "And then there's our lot. We're just the blacksmiths, I'm afraid, no halls, no estates, no money."

"What happened to Thurcroft Hall?" he asked. "You said the family seat *was* there."

"The last generation had no children. When the last owner died Thurcroft past to his sister so the name of the family changed after that."

"Ah, that sounds familiar. My mother's obsessed with making sure that very same thing doesn't happen to our family."

She nodded and looked at him,. "And how do you think she's going to do that?"

He looked uncomfortable and said, "I suppose, by marrying me to one of her friend's daughters and hoping we have sons."

"And us? How do we fit into that plan? "

"We don't, unfortunately," he admitted.

She turned to him. "You see, Pen, that doesn't sound like something she's going to give up very easily."

"No, it probably isn't. But surely I deserve a chance to be happy?"

She frowned and held his hand. "Oh, Pen, I agree. But what do you think your mother thinks?"

His gaze fell to the floor. "She would want me to marry and have heirs. If I can do that and be happy as well then all the better. If not...." He shrugged. "Happiness is a secondary consideration."

"And would a child of ours count as heir?" she asked softly, knowing she already knew the answer.

"Yes," he replied doubtfully. "If we were married he would be a legitimate heir."

"But would we be allowed to marry?"

He sighed, "Not without consent. Mother would take some convincing."

"I can imagine," she said. "I somehow don't think diluting your family pedigree with Mirfin blood is what she has in mind."

"She cannot force me to marry someone she chooses," he said. "My consent is required too."

"If, in order for you to marry, both you and your mother have to agree. Then I can't see it happening at all," she admitted. "Although she has more to lose than you. In the end she may conclude that any heir is better than none at all."

"Why do my family have to be so...difficult?" he complained. "Why can't they be more like yours?"

"Oh, believe me, I think Pa would have reservations about me marrying an Earl."

"But he wouldn't oppose it."

"No," she admitted. "He wouldn't. Not if that's what I wanted. If it made me happy."

"I wish I wasn't born an Osborne! Why couldn't I just be a normal person in Wales?"

"I wouldn't look twice at you if you were just a normal person," she said. "I know, I used to go out with John Bradshaw – when I told him I wanted to go to Paris he thought I meant Parwich in Derbyshire!"

He laughed, "I didn't know you'd been out with others."

She frowned, "I am twenty-two years old, Pen. Do you think I've just been waiting for you to arrive?"

"No, I suppose I'd just never thought about it. How long did you see him?"

"Oh, I don't know, a year or so. He wanted to marry me, but I told him he was too parochial. He didn't understand, of course.

I've always felt, I don't know...different. I'm only really interested in people who are different too."

He laughed. "Parochial? No wonder he didn't understand! Where do you get these words from?"

"Ma taught me how to read. I read her books, but she didn't have many. The biggest one was a dictionary. Not much of a story, but I learnt a lot of words!"

His arm tightened as he gave her a gentle hug. "You're amazing. How come your mother wanted you to read books?"

"Her father was a clergyman. He taught Ma to read. She taught me and Susanna. And Mary, my older sister, too."

"But not Henry?"

"I think Pa put his foot down with Henry. He's determined at least one of his children will follow in his footsteps."

"Good for him! Henry's turned out great. You all have. You're all such wonderful people. Well, compared to my family anyway."

"What was your brother William like?" she asked softly.

He looked distantly out across the valley. "Will was the perfect one, or at least everyone thought so. Healthy, good looking, clever, the family thought he was the messiah after the debacle they'd had with our father. They've been painting his portrait since he was baby. He's the one in the portraits with our sisters. I'm not in any. In other people's eyes Will was Germanicus to my Claudius. But to ourselves, we were like twins. We did everything together. He said we were like two trees blown over by the wind, somehow falling against each other and holding each other up."

"I wish I had met him," she said softly.

"You would have liked him, everyone did. And he would have liked you. He knew a good thing when he saw one." He grinned.

The wind had started to blow from the north, bringing with it an icy chill. Brooding, sullen clouds were starting to appear in the sky, obscuring the sun and driving the temperature down.

"It's getting cold. Maybe we should start back?"

"Of course," he agreed.

They managed to coax their horses away from the grass and rode them back up into Laughton then down the slight hill onto the common. Once there, they let them gallop down the hill, across the Dinnington Road and onto the pastures. The hooves thudded rhythmically against the ground as the horses threw their heads up with elation to be running free, if only momentarily. It was a contagious feeling and Elizabeth found herself laughing as Cyrene carried her swiftly across the common.

As they approached the Todwick Road they slowed the horses to walking pace, patting them on their necks in appreciation.

Peregrine turned to Elizabeth. "Why don't you come up to the house?" he said.

She shook her head, "Oh, I don't know. A confrontation with your mother wouldn't do anyone any good."

"You won't meet anyone. We'll go in through the back way. I spend days in that place and see hardly anyone from the family. I have my own rooms, they don't go in there."

"I don't know," she said uncertainly.

"I'll get the staff to bring us something to eat. We'll warm up and then we'll ride back down to Wales."

"You say there's a back entrance?"

"Yes, through Anston, up Dog Kennel Lane then down Lodge Hill Avenue and up into the South Pavilion. We won't go anywhere near the main house or stables.

"Alright," she said, but sounded reluctant. "I'll follow you."

"Good," he said happily.

Instead of following the road back to Todwick, they turned left along a small track leading to North Anston. The track led down between fields. To their left the ground rose suddenly into an escarpment, not high, but steep. North Anston itself was a just a series of cottages nestled at its base. Eventually, their track came out onto the Main Street and they turned right. Main Street then turned abruptly round to the left and, after a few yards, forded Anston Brook then continued up to meet the Sheffield Road. Technically, they were now in South Anston, the brook forming the boundary between the two villages.

At the junction of Sheffield Road they paused. Ahead of them, across the other side and beyond a wall was Kiveton Park. The rising land obscured any view of the distant hall. Sheffield Road itself was little better than the tracks they had just traversed, but it was wider. There was no other traffic on it as they turned left. The road began to incline up hill, drifting to the right. They were now passing the dwellings of South Anston and not far ahead they could see the impressive spire of Anston Church. About half way up the hill they turned the horses up a lane to the right which rose more steeply. They were now following the eastern most wall of Kiveton Park. At the top of the road it passed through a line of lime trees and, where it did, on their right was the Crow Gate. This was the original way that Peregrine had arrived at Kiveton weeks ago. Now they rode across the lime tree avenue without going through the Crow Gate, following the wall southwards. They were now on Dog Kennel Lane. They followed the road a further thousand yards to where there was a break in the wall on their right. Here, a straight road forked off right, through Kiveton Park. It was lined on both sides by lime trees and seemed to stretch towards the distant horizon for a huge distance. This was the eastern entrance to Lodge Hill Avenue. The straight road four thousand feet long was initially flanked by woods. It then crossed the small bridge over Lodge Hill Pond where Peregrine had previously skated. The road then continued, straight as an arrow, past the kitchen gardens until finally crossing a double line of scotch pines. So, finally, they emerged onto the South Lawn.

They turned the horses up the hill, galloping up the Lawn to the side gates of the South Pavilion. Here they dismounted, tethering their horses to the fencing and allowing them to rest.

Having ridden across the grounds, Elizabeth was even more nervous about entering the Hall. If the building itself was an imposing sight that made her feel small, experiencing the full size of the park and gardens had reduced her even further. If not for Peregrine's casual confidence she would have turned and run before anyone saw her. But he held her hand, drawing her across the south courtyard to the entrance to the South Pavilion.

Without a care, he opened the doors and entered. They were in a large stone vestibule adorned with paintings by unknown artists. There was no one around. They were alone. He led her up some stairs onto the second floor, then along a corridor before turning left.

He paused before a white door, "These are my private rooms. We'll be safe in here," he said with a smile and threw the door open.

The room beyond was a living room, but larger than the entire blacksmith's cottage. Pictures of strange landscapes hung on the walls. One wall was filled completely with a huge tapestry of a mediaeval woman in a garden surrounded by various animals, principally a lion and a unicorn. A huge marble fireplace was in the centre of another wall, a fire blazing away and heating the room to comfortable temperature. High windows on the far wall looked out onto the South Lawn. The walls were painted a pale green, a soothing, pastel shade that showed off the gold picture frames magnificently.

"Do you like it?" he asked with a grin. "These are the Green Rooms. This one, a bathroom through there and a bedroom through the other way."

"These rooms are all yours?" she asked a she stared around trying to take everything in.

"Yes, all mine." He threw his coat on a chair. "Make yourself at home."

She took off her own coat and gently placed it on the same chair. "This is like a room from a fable," she said. "From a fairy tale."

He sat down on a rug in front of the fire and warmed himself. "It seems a lot more like home now that you are in it."

She laughed, "It's nice of you to say, but I find that so hard to believe. Look at this place!"

"It's just stuff," he said with a disparaging tone.

"Expensive stuff," she replied.

"Of course," he agreed. "I appreciate them. But I'm alone with this luxury and I do not want to be alone."

"And if you are asked to choose between me and all this? I could not, in all seriousness, expect you to choose me."

"I do not know what it is to live without luxury, but I do know what it is to live without you and I will not go back to that."

"Ask yourself this. If your brother William had not died, would you even be aware I existed? Would you care? Wouldn't everything be just as good even without me here?"

He thought about it for a moment. "If he had lived then I probably wouldn't know you. But that would be my loss. I see now that William had to die so that I could meet you. Of course, I wish he hadn't, but, if I could turn back the days and rewrite events differently, I would not undo a single day. If asked to choose between him and you...I would choose you."

She sat down next to him in front of the fire. The heat was comforting without burning. They both sat there looking into the flames, watching them dance amongst the logs.

"So, is there something you would like me to do now?" she asked without looking at him.

He shook his head. "No, not really," he answered. "What do you mean?"

"Well," she said slowly. "The Earl of Danby takes me riding, says he can't imagine life without me and then we find ourselves alone in his bedroom and he tells me we won't be disturbed. I've got to think he's expecting me to do something for him."

"Ah," he smiled in understanding. He put his hand to her face and turned her gently to face him. "I don't expect you to do anything. I just invited you here because it was warm and we could be alone. Now, are you hungry?"

"Famished," she said with a laugh.

He got up and went to a large bell on a table and rang it loudly. A few minutes later there was a knock on the door and when it opened a tall man in a long coat came in.

"Could we have some bread, cheese and fruit, please. And some tea," said Peregrine then turned to Elizabeth. "Anything else?"

"No, that sounds fine," she answered.

"That'll be all," he said.

"Yes, my lord," said the servant and left.

Peregrine sat back down in front of the fire. "Now, where were we?"

"I think we were talking about me doing something." She leaned over, put her arms around his neck and kissed him passionately. His arms enveloped her, holding her so tightly he could feel the warmth and curves of her body. They gently probed each others mouths, enjoying the excitement of the intense intimacy. The smell of her hair filled his senses as it tumbled down carelessly from where it had been held up behind her head.

Elizabeth found his proximity intoxicating. She could feel his excitement building and knew it was because of her. She could feel how her touch thrilled him and that response, in turn, thrilled her. She felt her blood pumping as their kisses grew more desperate.

His hands explored her body through her clothes. Tracing the contours of her legs through her petticoat. His imagination raced ahead, filling in the details, increasing his excitement further. He wanted to see more of her body, feel her thigh under the palm of his hand. His fingers traced the outline of her knee. He felt her legs open slightly...

Then there was a knock on the door. They broke apart self-consciously, hurriedly straightening their clothing. Peregrine got to his feet with difficulty and went to the door. He opened it and a servant came carrying a tray of various fruits, cheeses, some bread and a pot of tea. He placed in on a table, asked if there was anything else and then departed.

Peregrine turned to Elizabeth, "Well, that should provide some gossip in the servants hall tonight!"

They both laughed.

12th January 1712

For the next few days the rain fell heavily from leaden skies, running down the road in ragged streams to empty into the Broad Bridge Dyke that ran through the valley to the south of Kiveton. It puddled on the South Lawn forming impromptu ponds where ducks flew in to frolic in the shallow water.

Peregrine gazed morosely through the weeping window panes at the watery landscape. It would not have been pleasant to go out in, either for a ride or a walk. They would have to wait for the weather to break. In the meantime, he tried to busy himself reading. Kiveton's large library was a fertile source of material and, normally, Peregrine would have found it easy to consume endless hours there. But now his thoughts kept drifting to Elizabeth. Every detail of his memory obsessed him. He found himself replaying scenes of their last time together over and over in his mind. Analysing every statement, every look and every gesture to try and determine how she thought about him.

Did she feel the same obsession? Was she now thinking about him as he thought about her? Was she staring through her own watery windows as he now stared impotently through his?

But her situation was not the same as his. She had relentless diversions to occupy her mind, chores to perform, meals to make, people to converse with. By comparison he languished in almost total isolation.

Inevitably, he turned to his imagination for succour. What if they had gone further that night. Maybe she would have allowed him to explore her body as he dearly wanted to. Perhaps he could have loosened her clothing. He fantasised of handling the soft mounds of her breasts through her shift, letting his fingers delicately caress the insides of her thighs. He lay on his bed in heathen nakedness, letting primeval, cavorting thoughts surge unfettered through his mind until he moaned in hot, wet, blessed relief.

Then abruptly, guilt would flood him, flushing his cheeks with embarrassment, soiling his delicate sense of pristine chivalry. What was he doing? How could he do this? To her? To Elizabeth? Reducing her to a derided object of animal lust.

Part of him was disgusted. But another part of him craved satisfaction so very much.

For days he had stalked his rooms, battling his demons. An endless conflict between opposing appetites of divinity and desire. Eventually, he could endure no more. He had to escape this prison. He had to quench his parched soul.

He had to see Elizabeth again.

So it was that morning he donned a heavy cloak with hood and sturdy boots and went out into the deluge. Stomping through the puddles in the South Pavilion courtyard he went out through the gate and onto the Todwick Road. The road was awash with mud and rain, in some parts a veritable quagmire. Instead, he walked directly across it and into the field beyond. Here was the most direct route to the Mirfin's cottage. The field sloped steadily down hill for a mile and there was the blacksmiths yard. As Elizabeth herself had said, he lived at the top of the hill and she lived at the bottom.

Surprisingly, the field was drier than the road, its natural drainage quickly removing the water from the surface. It was still soft going and he had to take care as he strode purposefully downhill. Mercifully, there was little wind to blow the rain in his face, but nevertheless his cloak was soon sodden. He jumped over the small stream that ran north to south down the field and then, when he was eight tenths of the way there, he came out onto the lane that ran towards the blacksmiths yard. He followed the lane to the field where he had played football weeks earlier. Then he left the lane and walked across the field. He climbed between the hedges at the far side and clambered out into the blacksmith's yard.

The yard was an obstacle course of puddles. The forge was open, its chimney coughing black smoke into the air. The clanging sound of work came from inside. Peregrine had no doubt that Robert and Henry would be busy inside. He made his way over to the cottage entrance. He paused before the door, steeling his sparking nerves. He drew back his hood and knocked.

The door opened and there was Elizabeth.

"Hello," he said, grasping fruitlessly for more evocative words.

She threw herself into his arms, wrapping her arms around his neck and hugging him tightly. He returned her hug happily. His heart leapt in his chest like a panicked bird as relief threatened to flood his eyes with tears. All was right with the world once more.

They parted, but her arms stayed around his neck as she grinned up at him. Rain was steadily drenching her hair, dribbling down her face. "I thought I wasn't going to see you again," she said. "I thought you had changed your mind...after the other night....when I didn't...when we didn't..."

He couldn't believe what she was saying. How could she think she could ever disappoint him in any way. He hugged her close, his face submerged in her wet hair, close to her ear.

"I could *never, ever* change my mind about you."

She pulled away, laughing as she said, "We are getting drenched! Come in before we catch our deaths."

They went into the kitchen. Peregrine's cloak was dripping all over the floor and Elizabeth was running her hands through her hair, desperately trying to dry it.

"Well, I can see you're glad to see each other," said Susanna with laugh. "Come over by the fire and get warm."

Peregrine took his cloak off and hung it up. His clothes

underneath were surprisingly dry. Elizabeth wasn't as well off. Her hair had come lose and hung in wet, curly strands, dribbling droplets onto her bare shoulders. He noticed, despite himself, how the clear, glassy drops trickled down her chest, scurrying between the curve of her breasts.

"I told you he'd come back," said Susanna. "She's been thinking all sorts."

"Forgive me," he said to Elizabeth. "I didn't know. It was just that the weather has been so bad. We couldn't go out or do anything so I thought that I'd wait for it to stop. But it didn't."

"So why now?" she asked.

"I couldn't wait any longer. I had to see you. Rain or no rain."

"It's so good to see you," she said earnestly. "I've been thinking about you..."

Susanna cleared her throat, "Well, I think I'll go upstairs and sort some clothes out... or something, uh, else." She wiped her hands on her apron and then went upstairs.

Peregrine turned to Elizabeth, "I think about you all the time. You are my obsession. I feel like an eternity has passed since I last saw you."

"I wondered if your mother had said anything?"

"No, not a word. I haven't told her anyway. I think Mary knows, after all she introduced us. But I don't think Mary would say anything to mother anyway."

"I guess your mother is bound to object?"

"I expect so," he said sadly.

"Even if she knew how we felt?"

"Even then. Probably more so. I don't think she would mind if you were just a flirtation. God knows, she's had enough to put up with with my father and she's managed that. But this - I'm sure she will see it as a threat."

"If we were being sensible we would stop seeing each other," she admitted.

"I don't feel like being sensible."

She put her arms around him and rested her head on his chest. "Me neither. I guess it's a path that can only lead to trouble."

He laughed, "The course of true love never did run smooth."

"I wish it did," she replied. "I don't want to lose you."

"Do you mean that?" he asked gently.

"Yes. Definitely."

His arms round her tightened perceptibly. "Then no one can stand in our way."

She wished she could believe that.

18th January 1712

Over the next few days the rain eased off and then stopped completely. Peregrine and Elizabeth were able to go out riding again.

Firstly, upstream along the river, towards Renishaw, following the shallow valley of the Rother through green hills before turning north eastwards and riding back through Harthill. The village of Harthill lay inside the Osborne estate and, more importantly, carried a spiritual significance as it was where Peregrine's grandfather had built the family tomb as part of the old mediaeval church.

On another ride, a couple of days later, they rode through the park to Anston then followed Anston Brook until it joined the River Ryton, which was itself little more than a brook. Following this stream through wooded valleys they reached Shireoaks before turning back through the old Osborne ancestral home of Thorpe Salvin, where Thorpe Hall now stood empty and desolate. Thorpe was the home of the Baronets of Kiveton, Peregrine's grandfather's original title, before he was elevated to be Viscount Osborne and then Earl of Danby. When becoming a Duke, he had decided Thorpe was not grand enough for his new status and had built Kiveton.

Elizabeth sighed, "Everywhere we go we seem to come across signs of your family. It's either their personal mausoleum, their park or their huge houses. It's all very humbling. Look at this place," she said, indicating Thorpe Hall as they passed its overgrown entrance. "It's a large, fine house, but it's just deserted and unoccupied. Locked up and abandoned. Does no one in your family care about it?"

"No, I don't think so," he admitted. "It's a relic of a previous time, when the family wasn't as omnipotent. They like their history to emphasise a glorious past not their humble beginnings."

"But it's so...wasteful. To just leave a house to decay because you don't need it any more. We're always reusing and mending. Before I throw away anything I ask myself if I could make use of it somewhere else."

He shrugged. "They're extravagant because they can afford to be. They don't have to care."

"It seems a shame."

"Perhaps," he admitted. The old Hall stood silent and empty. its tall towers, high walls and Tudor windows harked back to a distant time. It seemed to be waiting. Like a man who dies so suddenly that he just stands there, surprised, but not yet falling to the ground. Elizabeth was right, it was a shame.

They continued past Thorpe Hall towards Broad Bridge Dyke. Then, crossing it, they turned up Dog Kennel Lane before re-entering Kiveton along Lodge Hill Avenue. Then, as usual, they rode up the South Lawn and dismounted.

Peregrine led the horses into the courtyard. "I was thinking that we could walk back to your house later. That I should take the horses back."

She nodded then said hesitantly, "You want me to come with you?"

"No, just go up the my room. I won't be long. You know the way?"

She nodded, "Alright. Don't be long." She gave him a quick kiss and a smile and headed for the South Pavilion's main door.

He led the horses out through the gate onto the Todwick Road then turned right, up past the main entrance and the North Pavilion and then, through the gates, into the stable yard. As he walked across the yard he saw his sister Mary emerge from the stable managers office, adjust her garments slightly, push a stray piece of hair back into place and then start across the yard.

She stopped, with sudden surprise, when she noticed him looking at her. Then she smiled, looking relieved. "You ride two horses these days?" she commented with a grin.

"Yes, a mare and a spare," he replied lamely, unable to think of any better response.

She said mischievously, "Something told me riding would be good for you. It definitely seems to have lifted your spirits. A man your age needs a hobby," she said with a laugh. "I've been getting quite a bit of riding in myself recently. It must run in the family."

Over her shoulder, Peregrine saw Tom Crowther come out of the stable managers office too. Not in itself unusual, but there was something in the way he stopped when he saw Mary was talking to someone. A moment of...concern? No, more like a hint of panic. Then he walked briskly off in another direction leaving an unmistakable cloud of guilt hanging in the air.

"Well, be careful," said Peregrine levelly watching him go.

She stepped closer to him, her finger idly fastening a button on his tunic. "And you too, little brother. We both know how suspicious Mother can be," she said playfully. "I'm sure I can rely on your discretion. And you can, equally, rely on me not to disclose your....little adventures."

He didn't know how much she knew and how much was supposition so thought best to say nothing in case he unwittingly incriminated himself.

She smiled up at him, "You know that I know...and I know that you know... we're a very knowledgable pair of siblings really. But it's just between us, eh? " She placed an upright index finger over her lips, "Shh." Then she turned and skipped over towards the Hall.

He watched her go, somehow thinking that, in some obscure way, his sister had the advantage of him.

He handed the horses over to one of the stable hands and

then entered the Hall through the North Pavilion, making his way round to the South Pavilion and then up the stairs to his own rooms. He opened the door and entered. The fire was newly made and was heating the room nicely, filling it with a warm, amber glow. But there was no sign of Elizabeth. The bathroom door was open, he looked in, but it was empty. He went back across the main room and into the bedroom. The bedroom was almost a copy of the living room, the same pale green colour and adorned with various landscape paintings. The difference was that it was almost devoid of furniture apart from a four poster bed that dominated the room. Draped from the four thick oak posts was an olive green canopy edged in gold thread.

Elizabeth was laying on the bed, propped up on one arm watching him enter. She had a broad grin on her face.

"I wondered where you had gone," he said. "I thought you might have got lost."

"No, I found it easily. I made myself comfortable."

"I've noticed," he said. She had removed her shoes and stockings and now she lay, barefoot, wriggling her toes.

"I've left room for you," she said, indicating the bed next to her.

He threw his tunic over a chair carelessly and pulled off his boots and put them to one side. With a smile he jumped onto the bed next to her and propped himself up on an arm. Looking directly into her face. Her hair was completely down, falling in a cascade of black strands about her shoulders. She had removed her petticoats so that she wore only a light shift beneath the waist.

"I may need some assistance," she said softly. Her brown eyes never left his face, watching him like a hawk for a reaction.

"How can I assist you," he said., discovering that his mouth was suddenly dry.

Her eyes drifted down to the stays she was wearing that enclosed her ribs, and pushed up her bust. The pair of stays were worn like a waistcoat, tethered together behind her back and then laced at the front.

"I was going to undo the laces, but then I thought you may prefer to do it for me."

He reached across and delicately pulled at the bow knot tying the laces together. The knot fell apart easily, the two ends dangling down the front of her garments. He hooked his finger under the laces and pulled. The two ends wriggled through their lace holes to dangle loosely again. Continuing, his finger hooked under the lace again, freeing even more of the laces. He quickened, pulling lace after lace free. With every lace that was freed, the two sides of the stays opened more and more. Her shift was revealed underneath, crumpled, but tantalising. The mounds of her breasts could be seen, heaving gently beneath the material. As he pulled the laces loose, the back of his hand stroked her shift, it felt like a garment woven from softest down. More laces came loose, he looked up at her. She was looking at him intently, smiling gently that smile that he had first seen on her face in the Saloon. That smile had begun his infatuation with everything about her. She wanted to see the enjoyment on his face, the unadulterated pleasure that she was invoking in him.

The final laces came free. She sat up and pulled her arms free of the stays, discarding them on the floor. He looked at her hungrily. Through her shift he could see the outlines of her young body, the curve of her hips and long legs. Beneath the neckline he could see the gentle swell of her bust and the slight protrusion of her erect nipples.

His blood pumped through him, drumming a mad beat inside his head. He reached out and urgently pulled her towards him. Their lips met, anxious and unrestrained. His hands stroked down her sides, feeling the warmth of her body against his. He could not control himself, he kissed her cheeks, her neck, her ears wildly and with total abandon. He licked her face and neck, he could taste her, he could smell her. His breath was panting with intensity. His hand held her waist, then slid up her body and held her breast, squeezing its softness. He could feel her hard nipple pushing against his palm. She moaned softly, the sound only increasing his ardour.

He wanted her naked. He wanted to see and explore all of her. His hand descended suddenly to the bottom of her shift, sliding under the hem, stroking her thigh, going higher and higher.

"No, no," he said and pulled painfully away. "I can't do this. I can't treat *you* like this. I will not use you in this way!"

She came over to him, her hands holding his face, kissing him urgently. Her voice was gentle as if she spoke to a child. "You're not using me, silly. I'm using you." She took hold of his hand placed it under the hem of her shift, opening her legs and pushing his hand further and further upwards into her damp warmth. "Now, do what I tell you," she said. "And don't stop until I tell you to."

So he did as he was told. Initially using his hands and fingers to caress and arouse and later, kneeling by the bed with his head between her legs. She moaned with sincere enjoyment, her eyes tightly closed, her mouth open, her breathing laboured and pulsing. Finally, with her own fingers, and with his gentle urging, her body arched, stiffening at the moment of maximum intensity with waves of pleasure. She gasped as her climax washed over her like a comforting, hot, raging fire. Then, slowly it subsided.

Her body relaxed, her legs closed slowly and she found herself grinning and laughing involuntarily. He lay down beside her, excited and eager. His heart so full of joy as he saw her boundless excitement. Knowing he had done that for her.

Her eyes were still closed as she wrapped her arms around him. "That was amazing!" she gushed. "Probably the best..."

He grinned madly he was so happy. "I wanted you to enjoy it."

She laughed, "Oh yes. I enjoyed it alright!" She opened her eyes, looking at him with almost feral intensity. "And now it's your turn."

"My tu..?" was all he managed. She was already sat up in front of him, pulling her shift up over her head. Like drapes lifting to reveal a living work of art he stared mesmerised by her lithe nakedness. He couldn't close his eyes, he dare not obscure his vision and lose a single moment. "Sweet Helen," he murmured almost inaudibly. "Make me immortal with a kiss."

She leaned over him, kissing him with wet intensity, her breasts pushing against his chest. Raising herself up, she held his head with one hand and lowered her nipple into his open mouth. His lips closed tenderly. The feel of her breast against his face made him almost dizzy with desire. He strained painfully in his breeches...and then, suddenly, he was freed as her hand reached in and pulled him free. Slowly, she kissed her way down his body, opening his shirt step by step. Getting closer and closer, enhancing and building his anticipation. Until, throwing her hair back, licked him enticingly.

He could not move, he was frozen and helpless. Staring at the ceiling as he felt her mouth close around him. The idea of it was enough, it inflamed him, ignited him into a dizzying frenzy. He abandoned all hope of restraining himself and exploded in an unfettered, heart bursting rapture.

Chapter Seven

19th January 1712

It's the best day of my life, thought Peregrine to himself. He had awoken earlier than usual, long before dawn. He lay on his back in his four poster bed, surrounded by his luxurious bedroom. Elizabeth was sleeping next to him, her head resting on his arm, her hair falling across his chest. They were both naked and at ease with it.

As innocent as Eve, unsullied by guilt, he thought to himself. *We should cherish these moments while they last.*

For he knew they could not last. Nothing did. If his life had taught him any harsh lesson it was that. Happiness was that most fragile of things, so easily broken by a brutal world.

As dawn broke and soft light lit the room, he looked down at Elizabeth where she breathed so delicately against him. He must protect her from the future if he could. The forces ranged against them were formidable, his mother, his grandfather, even his father. But he must oppose them because he had something that mattered now. Something he could not allow them to tarnish. He must find a way to secure a life for them that could last.

She moved against him, sighing contentedly. "Good Morning, my lord," she said with a grin.

"Good Morning," he replied happily, kissing her forehead.

She ran her fingers through the hairs on his chest playfully.

"My very own earl. What a lucky girl I am."

"I am your slave, but I count myself the fortunate one."

She kissed his chest. "You enjoyed yourself, then?" she asked coyly.

"As I never thought I could."

She looked up at him with a questioning look, "Was that your first time? With a woman?"

He smiled, "No. It's happened twice before."

"Oh," she said, sounding disappointed. "I thought, well, never mind what I thought..."

"The first time was at school in the Netherlands. William got talking to two girls. I think they liked him, not me But there were two of them and two of us. It's seemed inevitable that we pair off. So we did. I guess it was all very clumsy, but it was enough for me. I fell madly in love that night. But that was the start and end of it - I never saw her again. So I guess she didn't feel the same."

"Ah, your first broken heart can really hurt," she said sympathetically.

"Months later, William told that she slept with him the next night. So I guess she got what she really wanted in the end."

"That's cruel. He shouldn't have told you."

"I was over it by then. But it did sting."

"And the second time?"

"A courtesan in Venice. For money."

"You mean a harlot?" she said with surprise.

"Aye. Well, we were two young men with money far from home...and everything's for sale."

"So, what was she like?" she asked. .

"She was well practised. And very at ease with the situation. Oddly, I was the one who felt soiled and degraded by the experience."

"It was better with me then?"

He scoffed, "Without the tiniest shred of a doubt! They are incomparable."

"But we didn't actually, you know, do it. Did we?"

"I couldn't care a jot."

"I couldn't, you see," she said quietly. "It's the wrong time. Only in the week after the start of bleeding. Then it's safe. The rest of the time...I could get with child. That would be a very foolish thing for me to do. What with everything so uncertain and all. I'm sorry, but you understand?"

"What are you apologising for? Of course, I understand. I count myself blessed if you chose to spend any time with me at all. Or even look in my direction."

"I didn't want you to feel let down."

"Look! Will you stop talking like this. There's only one thing you could do that could let me down. And that's stop seeing me."

She snuggled closer, "Then that's good, because that will never happen."

"It might, when your father finds out you've stayed here all night. We only said we were going out with the horses."

"It'll be fine," she said dismissively. "They know I'm with you. They won't worry. As long as I turn up sometime today."

"Well, we better have breakfast then. I'll get dressed and then ask them to bring us some up." He jumped out of bed and started gathering up his clothes.

"With tea? I loved that tea."

"Yes, with tea," he said. "But I hope you realise that I'm spoiling you. "

"Oh, I do." she answered sarcastically.

"The other girls I brought up here only got water."

She threw a pillow at him.

4th February 1712

Snow returned to Kiveton in late January. Some days it drew grey curtains of heavy flakes across the view from Peregrine's window, carpeting the South Lawn in wintry white. Other days it fluttered down like torn paper in the breathless air. In between the snowy days it would rain. Beating on the window and rattling the drains and transforming the roads into muddy paths where the endless trudge of cartwheels carved deep ruts.

Peregrine no longer minded. He saw Elizabeth most days, whatever the weather. It was no longer a barrier, simply an inconvenience. Most of the time it wasn't the weather for riding, or even walking, to any degree. So they stayed in. He would walk directly down the field to the blacksmith's yard. Usually, unless it was a Sunday, Robert and Henry would be working in the forge while Elizabeth and Susanna handled the chores around the house. He would spend hours in the kitchen as the girls busied around him. When Robert and Henry took a break he would share drinks or food with them. He became almost a house fixture, after a while they just expected him to arrive sometime during the day. He started taking some food and drink with him, mostly just essentials that he would take from the kitchen at Kiveton, but sometimes something special or hard to come by. It just felt good to make some contribution, as they were always willing to share what they had, however meagre. Although, the family were not poor, both men were skilled tradesmen after all who could command a decent rate for their work. In addition, Susanna helped out at the church and Elizabeth did housework for some of the older residents in the village.

That was how she found out about the Billam's Cottage. Mrs Billam lived across the road from the blacksmith's yard. For years her and her husband had lived in the cottage and grown various vegetables in the small holding at the back. They then sold their produce to people in the village or at the market in Worksop. They must have made a decent living by it, the cottage was half again as big as the blacksmith's cottage so the tenancy would have cost more. Then a few years ago her husband had died. For a while she persevered as best she could, but she wasn't getting any younger and there was a lot of work for one person. She had two sons, but they worked a farm in Aughton, about four miles away, and they came over when they could to help. Henry started helping out with the vegetables when he could find the time and Elizabeth helped out in the house. Mrs Billam paid them for their time, but eventually her health worsened and it became difficult to make ends meet.

It was after spending the morning across the road at the Billam's cottage that Elizabeth decided to go home. She stood in the doorway steeling herself against the rain. She pulled her shawl over her head and ran across the road to the blacksmith's yard. She deftly dodged the growing puddles, skipping and dashing as best she could until, with relief, she made it into the kitchen.

"Damn this rain!" she said, shaking the water off her drenched shawl.

"It's good for the garden," commented Peregrine with a grin.

"If it likes growing in mud perhaps," she replied. She went over and gave him a brief kiss. "Sorry. Bad morning."

"I brought some more tea," he said indicating a package on the table.

"Oh, Thank Goodness! That's a life saver." She picked up the package and then went over to fill the kettle.

Susanna came in from the living room. "How's things across the road?"

"Not good. Mrs Billam's leaving."

"Leaving? She's been there all my life," said Susanna.

"She's struggling to keep up with everything. I can't see her putting much work in in the field this year and, without that, she'll have no income. No income, means no money to pay the rent."

"Or pay you and Henry."

"Aye, I think we can forget doing any more work over there. "

"What can she do? Where can she go?"

"It makes sense actually. She's moving in with her sons in Aughton. Apparently, they've got the room. They can use some help on their farm and they can keep an eye on her. It's the best option really."

"So we'll be getting new neighbours?"

"Eventually, I guess. These places can take some time to find new tenants."

"I wonder what they'll be like?" asked Susanna dreamily. "Probably some young hunk with lots of muscles. In summer, he'll probably have to remove his shirt to work in the field. I wonder if we can see over there from our bedroom window..?"

"Oh, I think we can," agreed Elizabeth. "He might be an older man. About thirty would be...interesting."

"Thirty! That's ancient!" cried Susanna. They both started laughing.

"Don't mind me," said Peregrine. "I'd hate to think my presence was limiting your imaginations."

"Oh, don't worry," said Elizabeth. "It isn't."

"Of course, it could be an old couple, like the Billams," he said.

"I suppose," admitted Susanna. "Pen, you're such a spoil sport! Where am I supposed to find a husband when there's so little to choose from?"

"You?" replied Peregrine. "You've got lots of time yet."

"I'm fourteen. Some girls my age in Todwick are married already."

Elizabeth scoffed, "Well, I think that's awful. Those poor girls. They need to live a little first, not marry the first boy that looks at them."

"Well, I know," said Susanna. "But, then again, if he was really great I might want to make sure I got him before anyone else. Marriage does that, makes it permanent."

"I suppose it does that," said Elizabeth, distantly, as she made her tea.

Peregrine looked at her. He knew what she was thinking. Marriage looked very unlikely for them. Without it, there was no guarantee it was permanent. Things could change, especially with his family. If they were married, things would be different. Marriages were very difficult to break, often requiring significant expense, a court judgement and often, an act of parliament. His mother knew this only too well. She had originally been married at the age of twelve to her cousin,

John Emerton. In order to marry Peregrine's father they had to annul the first marriage and bribe Emerton so he would not challenge it. His father, as usual, had no funds of his own so the costs had to be met by *his* father and the prospective wife's family.

No, Peregrine had no doubt, that his mother would never allow him to marry Elizabeth. Ever.

He spent the afternoon with the Mirfins. As the sunlight began to fade he decided to start the walk home. It was easier to do it while it was still light. He kissed Elizabeth goodnight, promised to see her the next day and set off, over the field and up the hill to Kiveton.

The rain was a constant irritation, spitting in his face or running in icy droplets down his neck. He was glad to get back to Kiveton. It was nearly dark, he could see the windows in his room were flickering with the light from inside. The servants had lit the candles and probably made the fire by now. It would be warm and dry and a blessed relief.

He barged through the doors into the South Pavilion. He took off his muddy boots and soaked coat then carried them up the stairs. He opened the door to his room and was greeted with the welcome warmth of the fire. He entered, not paying much attention to anything, he put his boots down, threw his coat over a chair and went over to the fire to warm himself.

"Good Evening, Pip," said his mother.

He turned, startled. She was sat in the big chair by the fire, invisible to anyone until they stood where Peregrine now stood.

"Mother, you startled me." he said.

"Where have you been until this time?" she asked. It sounded like a loaded question.

She knows, he thought to himself. "Out. ...walking."

"In the rain?" she asked incredulously.

"I needed some fresh air."

"Where did you walk to?"

"Oh, just around. Nowhere special."

"Not into Wales then?" she asked.

She definitely knows, he thought. "Yes, as it happens, into Wales." He couldn't stop himself fidgeting under her gaze. His eyes didn't want to meet hers so they nervously darted around the room looking for somewhere else to rest.

"To the blacksmith's cottage?"

"Uh," no answer he could contrive seemed appropriate.

"I know about your dalliance with that blacksmith's daughter, Pip. It's my business to know. You can have no secrets from me."

He felt the colour drain from his face. "How did you find out?"

"A lot of people work in this house. I have eyes and ears everywhere. And some live in Wales too. You haven't been very discreet, have you?"

"She's helped me," he said, in what he hoped was his defence. "She's helped me get over William. I needed to do that, I couldn't go on as I was."

She smiled, but there wasn't a lot of warmth in it. "Oh I understand, Pip. There are times when we all need a diversion, something to get our minds off immediate events. We are all human, after all."

"She makes me happy," it sounded very lame in the face of his mother's disapproval.

"Well, that's good. You are my son, I want you to be happy." Peregrine suspected that she didn't mean that the way it sounded. "Lots of things in this world have the capacity to make us happy. Wine, tobacco, art, music even love. But we cannot allow them to distract us from doing what is necessary. Or even essential.

"For example, take your blacksmith friend, I'm sure he would rather be sitting in the sun, having a smoke and a drink than working in his forge. But he doesn't. Because his work is necessary for him to indulge in these other pleasures.

"And so it is with you too, Pip. I am prepared to overlook, even endure, your transgressions...provided you do what is necessary. "

"And what is necessary?" he said, almost afraid to ask.

"At this moment, it is necessary for you to go to Hereford-shire."

"I can't..." he began.

"Really? You have some other pressing engagement?" He turned and stared into the fire, but said nothing. "No, I thought not. You will deliver a letter I will write to the Earl of Oxford. He's a good friend of the family."

"A letter? Can't you post it?"

"It involves a little bit more than the letter. You will leave on Monday. You will stay at Brampton Bryan Hall, the Earl's residence. You should not expect to return until the end of the month."

"Is this to do with finding a husband for his daughter?"

"It's early days. We shall see how the wind blows when you return."

"And what if I don't want to?" he said, still staring into the fire.

"As I say, we all must occasionally do what we don't want to. That is the nature of things."

"And what if I say I won't?"

"You will." She said sternly, then sighed. "Please, Pip, I am trying to avoid any unpleasantness. Don't try and assert your-self over this. You really are not in a position to do so."

"Are you threatening me, Mother?"

"Threats are such distasteful things. I am asking for your willing cooperation. All I am asking is for you to go to Here-fordshire and let them see you. Nothing more."

"Not yet?" he said bitterly.

"Well, as I say, it's early days. We had an agreement that she would marry William, well, obviously that's not going to hap-pen now. But I am determined to salvage something from the project."

"I cant marry the Earl of Oxford's daughter. I love someone else."

She laughed, but without humour. "My dear Pip, you can love whoever and whatever you want. But understand this. Should it become necessary, you will *marry* whoever I tell you to and when I tell you to."

"Or what?"

She sighed, "Why do you have to make me force you like this?"

"I wouldn't want to think I had capitulated without knowing the nature of the compulsion."

"Alright, have it your way." She paused, gathering her thoughts. "Your blacksmith family don't really own the cottage they live in or the forge they work, do they?"

"They are tenants," he replied. "They pay to live and work there."

"So, we own their cottage and the forge? They're on Osborne property?"

"Yes," he admitted grudgingly.

"So they could be evicted, then? They would lose their home. Their livelihoods. What would happen to them then? It would be hard for them, especially this time of year in the rain and the snow. Very hard. And all because they met you, Pip. They might blame you for it. Might never forgive you."

"You wouldn't do that..." he said softly, but he knew she would.

She rose from her chair and came over to stand next to him. She placed an arm on his shoulder reassuringly, "You think about it tonight, Pip. I'm sure that, once you have, you'll realise where your obligations truly lie. And you'll have a few days to explain to your friends why you have to go to Herefordshire. I'm sure you'll realise that it really works out best for everyone all round. Good Night."

She left, closing the door gently behind her. Peregrine stayed, staring into the fire, his hand clenched into a fist.

5th February 1712

He walked down to Wales early next morning. He walked slowly, he was in no rush to get there. It was still raining, but he didn't care, his thoughts were elsewhere. He had come to Kiveton originally hoping to find somewhere he could call home, It had worked far better than he had expected. Now he could not contemplate leaving there at all.

He arrived at the blacksmith's cottage a lot earlier than he had planned. He hesitated then opened the door and entered the kitchen.

Susanna turned when he entered, "Hello, Pen. It's a bit early for you isn't it?"

But Elizabeth could read his expression. "What's wrong?"

"I need to speak with you," he said simply.

"Of course," she said. "Come into the living room. Pa and Henry are in the forge working."

Susanna looked worried, but said nothing. Elizabeth and Peregrine went into the living room and closed the door.

Elizabeth turned to face him, desperately trying to read his expression. "What's this about?"

"Mother wants me to go to Herefordshire," he said simply. "For a few days. I won't be back until the end of the month."

"Alright," she said slowly. "That doesn't sound too bad. I'll be here when you get back. I'll try and keep busy. I'll miss you, of course, but I'll look forward to seeing you. Is that it?"

He looked at her helplessly. How could he explain that his mother was trying to marry him to someone else?

"She's trying to split us up…"

Elizabeth frowned, "Hold on, your mother knows about us?"

"Yes. I don't know how, but she does."

Elizabeth nodded, "I see. So she's sending you to Herefordshire? Separating us?"

"Yes! Oh, why do I have to have a mother like her?!" he said angrily.

"Calm down. So, she thinks sending you to Herefordshire will make you forget me?"

"I suppose so," he murmured.

"Well, it won't work," she said firmly. Then she looked at him for confirmation, "Will it?"

He smiled, "No I couldn't forget you any more than I can forget my own name."

"So, why Herefordshire?" she asked.

"What do you mean?"

"What is there in Herefordshire that she's sending you there? Why not London? Or Wimbledon?"

"She wants me to meet the Earl of Oxford," he replied steadily and half truthfully. "I think she's wants to build relationships between the two families. They can't rely on my father to do it."

She nodded, "That's understandable. And your grandfather's an old man, I can see why they might want someone younger to meet them."

"But, I don't want to go."

"No, of course not. But you're going to be the Duke of Leeds one day and, when you do, you'll need some friends. Here's a chance to make some."

He sighed, "That's the sort of thing she would say. But I want to stay here with you."

"Yes, and I'd like that too. But, although I hate to admit it, she has a point. When do you go?"

"Monday."

"Good," she smiled. "We've got a couple of days together. Then you go to Herefordshire. Do what you need to do for a few days. Come back here and I'll be waiting for you. The weather will be better and we can go out again. We'll be happy. This Earl of Oxford will be happy and your mother will be happy. It'll all be over, right?"

"Yes, I suppose...sort of."

"Then there's nothing to worry about. Is there?" She could sense he was holding something back.

"No," he said as he took her in his arms and hugged her. "There's nothing to worry about."

She hugged him back. But, for some reason, she was worried.

8th February 1712

Monday morning came, as he knew inevitably it would. Friday had been great, Elizabeth had been really positive about Peregrine's Herefordshire trip. She saw it as a temporary inconvenience, but nothing they couldn't deal with. Susanna had been even more positive when she heard the news. She considered he should be counting his blessings, Herefordshire was a wonderful place and he was lucky to be going there. He should make the most of it and, before he knew it, he would be back. Peregrine found the two sisters attitude infectious. He had walked back to Kiveton later that day thinking that things may not be too bad after all.

On Saturday the weather wasn't too bad for the time of year. It was cold, but it wasn't raining. They had walked down through the wood to the river. They made it back to the cottage before dark and had some hot broth by the fire. Henry had gone out with his friends and was not expected back so Peregrine could sleep in his bed. It had been idyllic.

Then he had awoken and it was Sunday. He had breakfast then he went with the rest of the family to church. During the afternoon he walked with Elizabeth slowly up through the field to the hall. Elizabeth had told her family that she would see them tomorrow. No one had objected. That evening they'd sat in front of the fire and enjoyed each others company, but there was a lingering, ominous presence with them. He knew that tomorrow he would be going to Herefordshire. He tried to make the most of the precious hours they had left. They went to bed early, soothed each other with pleasure then clung together desperately. But still, the lingering presence was there. The hours were ticking past like trickling grains through an hourglass and there was nothing he could do to halt it.

Then it was Monday. At least Elizabeth was with him. That made everything bearable. Whatever was coming, whatever others decided, whatever his mother planned, they would face it together. He was not alone any more. Elizabeth was here. He could no longer conceive of a life without her in it.

He realised that she had woken and was looking at him. "How are you feeling?" she asked.

"Numb. Resigned to it."

"How long is the journey?"

"I'm not sure, three or four days."

"So, you'll have a long time before you have to face anyone. You'll get to see quite a bit of the countryside. I'd quite like that aspect, I have hardly seen anything."

"Oh God, I wish you were coming with me," he said desperately.

"Maybe next time," she said. But they both knew that that was unlikely. The Earl of Danby could not take any consort on any official visit. "I'll be thinking about you and wondering how you are getting on. And I'll be here when you get back. They can separate us geographically, but here," she tapped her temple with her finger. "And here," she put her hand on her heart. "We cannot be separated."

He hugged her closer. "Did I tell you that I love you?"

"Frequently," she said.

"Good. I just wanted to make sure you knew."

They got up, got dressed and had some breakfast brought to the room. Then, at the right time, they went down, hand in hand into the vestibule of the South Pavilion. Walking through the corridors they crossed into the main building. They saw servants busily running around going about the chores of the day, but they didn't see anyone from the family. Peregrine was relieved when they got through into the North Pavilion and then out into the stable yard. His coach was waiting, the drivers were busy finishing tethering the horses for the journey and loading his luggage. They would ride the horses to the first staging post then return with them and a new set would take him onwards. After a few minutes they were ready.

"Have a good journey. Hurry back," she said, tearfully.

He turned and held her in his arms. "I'm going to miss you very, very much.". They kissed and hugged then parted slowly and reluctantly.

He climbed into the coach and closed the door. As it pulled away he looked through the window, held up his hand in farewell, his face creased with emotion. As the coach pulled onto the Todwick Road and rounded the corner he fell back into seat. Despondent and alone.

In the stable yard Elizabeth watched his coach disappear. She still had her hand in the air where she had been waving franticly. She covered her mouth with her other hand as she felt the tears welling in her eyes.

11th February 1712

Brampton Bryan Hall lay between Ludlow and Knighton, close to the Welsh border. It was a very rural area of endless green fields set in rolling hills which, in the west, suddenly rose into the mountains of Wales. The nearest towns of any size were at least a days ride away, Hereford to the south, Shrewsbury to the north or Kidderminster to the east. The journey there took Peregrine four days, stopping overnight in Derby, Tamworth and Kidderminster. It was exhausting, uncomfortable and tedious. Worse, it left him with very little to do except consider his circumstances.

He realised that, though he may appear to live a life a privilege and wealthy indulgence, in reality he owned nothing. Everything was owned and paid for by the Osborne estate, his grandfather's estate. Peregrine himself, received an income from it and he could claim expenses from it, but he did not control it. He compared himself to John Lambert, his grandfather's steward at Wimbledon. Lambert also received an income from the estate, but he was regarded as an employee. Peregrine was family. But, apart from the fact that Peregrine could not lose his job, was there really any difference? Lambert had his role to perform and so did Peregrine. The estate paid them and demanded their obedience and servitude in return. Peregrine realised that Lambert had one big advantage – he could leave at any time. He had a choice, while Peregrine had no choice. If Lambert wanted to marry a blacksmith's daughter he was free to do so. Peregrine had no such option.

Peregrine endlessly debated with himself who was the most fortunate. He had to conclude it was not himself.

As the fourth day came to a close he finally neared Brampton Bryon Hall. The house was set in a large estate. Robert Harley, the Earl of Oxford, had recently been made Lord Treasurer and had risen to major influence in the country. He could be a very powerful ally to the right person. Peregrine could see why his mother might consider a link between the Osbornes and the Harleys to be a very good idea indeed. Harley had an unmarried twenty-two year old daughter and Lady Bridget had an unmarried twenty year old son. It seemed like an obvious opportunity to connect both families.

Peregrine realised grimly that his relationship with Elizabeth stood in the way of all that. Two of the most powerful families in England were ranged against a blacksmith's daughter. It seemed like a very uneven match. Elizabeth had been right, they were very small and what they wanted didn't count for much at all.

The coach drove through the Brampton estate for several minutes before they entered the small hamlet of Brampton Bryan. The road curved round a small wood and then they turned up a drive and, a few seconds later, there was the house itself. It was a large, square brick building in a modern Queen Anne style. It was not dissimilar to Kiveton's main building, but not as wide and it lacked the large, twin Pavilions that Kiveton could boast. It sat on a lush lawn, surrounded by extensive woods. As the coach pulled up along the drive Peregrine caught sight of a tower of white stones to its rear, the remains of a mediaeval castle now sitting like a magnificent folly in the garden.

The coach pulled up in front of the building. Peregrine got

out, feeling very nervous. A tall man in a red jacket and black breeches was waiting for him.

"Good afternoon, my lord," he said. "Welcome to Brampton Bryan. His lordship has instructed me to take you in to see him as soon as you arrive."

"Thank you," said Peregriine and followed the man up the stairs and through the main doors into the main hall. The room was two storeys high with an dark oak staircase leading up to a an upper storey. The rooms exhibited several statues from classical mythology mixed with portraits of the Harley family. The floor was a swirling pattern of brown and white marble tiles.

Peregrine was led directly across the hall and through two sets of doors into a smaller room. It was a darker, more intimate library or drawing room. The walls were covered in Tudor style oak panelling stained dark, almost black. Various forms of easy, relaxing furniture were positioned around, but a large desk dominated the far end. The desk was covered in papers and a selection of books, some open as if in the act of being read. It gave the impression of someone who was very busy, finding a small amount of time in his schedule to greet a visitor.

Robert Harley, the Earl of Oxford sat behind the desk looking very much at ease, almost a living part of the desk itself. He was a man in late middle age, his hair grey and thinning and his belly expanding about his midriff. He had a round, fat face with a sharp nose. His eyes were so dark it wasn't clear what their colour was. He wore a blank expression that carried with it a hint of continual assessment and disapproval. It wasn't the face of a man who smiled very often.

Harley rose from his desk with some difficulty and walked round it to greet Peregrine.

"Ah, Danby, isn't it? Leeds' youngest. Glad to meet you."

"I'm glad to meet you,sir," replied Peregrine formally and they shook hands. Harley did so without any warmth, his attitude was very business like. "My mother sends her regards and this letter." Peregrine handed over the letter.

"Oh yes, your mother, Bridget. Leeds is your grandfather, of course."

"Indeed he is, sir. My mother is his daughter-in-law."

"Yes, I remember now. Hyde's daughter." Harley sat back at his desk as if he was uncomfortable being away from it too long. He opened the letter with a knife and then studied it with his full attention.

Harley may not know much about Peregrine, but Peregrine knew a lot about him. He had been reading about him on the journey down. Like Peregrine's grandfather, Harley was a political animal, a member of parliament, quite at home in the cut and thrust of political life at Westminster. In the last two years he had been appointed Chancellor of the Exchequer, a poisoned chalice given the state of the country's finances after the recent war with France. But Harley, a clever business man and a devious and wily political operator, had proved up to the task. Last year had proved particularly advantageous, he was made a Baron and then elevated to the prestigious Earldom of Oxford even though his family had little connection to Oxford or the De Vere family who had traditionally held the title. He had also endured two assassination attempts. One early in the year when he was stabbed by the Marquis de Guiscard while he was being examined by Harley on a charge of treason. The second attempt was towards the end of the year when he was sent a hat box containing two pistols which were triggered by a thread.

All-in-all, Peregrine's impression was of an ambitious, unscrupulous but capable politician who dearly wanted to establish his family's credentials and create a dynasty. From Peregrine's family's point-of-view he was probably seen as an influential, wealthy and powerful ally. Disturbingly, Peregrine realised that what both family's may want from him was an heir. A combination of the two houses in a single individual.

Harley put down the letter from Peregrine's mother. "Please sit," he said indicating a choice of chairs arranged around his desk. Peregrine sat in one, although he didn't feel particularly at ease. Harley continued, "Now, as you may be aware, I have been in discussions with your mother over the last year or so with a view to a possible liaison between your elder brother, William, and my daughter. They had met, once, admittedly some years ago when they were teenagers, but, as I understood it, my daughter was quite taken with him. So, when I raised the possibility with her last year she was initially enthusiastic." He paused, looking at Peregrine closely, "Of course, as often happens, our carefully laid plans have been overtaken by events and, as you are no doubt aware, your brother is no longer with us. Which is a great shame, all things considered. The timing would have worked out well, him having just finished his tour of Europe. But, there we are, it is what it is. Nothing we can do about that. The point is that, apart from the obvious fact that one of the candidates is no longer available, the fundamentals of the deal are unchanged. An association between our family's would be advantageous to both. With this in mind, your mother has suggested you as a possible replacement."

Peregrine didn't know whether to be honoured or insulted that he was being considered in such an off hand manner. He felt like he was applying for a position on the house staff. While he didn't want to show any obvious lack of interest, in truth he had none at all. He kept silent being unsure what response was expected.

Harley continued, "Now, you are currently the Earl of Danby, is that correct?"

"Yes, sir," said Peregrine. "Since Will...my brother's death I now have that title."

"Your grandfather is a dear friend, but when he passes away, as inevitably he must, you will be...?"

"At that point I will become Marquis of Carmarthan. And, subsequently, when my father dies I will become Duke of Leeds."

Harley nodded approvingly, "Duke of...yes, that's interesting. And your son, he would also become a Duke?"

"My heir would be initially Danby, then on my father's death he would be Carmarthan and, on my death, ultimately Leeds."

"Interesting. Assuming this heir came about through a liaison with my daughter, you are saying that, if all went to plan, my grandson would be the Duke Of Leeds?"

Peregrine nodded, "That's a large assumption, but, yes, that is what would happen. Theoretically."

"Oh yes, in theory, quite. A long way to go yet, of course. And this theoretical heir would inherit all the Osborne estates?"

"Again, yes. In theory," agreed Peregrine..

"Um," murmured Harley to himself. "You and your mother dangle quite an enticing bauble in front of me, do you know that?"

"It is not my intention to tantalise, sir," said Peregrine. "Merely to answer the questions put to me and present myself in a favourable light."

"Oh yes, yes, quite," he replied with a wave of his hand. "Still, intentionally or not, you do tantalise me with the possibilities..."

Peregrine cleared his throat dramatically, "Would it be possible for me to meet your daughter, sir?"

"My daughter?" said Harley distantly. "Oh yes, of course, my daughter. Yes, you'll probably want to see her. Well, from your mother's letter I see that we can expect you to be with us for several days so there will be plenty of time for you to acquaint yourselves. But it is quite late now and, I have no doubt, you're exhausted from your journey. But, plenty of time to meet her tomorrow."

"That would be...useful," said Peregrine trying to walk a thin line between stating the obvious without being sarcastic.

"Yes, I suppose it would," said Harley. "Well, as I say, plenty of time for that. I'll have one the servants show you to your room and we'll get you settled in. We're not having any dinner tonight so, if you're hungry, ask one of them to bring you something in your room. Breakfast is in the Morning Room – just come down and ask someone where it is. Then we'll take it from there. Alright?"

Feeling like his interview was over Peregrine got to his feet. "Thank you, sir."

"Yes, yes, see you tomorrow," said Harley dismissively and was already turning back to the books on his desk.

12ᵗʰ February 1712

Peregrine entered the Morning Room quite hesitantly. The brightness of the east facing room's early morning light cast an unwelcome spotlight on his hesitant entry making it uncomfortably obvious. A long table dominated the room, which was only a little larger. The walls were painted a pale, sunrise yellow which added to the morning atmosphere.

Robert Harley was sitting at the head of the table while to his right was his wife Sarah. His second wife, Peregrine recalled from his briefing. All the children were from his first wife.

Robert beckoned him over with a wave of his hand. "Danby! Come in, take a seat. This is my wife, Sarah." He said absently to his wife, "This is the Earl of Danby, Duke of Leeds' youngest. He's staying with us for a few days."

"Welcome, my lord," said Lady Sarah formally.

"Please call me Peregrine. The title is unfamiliar to me – I still think of it belonging to my brother."

"Your brother...oh, yes, I remember now. I was sorry to hear about it." She added, "Elizabeth seemed quite impressed with him."

"Young Peregrine is his replacement," said Harley, in a cold hearted fashion, as he was stuffing some bread into his mouth. "He's the new Danby, so to speak."

"Well, I'm sure he will be eminently suitable," said his wife with what she probably thought was great sensitivity. It all just made Peregrine feel like some colt being appraised for stud.

At that point, two other people entered the room. A man and woman, both in their early twenties. He pushed in front of her playfully to enter the room first which caused her to slap his shoulder equally playfully.

They came over to the table without speaking to anyone and fell into seats on opposite sides.

Lady Sarah said "Edward, Elizabeth, this is Peregrine, the Earl of Danby. He's staying with us for a few days."

Elizabeth Harley picked up a plum from a selection on the table and bit into it thoughtfully while she examined Peregrine. "Danby? I met the Earl of Danby years ago. Was that you?"

"My brother," explained Peregrine. "Older brother."

"Ah, that explains it. I see the resemblance...vaguely. So, why's he not here?"

Robert Harley interrupted before Peregrine could speak. "The previous Danby sadly passed away last year."

"Oh," said Elizabeth idly. "Pity."

"The lengths some people will go to to get out of marrying you!" said Edward with a laugh. Elizabeth threw her half eaten plum at him which he dodged easily.

"Papa, tell him to stop insulting me," she cried.

"Stop annoying your sister, Edward," said Harley absently.

Elizabeth grinned brazenly at her brother, glad to have secured a minor victory.

"You must forgive them, Lord Danby," said Lady Sarah. "They're always at each other. Are you like that with any of your brothers and sisters?"

"I have only two sisters," replied Peregrine. "And they are both older than me. My brother and myself didn't grow up with them really, we were educated on the continent..."

"With foreigners?" exclaimed Edward. "Surely not in France? With the frogs! Oh, I couldn't do that. I hate the frogs. We've been at war with them for eleven years."

"And at astronomical expense," muttered Robert Harley. "By the time it's over we'll be lucky if the country isn't bankrupt."

"And there speaks the Lord Treasurer himself," said Edward. "So he should know."

"Don't worry," said Harley with a grin. "I have a cunning plan."

Elizabeth explained to Peregrine, "Papa has set up a company to sell Negroes to the Spanish colonies. As slaves. Buy them cheap in Africa, ship them to the New World and sell them for a lot more money. There's a big demand for slaves in the colonies. Isn't it a great idea?"

Harley said, "Well, it's a bit more complicated than that, dear. We've been doing that for years. But I've arranged for the South Seas Company to have a monopoly on trade of all kinds with the Spanish colonies. Only they can do it. But the really interesting bit is that I've financed it from the national debt. All the people that the government owes money to, I've persuaded them to exchange their debt for shares in the South Seas Company. That way they get dividends and their shares increase in value, a lot better than having the country owe you money."

"Which solves the national debt at a stroke," said Edward. "It's genius."

"Good enough to get me an Earldom," said Harley.

Peregrine was completely out of his depth, but he had a feeling that moving debts from one place to another wasn't really solving anyone's problems, just delaying them.

"I'm afraid I'm at a loss to appreciate your achievement," he said.

"And so are most people, so you're not alone," said Harley. "Halifax himself admitted to me that he was out of his depth."

"England is so lucky to have you in charge of it's finances, Papa," gushed Elizabeth.

"Are you in politics, Lord Danby?" asked Edward.

"No, my grandfather still handles the family's political commitments."

Harley said, "He's getting on a bit now, though. I'm sure he'll be looking for some young blood like yourself to step forward and take over."

"Oh, he is," admitted Peregrine. "Grandfather has big expectations of me."

"So what is it you do?" asked Edward.

"Do?"

"For a living? Do you see yourself in parliament or a naval career? What?"

Peregrine was at a loss for an answer. "Well, I've just completed a two year tour of Europe. Since then I've just been...riding," he replied sheepishly.

"Oh good!" exclaimed Elizabeth. "You like to ride? We are going riding today. You should come with us."

"I'd love to," he admitted, relieved to be off the subject of his plans for the future. Because he didn't have any.

So it was that later that day, Peregrine, Edward and Elizabeth were leading their horses out from the stable block and down the drive towards the road. Once on the road they turned left and went down into the village. Then they turned right and into the Brampton Bryan Park. The Park consisted mainly of open grasslands with occasional trees, sometimes clumped into small spinneys.

As the ground opened out, Edward let out a yell, kicked his boot heels into the sides of his horse and shook the reins madly. His horse leapt forward, launching into a full gallop across the grass.

A fraction of a second later Elizabeth followed suit, kicking her horse angrily and spurring it on with flicks of her riding crop. She was riding astride the saddle, her horsemanship was so excellent that she almost kept up with her brothers frantic dash across the Park.

Peregrine, who had been expecting a gentle ride, was caught completely by surprise and could only nudge his horse into a gallop to try and keep up. The two Harley siblings were already quite some distance off and getting further away all the time. All he could do was follow in their wake as they beat their steeds into a faster and faster pace.

They raced like they were being pursued by a multitude of demons, yelling, standing high in their stirrups as they used their crops wildly. After several minutes their horses were neck and neck, their riders urging them on and on to greater speed. The horses hooves pumped the ground like engine pistons, their veins standing proud on their necks as they strained to take the lead. Edward and Elizabeth both gritted their teeth, as stressed as their horses as each strived to beat the other.

Then suddenly, Elizabeth's horse stumbled. In a second she was down and gone. The galloping horse tumbled across the grass, legs flailing madly as it slid for several yards. Elizabeth was thrown free, landing rather ungainly some yards away.

Peregrine, who saw her fall from some way back, felt himself panic. It looked very painful. Drawing near, he pulled back on the reins of his own horse, slowing its pace to a walk. He approached gently, fearing what he would find.

Much to his surprise, Elizabeth was on her feet. He watched her storm angrily over the where her horse was lying prone on its side, its legs jerking powerlessly as it tried to get to its feet, but it could not move. Elizabeth stopped behind the fallen horse.

"Get up! Get up!" she shouted at the top of her voice. She raised her riding crop, bringing it down repeatedly and painfully on the horses hide. "Get up! Damn you, get up, you useless nag!" she screamed, beating the poor animal over and over again.

Peregrine dismounted and ran over. Her hand raised the crop again to deal out another beating, but Peregrine grabbed her hand and took the crop from her.

"The horse is injured. Leave it alone," he said.

She turned round, her face snarling with anger, "Don't ever tell me what to do!" She shouted and stormed off.

Edward rode up on his own horse. He patted the panting steed gently. "She lost ," he said with a wide grin. "She couldn't keep up with me."

Peregrine was more concerned with the injured horse. He managed to calm it down by patting and talking to it quietly.

"Her horse may be lame," he said sadly.

"That's a shame " said Edward. "But she's got others." Elizabeth was coming walking back over. Edward turned to her and shouted, "You lost!"

"It wasn't my fault!" she shouted. "It was that things fault. That stupid horse fell over otherwise I would have beaten you."

"No, I was winning," he shouted back. With that she turned round and started walking back the way they had come.

"What shall we do with the horse?" asked Peregrine. "We need to get someone out here."

"We'll just tell someone back at the stables and they'll come and get it. Shall we continue our ride?"

"What about the horse?"

"Like I say, we'll tell them when we get back."

Peregrine sighed, "I'll go back and tell them now. You continue, if you wish. I can't just leave the horse here."

"Please yourself," said Edward, with that he pulled the reins, dug in his heels and turned his horse round and set off at a gallop.

Peregrine rounded up his own horse, pulled himself into the saddle and headed off after Elizabeth. He caught up with her after a few seconds.

"Do you want a ride?" he asked, pulling up next to her.

She continued to stare straight ahead. "No thanks. I'll walk."

"I'm going back to the stables to get some help for your horse. You might as well come with me. I'll pull you up." He held out his hand for her.

"Just leave me alone," she said without looking up.

"Fine," he said, resignedly, and rode off back to the stable.

He was beginning to wonder if this family were actually worse than his own.

16th February 1712

The weekend had been dreary. It rained continuously which meant, apart from the occasional venturing out into the garden from some air, the weekend was spent indoors. Peregrine saw very little of Robert Harley who seemed to spend most of his life at home locked in the room where Peregrine had first met him. Harley wasn't at home that much, most of the time was spent at Westminster.

Lady Sarah seemed content to spend her days embroidering. Peregrine was impressed with some of her creations, but it seemed a totally absorbing and time consuming pastime.

The younger Harley's kept themselves occupied with games. During the lighter hours it would involve variations on Hide and Seek around the extensive rooms of the house or, in brief rain free moments, in the garden. Sometimes they enjoyed racing competitions, or they would combine this with Hide and Seek to create a chase game. When night fell, they would indulge in charades, card games or sometimes chess or other board games.

They included Peregrine when they could, but he felt that it was out of courtesy only. To them, he was a casual participant, not an adversary. Whatever game or pastime they were involved in Peregrine felt that, in some subtle way, their attention was always on each other, not him. Even when, very rarely, he found himself winning, it was as if they didn't care - as long as they were not beaten by their sibling.

The overall effect was to create a very edgy atmosphere. Peregrine concluded that he would never be able to relax with them, or more importantly with Elizabeth herself. The air around them always seemed charged and likely to erupt at any moment. Their activity was relentless and Peregrine found it wearing.

More importantly, he realised that his relationship with Elizabeth was no more developed than when she had first spoken to him at breakfast on the first day. She acknowledged his presence, but it was in the same way that she might acknowledge the presence of a piece of furniture. She spoke to him and interacted with him in a distant, distracted sort of way. But her focus was always elsewhere. He could not capture her attention for anything but a brief minute or more and, when he did, he got the impression that she longed for someone to rescue her.

For his own part, he struggled to find any commonality with her. She had no interest in history, even of the very house she lived in. The ruins of Brampton Bryan Castle which formed a huge ruin in the grounds directly behind the hall were a mystery to her. Even though the history of her own direct ancestors was intimately woven into the stones of that formidable fortress, she knew nothing of them. When, attempting to engage her attention, Peregrine had told her that she could trace her ancestry back to Henry II, William I and Charlemagne it drew no reaction at all. She did not know who they were and Peregrine could not find the enthusiasm to enlighten her. He spent some time admiring the various classical artworks and paintings that her father had collected and had exhibited around the house. When he asked her about some of the pieces, she dismissed them as just ornaments.

Perhaps unfairly, he could not help comparing her to his own Elizabeth back in Kiveton. His Elizabeth had no education at all apart from what she had read for herself in an uneven collection of second hand books but she had more appreciation of art, beauty, the world around her and history of it than Elizabeth Harley had ever shown. Where his Elizabeth *wanted*, even thirsted, to know, Elizabeth Harley was content, even writhed, in ignorance. The differences between the two women just made him yearn even more for home.

At the start of the week, Robert Harley had departed for London. The rain cleared, the sun came out into a blue sky. There was the slight hint in the air that Spring would be here soon. Winter would soon be over.

Relieved at the brightening weather and that they could go out once again, Elizabeth had had an exciting idea. "Let's go hunting tomorrow," she had said, clapping with excitement.

Edward had nodded thoughtfully. "Sound idea. Have you ever hunted, Lord Danby?"

He shook his head, "I can't say I have."

"Have you even ever shot a gun?" asked Edward with a touch of disdain.

"No, not at all. My father's more the military man."

"Then now is a fine time to learn," said Edward. "What shall we hunt? Geese? Deer? Otters?"

"Deer," said Elizabeth. "Let's ride into the Shropshire Hills and bag one or two. While the weather's not too bad."

"Alright," agreed her brother. "Let's bag some stags!"

And so, that morning, they had set off north westwards, crossing into Shropshire. They were not alone, they took several staff including an expert deer stalker. The weather was cold, but agreeable. The terrain became immediately hillier and they left the main roads and started up into the hills. They reached a small, abandoned, stone barn and there, they left their horses. From now on they would hunt on foot.

They walked around in the hills for hours, up to their knees in ferns and bracken, sometimes ankle deep in mud along well worn tracks. Eventually, the deer stalker had come to them from where he had been scouting up ahead and waved his hand to indicate they should make no noise.

"There's a herd up ahead, over the ridge," he said in a low whisper. "They're relaxed, not spooked. If we crawl up and keep low we'll be able to get a shot off from the ridge. There's one stag and a dozen doe."

"I'll take the stag," said Elizabeth eagerly.

"No," said Edward quietly. "Let Peregrine have the stag. It's his first. We'll take a doe each."

Elizabeth looked disappointed. "Alright," she agreed reluctantly.

The deer stalker continued,"We'll only get one shot then they will run. So we all have the fire together. So, choose your target, take aim, get your finger on the trigger. I'll lower my hand three times like this, once, twice, on the third time you all fire. Understand?"

They nodded. With their guns in their hands they crouched

down and crept up to the ridge. By the time they got there they were all on their stomachs. Below them a small herd of Red Deer were stood at ease some twenty yards distant. Most of the doe had their heads down, munching idly on the grass. One was laid down, apparently relaxing with just her head up looking around. The stag was standing upright, not eating, surveying the landscape with an eye for threats and competitors. A magnificent specimen, tall and proud, his shaggy reddish brown coat marked with the ravages of the challenges he had faced to acquire his position. Atop his head, his antlers rose two feet high like the branches of a tree. Two points close to the head, then two more half way up and finally topped on each side by a splay of four sharp points. Each point tipped in white bone.

Peregrine raised the gun to his eye, staring along the barrel at the unsuspecting stag. Aiming just behind the shoulder, straight into the chest. He felt the trigger, cold, smooth metal against his finger. He felt the resistance as he tightened his finger. Felt the trigger give slightly.

The deer stalker raised his hand then brought it down. Once. Twice. And then they fired. Startled, the herd panicked and started running in a mad, sweeping stampede up the opposite hill. The stag ran along with them.

"You missed!" exclaimed Edward.

"No I didn't!" shouted back Elizabeth indignantly, "You missed, I got mine." She stood up and ran down into the small valley to where a doe lay on the ground bleeding into the damp earth..

"Damn," said Edward with disappointment. "Looks like I did miss after all. And you missed the stag," he said to Peregrine. Then he cast a glance at Peregrine's gun. "You didn't miss. You didn't even fire! Your gun's still loaded."

"I couldn't in the end. He looked so proud. It seemed a shame."

"Proud? Yes, they're fine looking beasts," admitted Edward. "And they look just as proud when their head's on your wall back home. Then you can admire them all day."

Peregrine sighed. He and Edward always seemed to misunderstand one another. They understood each other's words, but somehow, between being spoken and heard, the meaning was translated into something else. Their cultural frames of reference were so different they could never be friends. Peregrine didn't dislike Edward, but he knew he could never really like him either.

He looked down into the valley where Elizabeth was stood proudly, gun in hand, and one foot on the dead doe. A huge grin across her face as she bragged of her achievement.

"It's venison for dinner, boys!" she shouted with a laugh. "Thanks to me."

Peregrine thought to himself how much he would rather be having some vegetable stew in the Mirfin's cottage with his Elizabeth sat next to him.

18ᵗʰ February 1712

On Wednesday Edward announced that he had been called away by his father to London and that he would be gone for the rest of the month. True to his word he was not at breakfast the next day. But neither was his sister, which left Lady Sarah and Peregrine dining together.

"How are you finding your stay here, Lord Danby?" asked Lady Sarah as they sat eating some, fruit with bread and cold meats.

"As is the case with many journey's, it has been a rewarding experience but I will be glad to get home."

"I often think the same," she agreed. "My husband seems quite at home amongst London's teeming masses, but whenever I am there I long for the green hills of Herefordshire. And where is your home, Lord Danby?"

It was a question he would have had difficulty answering a few weeks ago, but now he had no hesitation. "I live in Kiveton Hall, between Rotherham and Worksop. South Yorkshire, almost Nottinghamshire."

"I am not familiar with that part of the country," she admitted. "As is true of much of the country, I fear. In fact the country itself has changed. For most of my life I was content that I lived in England, but now I am told we live in the Kingdom of Great Britain. I don't know what that makes me, Great British, I suppose. But I am old fashioned and, I fear, I'll always see myself as English."

"You are not alone," said Peregrine. "I imagine it will be a very long time before the English and Scottish abandon their national identities. If ever."

"Well, the Welsh still haven't and they've been part of the English kingdom for four hundred years. I fear, there's a long way to go!"

"Indeed," he laughed.

"And how are you finding my step-daughter?" she asked carefully. "To your taste?"

Peregrine chose his words just as carefully. "She may be an acquired taste," he said.

"But hopefully one worth acquiring. She would be a valuable addition to your family, would she not? Her father is the Queen's Lord Treasurer."

"No doubt," answered Peregrine.

"But, of course, it is not her father's generation that concerns us here, is it? Or indeed, yours and hers. We are concerned with the next generation. Your son. He would be an Osborne and a Harley – that would be a powerful combination, don't you think?"

"All I would hope for any son of mine would be that he be happy in whatever he chose to do."

"Of course, as we all do. But it would be an error to miss the opportunity. Elizabeth's son will be a Harley, of course, but with your assistance he may also be a Duke of Leeds. That's also a taste worth acquiring, is it not?"

"I am not sure that Elizabeth finds me to *her* taste, I am afraid."

Lady Sarah laughed mildly. "Elizabeth and Edward were born at the same time. Not twins as such, they are not identical, but they were born and grew up together. Their mother died from smallpox when they were very young which left them competing for their father's attention. Even *craving* their father's attention. They will do anything for their father. So, you see, her opinion in this matter is of interest but, ultimately, irrelevant. She would do anything to give her father a Duke as a grandson."

"Even marry me? " asked Peregrine.

"Oh yes," said Lady Sarah with a sly smile. "Even marry you."

Chapter Eight

<u>22nd February 1712</u>

The best day of Peregrine's visit to Brampton Bryan Hall arrived. The last one. He had been looking forward to this day since the moment his coach pulled out of the stable yard at Kiveton. It seemed a wonderful day, the sun was shining, there wasn't a cloud in the azure sky. The signs of new growth were appearing in the plants around the garden as life began again. Birds flitted around between the trees that surrounded the house.

Peregrine couldn't tell whether it was his mood colouring the world or whether it really was a brighter, sunnier place.

He went down the breakfast in the Morning Room with a wide smile on his face and a light step. Lady Sarah and Elizabeth were already there. Robert Harley and Edward had not yet returned from London and were not expected for a few days.

"Good Morning," chirped Peregrine as he sat down.

"Good Morning, Lord Danby," said Lady Sarah. "Your last morning with us, I believe."

"Yes, indeed," he replied happily. "I start the long journey back northwards today."

"Well, we hope to welcome you again very soon," she said pointedly.

Peregrine missed the point. "You are very gracious," he replied.

"I would hope so. We have a reputation for holding fine events here."

"I'm sure you excel yourselves."

"Elizabeth's older sister, Abigail, was married here."

Peregrine finally got the point. "I see."

She continued, "And we always expected that Elizabeth would be married here too."

The bread Peregrine was chewing suddenly seemed much more difficult to consume.

Elizabeth was sitting directly across the table from him nibbling some fruit idly. Her eyes never ventured from his face as she studied him.

"I'm sure she will be," said Peregrine finally.

"Are you?" said Lady Sarah. "And why are you so sure?"

"It is difficult to imagine a more suitable venue for such a family event," he ventured.

"We would be very honoured to host such a momentous occasion."

"As proud parents I could expect nothing else."

Lady Sarah looked at Peregrine, then to Elizabeth and back to Peregrine. Finally, she pushed her plate away. "Well, I will get on and leave you two to talk. It has been a pleasure to have you here, Lord Danby. Please do come again."

"It has been a pleasure, my Lady," he replied formally.

With a final glance at them both she left.

"Was she too obvious?" asked Elizabeth. Her eyes were still locked on him uncomfortably. "Or wasn't she obvious enough?"

"I'm sorry," he said. "Regarding what exactly?"

"Marriage. Specifically mine. To you."

"To me?"

"That is what you're here for isn't it? That is what this is all about, isn't it?"

"I'm not sure," said Peregrine. "I was instructed to come here, deliver a letter to your father and then stay here for a while. I have done that."

"And meet me. Get to know me. So we could know each other and not be complete strangers on our wedding day," she replied.

"Our wedd...I think you are getting ahead of yourself."

"Oh no, Lord Danby. I think you are the one who is not keeping up. My father, your grandfather and your mother are all in favour of a marriage between us."

"And us? Do we get a say in this?" asked Peregrine.

Elizabeth laughed, "I suppose we do, otherwise they wouldn't be allowing us to meet at all, they would just arrange the wedding and tell us afterwards."

"So we can say no?"

"We could," she admitted. "Is that what you intend to do?"

He hesitated. Whatever Elizabeth might think, his mother had made it clear that saying no was not an option. "It's just...I hardly know you."

"You've been here over a week."

"Exactly! A week. Hardly any time at all."

She paused and took a drink of her coffee. "Enough time, I think, to form a view of each other. Can I be blunt?"

"Please do, you usually are," he said before taking a sip of his tea.

She smiled in amusement. "There you are, you see. You have formed an opinion of me. Do you find me attractive, Lord Danby?"

He looked at her closely for a second. She had a rounded face with high forehead, a pert, little mouth and large, expressive, blue eyes. Her hair was a very dark brown, like stained oak. It was thick, wavy and fell down her back and over her shoulders. Her long, thin fingers were perfectly suited for musical instruments as she had demonstrated several times during his stay. Peregrine had noticed at these times that she had very little interest or appreciation of music, only in demonstrating her ability to perform it.

"You are very beautiful," he admitted slowly.

Her forehead creased with annoyance,"There you are, you

see. I am afraid I find your evasive nature irritating. You say a little, but the answer lies obscured in what you *don't* say. I prefer plain speaking, as you have noticed. Can I ask again – do you find me attractive?"

"No. I do not," he said, looking straight at her. "Is that plain enough?"

She smiled like someone enjoying a game and who had just enticed a point from her opponent. "Refreshingly plain. So, allow me to speak plainly too. I find you an enigma, Lord Danby. Your thoughts never seem to be engaged with the present, they are always somewhere else. You don't ride very well, you don't enjoy games, you don't hunt, you don't display any ability or skill in any endeavour, as far as I am aware. You are a blank to me. I have to admit that I do not discern a trace of character at all." She gave him a very pale, emotionless smile, "So, no, I do not find you attractive either."

Peregrine shrugged, "Then we are in agreement. What else is there to discuss?"

"I am afraid you miss the point. Perhaps deliberately so. The aim of this exercise is to produce a legitimate heir to the Dukedom of Leeds. That has already been decided and agreed by our families. But they can only do so much. They can provide the venue, the arrangements, the funds, the title and the legal framework to elicit this. But the actual act of creation comes down to me and you. We must agree, between ourselves, how we are to achieve that."

Peregrine found her cold assessment of the situation chilling. But, he had to admit, probably accurate.

She took another sip of coffee, all the time assessing him to see if she was making her points successfully. "You understand what I am offering you?"

"Yes," he said. "Your hand in marriage."

"No!" she pounced. "You can take that for granted. I am offering you my body. Are you going to take it? Are you enough of a man to take it?" He looked up angrily. "Ah, good. It is possible for you to react like a man then?"

"When I am provoked," he replied.

She sighed and sipped more coffee. "Of course, this would be easier if we held each other in some rampant esteem, burned with some surging passion. But, given that this is not the case, the question arises...can you still perform successfully?"

"I don't know," he admitted. At that moment he doubted it.

"It shouldn't be a problem. You're what? Twenty? At your age you should be spraying your breeches if I just put my tit in your hand..."

"Why are you doing this so...eagerly?" interrupted Peregrine. "You are not just compliant, you seem enthusiastic?"

For once, her gaze slipped. She put down her coffee. When she spoke, her tone had a bitter edge. "My father has recently been created Earl of Oxford. When he dies, that title will pass to my brother Edward. He will become the 2nd Earl of Oxford. At a stroke he will be elevated to the peerage, but he will have done have nothing to earn it. As for me? Nothing. No elevation for me. No title for me. History will record him, but I will be just...*his* sister. I will be defined by him!" Her large eyes turned again to look, unwaveringly, at Peregrine. "But I do, yet, have a card to play. I am still in the game. When I marry you I will become Countess of Danby, will I not? At a stroke, I will equal his rank in the peerage. Your grandfather is an old man and, when he dies, I will become Marchioness of Carmarthan, I will rank higher than my brother. Ultimately, I will be Duchess of Leeds. He will not be able to beat that! His offspring may become Earls of Oxford, but mine will be Dukes of Leeds. So, you see, this marriage is very important to me."

"I see," said Peregrine quietly. He was thinking of complaining that he did not love her - but she did not care. She didn't love him either. What's love got to do with it? As his mother had essentially told him, love who you want...but marry Elizabeth Harley.

But there was one thing none of them had considered. In their headlong rush to secure their own or their family's advantages or privileges there was one person they had not considered. Him. Peregrine Hyde Osborne, Earl of Danby. No one had asked themselves what was in it for him. All he wanted was to spend his life with the one person in this world he actually loved. But that appeared to be asking too much.

He said, "And what do you expect our married life to be like?"

Elizabeth smiled, "Very physical initially, given what we must achieve. I will live with you to start, in Leeds, or wherever it is you live. But apart from that, I expect we will live completely separate lives. I don't really want to spend any time with you and you, no doubt, feel the same. Once I am with child I will move here, or somewhere suitable to give birth. We will appear in public together, I expect, but apart from that I don't think we should constrain each other too much."

Resignedly he said, "Then what is it you want of me, now?"

"I want you to ask me to marry you. That is customary, is it not?"

He gulped then looked intently at her as she stared equally intently back. He said slowly, "Elizabeth Harley, will you marry me?"

She gave him a wide grin, "Of course I will. I would be delighted. Now let's give Mama the good news."

26th February 1712

It took four days to get home and Peregrine seemed to spend every minute of it wondering what he had let himself in for. Marriage – he was to be married. And marriage to *her*! How had that happened? It had happened because people more important than himself had decided it would happen. That it must happen. Bizarrely, even Elizabeth Harley was keen on the idea and she liked him less than he liked her. It wasn't so much a marriage made in Heaven as a marriage made somewhere between Kiveton, Wimbedon and Brampton Bryan! No matter which way he twisted it round in his head he could make no sense of it. How could it work? How could he and Elizabeth

Harley possibly father a child? They could barely endure each other's company.

And then he thought, how was he going to explain this to his Elizabeth? That he was to marry a woman he couldn't stand and who couldn't stand him. That he was giving up Elizabeth for that seemed insane. How could he? What would remain of his tattered soul if he did? In a brutal, intolerant, selfish world she was the only thing that made any sense.

But his mother's threat was still there. Unless he complied, the Mirfin's would be made to pay. He could not allow that. At all costs, no matter what it took, he must protect Elizabeth from his family. Even it meant him marrying the Devil himself.

After four days of winding its way through the Midlands Peregrine's coach finally drove through the gates of the stable yard at Kiveton and drew to halt. He clambered out of his coach, aching from the long journey, and stood on the yard just wanting to make his way to his room and go to bed. But at that point Tom Crowther came out of the stable manager's office and came running over to him.

"My lord, my lord! I've been asked by Lady Bridget to tell you as soon as you arrive that she is waiting for you in the Drawing Room."

"Oh, alright. Thanks, Tom," said Peregrine. "Oh, Tom, I've been meaning to ask you something."

"Yes, my Lord?" Crowther asked.

Peregrine drew him aside, away from any listeners. "It's a little delicate. You're in charge of several aspects of the running of the estate are you not?"

"Indeed. The stables, of course, but also all the commercial arrangements."

"Including tenancies?"

"Yes, my Lord. I manage the tenancies."

"I thought so," said Peregrine surreptitiously. "In that case, I've a favour to ask. It isn't a large one, but it is an arrangement between the two of us. No one else needs to know, you understand? I rely on your discretion and you, of course, may rely on mine."

"Of course, my Lord," replied Crowther. "An arrangement between gentlemen, so to speak."

"Exactly," said Peregrine and went on to explain his idea.

Peregrine later made his way up to the Drawing Room. He knocked once on the doors and the entered. His mother was sat by the fire, her face glowing with its sanguinary radiance. He came and stood by her and handed her a letter from Lady Sarah.

"Please, take a seat, Pip," she said absently while she read the letter. Her face gave nothing away. She put it down and said, "It says here you have proposed to the Countess' step-daughter. "

"That is so, Mother," he replied. "As instructed."

She smiled finally, "Well, that's good. You have done well, Pip. As, no doubt, you have had explained to you several times by many people, a mix of our two families would be very profitable. A Harley-Osborne heir would be very desirable."

"That has been stressed to me on occasion."

"Everyone seems happy about it," admitted his mother. "Apart from you, Pip. I detect a certain reticence."

"Me? Well, who cares what I want anyway? When there's the possibility of a Harley-Osborne heir it's alright to ride rough shod over my reservations."

"You have reservations?"

"Well, apart from the bride and groom hating each other, it's a fine idea for a marriage!"

"Yes, I heard that the daughter could be a little testy. But then you are not a woman's dream husband either, are you, Pip? There must be compromises on both sides."

Peregrine tutted, "Has anyone thought about how we are supposed to conceive a child under these circumstances?"

"That is for you and your wife to make the appropriate arrangements. As always."

"It's a little more difficult when the participants don't even like each other."

"Come, come. Don't make more of it than it is. Men bed women they don't like all the time. For example, the woman you paid to sleep with in Venice."

Peregrine was stunned, "I didn't know you knew..."

His mother smiled her hollow smile. "As I have explained to you previously. It is my business to know. I received regular reports on your activities while you were on your tour."

Not from William, thought Peregrine, he wouldn't. But they were accompanied by a tutor who paid for everything...

"Quite," said his mother when she saw comprehension dawn on his face. "All the money is expensed from the estate. It all has to be explained. Anyway, I'm sure you'll be able to come to some agreement with your wife regarding sleeping arrangements."

"When is this marriage meant to happen?" he asked.

"I'll start looking into it immediately. I've got a lot of people to see first, including the Harleys. But I would like to think the beginning of September would be good – six months should be long enough."

Six months, he thought to himself. Six more months with Elizabeth before he had to give up everything.

"Well, you've got what you wanted," he said to his mother.

"Not until we have a male heir," she said.

"That's a problem I'll worry about in six months. Can I be left alone, now?"

"To spend time with your blacksmith family?" she asked mockingly.

He bit his lip as he felt his anger rising. "I think I've earned that much."

"Really? You haven't done anything yet."

"I've agreed to everything you asked for. I deserve you to give me something I've asked for."

"You deserve..." she began, then stopped herself and sighed. "I went very wrong with you, didn't I, Pip? I don't blame myself entirely, I spent very little time with you growing up. Your grandfather was very determined to get you and William away from your father's influence as soon as possible. Which, inevitably, meant away from my influence too. And, I suppose, we also tended to concentrate on William. You were left to fill your own head with whatever you chose instead of what we chose for you. Which meant silly romantic notions of myths, history, sculpture, art and *love*." She spat the last word scathingly. "Poor planning, you see, and this is where it has got us."

"I'm sorry to be such a disappointment," he scoffed. "I know one thing. If I do manage to have a son from this abomination of a marriage I'll be doing my level best to keep him as far away as possible from you, grandfather, father and everyone else in this family! That's the only way he's going to have any chance of happiness."

"Oh, no, no, I'm sorry to disappoint you, Pip. But you won't be playing any part in bringing up any son from this marriage. He will be far too valuable. He is, after all, what this is all for. He will be raised to do right all the things you have done so wrong. He will be a leader, a parliamentarian, a peer steeped in honours. He will plan, connive and, yes, even marry in order to further himself and his family. He will wield his power and his wealth in the service of his country. For it is *his* country, it belongs to him and those like him, not your blacksmiths. In short, he will be everything you are not. He will excel in everything in which you are such a dismal failure."

"And fail in everything that really matters," said Peregrine sadly.

"You think you know what matters? You think you know something of the world? You! You are cosseted and pampered in a life of luxury and indulgence someone else has provided for you? Your lifestyle has been purchased by the labours of the very people you condemn. You think you can give all that up, do you? Go and live some simple, idyllic life with your blacksmith's daughter? Perhaps you see yourself and your lover as some new Adam and Eve regressing to a modern day Eden?

"Wake up, lad! How would you live? How would you provide for your new family's meagre needs? Somehow I don't see you breaking your back in the fields or dirtying your hands in the soil to grow next years bounty. Or perhaps you see yourself as a blacksmith? Look at your hands, Pip! The most labour they have ever seen is opening a book or lifting a tea cup to your lips! Somehow I can't see them battered and bruised by the brutal hammering of iron and steel."

"I have knowledge. I could teach."

"Teach who? Teach the farm boys about Homer? Teach the milking maids about Rome? They aren't interested in anything but full bellies, beer and a roll in the hay in Summertime."

Her tone softened, "They aren't people like us, Pip. Their horizons are narrow and ours are broad. That's why we send you on a Grand Tour for years, to broaden them. I'd be surprised if any of your friends in the village have been as far as Sheffield! They know nothing of the places you have seen and why would they need to. Their lives are here, working their forges and tending their fields. But the life of a Duke is about fashioning the destiny of Kings. You misunderstand your own place in the world.

"We own this estate and every living thing in it. Every tree, blade of grass, every cow, horse, sheep...and even the men and women in our villages. Not directly like slaves, but indirectly as indentured labour. Their lives are in our hands because they own nothing but their own skins and a handful of chattels. Where as we own everything. We make use of all the living things on our estate. We work them, breed them, hunt them, eat them, we even, occasionally, fuck them. What we do not do...is marry them. You can no more marry this blacksmith's daughter than you can marry your horse or a sheep. It is a ridiculous notion. Even if..." she paused and sighed. "To do so, would make you happy."

Peregrine said, "You are wrong. They are people just like us. If their tastes and desires appear base and limited it is because people like you will not allow them to rise."

She lowered her head and looked distantly into the fire. "Alright, Pip, have it your way...for now. Enjoy yourself. While it lasts."

"Thanks, Mother, you're so gracious." He said sarcastically then turned and headed for the door. "Good Night." He opened the door and left.

27th February 1712

He woke early and had breakfast brought to his room. He was so looking forward to seeing Elizabeth again, but he also had worries. He wasn't sure how he was meant to tell her what had happened in Herefordshire. How could he say he wanted to spend the rest of his life with her, but unfortunately he had just agreed to marry someone else? Someone he didn't even get on with. His instinct was to dodge the issue, to not tell her. After all nothing would happen for months, there would be plenty of time later. But when that moment came, when he finally had no choice but to disclose everything she would inevitably ask why he had not told her earlier. Which brought him right back round to...what was he going to tell her now? He had to tell her as soon as possible. But how would she react? She was hardly likely to be understanding. She would feel betrayed. She would stop seeing him.

That would be more than he could bear. She was the only thing in his life he did not detest. Whatever happened. Whoever he married. What ever vile scheme his mother concocted. He must not lose Elizabeth. Or his life would be reduced to an empty, meaningless charade of intolerable contradictions. His very soul would become a vacuous shell, devoid of spirit. An empty existence that would have meaning only to others, but would have none for him. Asked to tolerate the intolerable he would have to seek escape in the only way left to him. In darkness...and dust.

After long hours of procrastination he resolved that the only way out of his dilemma was action. Trying to predict every possible eventuality was a route to madness. He had to tell Elizabeth and then deal with the result. Only then there would be certainty. Only then would he know whether she would stand by him or throw him away.

So he made his way down to Wales. He didn't ride, he walked down through the fields. It gave him time to think, to build his resolve and try, as best he could, to prepare himself for the ordeal he knew he surely faced. He felt he had started out on a sure path that could only end in his own inevitable self-destruction. She would not take it well. How could she? But what choice did he have?

He arrived at the blacksmith's cottage around midday. The weak late winter sun was doing it's best to heat the day, but Peregrine found no warmth in it. He shuddered, whether through cold or the surge of nervousness running through his veins he did not know.

He knocked on the door hesitantly.

It opened immediately, Elizabeth stood there. Peregrine felt his worries burning away. He could not help himself, he lunged forward, gathering her in his arms, desperately, longingly. He buried his face in her hair, all his senses filled to overflowing. He felt her, soft against him with her arms enclosing him, returning his embrace. He smelled her gentle, rustic sweetness. Her image was etched onto his eyes. He felt himself drown in her presence and he never wanted to be anywhere else.

They parted slowly, not quite letting each other go. "Welcome back," she said simply.

Henry's voice came from the kitchen beyond. "I've never seen anyone look so glad to be back."

"Aye, looks like he missed her, alright," said Susanna.

Elizabeth led him into the kitchen where the other two were sitting at the table. They joined them, sitting down next to each other. Peregrine kept hold of Elizabeth's hand, he wasn't quite ready to let it go yet. Peregrine looked from face to face, all smiling, all honestly glad to see him. He looked round the homely basic kitchen with its bare wooden ceiling beams and fire roaring in the hearth. He felt like he wanted to spend the rest of his life in this room. Safe from the aggressive world outside.

"When did you get back?" asked Elizabeth.

"Last night, late. Too late to come here."

Susanna chirped in, "And how was, where was it? Hereford?"

Peregrine smiled,"Herefordshire. I think we were maybe thirty miles from Hereford itself. It was where the borders of Herefordshire, Shropshire and Wales meet."

"Wales? There's another place called Wales?" said Susanna excitedly.

Henry laughed. "Don't show yourself up! Even I know there's a country called Wales. England, Scotland and Wales – that's the three countries on this island. That's right, isn't it, Pen?"

"Yes, you're right," said Peregrine.

"And is our Wales named after that one or that one named after ours?" asked Susanna.

"Neither really," said Peregrine. "The people who live there call it Cymru. Wales is the English name for it. I guess this village was once full of the same people, so the English called it Wales too."

"You mean this village is older than England?" asked Susanna with incredulity.

"Very likely," said Peregrine. "And I wouldn't be at all surprised to find that, even back then, there were Mirfins living in it."

"Really?" exclaimed Henry.

"You know everything, Pen," said Susanna with admiration. "Such interesting things too."

"My mother would disagree," he replied bitterly. *So much for not being able to teach them. So much for them not wanting to learn*, he thought to himself.

Elizabeth's hand tightened on his, "Some people can't see a good thing even when they are staring straight at it."

Peregrine grabbed hold of Susanna's hand so he was holding the hands of both sisters. He felt an odd tightening in his throat as his eyes turned suddenly watery. "I am so glad I met you all. I honestly don't know where I'd be without you."

"Will you stop that or you'll set them both off blubbering!" said Henry. "Somebody put some tea on."

They all started laughing. Susanna got up to make some tea.

They spent the day talking about Peregrine's trip to Herefordshire. He told them about how he had stayed in a large house with castle ruins behind it. He told them how they had gone horse riding and hunting. How they had played Hide and Seek all around the many rooms and in the garden. He left out a lot of detail, especially about the Harley's themselves. It wasn't the right place to go into that.

As the day wore on Peregrine made up his mind to go back to the Hall. "Are you going with him?" Susanna asked Elizabeth.

Elizabeth cast a look at Peregrine and said, "Yes, I think I will."

"And not coming back until tomorrow morning, I guess?" said Susanna.

"Probably. We shall see," she replied with a grin. She noticed that Peregrine looked concerned, but she didn't know why.

Eventually, Elizabeth and Peregrine left the cottage and started walking across the yard. Peregrine realised he had to say something now. He had to broach the subject that he had been sidestepping round all day. He stopped and looked at her.

"I need to speak to you," he said earnestly.

"Tell me when we get to your room," she replied.

"No," he said. "It can't wait."

She looked at him suspiciously then said, "Alright, come into the forge. There's no one in there."

They went through the door into the warm forge. Henry and his father had been working in it that morning and it was still pleasantly warm and comfortable. She turned to face him, bracing herself. She knew he had been holding something back and now, she suspected, was where she would find out what.

"You have something to tell me?" she asked gently. "Something that happened in Herefordshire?"

"Yes. I need to tell you because I don't want to deceive you. I want to be honest so that you'll trust me. The trip to Herefordshire wasn't just to introduce me to the Harley's. Well, it was, but there was more to it. My mother has raised certain expectations with them." He paused not sure how to continue. "There was a woman there..."

"The daughter?" said Elizabeth.

"Yes. A daughter."

"The one you went riding with? And hunting with? And played Hide and Seek with?"

"Yes. Well, not alone, but yes, she was there."

"And you spent just over a week with her?"

"Yes. As I say, she was there all the time...."

"And now you are in love with her?" asked Elizabeth shakily.

"No. No!" he shouted. "Absolutely not! I can't stand her. She's detestable. I was glad to get away from her."

Elizabeth looked relieved, "But you slept with her?"

"No, I did not! I didn't want anything to do with her. And I still don't."

Elizabeth looked confused, "So what is it then?"

Peregrine couldn't face her. His eyes fell to the floor. "I haven't slept with her...yet."

"What do you mean – yet? That you're going to?"

"My mother and the Harley's have arranged for me to marry her."

"What?" she said, visibly shaken. She sat down on one of the stools and tried to gather her thoughts. "But you said you don't like her?"

"I don't."

"Then how can you marry her?" she demanded in an exasperated tone.

"Because they don't ask me what I think and they don't care. They want an heir and, to get one, there must be a marriage."

Elizabeth struggled to get her thoughts in order. She had always known that she wouldn't be able to marry him, she had even considered that he might marry someone else. And not so soon.

"But how can they compel you to marry when you don't want to?" she asked. "Because, if you don't they'll throw you out? Because you live in their houses and on their allowance?"

"No," he said softly. "I am the only chance they have of producing an heir now William is dead. I only have sisters. They must keep me in the family. But they can get to me through you..."

"Me? How?"

"Your family are tenants of the Kiveton estate. You can be evicted. Unless I fulfil my responsibilities."

"Evicted? Pa's been living here and running that forge for twenty-five years."

"But not for much longer if I don't do as I'm told."

"Your mother said this?" she asked, dumbfounded.

"Yes. It's a sad thing to say about your own mother, but I am afraid she is vicious and uncompromising when it comes to the family."

She thought deeply, "It would be difficult if we were evicted. We could probably live with Uncle Jack for a while. Pa could even help him out. But he only has a small cottage. Pa would need to find work somewhere else. And there's Henry too, he would need to find work. I can't imagine what would happen to Susanna and me..."

He turned and held her shoulders, looking straight at her. "Don't worry. I won't allow that to happen. You won't be getting evicted. I won't allow it. I'll marry this damned Harley woman if that's what they want, I'll even give them this heir they want. But only provided they leave you and your family alone. If anything happens to your father or Henry or Susanna or, especially, you then I won't be marrying anyone and they can get someone else to give them their blasted heir!"

She sighed and looked crest fallen. "But where does that leave us, Pen? You're going to marry another woman, even going to have a child with her. Where does that leave me? Cast aside to placate your mother?"

"No," he shook his head. "No, no, I cannot lose you. Better to lose everything than lose you."

"How, Pen? That's the choice you've been given. Keep seeing me and we get evicted. Stop seeing me and marry this woman and we get to stay where we are."

He took a deep breath. "What if I got married and kept seeing you as well?"

"That would make me an adulteress."

"It would make you my consort. My concubine."

"Use whatever name you like, Pen, it amounts to the same thing. What would your new wife think about it?"

Peregrine shrugged, "I don't care what she thinks. Anyway, I get the impression that, as long she gets an heir from me, she doesn't care what I do."

"And what about what I think? I love you, Pen, and I want to be your wife, but I realise that probably isn't possible. But to expect me to put up with you sleeping with another woman so you can give her a child....I don't know. That's asking a lot. How's it meant to work? Three days a week in my bed, three days in hers and Sundays off?"

He laughed, "You're being flippant."

She sighed heavily, but remained serious. "I don't know, Pen, I really don't know what to do for the best. It's a massive mess! I'm going to have to think about it. A lot." She took his hands off her shoulders.

"I guess you're not going to stay with me tonight?" he said.

"No," she replied quietly. "I need to stand back from it and decide what I'm going to do."

"Yes, of course. I understand. I've let you down. The one person I should never let down."

She gave him a peck on the cheek. "You haven't let anyone down, Pen. Your family are the sort of people that have deposed a King, it was always going to be difficult for us to take them on."

"I suppose you wish you had never met me?"

"No," she replied. "Whatever happens I'll always be glad I

met you." She stood up and went to the door. "I'll be in touch when I've decided what's the best thing to do. I'll come up to your room."

"I love you," he said feebly as she turned to go.

"I know you do," she said and left.

She went back to the cottage, threw the door open and went into the kitchen.

"Back so soon?" asked Susanna.

"Yes," Elizabeth replied. "Change of plan."

4th March 1712

"Sometimes I think I'm going to spend the rest of my life making horseshoes!" complained Henry Mirfin as he tucked into bread and cheese in the kitchen. It was lunchtime and they were taking a break from their forge work.

"And what would be wrong with that?" replied his father, "It's good, honest work. And regular too." Robert put a match to his pipe and puffed air into it to get it lit.

"It's not exactly exciting though, is it?"

"Food's exciting and it's making horseshoes that pays for it."

Henry sighed, he said dreamily, "I'd like to do a really fancy gate. With a really good design on it."

"Wouldn't we all," agreed Robert. "But until then – there's always horseshoes. People will always need horses and horses will always need shoes. It's a job for life."

"Urgh," moaned Henry. "Well, I've spent all morning making them. I hope we're not making more this afternoon?"

Robert puffed on his pipe, "Well, we might..."

"I'm going to be dreaming of horseshoes!"

Susanna said, "Well, you could always go and collect some coal, we're running out."

"Coal? The excitement! It just never starts..."

Elizabeth put a cup down in front of him, "Oh, shut up and drink your beer."

"Beer? Can't I have tea?"

"We've run out," said Susanna. "Well, Pen used to bring it and he's not been coming, has he?" She cast a quick glance in Elizabeth's direction then looked away hurriedly.

"Best not to get a taste for expensive things," said Robert. "They don't last and you miss them all the more when they're gone."

Elizabeth sighed, "Could you spare me your fireside philosophy, Pa!" She put a cup of beer down in front of him slightly too hard, spilling a few drops.

"I'm only saying..."

"Well, please don't," she said.

There was an uneasy silence for a minute and then Henry said, "Well, I'm through with horseshoes. I'm going to look at a new place this afternoon."

"What do you mean? A new place?" asked Susanna.

"I'm thinking of moving out. Getting my own place. I'm fed up of sleeping on a bed in front of the fire. I need my own bedroom, my own space..."

"But you're not married," said Susanna.

"You don't have to be...to get your own house. Marriage can come along later."

"To Mary Parkin?" she said with a grin.

"No! Not Mary Parkin. She's just an irritating child who won't leave me alone. "

Elizabeth interrupted, "You said you were going to look at a place? Where?"

"He's not serious," laughed Susanna.

"I am too!" he said angrily. "I'm going to go across and look at the old Billam's cottage. It's available."

"That's just across the road," scoffed Susanna. "When you said you were moving out I thought you'd at least make it to the end of the lane!"

Henry remained calm. "I haven't decided anything yet. I just thought I'd take a look. It can't hurt. I've got to move out sometime. And it'd be...convenient. I could come across here for meals and to bring my washing..."

"You will not!" said Susanna. "Ask Mary Parkin to do it."

"Will you shut up about Mary Parkin," said Henry irritably.

Elizabeth said, "But how are you going to go and see it? It's locked up."

He smiled, "I have the key."

"Who gave you that?" she asked.

"I made it. I used to work over there, remember? Mrs Billam thought it would be a good idea if I had my own key. We do have the tools to cut metal, we're blacksmiths. So I made a duplicate..."

"And you didn't give it her back?" she said, astounded. "Why?"

"You never know when it might come in useful."

"But that's dishonest," said Elizabeth.

"Not really, she asked me to do it."

"She didn't ask you to keep it!" said Elizabeth, exasperated. "Oh never mind. So what are you thinking of doing?"

"Taking a look inside. I am a prospective tenant."

"Not really, you're just nosy," she said.

"All tenants start off just being nosy."

Susanna said, "Well, I'll come with you."

"Why?"

"Because I'm nosy too." she answered. "And you might need a woman's opinion."

"Well, when I do I'll get a woman to give me one. Not a teenager."

"I bet you don't talk to Mary Parkin like that. And she's not even old enough to be a teenager."

"If I hear her mentioned once more...." began Henry.

"Can you two stop arguing for a minute!" said Elizabeth sternly.

Henry said slowly, "Well, she may actually have a point."

"About what?" said Elizabeth.

"About a woman's opinion being useful to me. You would notice things I'd never think of."

"Are you asking me to break into Mrs Billam's old house with you?"

"It's not breaking in. We have a key."

"Which we shouldn't have." She paused and thought for a second.

He finished his beer and got up, "Well, I'm going over there now."

"I suppose I should really go," said Elizabeth slowly. "To keep an eye on you."

"Aye, me too," said Susanna.

Henry sighed, "Please yourselves."

All three of them set off out of the kitchen, across the yard and down the small drive to the lane. On the other side of the lane stood the cottage – the old Billam place. It stood behind a small wall that ended in two gates between two stone gate posts. They opened the gates and entered the wide open plot. The cottage itself was over to the left, side on to the road. It was a typical, two-up two-down cottage, similar in many ways to blacksmiths cottage they occupied. But it looked larger. To the right of the cottage, and set back from the road, was the Billam's vegetable plot. Around half an acre where they had grown different produce. At this time of year it was a pitiful sight and, with no one looking after it, it would likely remain so.

They went slowly up to the centrally set, wooden door with its large lock. Henry with drew his home made key, inserting it into the lock. There was a comforting clunk as the lock opened. He turned the handle and pushed open the door. Like their own cottage it led into a kitchen, but as expected, it was larger. The room was bare. No furniture, no cooking pots, no plates or cups and no fire in the hearth. An empty room, waiting to be filled with the next tenants belongings. Elizabeth had done housework in this room many times, but she had never seen it looking so naked. It seemed a lot larger than she remembered.

All three of them entered and looked around.

"It's bigger than ours," said Susanna.

"I've never seen it so...empty," said Elizabeth. "If you were to rent here, Henry, you'll need to buy a lots of furniture and pots to make it liveable. You could do with a decent table, and they're not cheap. "

"Oh I think it will do very nicely," said Henry. "You'll soon make it into somewhere nice and cosy, just like you have with our place."

Elizabeth turned to face her brother with a frown, "What do you mean?"

"I could never rent this place. It's already got a tenant. You. It's yours."

She laughed, "Mine? Don't be silly. How am I supposed to pay for it..." She stopped as enlightenment dawned. "Pen?"

Henry placed the key in her hand. "I didn't really copy Mrs Billam's key. Pen gave it to me, to give to you."

"You've been seeing Pen..." she said as she dumbly accepted the key.

"Of course," said Henry dismissively. "He's a mate of mine. Just because you don't see him doesn't mean I can't either."

"But he hasn't even asked me if I want it. I'm needed at home."

Susanna laughed, "You're across the road. You're not moving to Todwick!"

"But there's nothing in here. No furniture or anything."

"I think he'll sort all that out once he knows you want it," said Henry. He sighed, "Well, I better get back. Those horseshoes aren't going to make themselves – worse luck!"

"Yes, me too," said Susanna. "I've got...something to do. I think."

They both started for the door, Elizabeth ran after them. As they emerged into the sunlight Elizabeth suddenly halted. Peregrine was standing outside, he stood straight. Silent. His long coat hanging loosely to his black boots. His blonde hair, as usual, pulled back tightly into a pony tail.

"We'll leave you two to have a chat," said Henry. Then to Susanna, "Come on!" Susanna laughed and they both set off back across the road.

"Do you like it?" said Peregrine.

"Of course," she admitted. "But it doesn't change anything."

"For who?"

"Between us. You're still marrying the Earl of Oxford's daughter, right?"

"Unfortunately," he admitted. "But not for at least six months. I was hoping to have at least that time with you."

"And what's this cottage for? Your private bordello?"

He smiled. "You dishonour me, but I probably deserve it. This isn't mine. It's yours. I just pay for it - as a good husband should."

"You can't be my husband," she declared. "Anyway, you'll soon be someone else's."

"Soon, but not yet. We still have this time. They may be able to marry me to whoever they like, but in here," he tapped a finger to his temple. "And in here," he placed his hand on his heart. "We cannot be separated."

"So, what is this cottage for?"

"You once told me I was searching for a home and I said that, in my case, home couldn't be found, it had to be made. Well, this is me making a start. A home for you and, hopefully later on - if you can find space in your heart. - a home for me too. I need it now more than ever."

"It's very easy for you, Pen, with all your money and clever words..."

"I don't find any of this easy, believe me. My family breed me like a prize bull. But I will endure this abuse if it means I can provide for what is more important to me than anything - you. It is important to me that you are happy, whether that is with or without me."

"What happens to our cottage here when you get married? Do I get evicted back to live with Pa, Henry and Susanna?"

"Nothing happens. While ever they want me to do what they want, they will have to do what I want. And, that means, you stay in this cottage as long as you want to."

She sighed, thoughtfully. "I suppose, if they won't let us

marry then this is the nearest we are likely to get. Six months you say?"

"At least."

"I heard about this couple in Anston once, they got married and then she grew ill and died five months later. So, some marriages don't even last as long as we'll be together. At least this way I'm still alive at the end of it. And I'm getting you before that Harley woman does. *She* can be the other woman!"

He smiled, "You're being very practical about it. You're better at seeing the positive side than I am."

"Of course, I wish it was different," she said sadly. "I wish money grew on trees, every day was a Sunday and rain was beer. But it isn't! So we may as well get on with it."

"Shall we go in?" he asked hesitantly.

"Aye, because I need to talk to you about furniture..."

Chapter Nine

<u>**21st March 1712**</u>

Dawn was about to break. There was a lightening of the sky in the east and Elizabeth had started to hear the chirp of blackbirds announcing the sun's imminent arrival. The bedroom she was in was as dark as coal and the air on her arm had a snap to it. There had been a frost. She lay on her back, staring up at the ceiling beams, which were just visible in the gloom. Her arm was open to the air, but the rest of her was warm and snug under several layers of bedding. She could feel Peregrine's body touching her side. The gentle warmth where his naked skin touched hers. He wore no clothes and neither did she. They rarely wore clothes to bed. They both enjoyed the touch of each others bare bodies and the excitement that often aroused. He lay on his front. She could hear his rhythmic breathing, a constant, measured beat and reassuring presence.

It had all worked out so much better than she could have expected - or allowed herself to expect. It hadn't just become her cottage, it had become an extension of the Mirfin family residence, as if their original cottage had suddenly more than doubled in size. Elizabeth took the larger of the two bedrooms, Susanna had moved into the smaller one which allowed Henry to have their old bedroom to himself. His complaints about not sleeping in front of the fire any more and needing more space had been half hearted, but Elizabeth concluded they were valid. It sort of made sense for Susanna to move into the new cottage with Elizabeth. They had gone from sharing a bedroom to sharing a cottage. It left Henry and Pa in the old cottage and, since they worked together, that also made sense. It had suited Elizabeth too, she didn't feel like she was living in Peregrine's cottage any more. It felt more like hers and Susanna's. It also meant Susanna had her own bedroom for the first time in her life. All-in-all, there was just a lot more room for them all to spread out instead of being on top of one another. They all still met in the same kitchen for meals.

Furnishing the cottage had been ridiculously easy. The hardest part had been deciding what to have and where to get it. Affording it was simply not an issue, Peregrine had told her she could have anything she wanted and he would pay for it. By the standards she was accustomed to it was as if she had been given hugely abundant funds. In fact, after so many years of restricting her imagination, she concluded it simply wasn't up to being granted unlimited freedom and she had eventually settled on just slightly more lavish versions of her familiar things.

She had decided to call it Horseshoe Cottage. It was a bit of a joke considering Henry's complaints at the time, but it seemed to work fine. She had even had Henry make a sign to hang up on the gate. It was all a bit extravagant considering that only her, Susanna, Peregrine and the rector, as far as she knew, could actually read it! But it made her feel more like this really was her house.

Perhaps her biggest concern had initially been about her relationship with Peregrine. She hadn't been quite sure really what she was letting herself in for. Or, more importantly, what Peregrine thought she was letting herself in for. The country was littered with rich, married aristocrats who set up convenient love nests where they could drop in, when it suited them, for some carnal frolicking without it interfering with their real lives. To say she had had reservations would have been putting it mildly.

As it happened, it had felt very different. Technically, Peregrine wasn't married – yet – he was just, sort of, engaged. Which meant, at least for the time being, Elizabeth didn't feel like an adulteress, because she wasn't. And Peregrine always acted as if he was a guest in her house, not as if she was a guest in his. He stayed when she allowed him to and left when she asked him to. He still went back to his rooms in the Hall, unless she said she would like him to stay. He talked to Henry as much as he talked to her and they all ate together, as a family, over at the blacksmith cottage.

Peregrine had even started working on the vegetable plot behind Horseshoe Cottage. At first he was just helping Henry out, but Peregrine had a lot more free time and so he began to take on more and more. Originally, Peregrine didn't have a clue what he was doing, but Henry had taught him as much as he could, and Peregrine was a quick learner. After just a few weeks things were looking a lot more organised on the plot. Elizabeth got the impression that Peregrine was really enjoying growing the vegetables, he had never really had any direct involvement before with anything like that. It was gardeners work.

As the sun rose, its pallid heat made little impact on the frosty lanes and hedgerows, but its light filled the bedroom. Elizabeth tried to make sense of her feelings. She felt different. It was more than contentment. She had always thought she was contented, but she realised now that she hadn't felt as contended as she did now. She had never really thought much about improving her situation, but all of a sudden, it had improved so drastically that she realised now how impoverished she had previously been. Suddenly, she was allowing herself to look ahead to a future. She was daring to dream.

She told herself that was such a dangerous thing to do. Ultimately, Peregrine and herself had no future, he had said as much to her. He had been forced to sell their future to keep her safe. He regretted it more than she did, but nevertheless, that was their destiny. Anyway, did anyone really have a future? Even when they thought they did? Weren't they just fooling themselves? There was no way to really know what might happen. In some ways Peregrine and herself were more fortunate – they knew what was written in the future for them. They could anticipate it. Plan for it. Be ready for it. And make the most of now, because they knew, for a fact, it would not last. As Peregrine himself had said, they had a few months to be happy. They had to grasp whatever happiness they could with both hands and make the most of every day. Because that was all they were likely to get.

"A penny for them?" he said.

She smiled, she hadn't realised he had woken up. "I was just thinking. I think I might be happy."

"Oh no. Do you need a doctor?"

She snuggled up to him, putting her head on his chest. "No, I think I'll just put up with it."

"That's probably the best course of action," he agreed.

"How about you?"

He thought for a second, "You know, I think I might be happy too. It must be contagious."

"I suppose we'll get over it eventually. Do you think it might take a while?"

"Oh God, I hope so!" he said fervently.

"In that case we aught to make the most of it while we can." She leaned on her elbow and looked at him intently. "I want you," she said in a whisper.

"You've got me," he replied happily.

She didn't smile, she just continued to look at him intently. "I mean I want you completely. Right now. I want to feel you inside me."

He was startled. Then excited. "Is it safe?" he murmured distantly.

"Yes," she said with certainty. "It is now."

She climbed over on top of him, straddling him. She smiled as she saw his escalating excitement. She felt him swell beneath her. Taking control, she guided him inside. Then she rode him, gently at first and then more intensely. She watched him...watching her. Felt him respond to her every touch, her every movement. Until he closed his eyes, writhing and moaning. His excitement fed her own.

And afterwards, she laid down next to him and her hand gently stroked the side of his face. "We're as good as married now," she said. "You were with me before her and you're mine now. Whatever happens with anyone else, I was first, they will always be second. You belong to me."

"Yes," he murmured helplessly. "I belong to you."

It was nearly an hour later that they were dressed and left Horseshoe Cottage to cross the road to the blacksmiths. Robert and Henry had already started work so they had some breakfast with Susanna.

"We're running out of tea...again," said Susanna when they all sat down. "It never lasts very long with all of us drinking it."

"Except Pa," corrected Elizabeth. "He calls it *foreign muck*."

"Well, it's definitely foreign so he has that bit right," said Peregrine. "I think it's dried plant leaves."

"Like tobacco. Which is also foreign," said Susanna. "And he gets through enough of that!"

Elizabeth laughed," He probably thinks they grow it in Rotherham or something."

"Best not to tell him and spoil it," said Peregrine. "He likes it too much."

"So, what are you two planning to do today?" asked Susanna.

"Well, I thought we might take the horses out," said Peregrine. "We've not done that for a while."

Elizabeth said, "Do you mind. I have chores to do!"

Susanna laughed, "Nah, there's not much and I can handle it. Go and have a good time."

"Well, if you're sure..." said Elizabeth.

"Why should we both be stuck in?"

Elizabeth sighed, "Well, alright. But only if you let me cover for you so you can go out another day."

"It's a deal. Now go and enjoy yourselves."

Peregrine said, "I'll bring some tea back."

So, Elizabeth and Peregrine grabbed their coats and began the walk up through the field to Kiveton Hall. She was always apprehensive when approaching the Hall. It felt like some forbidden place where she wasn't allowed and here she was sneaking in and hoping not to be caught. The closer it got the more nervous she became.

"There's no chance of us meeting your mother, is there?" she asked apprehensively.

He shook his head. "I think she went off to see one of my aunts or the Harley's or something. She said she wouldn't be back for weeks. She said she was going on Monday..."

"That's today," she said in alarm.

"I thought today was Tuesday?"

"No, today is Monday," said Elizabeth. "I just hope she's gone already."

By the time they got to the top of the hill Elizabeth's nerves were shredded. She really wished she had just sent Peregrine to get the horses and then she could have stayed at home and waited, They walked along the front of the Hall, past the North Pavilion and then they turned into the stable yard.

Elizabeth's heart sank.

There was his mother's coach waiting to leave. Panic rose like bile in her throat, if it hadn't been for Peregrine's firm hold of her hand she might have turned and run. Even so, she found herself hanging a step behind as he marched forwards unconcernedly. He didn't acknowledge the coach was there at all, but just made a straight line to the stables where the horses were.

Elizabeth closed her eyes and prayed, *Please let us reach the stables without seeing her.*

"Ah, Pip, have you come to see me off?" came Lady Bridget's voice. Elizabeth's blood seemed to turn to slush in her veins.

Peregrine stopped and turned. His mother was sitting in the coach with the door open. Elizabeth kept her eyes down on the court yard, she dare not raise them and risk catching his mother's gaze.

"No, Mother," said Peregrine, calmly. "We were rather hoping that we had missed you."

She smiled, but there was no warmth in it. "Well, I'm glad I waited. I wanted to make sure you were alright, I haven't seen you for weeks. I didn't want to spend all this time arranging a wedding just to find the groom had bolted."

"Where would I go?"

"Exactly. There is no where to run to, is there? And why would you want to? It's every young lad's dream to bed the daughter of an aristocrat and, here you are, marrying one. You don't appreciate how lucky you are, Pip."

"Oh I think I do," replied Peregrine levelly. His hand tightened on Elizabeth's.

"Well, it's good to see you're keeping yourself...how should I say it? Entertained, in the meantime. Is this one of that blacksmith's trollops that you're fucking?"

Elizabeth felt an angry fire rise and quench her nervousness. Slowly, she raised her eyes from the floor until she was looking directly at Lady Bridget. She spoke slowly, purposefully, pronouncing every word like a challenge. "My name is Elizabeth."

It was greeted with an uncomfortable silence. The two women's eyes held each other's gaze and neither flinched.

Finally Lady Bridget turned to Peregrine. "Well, Pip, I shall see you in a few weeks with details of your wedding. In the meantime...enjoy yourself."

She closed the door of her coach and then tapped on the roof and the horses set off through the stable yard gates. And she was gone.

Elizabeth felt she could breathe for the first time in several tense minutes. Relief flooded her like a cool wave and she breathed out a huge sigh.

Finally, she said, "I'm sorry to have to say this, Pen, but your mother is a bitch!"

"That's what I've been telling you," he said.

They looked at each then laughed with unfettered relief.

25th March 1712

"So, a new year," said Elizabeth quietly to herself as she opened the door of Horseshoe Cottage to let it in. The new year blew in with a cold wind that swept through her hair and threatened to blow open the blanket she had wrapped around her. The weather was restless, grey clouds threatened rain, but there was also some blue that held a promise of Spring sunshine. A brisk wind toyed with the remains of autumns leaves, throwing them around in the yard like a children's game. "I wonder what this one will bring?" - but she knew the answer to that question well enough.

Today was Lady Day, officially the beginning of the new year. It was also Good Friday, the start of Easter. It felt like the an important day, the beginning of something important.

Peregrine had felt it had been such a momentous year, that the last night of it really aught to be marked. So, last night, he had brought some wine down from the Hall and Elizabeth had made some seed cake. Elizabeth, Peregrine, Susanna, Henry and Robert had all stayed up much later than usual. The wine had received a mixed reception, Peregrine and Henry liked it but everyone else wrinkled their nose at it. Susanna had remarked she had expected it to taste sweeter. Everyone seemed to enjoy the seed cake. Eventually, as they all grew tired, Elizabeth, Peregrine and Susanna had set off back to Horseshoe Cottage.

Peregrine had shivered as he climbed into bed, it was like clambering into a bath of cold water. He promised himself he really should bring a bed pan down from the Hall. Some luxuries were really not worth doing without.

Elizabeth had come into the room and started, absently, taking off her clothes. He had suddenly forgotten completely about his cold bed as he watched her slowly remove layer after layer in the candle light. It was all the more enticing because she was oblivious to how he watched her. When she was down to just a thin shift, she reached up and removed her cap, letting her hair tumble down across her shoulders. She casually removed her shift to stand naked in the flickering light. As she had turned around to get into bed she had seen he was looking at her and stopped.

Her eyebrows had drawn together questioningly, "What?"

"Nothing. I'm just counting my blessings." he had replied.

In the morning, the bed that had seemed so cold as she climbed into it that night was now warm enough to make it an effort to leave. But she had wrapped herself in a blanket, gone down stairs and let in the new year.

She had hurried back upstairs. Thrown off the blanket and climbed into bed again, cuddling up to him as he lay staring at the ceiling.

"That's the New Year let in. For better or worse," she said.

"Lady Day is just an arbitrary day designated as the start of the year, you know. It means nothing really. In Scotland, and most of Europe, it's January 1st."

"Well, it feels like the start of a new year. Always has, ever since I was a girl. Everyone's leases renew then for another year."

"Speaking of which, I've paid the lease on this cottage for a year."

"But you're leasing it from yourself?"

"Not strictly true. *You* lease it from the Kiveton estate but I pay for it. I also had to pay Tom Crowther to set it all up. Anyway, all done for another year."

"This time next year, you'll be married, I suppose," she said distantly.

"Who knows? Maybe that Harley woman will fall off her horse, have a hunting accident or change her mind before then," he said.

She laughed, "It wouldn't solve anything. Your mother would find someone else."

"I suppose so."

"No, the more I've thought about it, the best thing is to go ahead and marry her."

"How do you figure that?" he said incredulously.

"Because that gets it over with. Once you give them what they want, a legitimate heir, they'll leave you alone. They won't care any more and you can come back to me."

"As a married man."

"That's just some legal waffle. I found you first and between you and me, where it counts, we are married. This second marriage is only possible because they won't let you have the first. It's just an arrangement to get an heir. It's like you said about Lady Day – it's just arbitrary...designated...meaningless. Where it counts, between us, is the real marriage."

"It's a way of looking at it, but I prefer not to think about it."

"I see it a bit like when your mother originally asked you to go to Herefordshire. You didn't want to and I didn't want you to go. But you went, you did it and we got through it. Now, they've left you alone to do what you want. This marriage can be the same..."

"Excuse me, there's a little more to it than two weeks in Herefordshire."

"I know. But if we can get through this then, when it's over, we'll have what we want. They'll leave us alone."

"Maybe. Or maybe they won't stop at one heir, maybe they'll want two or three or a dozen! Maybe the first child is a girl, or what if the child dies? No, I can't see me ever being free of her!"

"But there's a chance. Probably not much of a chance, but a chance just the same. And it's one that's easy for us to take because we have no other choice. It's like the ceiling above the staircase in Kiveton Hall."

"What? You, mean the Creation of Pandora?" he said, completely lost.

"Yes. You told me she released evil into the world. But also Hope. That's like us. We have to do this thing, but we can also hope. Hope that we can survive it and overcome it."

He gave her a gentle kiss. "You're so wonderful. You know, that Harley woman would never appreciate something like the

Creation of Pandora. She might like the colours, but it would have no meaning for her. Not like it has for you. It's wasted on people like her! But not on you."

"*You're* wasted on people like her," she said softly.

He heaved a sigh. "Can't we just run off somewhere? Somewhere they'll never find us?"

"As you yourself told your mother, there's nowhere to run to. Besides, they would take it out on Pa, Henry and Susanna."

"They could come with us."

"Oh yes, they would thank us for that! And anyway, your family and the Harley's run the country. Do you really think you can hide from people like them?"

"No," he admitted sadly. "Probably not."

"Then we will use this time. These few months. We will be happy and enjoy our lives together. We will make the bond between us so strong that when you have to leave, it will not be broken. You will survive the ordeal. You will do what you have to do and then, when it's over, you will come back to me. And I will be here waiting."

He looked at her through watery eyes. "What was I before you? Nothing. If I should ever lose you then that is all I would become. Dust. As long as I know, that somewhere you are still waiting, I can withstand anything."

12th April 1712

Elizabeth pulled open one of the heavy oak doors that led out of Kiveton Hall onto the East Prospect. She stepped out onto the top of a set of stone stairs that led down, left and right into the gardens. Before her the ornamental terrace stretched out before her. Four square lawns, adorned with statues of classical heroes and, to the side of each, a further square of flower beds where clumps of daffodils stood tall, facing the rising morning sun. The remains of earlier snowdrops dribbled in swathes through the beds, their gleaming white heads creating pleasant contrast with the yellow narcissi. Beyond the ornamental terrace the level dropped again to the formal terrace where two intriguing mazes sat either side of the central path, their high hedges obscuring the view of what secrets they held within. Beyond that, the lime-lined main avenue cut through Kiveton Park, reaching with arrow like linearity for over a mile towards distant South Anston.

The mid-spring sun was rising high above the gleaming limestone spire of Anston church, bathing the gardens in abundant radiance. An early morning shower had dowsed the grass and now, as it warmed, the vapours rose like misty phantoms huddling nervously in the morning light.

Elizabeth looked to her left where, beyond the edge of the gardens, began the mixed woods of ash, beach and oak that stretched up to Todwick village. She had ridden with Peregrine through those woods many times, northwards to where they eventually met the boundary wall.

It's an awesome sight, thought Elizabeth. A personal garden and pleasure grounds that covered a larger area than Wales village itself. And yet, as far as she could see, vacant. Even the house itself only had a dozen people cleaning and maintaining it. Peregrine was the only family member here. It was an empty palace, just over a decade old, finished and maintained, but now waiting. Waiting to be inhabited, to be put to the grand use for which it was created. Waiting for the guests to attend its parties, to occupy its bedrooms, to gasp in admiration at its treasures and gardens. Created as a grand family home for a family that preferred to avoid each other. The current 1st Duke of Leeds had built it, but it would be left to his successors to populate it and to realise its potential. From what Elizabeth had been told Peregrine's father, the likely 2nd Duke, wouldn't be doing it. And Peregrine himself, the likely 3rd Duke, would, thanks to her, now be happier living in Horseshoe Cottage with her instead of entertaining family and friends in his vast pleasure palace.

That responsibility would probably fall to the 4th Duke – and he hadn't even been conceived yet! Elizabeth had to admit, grudgingly, that was where the Harley woman came into it. Only she, or someone like her, could bear the future 4th Duke. The future of Kiveton now depended on it.

She felt a sudden pang of guilt. Hadn't she played a significant part in diverting Peregrine from his responsibilities to this place? Wasn't she the reason he now dreamed of a very different life to the one he was born to? But no, she couldn't take all the responsibility, his family themselves had played a bigger part in pushing him down that road. And, to be fair, Peregrine was no one's idea of what a Duke of Leeds should be. He was simply a different sort of person to the one his family desperately needed him to be. He could never be the Duke either his family or Kiveton deserved, but he could be her loving husband, if they would just allow him to be.

Peregrine came out and stood next to her. He took a deep breath of the fresh morning air. "It's a lovely day today," he exclaimed, happily. "Good idea to show you the gardens. Do you like the terraces?"

"It's impressive to put it mildly. Everything is just so...big."

"You haven't seen the other bits yet, come on."

He led her down the steps to the first terrace. The surface was a fine gravel that crunched under their feet. They crossed it and then down a further set of steps onto the main terrace. It was huge, symmetrical design based around four square lawns, each one flanked on either side by swirling bed of flowers. When they reached the very centre of the design, surrounded by the four square lawns, Peregrine turned right and led them down through a further set of steps into the Kitchen Gardens.

High walls rose to the left and right on the side of the path. They continued down the path to where there was a break in the right wall. Peregrine turned in. Rows of furrows were neatly dug in an enclosed area perhaps a quarter of an acre in size.

"Here's where they grow the vegetables," announced Peregrine proudly. "There are twelve enclosed spaces like this one.

I'm hoping that the vegetable patch at the cottage will look similar by the time I've finished. I've been getting advice and seed from the gardeners here."

"There's nothing in the furrows," she said.

"It's all been newly planted. You won't see anything growing for a while. But it will."

"Twelve areas like this?"

"Aye, this is the biggest. There are three smaller square plots and eight triangular plots. There's also a fish pond where fish can be kept fresh. There's also the Orchard which is as big as all these plots combined."

"That is a lot of space for growing fruit and vegetables," she said.

"Kiveton is self-sustaining. The estate grows more than necessary to feed everyone who lives and works here. The rest is sold off. There's a lot of variety as well, far more than I would hope to grow on our plot in the cottage."

"But there's only you and your mother live here?"

"As far as family, yes, but there's all the others who live and work here. Performing all the household duties, cooking, cleaning and repairs. Then there's the stables and the maintenance of the outer estate. We have three mills. Then there's the management, of course, like Tom Crowther and the gardening staff. The estate is very active whether there are any family in residence or not."

"But no guests?"

He frowned. "Apart from the occasional visitor, mother doesn't invite many people here. There certainly aren't any large events. Mother tends to visit other people's parties."

They went out of the Kitchen plot and turned right, walking down between another set of Kitchen Gardens before reaching a set of black iron gates hung between large limestone pillars topped with depictions of acorns. Peregrine opened the gates and they emerged onto the double tree lined track of Lodge Hill Avenue. They walked across the Avenue and down a small path between sets of raised beds, filled with an array of various shrubs and herbs. A dizzying number of fruit bushes that would, no doubt, produce an abundance of soft fruit in the autumn.

"This estate is producing as much as a farm!" said Elizabeth.

"Aye, it's very productive," he said proudly.

She put her arm around him, "And it will all be yours one day."

"I suppose," he admitted. "But I doesn't feel like it's anything to do with me. If I wasn't here it would carry on just the same. Just as it did before I arrived. If I grow something at the cottage it seems much more like mine than everything that's grown here."

She looked around, "It's all so big, so impressive and so beautiful. What is going to happen to it all?"

"What do you mean? Nothing. It's too big for anything to happen to it."

"Who's going to care about it? Not your grandfather, who's in Wimbledon all the time. Not your father, who cares more about the Navy. And not you, who cares more about a cottage in Wales. You're making your home with us – and I'm so glad that you are. But I do worry about who is going to make a home of this place. It seems like it needs someone to love it."

"Well, there's my mother..."

"Who won't be around forever. And, as you say, she spends a lot of time elsewhere and doesn't entertain anyone here." She paused in thought for a second and then said, "I once went with Susanna up to Wales church and we were the only ones in there, no one else. It was strange. I'm so used to seeing it when there's a service and it's full of people, talking and singing. To see it with just me and Susanna. It was a great opportunity to admire it, but somehow it seemed vacant, empty and unused. As if its purpose was unfulfilled until there were people in it. This estate has the same feel to it."

"I know what you mean," admitted Peregrine. "It's a family home without a family."

"Perhaps your son's family will live here and bring it to life," she said softly.

"My son?"

"The future 4th Duke. Perhaps he'll love it. No else seems to."

He looked at her, "Are you agreeing with my mother?"

She sighed, her lips tightly closed as if she didn't like the thought of it. "I don't agree with her when it concerns you, but concerning the future of Kiveton, I can see her point of view. There just seems such a lot here to put at risk. If you had no heir, who would inherit it?"

Peregrine hadn't thought about it before. "I don't know. My sisters don't have any children of their own. Next in line is probably my cousin, Thomas, Aunt Sophia's son."

"Not an Osborne then?"

"No, his father is William Fermor, Baron Leominster."

"So, the only way someone called Osborne can inherit Kiveton is if you have a son?"

Reluctantly, he nodded. "Aye, that's about the shape of it. My mother and father aren't going to have any more children. My sister Mary has two step-children, but I don't think she's very likely to have any more either."

"I see. Which is why they are very interested in you."

"Of course, if they would just allow us to marry then everything would work out. They would get their heir...our son. But they won't."

Elizabeth looked round at the huge estate. Would she want a son of hers to inherit this? And all the problems that came with it? She wasn't sure.

"Come on. Let's walk back," she said and, with their arms around each other they started back.

Chapter Ten

As April wore on it's refreshing showers gave way to bright, late Spring sunshine. Wild flowers painted the hedgerows and meadows with a delicate brush of colour. As the temperatures lifted, so too did the spirits. As Winter's grey grip receded into memory a bright, restless optimism slowly replaced it. Peregrine began to feel a need to go somewhere. To venture beyond the invisible boundaries of the little world they inhabited and experience the places beyond. More often than not, at these times, the same idea surfaced. A promise he had made to Elizabeth some time ago that, ever since, had gnawed annoyingly on the edge of his consciousness. When he innocently suggested it to Elizabeth he noticed that, like an optical illusion, what had seemed so simple, while it hid half-seen on the edge of his mind, seemed to grow in an unsettling fashion as it emerged into the light.

A few days later, he was sat with Elizabeth, Susanna and Henry in the kitchen of the blacksmith's cottage.

"Pen and I have a bit of an announcement," Elizabeth said when she had Susanna's attention. "We are going to go on a journey for a few days. At the beginning of May."

Susanna had said. "Where are you going?"

"We are going to see the sea," Elizabeth said, as if she was describing a pilgrimage. Which, in a way, it was.

"Oh, really? The sea? That'll be wonderful," enthused Susanna. "I'm going to do that, one day."

"Well, actually," began Elizabeth. "We would like you to come with us. If you want to?"

Susanna jaw dropped open. "You want *me* to go?"

"Ur, yes," said Peregrine. "It'll just be for a few days. If you can spare the time and if you want to..."

"Do I want to? Yes, yes, I definitely do want to! Don't worry, I'll find the time. When are we going?"

Peregrine paused before answering and turned to Henry. "And we'd like you to come too?"

"Me? To the sea?"

"Yes, you!" said Elizabeth with irritation. "We want all four of us to go. What do you think?"

Henry thought about it for a while. "If it's all the same I think I won't. Not that I wouldn't like to one day, but I'd prefer to do it with my mates, or with a girlfriend. Not with my sisters. You understand, right?"

"I understand," admitted Peregrine. "I did the Grand Tour with my brother and it was fabulous. I somehow think it wouldn't have been the same with my sister!"

"I guess I'm a bit old for family trips out." he said.

"Well, I'm certainly not! I'd love to go." exclaimed Susanna.

"That's settled then," said Elizabeth with a smile. "I'm sure Pa and Henry can manage without us for a week and Pa hates travel anyway."

"But how are we getting there?" asked Susanna. "Where are we sleeping? Where are we going?"

Peregrine grinned. "That's alright, leave all that to me."

It took two or three weeks to organise everything. As April's brief bouts of sun and frequent blustery showers abated, the days slipped gently into May. The woods were decked with carpets of Bluebells and the Hawthorne hedges started to turn snowy white with their early buds. Noisy gangs of pale brown, newly fledged starlings made a riotous cacophony throughout the villages. The woods echoed to the tap tap of woodpeckers and mating calls of wood pigeons. In the evenings, blackbirds secured the highest perches and sang their lilting songs to herald the approach of Summer.

In the early morning sunlight, Peregrine's coach made it's way down to Wales. Following the road, it eventually turned into the blacksmith's yard and pulled to a halt, it's two horses chomping at their bits.

Elizabeth and Susanna came out, wide smiles on their faces. Each carrying a canvas bag. Peregrine opened the door of the coach while the coachmen loaded the bags onto the back of the coach and secured them in place.

"It's just so, so exciting," said Susanna with a wide grin. "And I don't even know where we are going!"

Peregrine laughed. "We're going somewhere else. And that is always exciting."

"It is when you've spent your entire life in one village," replied Susanna.

"Yes, it's always good to get away for a while," replied Peregrine. Their enthusiasm was infectious. It made Peregrine happy to see them happy. He had experienced a lot of travel before, but they hadn't, and he enjoyed watching them experience it for the first time.

Elizabeth came up to him once her bag was loaded. "I was right about you, Peregrine Osborne," she said with a grin. "There is something about you that could turn a girl's head"

"You don't think it's just because I own a good set of wheels?" he asked indicating the coach.

"Um, that might be it, actually," she replied and climbed aboard.

Once they were all aboard, the door was slammed shut and the coach set off, the horses clomping up the lane towards the village centre then turning left towards Kiveton. Susanna was looking eagerly out of the window as they went through the village, waving to people she knew, but who then didn't recognise her at all.

The coach made it's way across the crossroads at Kiveton

before descending down Red Hill then turning left and pro-
ceeding up Dog Kennel Lane towards South Anston. They
crossed the main drive, in front of Crow Gate, and then went
down into South Anston. Then along the Sheffield Worksop
road and then right, going over the Anston Beck bridge then
up the main street hill in North Anston. The road climbed
at a twenty degree angle up the Anston hill and then turned
left and flattened out. They proceeded through open fields before entering the small village of Dinnington. The village sat
on a crossroads where the road from Laughton Common met
the north-south road to Anston. The coach continued across
the crossroads and headed north towards Throapham. At
Throapham they met an east-west road and turned east, travelling once again into open, undulating countryside.

"Well, I'm now completely lost," announced Susanna.
"Where are we?"

"On the Oldcotes road," said Elizabeth. "I think."

Peregrine nodded, "Aye, the road to Oldcotes. "

"It's a bit of an adventure, isn't it?" said Susanna.

"Yes, Pen, where are we going exactly?" asked Elizabeth.

"The seaside," replied Peregrine. "But it will take two days to
get there, so we're breaking the journey up in York."

"York!" the other two chorused.

"York is a really big town. That's really exciting," said Susanna.

"I never thought I'd ever go there," said Elizabeth dreamily.

Peregrine shook his head. In an age where people could sail
to the New World it seemed unjust that the girls had never
been to York or even seen the sea! It made him feel good to
know that he would be putting that injustice right.

The coach continued along the road between Firbeck and
Letwell before turning left into Oldcotes. The coach crossed
the crossroads and continued northwards, eventually entering
Tickhill.

Elizabeth and Susanna marvelled at Tickhill, the largest
village any of them had seen. Far larger than Wales or Tod-

wick, Tickhill had been a local market town for centuries and boasted a castle. Although the castle had been partially destroyed in the wars between the King and Parliament eighty years previously.

Tickhill marked the limit of the girl's experience of the world. They had been twice before, to the market, but that was years ago. From now on they were entering the unknown.

The coach followed the road northwards through the quaint village of Wadsworth, then Loversall and Balby before turning right into Doncaster. Doncaster was about the same size as Tickhill. Besides being a market town it was one of the few places where the River Don could be crossed, something they had to do if they were to continue north.

Once on the other side of the river they followed the road north towards Skelbrooke and Barnsdale. By now it was lunchtime and Elizabeth handed out some snacks she had packed. They also had some beer in flasks that proved very welcome for their thirst.

"This area we are passing through is Robin Hood country, " said Peregrine. "Allegedly."

"Robin Hood? I remember those old songs," said Elizabeth. "But, isn't he to do with Nottingham?"

"Ah, that's his enemy, the Sheriff of Nottingham," replied Peregrine. " According to legend he lived in Barnsdale Forest, which is just up this road on the other side of Skelbrooke."

"Is Robin Hood a real person, then?" asked Susanna.

"No," said Elizabeth. "It's just a few old ballads."

"Oh, you should teach me some. I like singing."

Sure enough, eventually the road entered a wooded area where trees closed in on either side of the road. Although, it was a stretch to call it a forest, more like a patch of woodland.

The road continued northward through Sherburn and Towton.

"There was a huge battle at Towton two hundred and fifty years ago," said Peregrine, who had adopted a sort of tour guide role just to break up the monotony of the journey. He noticed that after many hours in the coach even Susanna's enthusiasm was fading.

"You wouldn't think so, " said Susanna. "It's only about the size of Todwick."

"For a battle they don't need a big town," said Peregrine. "Just a big field."

The road carried on to Tadcaster which was slightly larger. It's mediaeval bridge crossed the River Wharf, as it had for hundreds of years, from which the road continued on to York. It was fairly straight road that headed north east, toward York and then onward towards the coast. It was mainly open common area, some strip fields, but mainly larger plantations and small woods. Ironically, it's most noticeable feature was it's lack of features and it's level appearance. Gone were the undulating hills and dales of Kiveton. This was the Vale Of York.

The day was beginning to get into the late afternoon by the time they approached York. Everyone was quite tired after having spent most of the day travelling, but the prospect of nearing the first real city they had ever seen had reignited the girl's excitement. The houses along the Tadcaster Road that had been few and infrequent began to increase in number and become steadily closer together. They also became subtly wealthier. Thatched roofs were replaced by slate and tiles until their numbers dominated. They found themselves following other coaches and dodging ones coming the other way. The number of pedestrians increased dramatically. Eventually, it took on the feel of a town rather than a series of houses. Buildings were now closely grouped together, people milled about on their daily errands and horses pulled carts, wagons and coaches of various shapes along the roads.

"I've never seen anything like it," said Susanna. "It's a lot, lot bigger than Tickhill!"

Peregrine laughed, "Yes, you could say that." For someone, like himself, who was familiar with London, Paris and Rome, York seemed provincial. But, to Susanna, who had never seen a human habitation larger than five hundred souls, it was a sprawling metropolis.

As they approached Micklegate Bar, the shouts from his companions were so loud Peregrine almost expected one of them to faint with excitement. The Bar was what remained of the mediaeval gate through the city wall. A castellated tower of stone complete with battlements and mediaeval cross slits and, at it's base, the arched gate through which traffic passed in single file. In front of the gate a further barbican gate stood as an outer defence. It stood like a scene from the eleventh century brought to life.

"We're entering a castle!" shouted Susanna.

"No, just one of the city gates," said Peregrine. "Micklegate."

"It's like living history," breathed Elizabeth. "Like we have been transported back in time."

"It's an old city," said Peregrine. "It's been around since Roman times."

"Roaming times?" asked Susanna. "When's that?"

"Roman," he said. "Seventeen centuries ago."

"I didn't know anything could be that old," she said. "Except in the Bible."

"York was four hundred years old when Christianity arrived in England," he replied.

"We're going through the gate!" shouted Elizabeth excitedly as they passed through the outer barbican gate and then through the arched gate beneath the ancient stone tower. Then they were inside the city. Buildings packed closely together presenting a continuous frontage to the street. Compared to the countryside the city seemed to bustle even in the early evening. People were everywhere, crowding the streets, hanging out of windows, entering or leaving houses or simply wandering around. Coaches and wagons rattled loudly along the cobble stone streets, but the city was also an assault on the senses.

"Uh, it's smelly," complained Susanna.

"That's what happens when you put a lot of people in one place," said Peregrine.

"There are churches everywhere," said Elizabeth who was used to every village having a church, but where the villages were far apart.

Sure enough, the Micklegate Road passed between two spires at the crest of the hill and then four further, flat roofed churches as they descended the other side. But as the road curved right then left they came into view of the river.

The Ouse was a hundred yards wide, a steely carriageway of water hurtling towards the sea. The densely packed houses halted abruptly on its bank and the road continued across a mighty limestone bridge which carried it's own selection of small shops.

"It's huge," said Susanna, commenting on the river. "It makes the Rother look like a stream."

Elizabeth agreed, "It's even wider than the Don was."

Certainly, recent rain had swollen the Ouse into a formidable presence that raced along only a few inches below the height of its banks. The coach continued up into the city, past Tudor style timber framed houses. It turned left along Coney Street, running parallel to the river. The houses here were a mixture of modern red brick and stone and older Tudor style properties creating a pastiche of designs all crowded together with no space between and enclosed, narrow alley ways that ran beneath them.

About halfway along the street the coach suddenly swerved left, pulling into an archway to the side of a large black and white, timber framed building . The coach ran through into a large stable yard behind the building where it stopped.

Elizabeth had noticed a black and white sign outside proclaimed *The Black Swan*.

The stable yard was surprisingly large, from the street no one would have suspected it had facilities of that size behind. Here the horses and coachmen would be fed and rested and then, tomorrow start their journey back to Kiveton. But Peregrine's coach, with fresh horses and men, would continue on.

Peregrine opened the coach door and stepped out. "And

here's where we rest and get something to eat for tonight."

"Here? Right in the centre of York?" asked Elizabeth, astounded.

"Aye, it's a good stop. We'll continue tomorrow."

"We're staying overnight in York?" asked Susanna. "Wait till I tell Pa, he won't believe it."

Peregrine led the way into the inn and at the bar told them they had a reservation. The inside of the inn was dark, light streamed in through the windows if you were fortunate to be near one, but the interior was a maze of small corridors that didn't get sufficient benefit. They were shown to a room on the first floor. It was a large room with a small window, two frail looking chairs and one large bed.

"And guess who's sleeping with who?" asked Elizabeth coyly.

"Oh dear," said Peregrine, alarmed. "I thought there would be two beds."

"Sure you did," replied Elizabeth sarcastically.

"What's the problem?" asked Susanna innocently. "It's certainly big enough. Me and Elizabeth have shared a bed all my life."

"I'll sleep on the floor," announced Peregrine with conviction.

"Oh no," said Elizabeth. "You're paying for this so you'll be sleeping in the bed you've paid for. With us, by the look of it."

Peregrine looked at Susanna. She was wearing a huge grin. "Alright, alright," he capitulated. "If everyone's happy then there's no problem."

"Well, I'm happy," said Elizabeth.

"And I'm very happy," said Susanna.

"Well, I'd be happier if we had two beds, but since we haven't..."

"Can we go out now?" asked Susanna.

"Out? What about food?" asked Peregrine.

Elizabeth joined in, "Oh, please, Pen. It'll be light for a while and we don't get to York much."

"We don't get to York at all!" said Susanna. "And probably never will again. So who cares about food!"

"Alright, we'll go out and eat later," he said.

They made their way back into Coney Street. It was pleasant late Spring evening, comfortably warm with the low sun shining bright and unhindered into the streets. Peregrine took a second to get his bearings then pointed to the left.

"That way," he said and set off. The two girls followed him, almost skipping along the road. It made him feel good that they trusted him so much. He had never had people really trust him before. He was always expected to trust other people. It made him feel important, for the first time in his life. That feeling was euphoric. And maybe addictive.

At the end of the road they found themselves in a small square where several roads converged in front of a small church.

"St Helen's Church," said Peregrine in his tour guide role.

"Helen, as in of Troy?" asked Elizabeth, smiling.

"No, different Helen," he replied. "And now we go up Stonegate by the side of the church."

Stonegate was a very narrow street, even narrower than Coney Street, where their Inn was. The three storey mediaeval timber houses were mixed with more modern brick ones. But, they all had shops on their lower levels. This was a merchant area during the day. During the evening, though, the shops were closed. The street had its own coaching inn, *The Olde Starre Inn.* They carried on up to the junction with Petergate and then, directly across and up a small alley where Stonegate continued.

They emerged at the end of the street into a large, open area. Peregrine smiled as he heard sharp intakes of breath from Elizabeth and Susanna at the sight before them. He looked at them and saw both their faces tilt backwards as their eyes struggled to take it all in.

Before them was a smooth facade of Gothic stone, rising like a mountain, intricately carved and adorned with huge stained glass windows. A monumental man made alpine barrier that stood in their way. Everything about it was oversized, from the gargantuan doors to the vast arrays of glass that formed the windows. At the top, in the centre of its triangular peak was a rosette of glass and stone perhaps forty feet in diameter.

"York Minster," said Peregrine. "Impressive, isn't it?" he said in a feat of understatement.

"It's the largest thing I have ever seen," said Elizabeth. Before it, Kiveton Hall seemed small scale, entire churches such as the ones at Wales and Todwick looked like they could easily fit in a small corner of it. "It's absolutely enormous."

Susanna said, "It must the largest church in the world."

"There are bigger ones," said Peregrine. "But they are newer. This is two hundred and fifty years old. Mind you, it took them centuries to build it."

"I am not surprised," said Elizabeth. "I cannot conceive how they could begin to build such a thing."

"This is the Southern transept - just the side door. There's a tower behind this, which we can't see, that is twice as high. Let's go round to the front."

He led them to the left, walking around the imposing edifice. With every corner they were greeted with more stone and even more glass. Just one of the stained glass windows would have been a magnificent addition to any church back home, but in the Minster there were countless numbers of them, piled on top of each other into mind boggling displays of grandeur.

As they drew around the corner of the huge building they were suddenly faced with the front prospect. Two mighty, square towers soared into the air, twice as high as the steeple on Laughton Church. Elaborately carved with endless intricacies. Grotesque gargoyles stared out from every side, alongside statues of saints and other notables. Huge stained glass windows spanned the entire height. In the exact centre of the building, above the huge, wooden door, rose another window twice as high as the others, elaborately carved with floral designs in the top arched section.

"It is so incredible my mind cannot hold it," said Elizabeth. "What a wonder of the world!"

"There are many buildings like this throughout England," said Peregrine. "Lincoln, Durham, Canterbury, Salisbury. They are all magnificent creations. Works of art."

Elizabeth put her arm round him. "Thanks for showing it to us, Pen."

"Yes, thanks, Pen. It's amazing," said Susanna, also putting her arm around him.

He grinned, "I'm glad you like it," he said quite truthfully. He had seen the Minster before, but on his own when he was much younger. And it hadn't been his first so he was less impressed than he might have been. But, for Elizabeth and Susanna, it was their first time and they had never imagined that such buildings existed, let alone that they would ever see one. They were awestruck and, because they were, he enjoyed it all the more. The wonderment they transmitted magnified his own experience.

"Let's go for something to eat then," he said.

He led them back down Petergate, turning right into Stonegate and then into Coney Street where their inn was located. They entered a dark corridor, but instead of going to their room they turned into the public bar. It was a low room of wooden beams and stone flags with a large window on one wall that let in the last of the fading evening light. There were several groups of people in the room, but it was only about a third full. So, Peregrine and the girls occupied a vacant table.

After some minutes a serving wench came up and they ordered three beers and three portions of stew.

"Imagine what it must be like to live somewhere like this all the time?" said Susanna dreamily. "Surrounded by people. Streets full of shops and a large market. And amazing things to see like the huge river and Minster. It must be like living in a dream."

"There are great things to see in large towns," said Peregrine.

"But somehow I've always felt more at home in villages."

"There are so many people here," said Elizabeth. "I have trouble remembering all the people in Wales, if I had to remember all these...well, I'm not sure I could."

"They don't bother," he admitted. "They are all just strangers. They keep to themselves and ignore everyone else."

"How odd. To be amongst so many people and not know any of them."

He shrugged, "They know their family and their friends. Everyone else is just...furniture. It has to be like that once you move outside a small community. Like you say, you can't remember everyone."

"Well, I'd love it," said Susanna. "It's just so full of life! It makes our place seem really boring. Look at just the people in here. I bet if you talked to them it would turn out they had come from all sort of places you had never heard of and done things you never dreamed of. Not like back home where no one's been anywhere or done anything." She looked across at Peregrine. "Apart from Pen, of course." she said with undisguised admiration.

The food was the usual inn fare to Peregrine's experience, warm and satisfying, but fairly basic. The beer was good though, and they had another round before deciding to go to bed. With a couple of candles they made their way to their room. They placed the candles on each side of the bed. Then, unceremoniously, they all stripped down to their underclothes.

"Who's sleeping in the middle?" asked Susanna with mock innocence. "Just because they have to get in first."

"I will," said Elizabeth. "Obviously."

"We should take it in turns," suggested Susanna, controversially.

Elizabeth smiled. "We'll see."

Peregrine blushed. He decided not to comment. "Uh, if you're in the middle then can you get in please?"

"Of course," said Elizabeth and climbed in, making her way

to the middle. "Ooh, it's cold. Hurry up and get in, you two."

Peregrine climbed in one side and cuddled up to Elizabeth. The sheets were cold, so he was glad for the warmth her body gave him. Susanna did likewise on the other side of the bed.

"Pen?" asked Susanna. "Does this mean we have slept together?"

"Only in a very literal sense," he replied.

"Shh, you two!" said Elizabeth. "Go to sleep."

They wished each other goodnight, put out the candles and soon they were asleep.

10th May 1712

A loud noise woke Peregrine the next morning. Light was pouring through the small window in their room. In its cold, revealing light the room appeared austere and bare, like a wooden cell or dungeon. Large beams hung like bare ribs across the ceiling, supporting counter running dark floorboards. The walls were a pale cancerous yellow, stained with numerous previous occupant's tobacco stains. Still, the bed seemed warm, clean and comfortable.

Then more noises came from beyond the door. Heavy stomps. Doors banging shut. Peregrine recognised them as the familiar noises of a coaching inn's guests starting their day. He had heard them far more times than he could remember.

At his side, Elizabeth was sleeping soundly on her back, the bedclothes pulled down, her arms laying on top. To the side of Elizabeth, Susanna was laying on her side, facing them, the bedclothes pulled up to her shoulders. Lying there together, wrapped in bedclothes, the two sisters looked very similar even though there was seven years between them. Susanna's face was a little thinner, her frame smaller, her height a shade less, but still she bore a strong resemblance to her elder sister. Both girls had thick, black hair which tumbled loosely down to their shoulders...provocatively...

Stop it! He told himself as unwelcome thoughts bubbled embarrassingly to the surface of his mind. He must keep his self-control, his dignity and his fragile self-respect. *She's only fifteen, for God's sake. And she's Elizabeth's sister.*

Elizabeth stirred, her eyes opening slowly with a yawn. "Good Morning," she said with a warm smile.

He kissed her. "Morning."

He looked across and found Susanna was also awake and watching them. "I can't wait till it's my turn in the middle if that's how you get woken up," she said.

"Not always," replied Elizabeth. "Now, unless one of you get out, I am trapped in here."

Peregrine got out first. "I'll go and get us some water for a wash and then we can have breakfast."

He got dressed hurriedly then took one of the buckets that were provided for the purpose and went downstairs, into the back of the inn and filled it from a trough. He went back upstairs and into the room.

Susanna had opened the window and was stood on the tip of her toes leaning out, her elbows on the window sill. Her shift had ridden up above her knees. Peregrine's eyes rose slowly from her shapely ankles, up her young legs to where her shift clung closely to her pert bottom.

He put his hand in the bucket, pulled out a handful of water and threw it on his face.

Elizabeth shook her head, "You're meant to put it in the bowl first. Didn't they teach you anything on the continent?" She took the bucket from him and poured some into the bowl.

"I'll wait downstairs for you two. Give you both some privacy," he said.

"We're all sharing the same room and the same bed," she said. "It's a bit late for worrying about privacy."

"Anyway. I'll wait. Downstairs. Don't take too long." Peregrine left the room and heaved a sigh of relief.

After breakfast, with fresh horses and coachmen, their coach pulled out of *The Black Swan* and turned left down Coney Street. It followed the same route they had walked the night before. At the end of the street turning up into Stonegate. Where it crossed Petergate, the coach turned right and then left into Goodramgate, heading north eastwards. The street twisted right and left between tightly packed houses and then, ahead, they saw the rectangular four storey block of Monk Bar, the gate through the city wall. They rode through the narrow gate directly underneath the building and then they were beyond the wall.

Straight away the character of the buildings changed from town houses into small holdings, set in larger plots with areas to grow crops and raise animals. Then, after a few minutes, they crossed over the River Foss on a stone bridge and they were in open countryside and racing across the Vale of York towards the coast.

The coach climbed up onto Stockton Moor then though a village called Little Flaxton which turned out to be just a handful of houses. As they progressed the flat farmland gave way to the undulating landscape of the Howardian Hills. Woods seemed the dominate more than farmland.

"The hills are named after the Howard family," said Peregrine to try and break the monotony of the journey. "The Earls of Carlisle. They own most of the land round here."

"Are they richer than your family, Pen?" asked Susanna.

"No, I don't think so. Although, the Earl is in the process of having a new house built somewhere over to our left. It's meant to be quite a big place. They've been building it since the turn of the century and I heard that he didn't expect to complete it in his lifetime."

"What is the point of starting building something you won't live to see completed?" asked Elizabeth.

"They don't think in terms of lifetimes," replied Peregrine. "They are creating something for posterity."

"What's posterity?" asked Susanna.

"A legacy," he replied. "Something you leave for people in the future."

"Oh, alright. Thanks. I must seem really stupid."

"No. It's not stupid not to know something. We're all born knowing nothing."

Beyond the Howardian Hills the ground levelled off again and they approached Malton. It was lunchtime by then and Peregrine decided they should stop for some lunch and a break.

Malton was actually two villages separated by a couple of miles of open countryside. Old Malton, up the road, was the original settlement near Malton Common. New Malton was the larger village and was as large as somewhere like Tickhill or Doncaster. The importance of the town lay in its market place and the fact it was where two major roads met, a north easterly road to Scarborough and a northerly one that went up to Thornton-le-Dale and then Pickering.

Their coach stopped for refreshment in Malton market square in front of St Michaels church. The church was a small, basic affair similar to the one in Wales, but constructed of white limestone. It dominated the square, situated right in the centre surrounded by open space and market stalls and much larger than the surrounding properties. Three storey houses with a mixture of styles squatted around the square. Some with wide large windows and white painted render, while many were a lot simpler brick or older black and white timber-framed.

Leaving the coach, they wandered round the market and purchased some pork pies and cheeses for the journey. They bought a round of beer at a local pub then sat outside in the sun, drinking while they ate their pies.

"It's so lovely here," said Elizabeth, putting her head back to enjoy the sun.

"Where are we?" asked Susanna. "Anywhere near the sea yet?"

"I think we are about half way there. Still a few hours away," said Peregrine absently.

"I can't wait to see the sea," said Elizabeth. "Imagine that much water!"

"I suppose so," said Peregrine. "I guess I've taken it for

granted, really."

"Do you think anyone from back home has ever been here?" asked Susanna.

Elizabeth said, "Pa said he'd been to see the sea with Uncle William when he was younger. I don't know whether he came this way though. Where are we going, actually, Pen? I know to the sea, but anywhere in particular?"

He smiled innocently, "We're going to Scarborough."

Susanna turned round quickly, "Scarborough? Really? As in the song? Scarborough Fair?"

Peregrine nodded happily, "The same one, yes. No fair there at the moment though."

"That's really will be something to tell people back home," said Elizabeth. "I doubt if anyone's ever been to Scarborough. It's so fashionable. It's where posh people go."

"Ideal for two posh girls then," said Peregrine idly.

"You're joking. We'll stand out like sore thumbs. I wish I'd packed my blue dress now."

"I don't even own a dress as good as that," said Susanna.

"Stop worrying," said Peregrine with a laugh. "You'll be fine. We're going there to enjoy ourselves. Who cares what we're wearing?"

"Um, well, us," mused Elizabeth, but then she shrugged and smiled. "But thanks, Pen," she said and kissed his cheek.

"Yes, thanks, Pen, you're the best," said Susanna and kissed his other cheek.

After lunch they reluctantly climbed back into the coach. It took the eastern most road from Malton towards Baronet St Quintin's estate at Scamston. The road crossed the estate using a bridge that crossed a dammed lake. They caught brief glimpses of the distant Scamston Hall as they passed by. The road now ran parallel to the River Derwent as it made its way towards the sea on the east coast. The girls kept lookout for the first glimpse of the sea now, although Peregrine assured them it was still some miles away. They passed through a series of small villages, East Hesterton, Sherburn, Ganton and Willerby before arriving at Staxton. Here the road forked, the right going towards the coast at Filey, but they turned left towards Scarborough. Crossing the River Derwent the condition of the road improved. They went through the turnpike on the other bank and paid the necessary toll. Then northwards through Seamer, the last village before the coast.

Excitement grew as they passed through a wooded valley with a large hill to the right – Olivers Mount. The air seemed fresher, the light brighter and more intense. They came into the town along the old Castle Road, ahead Scarborough Castle stood imposingly on the high escarpment of Castle Garth.

"The sea!, The sea!, I can see it," shouted Susanna. She had been sat on the right side of the coach and caught her first glimpse between the houses of the town as they came into the wide sandy bay.

Elizabeth rushed over to that side and they both stared out of the right hand door window. Sure enough, there it was, the North Sea. Between the gaps in the houses they could look down the streets that sloped away to the east and, in the near distance was a vast, grey expanse of water stretching right to the horizon. Like a river, but so incalculably wide that it stretched out and fell over the end of the earth.

The coach turned right, removing their view of the sea, but heading in that direction. Then it turned left along a long straight lane before turning right, half way along and going down quite steeply, following the line of the hill. It pulled into a coach park on the right and stopped. There were several other horses in the yard and another coach.

"And here we are," announced Peregrine. "Welcome to Scarborough."

They opened the door and jumped out into the sun. They were in the middle of town, amongst rows of closely packed, small cottages. There were no gaps and they could no longer see the sea, but they could smell it. The air was fresh and carried the tang of fish. It was different, but not unpleasant. Just one of the small signs that told them they were not at home.

This was different. This was somewhere else. The inn they were staying in was across the road. A white stone large cottage with four large windows and a central door.

"*The Leeds Arms!*" exclaimed Elizabeth. "How appropriate."

"This town's lopsided," said Susanna as she saw the inn.

Peregrine knew what she meant, the road was built on a twenty degree slope with each house several feet lower than the one next to it. Each house was level, but just built fractionally lower down the hill.

"Yes, the town is built on a hill that goes down to the sea," he said.

The inn's door opened into a oak lined room, filled with brass ornaments. A bar was along one side with numerous wooden tables filling the rest of the room. As usual, Peregrine had reserved a room and they made their way up to the first floor. The room was on the front, overlooking the road and had a large window giving it an airy, light feel even though it had the usual dark timber roof and walls. There was a dressing table with washing bowl, some chairs and one bed.

"Looks like we're sharing again," commented Elizabeth.

"I'm just glad Henry didn't come with us." lamented Peregrine. "Three in a bed is challenging, four would be disastrous."

"Aye, and he snores too," said Susanna, opening the window and looking out. "I can see the sea from here! It's amazing!"

Elizabeth joined her and looked out. The sea was just visible between the rooftops. "It's strange. Like you grow up thinking the world is land, but then someone shows you that the world is really all water and your little bit is just an island. It's disconcerting."

Peregrine laughed, "I suppose so. I'd never thought of it like that. Shall we walk down to the sea."

"Oh yes!" shouted Susanna.

They emerged from the inn and turned left, down the hill to a crossroads. They went across, down a narrow, cobbled road which descended at a leg-straining forty degrees angle. The road veered right after fifty yards and then came out onto another road. From there it was just another few yards and then they had arrived.

Ahead of them a broad field of sand reached out towards the sea twenty yards distant. It shone with a golden glow in the bright May evening sun. Beyond it, the sea's gentle ripples rolled in. The sea reached out to the horizon, as smooth as pale, steel blue glass. A monumental expanse of water, it eventually disappeared from view. Not because its limit had been reached, but because the eye could not discern something so far away. It gave an unnerving impression of something that was without end, that could only be constrained by the very dimensions of the earth, where it fell over the world's edge to tumble into oblivion.

To the right, the coast curved round for several miles in a moon shaped bay, extending its embracing arm out in a long distant headland towards the far horizon.

To the left, a row of buildings appeared perched, precariously where the land ended. Behind them rose a steep buttress of rock, bristling with trees and coarse vegetation, Castle Garth. And on its very crest the formidable walls of Scarborough Castle.

"It's incredible," said Elizabeth as she stared at the sea, trying to take in the sight before her. "I'm not quite sure what I'm seeing."

Susanna had already moved across the narrow road and was stood on the beach. She reached down and picked up and handful of sand and let it slip through her fingers.

"It's grains, like fine yellow soil," she shouted.

"It's sand," Peregrine shouted back. "This is called The Sands."

Elizabeth said, "You mean like they use for building? I've only ever seen a sack full." Her eyes followed the line of the beach where it curved round the bay, so far that it became indistinguishable from the rest of the headland. "But here there are miles of it. Countless millions of sack loads."

Peregrine grinned. "Yes. A river of sand."

"It feels good on your feet," shouted Susanna who had taken her shoes and stockings off and was walking on the beach in bear feet. "It sort of tickles."

Peregrine and Elizabeth removed their shoes and stockings and joined Susanna on the Sands. She was right, it did feel good beneath your feet. Peregrine held Elizabeth's hand and together they walked down to the edge of the sea where Susanna was already running around, dodging incoming waves.

The small waves were breaking and running up the shore towards them then falling just short of where they stood. All three of them moved slowly forward, ready for the next wave. The tiny wave raced towards them then broke across their feet. Susanna screamed, Elizabeth lifted her feet out of the cold water, but it was everywhere and she was forced to step back into it.

"It's freezing!" screamed Susanna.

Oddly enough though, the next wave didn't seem as bad and the one after that was unnoticeable. In fact, after a few seconds the water seemed cool and refreshing. One by one they went in further and further until the water was lapping at their knees.

"It feels really good," said Elizabeth. "Although I hate to think what we're treading on."

Susanna was kicking her legs and sending water splashing and spraying.

They paddled around in the water for several minutes then slowly made their way back to the shore. With their feet caked in sand they sat down on the beach. Waves were lapping gently onto the beach in front of them, the sound was strangely soothing.

Peregrine said to Elizabeth, "Once, on one of our rides, I promised to show you the sea and you asked me not to tantalise you. Well, here we are."

She nodded thoughtfully, "Yes, I think you can say you have delivered on that promise. Although, I still can't swim."

"I suppose we can try that tomorrow," he said.

"I'll think about it," she replied. "That water's freezing."

Susanna was making shapes with the sand, making them into small hills and valleys. She said, "Teach me to swim, Pen. I'll try it."

"Alright, I will. So that's something to try tomorrow, then."

Elizabeth said, "You said you watched the sunset over the Ligurian Sea."

"Yes, so I did. I'm impressed that you remembered."

"But the sun's setting behind us. It's not setting over the sea."

"Yes. The sun sets in the west so to see it you have to be on a west coast. The Ligurian Sea is off the west coast of Italy. Scarborough is on the east coast, so the sun sets behind us. I may have to take you to Italy to show you that."

"More promises?"

"Aye, why not? So far I've a good record of keeping them."

"I suppose if someone had told me last year that this year I'd be here I wouldn't have believed them. "

Susanna said, "Isn't Scarborough simply the best place in the entire world. The sea is just so big, and all this sand and everything. It's just...magical."

Peregrine said, "Well, Happy Birthday, even if it is a month late."

"Well, it's the best birthday present I've ever had. So it was worth waiting for."

"It's a pleasure," he said. And he really meant that. He had seen the sea hundreds of times, but he couldn't recall ever being so happy to see it and he was pretty sure that was because they were there too.

Elizabeth looked at him, "You know, we both think *you're* pretty magical too."

"Yes, we really do. Thanks for bringing us here, Pen." said Susanna.

"It's good of you to say so," he said wistfully. "My own family think I'm a bit of a failure."

"They don't appreciate you like we do," said Elizabeth.

As the sun set behind the hill they started making their

way back to the inn where they were staying. Once there, they went into the bar and ordered a plate of slices of beef in gravy with some vegetables. A round of beers washed it down nicely. And another two rounds was even better. As they made their way back to their room, Peregrine felt so relaxed that he just wanted to get in bed as soon as possible. He didn't wait for the others, he threw his clothes off and jumped into bed, making sure he was on the left side.

By the time Elizabeth and Susanna were ready Peregrine was fast asleep.

"You're in the middle again then?" asked Susanna.

"Of course."

Elizabeth climbed in, snuggled up to Peregrine and then Susanna got in on the right side.

"Elizabeth?" whispered Susanna quietly when they were settled in with the candles out. "Do you love Pen?"

There was a slight pause and then Elizabeth whispered, "Yes. I do. It's difficult not to. He's so different to anyone else I've ever met."

"You mean he's got a lot of money?"

"That's true. But I guess it's more because he knows about things I've never heard of. He talks about places I didn't even know existed. It's like he opens a window to another world."

"Would it be wrong for me to love him too?"

"No. But Pen will eventually go away and, when he does, those who love him will be hurt. He wouldn't want to see you hurt."

"But you will be hurt?"

"Aye, I suppose so. I've reconciled myself to that. I'd rather enjoy what we have now even if, losing it later, will hurt."

"Like being in Scarborough," said Susanna. "We need to enjoy it now, because soon we'll have to go home."

"Yes. All things end. Even the good things."

"Then I think I'll let myself love Pen," said Susanna. "Then, when he's gone, I can hurt along with you and you won't be on your own."

Elizabeth took hold of her sister's hand. "Thanks. I'd appreciate that."

11th May 1712

The morning sun lit their bedroom window, but it wasn't that that woke them. From the earliest morning hours a persistent tumult of raised voices and screeching gulls filled the room. Scarborough was essentially a fishing village and the harbour was a centre for bustling activity. Boats that had been out all night came in and unloaded their catches or boats that were readying to go out for the day were prepared early and set off. The activity on the harbour spilled out into the surrounding town as men made their way to work or made their way home.

As usual, Peregrine went and got some water for them to have a wash, then they all dressed and went down for breakfast. As they were near the sea, Peregrine suggested smoked herrings. They had never had them before. Elizabeth like them, but Susanna complained that the bones made them too fiddly. Peregrine had to agree.

Once dressed they headed back down onto the Sands. As before, they walked barefoot onto the beach and down to the water.

"The water's further away," said Susanna.

Looking along the sand, the houses now seemed much further from the sea and a couple of fishing boats were now completely out of the water, stranded on the land like beached whales waiting for the tide.

"It doesn't stay where it is. It flows forwards and backwards throughout the day," explained Peregrine.

"That's a wonder in itself," said Elizabeth. "Look how much water there is. It would require the application of immense force to drag so much forwards and backwards."

Peregrine nodded, "You're right. I believe it is to do with the Moon. At least, the tides coincide with the movements of the Moon."

"How can something in the sky cause the water to move?" asked Susanna incredulously.

Peregrine shrugged, "I admit I do not know."

"You don't know everything then?" asked Elizabeth jokingly.

Susanna interjected, "Because no one's told you. You can't know it if they don't tell you."

"Quite right," he replied. "And no one has illuminated me on that subject."

"No one's told me anything, apart from you, Pen," said Susanna. "That's why I don't know anything."

"Then the next thing you shall learn is about the healing waters of Scarborough Spaw House." He pointed way down the beach, away from the town and towards the headland. "It lies in that direction at the base of those cliffs."

They started walking, splashing through the shallow incoming tide. "And what are the healing waters?" asked Elizabeth.

"Some years ago they noticed that the water from a spring at the bottom of the cliffs stained the rocks red. They found that if they drank it cured all sort of illnesses. It's supposed to be good for you. Now they bottle it and sell it in London. "

"Good for you? Who says that? The people selling it?" replied Elizabeth sceptically.

He laughed, "I guess some people have given good reports."

"Well, they would. Or look foolish for wasting their money."

"Anyway, while we are here I thought we might partake in a small taster. It has put Scarborough on the map. People come from miles around to drink it."

Susanna sounded sceptical too, "Anything that turns rocks red doesn't sound like something you should drink."

They continued walking southwards along the beach. Soon they came within sight of a cube shaped building that clung to the base of the steep cliffs. As they drew nearer they saw that a small crowd had grown outside the building. The building itself was unusually grand, it was square shaped, but of white stone with two storeys of eight windows and a balustrade around the roof. They walked up the beach towards the building and joined the crowd. They were all listening to a man raised up on a small stage.

"Come all, come all," he shouted. "Come and taste the invigorating waters of the Scarborough Spaw House. Dicky's Castle they call this place round here. I'm Dicky Dickinson and this is my Castle. I'm well known round here. Ask anyone. This miraculous water has been reported to cure many ailments in this town for many a year and now it is available for general consumption by your good selves. All for the smallest of prices. Even the healthy will benefit and feel immediately vitalised. " He put his hand to his mouth as if speaking consiprationally to selected members of the crowd, "I have even heard that it has been successful in hardening an older gentleman's ardour if he's been suffering from unintentional droop, if you know what I mean. Can't say myself, I've never had need of any help in that department."

"What does he mean?" asked Susanna

"It's a man thing," said Peregrine. "Nothing for you to worry about."

"So, come all, come all! Don't you want be healthier? Of course you do. So, come this way and start your journey to a better, healthier you. There's a mountain to climb, but this is the stuff that's going to get you there. Dicky Dickinson's my name. I'm well known hereabouts for honesty and fair dealing. Just ask anyone. So come along and change yourself for the better." Then he said quieter, "Terms and conditions apply, available on request for those that can read."

People started moving forward, coins in hand which the man collected eagerly. He then directed them towards the door of the Spaw House. Peregrine and the two girls shuffled to the front and then it was their turn.

Peregrine handed over the money. "Three cups, please."

"Three cups it is," said Dickinson. "It'll put some colour in those lovely ladies cheeks, this will. And, as a man with two ladies to look after, you'll probably be glad of a good slurp before long to keep the old flag flying, if you know what I mean," he laughed and gave Peregrine a knowing wink. He handed them all a cup each.

"Thanks," said Peregrine abruptly. The man's crude asides were beginning to wear his patience very thin.

They walked off towards the Spaw House to join the queue for drinks. At the door a woman was taking the cups or bottles from people, taking them inside and filling them from a small trickle of water that emerged from the rock face in the room. The spring was surrounded by a stone surround, like a fireplace, with drainage to deal with any unused water.

With their cups filled, Peregrine and the girls found somewhere to stand then looked at each other expectantly.

"Alright," said Elizabeth with a smirk. "Are you going to drink yours first, Pen? It was your idea after all."

"Yes, of course," he said unconvincingly. He took a hesitant sip while they watched him intently. "Ummm, lovely, it tastes like fresh strawberries," he lied extravagantly. With that he took a big gulp, finished his cup and wiped his mouth with the back of his hand.

Susanna took a sip. Her face creased up, "Urgh, it tastes awful. Like drain water."

Elizabeth said, "It's not too bad. A bit chalky. And metallic. No unpleasant." She drunk hers completely too.

Susanna had another go, but gave up. "No, I can't. It's like licking a rusty horseshoe."

Elizabeth took Susanna's drink and downed it in one go. "Any colour in my cheeks yet?"

Peregrine nodded, "You do look healthier, somehow. Unless that stuff's affecting my eyesight."

They walked back along the beach. There were a few people on the sands now, they were spread sparsely along its formidable length. Some were bathing. They seemed to just take their clothes off, leave them on the beach in a pile and then walk into the water. The men stripped completely naked, but the women bathed in a shift to retain some dignity. A few were swimming, most weren't.

Wiping the sand from their feet they donned their shoes and stockings and then left the Sands and walked along past the Sandside shops. The buildings formed a rough line along the waterfront with a small road in front. Behind them the ground rose sharply into town and the huge cliff of the castle formed an impressive backdrop. In front of the buildings the harbour pier stretched out from the base of Castle Garth into the sea. There was an all pervasive smell of fish and salt in the air. Boats of all sizes were tethered to the pier from small one man affairs to larger three-masted fishing schooners.

"Where do these ships go to?" asked Elizabeth, who had never seen a sea vessel and certainly no boat of any kind this large.

"Mainly fishing in the North Sea," said Peregrine. "Although the larger ones are transporting farm produce and some minerals down the coast to London."

"London is across the sea?"

"No, the same sea, the same coast. Just further along and up the River Thames. The ships can carry a lot and it's quicker than trying to take dozens of wagons by road"

"London must be a fabulous place," said Susanna dreamily. "The Queen lives there so it must be like Heaven."

"It's a far cry from heavenly to my experience," said Peregrine sourly. "Although it's not without some novelty."

"Is it bigger than York?"

"Yes, a lot bigger with more bridges, bigger buildings, bigger churches..."

"What? Bigger than York Minster?" asked Susanna in disbelief. The Minster was so incredibly large in her experience she could not envisage something larger.

"They have just completed building the largest cathedral in England, St Pauls. It has a domed roof three hundred and sixty-five feet high, the highest in the world. In fact most of London has had to be rebuilt, it burnt down forty-odd years ago. So a lot of it is new."

Elizabeth shook her head in disbelief. "I can't imagine something that big."

Susanna said, "I'm going to go to London one day."

Elizabeth sighed, "Not many people from Wales go to London. Although, Aunt Bett managed to go and live in Somerset so it's not impossible."

"Perhaps Pen will take us," suggested Susanna cheekily.

Peregrine looked out to sea, but his thoughts were elsewhere. "Believe me, next time I have to go to London I really do wish you both could come with me."

Susanna held his arm and rested her head on his shoulder. "Well, I'm sure we can make ourselves available."

Peregrine smiled, "If only it were that simple."

Elizabeth held his other arm and said suddenly, "Come on. Let's get something to eat."

They managed to get some pastries at a shop on the sea front and sat on a small wall and ate them.

After lunch they made their way back down onto the Sands. They walked along the beach a little way until they found a space well away from anyone else. It was easy to do, only a few dozen people were on the Sands and it was so huge it could easily accommodate them.

"Right, let's do it," said Susanna happily and started taking her petticoats off.

Elizabeth sighed and started doing the same. Peregrine stripped down to his underwear, so he was naked above the waist. The girls stopped once at their shifts. Together they walked into the water. At the beginning it was easy as the water rose up their calves. They had spent most of the morning walking through the sea. But, as they pushed on though, the water rose above the knee and it became a little more disconcerting. The girls held Peregrine's hand for reassurance as they moved forward, more slowly. By the time the water was at their waists their progress had slowed to step by step. The parts of their bodies that had been immersed for a time were warm enough, but any water that splashed up gave them a sudden shock of cold.

"We'll stop here," said Peregrine. "There's no point going any deeper if you've not been in deep water before. You can lower yourself in if you want and then, if you're not comfortable, you can always just stand up."

They were both gripping his hands tightly. "What if I fall over?" asked Elizabeth looking a bit shaky, "I might drown."

"You won't drown," said Peregrine. "I'm here, I won't let you."

"I'm smaller," said Susanna. The water was coming up to just below her bust, the occasional wave went even higher.

"I won't be letting you drown either. Anyway, the water holds you up if you fall over." Still holding their hands he lowered himself into the water until it was above his shoulders and then he raised his legs up until he was floating. "See?" he said, standing up again.

They both laughed rather nervously. But they looked a little more relaxed.

They spent all afternoon either in the water or drying off on the Sands. Their confidence gradually grew, not enough to swim, or even completely trust the water, but enough to be more at ease with it. Enough to enjoy it. Drying off was made easier by the late Spring sun being surprisingly warm. They went into the sea several times, each time they became more accustomed to it.

Eventually, the afternoon wore on and the sun lost a lot of its heat so that it took a lot longer to dry off after being in the sea. So they gathered up their belongings and made their way back to their inn up the hill. They had a wash to get rid of the last remains of the sea water and freshen up. Then they changed into clean clothes.

"We'll need our best clothes tonight," said Peregrine, rooting around in his baggage.

"Why?" asked Elizabeth suspiciously.

"I thought we would eat at the Long Room."

"The Long Room? What's that?" asked Susanna.

"It's a bit like Mallander's Barn."

"Like on Twelfth Night?" she said excitedly.

"Sort of. A place for people to get together. Have something to eat and drink. Maybe a dance. It's supposed to be fashionable thing to do in the evening."

"Right," said Elizabeth decisively. "Time for my green dress."

"And what am I supposed to wear?" asked Susanna.

"Your best clothes will be fine," said Peregrine. "At the end of the day, it's a type of inn. Just a posh one."

"I wish I'd brought my blue dress," complained Elizabeth.

"Aye," replied Susanna disdainfully. "Then I could have worn your green one."

Peregrine shook his head. *Women!*

They walked down the hill from their inn as usual. When they got down to the beach, Peregrine led them left along the row of buildings. The tide had now come in completely and was lapping very close to the edge of the road they walked along. About two hundred yards along a wide rectangular building was positioned at an angle, facing towards the sea. It had several large windows along its front. It had an elegant facade with open arches and it had been painted a bright white. A warm, inviting glow was coming through the windows from the candles within.

They went up to the door, Peregrine opened it then stepped aside to let Elizabeth and Susanna enter first.

They were greeted by a well dressed man in a royal blue coat and frilly shirt. "Evening, sir, are you members?"

"No, I'm afraid not," said Peregrine. "We're only here one night."

"Members only, but that's no problem," he replied. "Membership is five shillings and lasts a year."

"Five shillings? That's expensive for one night."

"Each," said the man. "Fifteen shillings for you all."

Peregrine thought if he hadn't already promised the girls they would go he would have told the man what he thought of him. But, nevertheless, since he had made a commitment he got together the required money.

The man started writing in the membership book, "Name?"

"Danby. The Earl of Danby," said Peregrine.

The man looked up at Peregrine. "Well, we can forget those formalities. Please follow me."

Peregrine offered him the money.

"Please, your Lordship, there will be no charge. We are honoured to have you frequent our establishment. Would a window seat be alright?"

"Thanks," said Peregrine as they were led to some seats and a table which were set into a window alcove. The window looked out onto the Sands and the sea. "This will be perfect."

"There are some card and gambling tables over there," said the man. "The band will be starting shortly. Someone will be over soon to bring you any drinks or food. Anything else you require, your Lordship, please ask. I hope you and your friends have a pleasant evening." And he left.

"Your name carries a lot of weight round here," said Elizabeth.

"And everywhere, " said Peregrine. "It is our country after all, as my mother often reminds me."

"Well, it's certainly useful," she replied.

A serving girl came up with a menu and gave it to Peregrine. "Would you like some drinks, sir?"

"Would you like some wine?" asked Peregrine. When they confirmed he said to the serving girl, "Could you bring a bottle of claret?"

"Of course."

"And three glasses."

"Of course, sir," and she went away

Peregrine gave the menu to Elizabeth. "You can choose."

She and Susanna studied the menu.

"Of course, I forgot, you can both read."

Susanna said, "Yes, of course. I'm not stupid, you know."

"No, certainly not," laughed Peregrine.

Elizabeth decided on the capon, Susanna on the pork. Peregrine decided to have mackerel. When the girl came back with a glass of claret, Peregrine ordered the food. He then uncorked the claret and poured it into three glasses.

"This is claret. Should have more of a fruit taste than the wine we had before." he said.

Elizabeth said. "I find with wine that it seems to taste better the more I have."

"I've never heard of claret," said Susanna.

"Well, sip it," said Peregrine. "Don't swallow it straight away. Enjoy the taste for a while before you swallow."

"You're right. It does taste fruity," said Susanna. "I like it."

"Very nice," said Elizabeth. "Is it French?"

"Yes, all claret's are French. From Bordeaux."

"Have you been to Bordeaux, Pen?" asked Susanna.

"Yes, when I was at school. It's a beautiful city in south-west France. Surrounded by wine growing fields."

"You went to school there?"

"No. I went to school in the Netherlands. But we went on a trip to Arcachon which is on the coast near Bordeaux."

"Is that like Scarborough?"

"Well, it is a seaside town. But Arcachon has a very large natural harbour, as big as the bay Scarborough is in. So, from Arcachon you can't see the horizon, just the other side of the bay. I remember that the fishermen's boats are painted bright colours. There is a massive mountain of sand there, a sand dune."

"You've seen some wonderful things," said Susanna. "You're very lucky."

Peregrine nodded thoughtfully, "Not so long ago I thought I was very unlucky. But meeting you all has made me appreciate what I have and I now feel very lucky."

After some time the food arrived and they all tucked in, washing it down with glasses of claret. By that time a string quartet had started up and some of the other people were starting to dance.

"What dance are they doing?" asked Elizabeth.

"I think it's a gavotte or maybe a rigaudon. But I'm not an expert," said Peregrine.

"It's all very formal compared to the dancing we do back home."

"Yes, there's a definite pattern to it," admitted Peregrine. "Do you want me to teach you?"

"You can dance?"

Peregrine pretended to be insulted, "Well, of course I can dance. I'm an Earl, you know, not some farm boy."

"And you could teach me?"

"Us," added Susanna.

"Yes. I'll show the minuet, they're bound to do those and then we can have a dance."

So, after they had finished eating they all stood up and Peregrine said. "Alright, the minuet is this series of six steps. Place the feet pointing apart with the knees slightly bent. Take weight on your left foot and move the right foot forward and move your weight on to the ball of the foot. Move the left foot beside the right. Move the left foot forward and take the weight on the ball of that foot. Then do the same with the right foot. Then do the same on the left foot. Then move the right foot to the left and then bend the knees to be back in the original position. The couple usually circle each other, moving slowly together and then back away and start again. After a bit of practice and if you watch others you'll see how it's done."

They practised, got it wrong several times, but eventually began to get it.

They waited until Peregrine said that the string quartet were playing a minuet and Peregrine and Elizabeth walked out onto the floor with the others. As the music played, they performed, roughly, the steps they had practised. It wasn't perfect, but neither was anyone else, but they didn't go terribly wrong either.

For the next minuet Peregrine took Susanna onto the floor and danced with her. Again, not perfectly, but not disastrously either. And so they alternated throughout the night. Dancing whenever the band played minuets, resting when they didn't. Finishing one bottle of claret and starting another.

Eventually, the evening drew to a close and they left the Long Room and made their less than steady way back up the hill to their inn. The claret was beginning to have an effect by now and they held onto each other for support. On reaching the inn they went in, then up the stairs and into their familiar room. They virtually fell through the door with a burst of inebriated laughter.

Elizabeth and Susanna sat on their sides of the bed and made brave attempts to get ready for bed. Peregrine, fiddled with the buttons of his shirt for several minutes before giving up and pulling it off over his head and throwing it in the corner. He took off his shoes and, by that time, his head was spinning so much that he had to lay down. As the girls were both sitting on both sides of the bed, he decided the easiest route was to just throw himself between them. So, he threw himself on the centre of the bed, still half clothed but totally uncaring. And there he fell asleep.

12th May 1712

Susanna awoke to the usual morning cacophony from the streets outside. The bed felt warm and comforting. Peregrine's arm was around her...

She opened her eyes with a start. It was true. Peregrine was lying on his back next to her with his arm around her shoulders. She could hear the slow, steady rhythm of his breathing. Her head was resting on his chest, so close that she could see the fair hairs. She smiled to herself and snuggled closer. It felt very comfortable. She could almost imagine that he was hers...

Peregrine's eyes opened. *Oh God, no,* he thought. With relief he realised he was still wearing his breeches from the night before.

"Good Morning," said Susanna in the most sultry voice she

could manage.

"Susanna?" he asked with a touch of alarm. "Where's Elizabeth?"

"She's on your other side. We're sharing you. Well, you didn't give us a lot of choice, you got in bed first."

"I'm so sorry. I was drunk, I didn't know what I was doing..."

"Don't apologise. I was beginning to feel left out."

Elizabeth awoke and turned over to the face them. With a smile she snuggled up to put her head on his chest too.

"Good Morning," she said happily.

"Elizabeth," began Peregrine. "Look, I can explain..." With a sigh, Elizabeth put her hand across his lips to shut him up.

"Is he always this noisy in a morning?" asked Susanna.

"Yes, quite often," admitted Elizabeth idly. "He's always feeling guilty about something or other."

"About what?" Susanna asked as she played with his chest hairs.

"Something he's done, or not done, or thought about doing. All sorts of things."

"That's silly," giggled Susanna.

"I know, but kind of endearing," said Elizabeth.

"What's the problem?" asked Susanna. "We're all friends aren't we? I'm very fond of you..."

Peregrine sighed. "I'm very fond of you too. And it's a big compliment. But, well, some day a very lucky man is going to come along..."

"It's all very well saying that," replied Susanna. "But, I'm afraid, we don't get many men like you in Wales."

Elizabeth said, "She means that you're a hard act to follow. And I tend to agree."

"I really am not," said Peregrine. "It just seems like that to you because you haven't met many people."

"It is true that we don't get out much," admitted Elizabeth. "Well, not until you came along."

"Anyway, we haven't done anything to be guilty about," said Susanna.

"Yes, and I would rather it stay that way," said Peregrine. "I don't trust myself and I just know I would regret....um"

"Regret what?"

"Never mind. I would regret it, that's all. I just don't want anyone to get hurt. Principally me, but especially either of you."

"Well, it looks like we both love you, Pen," said Elizabeth jovially. "And I'm afraid there's nothing you can do about it."

He sighed resignedly.

Chapter Eleven

3rd June 1712

As late Spring gave way to early Summer the days lengthened and Peregrine and Elizabeth's occasional horse rides grew longer. The rising temperatures meant coats were unnecessary and hats became essential. They still rode the same horses, Theseus and Cyrene. The animals themselves were like old friends now, accustomed to each other and the regular rides on familiar paths.

They rode the horses out of the stable yard and turned right, along the road through Todwick to the crossroads with the Sheffield road. Crossing it, they carried on up towards Laughton-en-le-Morthern. As usual, they let the horses gallop across Laughton Common in an exhilarating chase. The horses seemed to enjoy the chance to run, going flat out before being gently reined in before they reached the common road.

Crossing the road, they took the horses up the gentle hill towards Laughton. Once in the village, they crossed over and then followed the lane which descended down into a small valley. They had been here before, months earlier, but then in winter they had stopped, but now they continued. Down the valley sides towards the hamlets of Brookhouse and Slade Hooton.

"Mirfin country," said Peregrine with a smile.

"Yes, I'm glad you remembered," replied Elizabeth. "We do seem to be concentrated here for some reason. We've probably been around here in these villages for centuries. As you saw, we don't get around much."

"But your wealthier relatives are here?"

"Certainly, the Mirfins at Thurcroft Hall have been farming round here for a very long time. But seventy years ago Robert Mirfin died childless, so the estate ended up with William Beckwith who married into the family."

They reached the bottom of the valley and crossed the narrow beck of Hooten Dyke where the road began to climb the other side towards Slade Hooton. A side road forked off to the left after a hundred yards.

"That way leads to Brookhouse and Uncle Jack's house," said Elizabeth. "Pa's brother. His real name is Jonathan, but everyone calls him Jack."

"Just two brothers?"

"Three. There was William as well, but he died a couple of years ago. There's a sister too, Elizabeth, but everyone calls her Bett. She's a cook. She married a Quaker and moved to Gloucestershire. I still get a letter from her now and then, her husband writes it for her."

As they continued up the hill, they found themselves riding along a wall on their right.

"Slade Hooton Hall," said Elizabeth. "Some other branch of Mirfin's, not sure what the connection is to us though."

The road turned abruptly to the right, ran for fifty yards and then forked at a crossroads. They stopped where the road diverged. On the right, the wall they had been following ended at two limestone pillars topped with stones spheres. Between the gates hung a magnificent set of ornate, black iron gates, topped in gold. On each gate was a golden M and, at the top, a large, golden, elaborate device – a large M. Beneath it the date, 1698. Through the gates, down a drive could be seen a square, limestone William and Mary mansion with Cornish slate roof. It had two floors and five windows across each side.

"I guess the people living here have a name beginning with the letter M?" said Peregrine with a laugh commenting on the gates.

Elizabeth laughed. "Uncle Jack, Pa and Uncle Will made the gates. Mirfins making gates for Mirfins, so to speak."

"Do you think they're trying to make a point to your family?" he asked with smile.

"Well, if they are, we had the last laugh. That large M device at the top, if you look close you can make out, apart from the M, also the letters R, J and W. Pa and his brother's initials."

Peregrine laughed, "Oh yes! There's a lesson. Never get a blacksmith with the same name as you to make your gates."

"Funny thing is none of them can read or write. Just the first letters of their names."

"It's what you might call making your mark," he said with a laugh.

They walked the horses along the road through the tiny hamlet of Slade Hooton. The village consisted of just a handful of buildings nestled near the hall, three of them were farms. Then they were riding on a slender track that snaked its way between open fields. After a mile the road dipped and they took an even smaller track to the right, following a trickling stream through a dense wood. Finally, after another quarter of a mile, the wood parted into a flat, open expanse of grass and there were the ruins of Roche Abbey.

The abbey was once home to fifty monks, but it was destroyed in the 16th century and, since then, its ruins had laid as a reminder to its previous glories. For the most part, all that was left was the foundation stones that gave some insight into the size and shape of long gone buildings. But, in one corner, the twin transepts of the Cistercian monastery still soared in their Gothic splendour. Towering arches of limestone built one upon another three floors high, after nearly two hundred years of desecration still commanded respect.

Elizabeth and Peregrine dismounted, letting Theseus and Cyrene graze idly on the grass. They had brought a blanket, some snacks and a bottle of sack with them which they unpacked and set down on the grass overlooking the tumbling water of the Maltby Dyke.

A light breeze stirred the newly grown canopy of the nearby trees. The Summer sun high above beat down making Peregrine open his shirt to cool off. They had brought some fruit, bread, butter, cheese and some cold ham. Elizabeth split it between them and then tucked into her own. Peregrine poured them a glass of sack each. He would have preferred a bottle of wine, but Elizabeth was more taken with the sweeter sack. He had to admit that it tasted great. He lay back on the blanket. Behind them the towering ruins of the abbey created a suntrap, raising the temperature even more.

"I haven't been here for years," said Elizabeth, undoing the laces of her stays. "I'm pretty sure it wasn't this hot last time."

"It's a great place," agreed Peregrine. "So peaceful. There's something about old ruins that gives a place a lot of atmosphere."

"Do you think their ghosts are still here?"

"If they have any sense, there are worse places to haunt. Some old castles claim to be haunted and they're just cold piles of stone. Believe me, they're better off here."

Elizabeth sipped her sack. It reminded her of Christmas Day, the first time she had tasted it when Peregrine brought it to dinner. "Yes, I love it here. Our own little bit of paradise."

It reminded Peregrine of something his mother had once said to him, "We are a new Adam and Eve regressing to a modern day Eden."

"There's nothing *modern day* about this place," she replied, absently looking at the wispy, high clouds against the remains of the abbey transepts.

"Just something my mother once accused me of."

"Oh, not *her* again!"

"Aye, her again. But on a day like today she seems like a very distant problem. We are alone in the world, right now. Just you and me in our Eden."

"As I recall, it didn't work out too well for them."

"Well, it depends on your point of view. I suppose it messed up God's arrangements so he wasn't too happy about it. But, from their point of view, they lost Paradise, but discovered each other – which was more important." He paused then said dreamily, "How can I live without thee, how forego thy sweet converse, and love so dearly joined."

"Who said that?" she asked.

"I did, just now."

"I mean *originally*," she said and slapped his leg playfully.

He laughed, "Milton. It's from *Paradise Lost*."

She lay back and sighed happily. "I like the way you keep quoting the books you've read. It's like I have a library and I can read choice pieces whenever I like."

"They just tend to stick in my mind, they always have," he said raising himself up on his elbow to look at her. She was laying back on the blanket, the sun bathing her in its spotlight. She had removed her stays and opened the top of her shift slightly. His eyes couldn't avoid drifting down from her neck to watch the slow rise and fall of her bosom. The tiny cotton buttons of her shift so tantalisingly open.

"Quote me something else," she said without opening her eyes. "Something about Summer."

He thought for a second. "Shall I compare you to a summer's day? You are more lovely and more temperate. Rough winds do shake the darling buds of May, and summer's lease has all too short a date. But your eternal summer shall not fade, nor lose possession of that fair you own."

"And that was?"

"Shakespeare. One of the sonnets, I forget which. It seemed...appropriate."

She opened her eyes and looked across at him. "Alright, I'm in the mood. You can kiss me now."

He did so. In the hot sun, listening to the gush of the beck and surrounded by the gentle, guarding ruins, love was made. And, it seemed to him, in some way, Paradise was regained.

15th June 1712

Peregrine wasn't surprised, but he still felt his heart plummet like a heavy stone and his bowels tighten. Ever since he had realised that he had found contentment, deep inside, a dark core of his being had been waiting for it inevitably to end.

For end it must. Happiness was a transient thing, fleeting. To be cherished while it lasted, because its timespan was limited. The natural course of the world was an entropic descent into decay and despondency. A man could expend his energy, battle the relentless current of time and, with luck, even achieve a brief victory of intense joy. But the torrent was persistent, and soon, he must tire and surrender to the inevitable power of the flood.

And so it was, as he stood before one of the windows of the North Pavilion, looking down into the stable yard, that he felt the first chill winds of Autumn shake the golden wheat fields of his Summer. The natural order of the world began to reassert itself.

His mother's coach pulled into the yard and stopped. The door opened and Lady Bridget climbed down, back from her months long journey to arrange his future. Her return meant only that her mission was complete, that his future was now set. And imminent.

That evening he had walked down to Horseshoe Cottage to be with Elizabeth. They had sat in the kitchen, not the kitchen where everyone else sat, but their own kitchen in their own cottage where they could sit with just each other by the fire and sip tea. They just talked. Reminiscing on how wonderful the last few weeks had been. Expressing earnest hopes of how wonderful they could still be. Taking comfort from each other's proximity and knowledge that, whatever the future held, they would face it together.

She had asked him to stay that night and he had agreed whole heartedly. Neither of them wished to sleep alone that night.

But, come morning, after a light breakfast he had begun the walk back to the Hall. He knew his mother would be waiting. Ever watchful for a sign of his appearance. She had news too impart. She would be determined to take the necessary action to set him on her chosen path. Reluctance knotted his insides, but he knew she had to be faced.

. As usual he entered the Hall through the South Pavilion and made his way up to his room. He entered his rooms hesitantly, checking ever room and every piece of furniture to ensure he was alone. It was with some relief that he discovered he was. He relaxed a little. He took off his coat and changed his clothes. He sat in a chair, alone with his thoughts for several minutes. Then he realised he was just postponing the inevitable. Waiting wasn't easing his nervousness, it was heightening it. The unknown was more fearsome than the reality itself. His imagination conjured monsters and situations far more terrifying than any his mother was likely to disclose.

Eventually, he resolved to go and find her. If nothing else, it would calm his nerves, make him feel that he was doing at least something on his own terms. Create the illusion, however fragile, that he was in control.

He left his rooms and headed to the most obvious place to find her, the Drawing Room. He opened the door slowly, as if he was about to undergo surgery. He looked around the door gingerly.

His mother's voice sliced through any composure he might have had. "Come, come, Pip. Stop hiding behind the door and come in. I've been waiting for you."

With his shoulders stooped and, with them resisting any attempt to straighten, he made his way over to the fire where his mother was waiting. A chair had been positioned opposite her own. All other chairs, were at the other side of the room away from the fire. This was deliberate, he was sure. He assumed his place.

"Did you have a good journey?" he asked, when he found his

voice.

"I always find the actual journey a detestable bore," replied his mother. "But the places I stayed were very welcoming. Your aunts were overjoyed to hear your news. Your grandfather was very relieved. We're all very keen that you take up your rightful place and fulfil your obligations."

"I know you are," was all he could say.

"I went to Brampton Bryan too. I met your bride." She paused and examined him for a reaction, but he gave none. "She's a wilful girl, it has to be said. I personally think that her father has let her have too much of her own way. Her spirit needed to be reined in when she was younger or you'll struggle to get it to take a bridle now. But, that's by and by, I am sure she'll be a worthy addition to the family. She's keen…"

He scoffed. "Keen? She doesn't even know me. And what she does know she doesn't like!"

Lady Bridget continued, "I was about to say, she's keen to have children. Which is, after all, our primary concern here. She's very healthy with a robust constitution, there's no obvious reason why she shouldn't successfully bear them. Of course, one can never tell. Some women can conceive with little more than a single spurt of a man's cream and then drop them in the fields like peas from a pod. Other women have to be doused in the stuff and the fruits teased out from their reluctant wombs. There's no way to say which she is. Our own Queen has been with child seventeen times and still we have no royal heir."

Peregrine felt his spirits dampen with every sentence his mother uttered. His desperate hope was that the Harley woman would get with child at first sitting, so to speak, and bear a son straight away so he could consider his role over and he could get back to Elizabeth. He suspected his hopes were forlorn, but he had to hold onto them.

His mother continued. "Still, the Harleys are generally enthusiastic. But finding an opportunity in Robert Harley's busy schedule proved a challenge. I was initially hoping you would be married by September, but that proved not possible. We eventually set a date of 16th December at Wimbledon House.

Peregrine's heart missed a couple of beats with relief. That was still six months away! Six more months with Elizabeth. Six more months of life before being sentenced to perpetual husbandry.

His mother picked up on the slight sign of relief. "You approve?" she asked with a touch of surprise.

"I approve of the delay," he admitted truthfully.

"Yes, of course you do. Six more months of freedom before you have to take the yoke. I, truly, don't understand you, Pip. I have seen your bride. She is comely, in good health and wealthy. Despite your obvious shortcomings, she is more than happy to allow you to bed her every night. She expects very little or nothing from you in return. I'm sure there are hot, steaming multitudes of young men in this country who would happily take your place with little persuasion. But you, who cannot be substituted, are...reluctant. Even opposed. Why?"

"I do not like her," said Peregrine, limply.

"I could understand it if she was my age, or older. Or fat. Or hideously ugly. But she is twenty-two and easy on the eye. Alright, you don't like each other. I am not asking you to write endless verses of passionate prose to each other. I'm asking you to do what any boy in the street is more than capable of doing. Can you manage that, Pip?"

"I will do what is necessary," was all he could say. What was the point trying to explain to his mother that to marry at all would mean betraying the only thing in his life he actually valued. There was only one person in the world he wanted to sleep with and no wife his mother could arrange would ever be replace her. He didn't try to explain. His mother would not, and could not allow herself, to understand.

"Well, let's hope you can manage a little more eagerness when she spreads her legs for you! I feel sorry for the poor girl, I really do! " She sighed in frustration, "Oh, get out, Pip, you depress me."

Without a word he got up and left. Something he could do eagerly.

30th June 1712

Summer inexorably progressed. The days lengthened until cool, dewy mornings stretched through warm, sunny days into long, gentle evenings. Peregrine spent most of his time at Horseshoe Cottage now. Any appeal that Kiveton had when he had it to himself had diminished with his mother's return. Not that he saw much of her, even when there – it was more than large enough for them to avoid one another. Also, she had her own rooms and he had his. Avoidance was easy. But, when he was there. he was always aware of her presence and the possibility she may appear. It made the experience of going to Kiveton into one worth avoiding.

Besides, he didn't need Kiveton any more. He felt more and more like he belonged down the blacksmith's lane in Wales. At Horseshoe Cottage with Elizabeth or over the road with Henry, Susanna and their father. The vegetables he had planted in the plot behind the cottage were beginning to show their first shoots. It was a sight that almost made him choke with pride. To see all that life appearing in those ordered rows, directly as a result of his efforts, gave him a sense of creation. He had done this. No one had cajoled him or compelled him, he had chosen to prepare the ground, to plant and tend the seed and now, life had appeared in abundance.

He found himself spending an inordinate amount of time simply admiring that garden, watching his workmanship grow and mature towards the promise of a future bounty.

"And the earth brought forth grass, herb yielding seed and tree bearing fruit," he murmured. Then he grinned to himself, "And I saw that it was good."

When he had told Elizabeth that his mother had only managed to arrange his marriage for the middle of December it hadn't had the effect he had expected. They had originally thought he would be married in September or just after, now that was to be put back three months. He had told Elizabeth what he thought was good news. But she had greeted it as just a reminder that, eventually, their relationship would have to end and the uncertainty would begin.

"You are to be married at Christmas?" she had said. That hadn't occurred to him. "Nine days before Christmas Day? No one gets married at Christmas!"

"I imagine that's the only date they could find when everyone was free," he explained with a shrug. It did seem strange when he considered it. "I imagine they are in a hurry."

"Well, I am in no hurry!" she shouted and sat down at the kitchen table in Horseshoe Cottage with her forehead resting on her hand. He sat down next to her and put his arm around her reassuringly. She said, "It's almost a year, to the day, from us meeting."

"Oh aye," he said. That hadn't occurred to him either. "But we've had longer together than we expected to have. I was glad to hear it was delayed."

"Delayed, but inevitable," she had said sadly.

"We always knew that," he said, but it sounded like a weak and pale excuse.

They had carried on with their lives as best they could. As they always had. But something seemed different. The threat of his forthcoming marriage had always been there, but it had been indistinct, unresolved and in doubt. Now it was suddenly as solid as a gravestone with the date already scratched into its surface. No longer an eventuality, it was now a certainty. It lingered in the backs of their minds like a tumour. Knowledge of its presence was enough to discolour their every day.

Everyone knows they will die, but the absence of precision grants them the tiniest hope and allows them to forget...and to live. But that changes should they are discover the precise date they will die. From that point they are waiting. And living becomes a conscious effort of will.

Peregrine went back to Kiveton Hall to sleep every three or

four days. Elizabeth would have willingly allowed him to stay, but he made his excuses and went back. He needed her to feel that it was her cottage, not theirs. That he was a visitor, a welcome one, but a visitor none the less. If it became their home he was afraid that ,when he was gone, it would become a lonely mausoleum to hold her pain. He didn't want that. He didn't want her memories of what they had had to haunt this place like his ghost. He wanted her to still feel it was her home. She had to have a life after him.

So, as the long Summer evening finally darkened into twilight he made his way up the hill, through the fields to Kiveton. The Hall stood proudly on the top of the hill, candlelight casting a soft glow from its many windows. He made his way up through the gate into the courtyard of the South Pavilion and then towards the main door.

The door opened silently, as usual, and he entered the gloomy, empty corridors. Not a soul stirred. The rooms of the South Pavilion were largely unoccupied. Apart from himself. A fact that he relished, it made it seem much more like his own private piece of the mansion.

A distant woman's scream cut the night.

His back tensed rigidly as cold fear trickled down his spine like cold water. His heart fluttered erratically. Eyes wide, he turned to look around, but there was only the empty corridors of the South Pavilion. There was nothing to say it hadn't been his imagination. Perhaps cats? Or a bird? But his rational mind said otherwise. It had appeared to come from inside. From the south east wing.

He grabbed a candle from the table, its moving light caused the corridor's shadows to reach and stretch alarmingly. Slowly, he headed off into the dark corridor, carrying the only source of light. It wasn't enough, a small circle of illumination and up ahead, beyond the pitiful light, a wall of darkness and... who knew what.

He knew he should progress quicker, stride undaunted through a corridor that was so familiar in the revealing daylight. But his legs refused to move any faster, so he proceeded with extreme caution.

As he turned the corner into the south east wing he noticed that there was light further down. The corridor at the far end was illuminated by wall mounted candles. The staff only did that if the rooms were occupied. But Peregrine had thought they were vacant. But all the doors were closed.

He continued down the corridor, faster now that he could see more clearly. Still, there was no sound. No sign of habitation. Perhaps the noise had been nothing. Maybe the result of some playful jollity by whoever now occupied these rooms. Some unbridled expression of gaiety…

Then a door further down burst open and a girl came running out into the corridor. The top of her shift was ripped and she held it closed with one hand as she ran. Peregrine's candle lit her face as she ran towards him. Her eyes were wide with fear, her cheeks stained with weeping. As she hurtled towards him she pleaded for his assistance.

He hurriedly pushed her behind him, raising the candle he held, peering into the gloom. A large man came charging out of the open door into the corridor. Above the waist he only wore a shirt and that was open half way to his navel. He turned in Peregrine's direction, anger flaring in his eyes.

"Where's that little bitch gone?" he stormed.

"Father?" exclaimed Peregrine with surprise. He couldn't have been more surprised if Jesus Christ himself had emerged from the room. "What are you doing here?"

The Marquis paused and looked at Peregrine unsteadily. "I live here!" he shouted. "This is my vessel. I am the master here! Now, where's that…"

"Stop, father," said Peregrine holding up his hand. "Let her be."

His father looked at him with a withering gaze, "You dare to tell me what to do!"

"You're drunk, father."

The Marquis laughed. "Yes, indeed, and I don't intend to let a snivelling little shit like you stand in my way. Now, stand aside!"

Peregrine found his breathing quickening, but he still felt out of breath. "No, I can't. I won't."

"Oh, yes, you can," grunted the Marquis angrily and started forwards.

Peregrine turned round, flinging the girl back up the corridor. "Run! Run!" he screamed at her as he felt his father's large hands grab him and spin him round.

Not knowing what to do, he hung helpless in an iron grip as his father raised a mighty hand. It came down across Peregrine's face with ferocious force, sending the world spinning out of control. Before he could recover, the same hand hit him again on the backstroke, hurling him across the corridor and crashing into the wall.

The Marquis stomped over to Peregrine's prone body. "Think you can best me, do you, lad? Have you any idea how many bar room brawls and whorehouse fights I've been in?"

He grabbed Peregrine's coat and effortlessly pulled him to his feet then thumped him hard in stomach. Peregrine crumpled to the floor like a broken doll, gasping painfully for the slightest breath of air.

"I am Captain here! This is my ship and I'll not have boys like you thinking they can command me!" He kicked Peregrine viciously in the back causing him to groan in agonising pain. "If we were at sea I'd have you flogged until the blood stains your back red or hung like game meat from the arm!" He kicked him again, this time between the shoulders. Then he reached down and picked up Peregrine's crumpled body by his coat. He raged into Peregrine's blood soaked face, "I should break every bone in your body for interfering with my sport!"

But then, surprisingly, he paused and looked up the corridor where the girl had run. He frowned. "But what's the point? The quarry has flown," he said and threw Peregrine's motionless body to the floor and then stormed back into his room and slammed the door shut.

How long Peregrine lay there he didn't really know. He was submerged in an ocean of pain. It took all his effort just to breathe. He dare not try to open his eyes. His head pounded with agony and spun in a dizzying whirl even with his eyes tightly closed. He lay there sleeping for hours until eventually he realised that he needed to move. He didn't want to be still there should his father come out of his room again. His father was unpredictable, certainly abusive and potentially deadly. He had to get out of his way.

He tried to open his eyes, but only one would open and then only partly. It was enough to see by. Getting to his feet proved more difficult. Every nerve and muscle cried out in protest as he tried to get up. He groaned loudly, but managed to get half way to his feet. Holding onto the wall and crouching, he staggered his way back along the corridor. Without candles, and in the dark, his only way back was to follow the wall. As it happened that was the only way he could actually remain standing. He made his way up the stairs and, after an excruciatingly long amount of time he stumbled into his room and made his way to the bed. He threw himself on it with relief, fully clothed, and surrendered completely to healing sleep.

2nd July 1712

The first sensation he remembered was cold water against his face, soothing his wounded eye. Then the touch of a hand on his head that made him flinch with pain. He tried to stir, but it was in vain, the pain of his bruises was too intense and he succumbed and fell back onto the bed.

"Pen, can you hear me?" said Elizabeth's voice. But he could not reply. "My God, Pen, what has happened to you? Who did this?" Her voice shook with concern.

Once again there was the soothing water on his face. He licked his dry lips and with great effort managed to say, "Father. Father is here."

Then panic stirred in him. Father was here, in this building.

And they were here in the same building. They were in danger. They had to get out of here! He tried to command his body to get up, but an avalanche of pain buried him and he could not move.

"Shh," came Elizabeth's calming voice. "Don't try to move. You need to do a lot of healing first."

"Danger. Here," he gasped out.

"We seem to be safe here for the time being. Is your father looking for you?"

"No."

"Then rest here for now. As soon as I can, I'll fetch Henry and we'll get you home. But, for now, just rest."

He didn't like the idea of Elizabeth being in the same house as his father.

"You. Leave," he said.

"Oh no," she said. "I won't be leaving you. Not until I'm sure you'll still be alive when I get back."

"Danger...ous," he managed with his last spasm of effort, then fell back to sleep.

11th July 1712

Recovery was slow, but steady. By the next day he was awake, although still weary. Elizabeth had gone to fetch Henry and they had returned with the wagon. By that time Peregrine was able to stand for small amounts of time and, together, they had manhandled him across the South Pavilion's courtyard into the wagon. The wagon then trundled back down to Wales. As they lowered Peregrine into the bed in Horseshoe Cottage he felt tremendous relief. For the first time since it had happened he actually felt safe.

For three more days Peregrine stayed in bed and was fed warm soups and vegetable broths. At first he had vomited them back, but Elizabeth persisted and eventually his condition steadied and he began to enjoy them. Elizabeth and Susanna cleaned his cuts and applied honey to them to help reduce the inflammation. Every day there was improvement. After several days, he could get out of bed and stand unassisted, although he still ached atrociously. By the next day he had navigated the stairs and sat in the kitchen in front of the fire. His body was heavily bruised, his face was swollen and, at first, he had been unable to open one eye. But, as days passed, the bruising steadily cleared.

Nine days after the encounter with his father he began to feel something like normal again. His back still ached, but even that seemed to be fading. He sat in the kitchen at Horseshoe Cottage and examined himself in a mirror. The swelling on his face had subsided, there was still a lot of yellow bruising, especially around one eye, but that was also improving.

"Luckily you weren't that good looking to start with," laughed Henry.

"Thanks," replied Peregrine sarcastically. He put the mirror down. "Yes, I'm feeling a lot better. Thanks to you lot."

"I don't understand why your father would do that to you?" said Elizabeth, shaking her head.

"I don't know," he admitted. "To be honest I don't really know him. We lived with him when we were children and I always remember him drinking a lot. He had a reputation for a temper. But I just remember him being very distant, not being this violent."

"Did he know it was you?"

"I called him father, but I'm not sure he heard. He was angry for some reason."

Henry said, "I blame the drink. It affects people differently. It always makes me want to go to sleep but I've seen it send others into a mindless rage."

"He had definitely been drinking. I could smell it."

"Suddenly, I feel sorry for your mother," said Elizabeth.

"I think mother knows how to handle him. My father has bigger problems than drinking. He's perpetually bankrupt. He always has been. And mother controls the purse strings."

"That doesn't make sense, he's the Marquis of Carmarthen!"

she said. "How can he have no money?"

Peregrine shrugged, "It's just a title. Grandfather owns everything, not him. Whenever he *has* managed to earn anything it's always been exceeded by his spending. Grandfather supported him when he was younger, but was always looking to marry him off to someone with money. Eventually they found Bridget Hyde, my mother, she was an heiress to a fortune. But she was already married to her cousin. It cost grandfather thousands of pounds to get that annulled. Ever since, father's been living off mother's money. I imagine the reason he's here now is because he's broke."

Elizabeth shook her head. "Imagine being continuously reliant on your mother for handouts? No wonder he drinks. Anyway, I thought he was an Admiral in the Navy?"

"He is. When he first became an Admiral he had to borrow the money from Grandfather just to afford it. He once met Peter, the Tsar of Russia. They got on very well indeed, both being hard drinking men with a love of ships. The Tsar even gave my father the exclusive right to import tobacco into Russia. But, typically, he sold the right because he needed the money."

"Your family are an interesting lot," said Henry.

"That's one word for it," replied Peregrine with a sigh. He reflected how his real family manipulated and abused him and it was left to his adopted family to rescue and care for him. He looked at Elizabeth, "I don't want to go back there. Ever."

She took his hand in hers, "Of course. Stay here with us."

But they both knew that, whatever they might want, that was the most unlikely outcome.

As the day wore on Peregrine felt a lot better. He still let out the occasional groan as he moved around, but at least he was mobile. It was still gentle relief to get into bed at night, knowing that another night of rest would put him even further along the road the recovery.

Elizabeth slid into the bed beside him. The first couple of days after he came back she had been sleeping with Susanna so as not to antagonise his bruises, but after that, she had started sleeping with him again and he was so glad she had. He needed her reassuring presence near him now.

"How are you feeling?" she asked as she lay beside him. There was just a single candle on the table next to the bed. The circle of it's light created a small, protected world where they were the only inhabitants.

"A lot better," he admitted. "I feel even better than I did this morning. I think I'm getting there."

"Good. Because I wanted to wait until you were feeling better."

"Why?" he asked suspiciously. "Not more bad news?"

"Well, no, it might be good news. It depends on your point of view. A bit like the Adam and Eve story."

"Oh yes?"

"I've been feeling sick myself recently," she said slowly, looking at him intently.

He sighed, "Not you as well? Do you think you're sickening for something?"

"No. In fact I've probably never been healthier."

He frowned, "Now, I'm lost."

"I think your heir is going to arrive sooner than expected." Her eyes searched his face for signs of a reaction. "Or she might be an heiress. Difficult to say."

His eyes widened, "You mean you're...you're with...we're having?"

"A little Mirfin-Osborne," she said with a grin.

He pulled himself up in bed, wincing with the effort. He couldn't seem to help grinning like a buffoon, even though the bruises on his face complained loudly. "That is fabulous news!" he laughed. "But how?"

"If you need me to explain that then we really do have a problem."

He laughed again, loudly. "No, no, I mean I thought you didn't want to..."

"No one usually takes any notice of what we want, why

should he be different?"

He hugged her tightly, he didn't care if it hurt. He laughed, "You've made me so very happy. It just feels so right. We've done something amazing!"

She laughed with relief as her own feelings reflected his elation. "I'm so glad you're happy. Because it could be seen as a problem..."

"He or she is not a problem," he said. "The rest of the world is a brutal, heartless mess. That's the problem. This is someone we have created together because we love each other. That is something wonderful."

She hugged him even tighter as she felt tears welling up.

13th July 1712

It was all Peregrine could think about for the next two days. He was going to be a father. But not as the result of one of his mother's breeding programmes, but because he and Elizabeth loved each other and had created new life together. They had chosen each other and their child would be evidence of that. In his view that made it more valid than any concoction dreamed up by his mother and the Harley's. This child would be his first born, his rightful heir – but not his legitimate one. That would be the entire point as far as his mother was concerned. Unless he made it his legitimate one. By marrying Elizabeth before the child was born.

He felt so positive since Elizabeth had given him the news. This changed everything. While ever there had been no heir he could see that the future was in doubt. But now, that doubt was removed. Surely that made sense to everybody? Mother would have an heir. He and Elizabeth would be husband and wife. He could marry someone he loved rather than someone he detested.

Anyway, it was a question of certainties. If he married Harley's daughter there was no certainty they would even have a child. He tried not to think too much about the tribulations of a possible wedding night with the Harley woman. Besides, she may not even be fertile, in which case his mother would have steered the succession straight down a dead end. There would be no prospect of a child and no possibility of divorce or another marriage either. Meanwhile, here was his Elizabeth, already having a child. An heir was already on the way. It seemed insane to pass up on this certain opportunity just to risk everything on an uncertain future.

It was in this positive mood that Peregrine found himself making his way back up the hill towards Kiveton Hall. A few days ago it would be last place he wanted to go, but now he saw that it was something that had to be done. He had to tell his mother his decision, convince her of how sensible it was. That this was the way forward for all of them.

He was still nervous about the possibility of meeting father. The Marquis would still be lurking in the Hall somewhere, probably in his rooms in the south east wing, which meant it would be risky to enter through the South Pavilion. Peregrine's own rooms were in the south west wing, a little too close to his father's.

Peregrine finally decided to enter through the stable yard. This would bring him into the North Pavilion, hopefully as far from father as possible. He didn't know where mother was, she could be anywhere, but odds were that she was either in the Living Room, the Drawing Room or, most likely, her own study which were all in the main building.

As it happened, she wasn't in any of those places. The first room he entered from the North Pavilion was the Saloon and there she was. She was sitting in one of the large loungers scribbling on pieces of paper.

She looked up as he entered, a look of surprise drifted across her features like a shadow in front of the sun. "Pip! You are the last person I expected to see..." She noticed the bruises on his face as he came nearer and her eyes narrowed. "What has happened to you?"

"Father happened to me," he replied sternly.

She looked genuinely concerned, an emotion that looked out of place on her. He wasn't used to seeing it and wasn't sure how to react to it. "Are you alright? Do you need to sit down?"

"Sitting down seems like a good idea," he admitted as he lowered himself gingerly into another chair. "We need to talk somewhere privately. I have some news."

"Alright," she said slowly. "Let's go into the Drawing Room..."

"Where's father?" he asked.

"It's alright. He's gone out hunting with the dogs. He won't be back until much later."

"Alright," he agreed and they made their way upstairs and into the Drawing Room.

The room was completely empty and his mother closed the door firmly shut behind them. Then they went to sit by the window. It faced eastwards giving a tremendous view over the garden terraces and park. On a clear Summers day like today it was possible to see for miles. All the way down the main coach road to Anston church. Beyond that the distant church at Shireoaks and beyond that, Worksop. To the right the sun reflected off the water of Lodge Hill Pond and then, on top of the hill that rose beyond the boundary wall, could be made out the old family Hall at Thorpe Salvin.

"You have something to tell me?" asked Lady Bridget when they were seated.

"Yes," he said slowly. "There's been a development."

"Really?" she replied cynically. "And what would that be?"

"Elizabeth. My Elizabeth...is having a child. We...are having a baby."

His mother nodded her understanding. "So?" she said dismissively.

He was taken aback by her lack of reaction. "I mean that there's no need to marry Elizabeth Harley any more. I'm already having a baby."

"No need?" She laughed, it was a very hollow sound. "There is every need – this family needs a legitimate heir. This changes nothing."

"But I'm having a child," he insisted.

"A child? Yes. An heir? No. You are having a bastard, that is all."

"Not if I marry her..."

"Marry her? You can't marry her, Pip. I won't allow it and there's no church in the country that would marry you against the wishes of the Duke of Leeds. It won't happen."

"But that will give you what you want? An Osborne heir."

"Pip, there's a little bit more to creating an Osborne heir than getting the local village trollop to drop a pup. The heir you will produce will bring the Harley bloodline into the Osborne family. He will be able to trace his ancestry back to Charlemagne. Do you think we would prefer an heir that is a descendent of some blacksmith in Yorkshire? One day you will be the Duke of Leeds! Do you think I would sell you so cheaply? Do you think that is a prize I would give away to the first slut that drops one of your bastards?"

"He will be my son or daughter, as much as any offspring of Elizabeth Harley."

"Of course. But we do not want just any of your sons or daughters. We want the one by Elizabeth Harley. This...child...is nothing. An aberration. The product of a pastime. Worse. It is the base, unwanted result of a frivolous error. It is destined only for a life of grinding poverty. It would have been better if this...thing...was not allowed to survive. If it was erased before it existed. You think you are doing the right thing, but you do it no favours to bring it, fatherless. into this world. Better that it never took breath at all."

"This baby is not the product of an error, it is the deliberate testimony of our love..."

She laughed mockingly. "Love! You are in love, are you? How touching. Will your love wash away the stain of being born out of wedlock? Will your love dry its tears from the stings of a lifetime of abuse? Will your love salve the raw wounds of a fatherless life. Your romantic dalliance condemns this child to a life sentence of bastardy from which there will be no escape. And you say you love it? Would anyone be so cruel to something they really loved?"

"My child will not be fatherless. Elizabeth and I will not allow him or her to grow up unwanted and unloved. As I have."

"You are very much wanted. I want you to fulfil your destiny. To take your rightful place as a Duke of England...."

"No, mother, not me. William. You wanted William to do that. It was never my destiny or place until William died. Well, I reject it. I don't want it. I want something else. Something better for me and my children. "

"So what do you intend to do?" she asked slowly and deliberately.

"I intend to marry Elizabeth and live as normal a life as possible. If you refuse to grant that and I cannot marry her, then I will live with her unmarried. I still choose to be with her and our children. I will not be marrying a daughter of Robert Harley, or anyone else. I have only one life and I choose to live it. For me. Not for you, the Harleys or anyone else."

"Would you risk their eviction? Would you face challenges of that magnitude on their behalf, Pip? You really think your pampered upbringing has prepared you for that?"

"No, it hasn't. In fact, I seem singularly unprepared for any of the hardships I have to endure, no matter which course I take. However, I am resigned to face these hardships with the people I love. It is, in my view, to your lasting shame that you seem intent to inflict them on us."

Before his mother could speak he got up and walked out.

She didn't move for a minute. She just stared out of the window in the direction of the expansive parklands, but she didn't see them, her thoughts were elsewhere. Eventually, she rose from her seat and rang a bell for service. After a few minutes, the Drawing Room door opened and a servant entered.

"Has the post to Wimbledon gone yet?" she asked.

"No, my Lady.," he replied.

"I need to add a letter. Make sure it does not go before I give it to you."

"Yes, my Lady. Will there be anything else?"

"No," she said absently. "I'll be in my study."

Chapter Twelve

Wimbledon was beautiful at this time of year, thought Peregrine's Aunt Sophia as she took her daily exercise along the middle terrace of Wimbledon House. From here the parkland stretched endlessly towards the distant horizon, the private gardens mixing seamlessly with the common beyond and then into the Queen's larger estate. The eye could not grasp it's full extent with any clarity. The impression was of a small country laid out like living tapestry before the Osborne family's mighty sepulchre of Wimbledon House. The sensation of immense authority was almost overpowering. From this vantage point, set high up on the House's terraced hill overlooking the subdued domain she felt a deep pride, as the gods surely must, when they looked down upon their work.

Sophia loved her morning walks. Sometimes she would range far into the park, amongst the trees, listening to the birdsong and ever watchful for the elusive deer. She felt connected to nature here in a way she never quite seemed to back at her home in Towcester. Although she had to admit that the one thing Wimbledon lacked was water. At their house at Easton Neston they had built a canal called the Long Water that ran out along an axis from the entrance. It had been a powerful idea. The presence of water added a great deal to the garden and also, in a subtle way, demonstrated their mastery of nature. Yes, she thought, Wimbledon would benefit similarly from a canal or a lake in the foreground.

She turned and climbed the staircase to the upper terrace, The views were even more impressive from here, improving with height, but somehow it felt more disconnected from the scene. As if the additional height had added a remoteness that gave a better appreciation of the view but, at the same time, isolated the viewer from it.

A servant came over to her while she was admiring the view.

"My lady. His Grace requests that you speak to him in his study urgently."

"Alright, when would be convenient?" she replied.

"I have been told to fetch you immediately."

"Alright. Please accompany me and show me the way."

He led her into the House and then through one of the long galleries and up the main staircase. Opening a door he directed her into a room and closed the door behind her.

The Duke of Leed's study was a large room. The walls were covered with huge tapestries depicting battles such as Towton and Bosworth. The floor was red deal with an occasional brightly coloured rug for contrast. A huge window dominated one wall, stretching from floor to ceiling, split into a hundred smaller panes and held in place by black leading. The window overlooked the northern side of the house, the street beyond and the small village of Wimbledon that huddled at it's feet. And offered a view north over Surrey towards the distant Thames and London. The Duke's desk was set in front of the window. It was a huge rectangle of dark wood, thick and robust, standing on four legs as thick as a man's waist.

The Duke sat behind his desk, his back to the window, looking into the room at approaching visitors. It took Sophia several seconds to do the long walk to the Duke's desk. It was intended to invoke the impression of having an audience with an obvious superior.

The Duke looked up from a document he was reading, his

hawkish features frowning. "Ah, Sophia. I may need to go to Yorkshire and it obviously makes sense for us to go together as Easton is on the way. So I was wondering when you were thinking of going home?"

"I was planning to spend another week here and leave next Saturday. It will take three days just to get to Easton. Stay overnight in London, then St Albans."

"Yes, it's a hell of a way to Kiveton, but I think I need to go up there. Starting off in a week sounds fine."

She lowered herself into a seat. "I thought you didn't like going to Kiveton, father?"

The Duke scowled, "I love Kiveton, but there are two problems with it. Firstly, it's a long way from London. And secondly, there's the chance of meeting your brother."

"I didn't think he was there any more."

"Well, he is now. I got a letter from his wife to say he was staying there. Apparently, he's run out of money again and lost his place in London so he had nowhere else to go."

"So, if you go to Kiveton you'll definitely run into him then. "

"It seems so. But I plan to send some people ahead to make the appropriate arrangements so that your brother and myself will never meet. I shall have my own separate apartments and he shall have his. Provided we stick to the arrangements I can't see any reason why we should ever see each other. Because of this requirement to send some people on ahead, it seems perfect for me to depart with you in a week. That will give me time to finalise some other matters, for Kiveton to get things organised and for me to travel up there."

"Can I ask," said Lady Lady Sophia. "Why is it so urgent that you go to Kiveton?"

"Ah, of course, I haven't told you. I only found out myself today because it was in Bridget's letter. Apparently, young Pip has become involved with a local girl during his stay at Kiveton."

"Oh dear," said Sophia. "I thought he was betrothed to that daughter of Robert Harley's?"

"He is! The wedding is arranged for Christmas. Now Pip refuses to go through with it."

"Because he wants to marry this local girl?"

"Exactly! She's having his child."

Sophia sighed. "Presumably Bridget has explained that he can't be allowed to marry this girl and, without that, this child will be base begotten?"

"I imagine so," said the Duke tiredly. "His mind is set though. I was hoping that he had sown all his wild oats on his Grand Tour and that he could now knuckle down to doing what was right by the Dukedom. But, he must have had some more to sow."

"He can sow what he likes," said Sophia. "My brother has a string of bastards across south east England. But who he marries is something we must control. "

"Indeed, even your brother understood that!" said the Duke with sigh. "So, that is why I need to get to Kiveton. Bridget says she can't control him any more and your brother's useless of course. So it's up to me to talk some sense into him."

"Good luck with that," she said earnestly. "But anyway, yes, you can come with me to Easton and then continue your journey."

"Alright then. I'll send John Lambert up to Kiveton straight away to get things prepared and we can start in a week."

The Duke swore silently to himself. As if he didn't have enough problems to worry about, now he had another. Why did Pip have to be so difficult!

23rd July 1712

Lady Bridget dined alone in the Dining Room at Kiveton, as she did most of the time these days. Both her husband and her son were in residence, but in practice she rarely saw either. But then this was nothing new. Her husband had been absent for most of their marriage, as both her sons had been since they were spirited out of her grasp by their grandparents when they were school children. They had let her keep her daughters, but it meant that she had spent most of her life without male company. Perhaps that was why she was so poor at steering men in her desired direction. She had been relatively successful with her daughters, arranging suitable matches for them all, sometimes more than once. But the men in her life always seemed to resent her. William was the only one she had dared to pin any hopes on, so it was a cruel irony that, of them all, he was the one to be lost.

She finished eating and retired to the Drawing Room. She looked at some letters she had been composing earlier, concerning litigation she was engaged in. The work kept her occupied...and distracted. She studied them intently, settling in for another lonely evening.

So she was startled when the door burst open and her husband entered. Although he looked tidy and well-dressed, there was something about the off-centre way he walked and strange look in his eyes that told her he had been drinking. As he did every night.

He stood in the doorway, supporting himself against it. "Well, good evening, lady wife," he said mockingly. "And how is my dear spouse this night?"

"You've been drinking," she said flatly. "You drink too much."

He came into the room, slamming the door closed behind him. "On the contrary, my dear, I haven't drunk anywhere near enough." He flopped into a chair. "I fancy a nice Burgundy."

"I shall ask for some," she replied and rang a bell on the table next to her. The door opened again and a servant entered. "Could you fetch us a bottle of Burgundy."

"And Brandy," said the Marquis.

"And a glass, my Lord?", asked the servant.

"Yes, two glasses. And bring the bottle," he said and servant left. The Marquis looked at Lady Bridget. "Well, this is pleasant, eh Bridget? Probably the most time we've spent together in years."

"I think the separation has been mutually beneficial for us," she replied. "We do not savour each others company."

"It wasn't always like that, though, was it? I seem to remember in the early days there was affection, wasn't there?"

"No, you are mistaken."

"Well, there was on my side. I felt something for you then, Bridget."

"You've always found pleasure in abusing others, Peregrine. That is not affection."

"Perhaps you find me too uncouth for your tastes?" he replied angrily. "I don't think you examined me as closely when you married me. No, you were blinded by the possibility of marrying a future Duke then. Quite a leg up from your father. What was he? A Baronet?"

"I had hopes for you then. We all had. I've learned to live with the disappointment."

A servant entered with two bottles which he placed near the Marquis with two thick stemmed leaded crystal glasses. After asking if there would be anything else he left, closing the door behind him. The Marquis poured himself a Burgundy and took a gulp of it.

"Aye, my father wanted me to be a *member of parliament*," he spat the last words as if they left a sour taste. "To spend my days chatting and smiling with a barrel of two-faced, conniving back stabbers. I was too plain speaking and too obvious for it. Not like my father."

"Your father is a great man."

"Oh aye, I'm sure history paints him as such. But then he wrote it, so it should. He plotted to overthrow his King, an act that should see him hanged as a traitor. Except that he was successful, so now he is the *hero* of the Glorious Revolution. He arranged for his own country to be invaded by the Dutch, but because they won, we must don our smiles and praise his great foresight. Well, not me, I cannot look him in the face – I don't know which face he is wearing."

"I didn't know you were a Jacobite?"

He took another gulp of wine and refilled his glass. "I have... sympathy...with their point-of-view. He was our King and people like my father waged a war to overthrow him. Where is their loyalty? Or is that just a badge they wear when it suits them?"

"The King was a catholic," said Lady Bridget firmly. "And his son would have been another. England is a protestant country. They were...incompatible."

"But Ireland was catholic and so were large parts of Scotland. He was their King too."

"Ireland! Scotland!" she mocked. "Poverty stricken backwaters. It is England that counts. It always has been and always will be."

"You dismiss them at your peril. Sympathy for the old King still festers there and it will not be easily lanced. It may come to a head when this Queen dies. And she will die soon. Then, who knows what? A civil war with Scotland? A Jacobite Army burning Kiveton? It's possible. We are only a hundred and thirty miles from the border."

"Well, Peregrine, you never fail to disappoint," she mocked him. "It turns out that you harbour sympathies with traitors."

"I am no traitor!" he shouted, but then continued more calmly. "As an Admiral in the Royal Navy I am loyal to the monarch. I leave it to others to decide who that monarch is and to fabricate a plausible explanation of why it must change."

"You are a simple man born into a complex world. How could you do anything but fail?"

"Unlike you, eh, Bridget? You seem to relish these endless contrivances. These confrontations have become your sustenance. You enjoy them."

"I have faced up to my responsibilities. Not avoided them. Like you have. Like Pip is."

"Pip?" He laughed. "Oh yes. Poor little Pip. Not really cut out for the role you're trying to land him with, is he? All your scheming isn't really working out very well is it? The 1st Duke is an old man who can't last much longer. And when he goes, then I'll be the 2nd Duke, not really an ideal choice, but then no one's giving you a choice, are they? Then, after me, it looks like Pip will be the 3rd Duke. Oh dear, he must be another disappointment for you. I really can't see him becoming the King Maker you'd like him to be."

She nodded solemnly. "To be honest I have given up on you and Pip. As you say, we don't really have a choice so we'll just have to live with it. But I'm thinking beyond Pip now, to the 4th Duke. He will have to fulfil the family's aspirations."

"The 4th Duke? Who's that?" he frowned in thought. "Sophia's lad. Thomas Fermor. But what about his father, Baron Leominster? The son would be a Duke, the father a Baron."

"That's not a problem," replied Lady Bridget. "His father died last year. Thomas is already the 2nd Baron Leominster. But he isn't really suitable. He's not an Osborne for one thing. I am hoping Pip will have a son..."

"He's not even married," scoffed the Marquis.

"Not yet. I've arranged for him to marry at Christmas."

He laughed, "Have you told Pip yet? I'd like to see his face!"

She looked down, "Yes. He has refused..."

"I'm not surprised."

Lady Bridget was suddenly angry, "If you were any kind of father, let alone a future Duke, you would talk to Pip and convince him that it's for the best. But, once again, you fall woefully short."

"Why? Because me and Pip aren't following the script you and father have written for us? If I could, I would give Pip my full support."

"Like you did the other night?" she asked coldly. "He was still sporting the bruises days later when he came to see me. No, I don't think he wants the sort of support you can provide."

The Marquis grinned and finished another glass of wine. "It was just a few lumps. It will toughen him up. Maybe even make a man of him."

"A man like you, perhaps? Let's hope not."

The Drawing Room door opened again and a servant entered. "My Lord, My Lady. There is a gentleman here from the Duke."

"From the Duke!" spat the Marquis. "What's he want?"

"He says he is here to prepare for the Duke's visit, my Lord."

"What does he mean? The Duke's visit?" stormed the Marquis hurling his glass at the wall where it smashed into a myriad of fragments.

"I've been meaning to tell you," said Lady Bridget in an attempt to quell his rage. "I've asked your father to come here. To speak to Pip. Well, you wouldn't, would you?"

"The Duke coming here?" he said as if he was having difficulty comprehending what he was being told. "There'll be no Duke coming here. I am in command here. Not him!" He turned to her with fire in his eyes, "And certainly not you!" He turned to the servant angrily, "Where's this Duke's servant now?"

"The stable yard, my Lord. He has only just arrived."

The Marquis jumped out of his chair and rushed over to the door. "This servant of the Duke's must not be let into the House, do you understand me, lad?"

"Yes, my Lord," said the servant although he sounded uncertain.

"I'll come with you, lad, and help. Do we have any pistols nearby?"

"Perhaps in the Gun Room..."

"Good. We'll stop there first and pick up some weapons."

Lady Bridget ran across and grabbed the Marquis' arm, "Stop, stop! What are you doing, Peregrine? It's your father..."

"Get off me, woman!" he yelled and threw her off onto the floor. "We are being boarded! Well, no one boards my ship, not while I'm its Captain! Come on, lad, show me the Gun Room." He marched out with servant, leaving Lady Bridget lying on the floor on the edge of tears.

They marched down the stairs and then down into the North Pavilion. The servant indicated a room to the left. "This is the Gun Room, sir," he said.

"Right. You proceed to the stables and hold them off as long as you can. I shall follow presently."

"Aye, sir," said the servant and ran off down the corridor.

The Marquis entered the Gun Room. It was a small room, but its walls were mounted with an array of pistols and flintlocks used for hunting. He found some gunpowder on the table and poured some into a couple of pistols. He pushed a pistol into his belt and then, with the other in his hand raced out of the room and down towards the stables.

He emerged into the late Summer evening. It was still light and would be for another hour or so. A couple of the house servants were stood in front of the door leading into the Hall. Tom Crowther was stood to one side looking perplexed.

John Lambert stood in front of all of them, his clothes ruffled and dusty after a days ride. He smiled as he saw the Marquis appear. "Ah, my Lord, there appears to be a misunderstanding..." he began.

Tom Crowther interrupted, "These boys say they have been told not to allow John to enter the Hall..."

"Yes," growled the Marquis angrily. "Those are my orders. I will have them obeyed on my ship, Mr Crowther."

Lambert said, "This is not your house. It belongs to the Duke and I am here on the Duke's business. Now let me enter."

"Get back on your horse and leave," said the Marquis. "No servant of the Duke is welcome here."

Frustration showed on Lambert's face. "I understand that there is a certain animosity between yourself and the Duke. That is why I am here. To make preparations so that you and the Duke are sufficiently separated during his visit."

"The Duke won't be coming here, so there's no need for you to bother yourself."

"I assure you the Duke will be here in the next few days..."

The Marquis raised his pistol and pointed it straight at Lambert's chest. "Leave. While you still can."

Lambert stood firm. "If you harm me the repercussions could be severe..."

"Never threaten a man holding a pistol," said the Marquis and fired.

There was a loud bang, a burst of fire from the lock of the pistol and a cloud of smoke. Lambert fell back onto the floor, clutching his chest.

"Oh my God!" exclaimed Crowther, running over to the fallen Lambert. He put his arm around Lambert to support him. "Are you hurt?" it seemed like a stupid thing to say, but that was all he could think of.

Lambert slowly removed his hand from his chest and looked at it. He expected to see blood, but there was nothing. He fingered his waistcoat, but it was unharmed. "No, I don't believe I am," said Lambert slowly, not really understanding.

The Marquis threw the spent pistol on the floor. "I forgot to put a pellet in that one. Just a noise, but no one's hurt." He drew the second pistol from his belt and pointed it at Lambert. "Should we see if I made the same mistake with this one?"

Lambert got to his feet. "I'll leave. But I'll have to notify the Duke."

"You do that," said the Marquis. "And you tell him that this is my house and I'll shoot him, or anyone that works for him, that sets foot here. "

Lambert knocked the dirt from his clothing and went over to where his horse was still waiting to be unsaddled. Crowther went with him.

When they were out if the Marquis' earshot Crowther said,"The nearest inn is in Worksop, and they'll probably have room. What's going to happen now?"

Lambert shrugged, "I really don't know. Tomorrow I'll travel down to Easton Neston and intercept the Duke. I'll explain the situation and see what he wants to do. He probably can't come here while ever the Marquis is here."

"No," agreed Crowther. "I'll tell Lady Bridget what has happened and that the Duke is most likely not to visit as expected."

Lambert nodded. He climbed onto his horse and, with a final grim look towards the Marquis, rode out through the stable yard gates.

The Marquis watched him go and smiled. "Stand down, lads. We've seen them off," he said to the servants who stood next to him.

26th July 1712

It was a long, hard horse ride for John Lambert. He had already spent five days in the saddle before he arrived at Kiveton, only to turned away and find himself facing another three days back to Easton. He found an inn in Worksop easily enough and spent the night there, obtaining food and lodgings for both himself and his horse. He had already stayed at Easton on his outward journey so he simply repeated his original route in reverse, even staying at the same inns. So, the next day he had made the journey to Nottingham, to another inn for the night. After that he rode to Leicester and then, finally he made the journey to Northamptonshire, to Towcester where Lady Sophia's house of Easton Neston was situated.

Lady Sophia, the Duke's daughter had originally been married to Donogh O'Brien, Lord Ibracken, an Irish nobleman when she was eighteen and he was only sixteen. He had died three years later. When Sophia had married again, this time to William Fermor, Baron Leominster she moved to Leominster's house of Easton Neston which he was in the process of re-modelling completely.Sophia was his third wife, but the first to bear him a son, the others only bearing daughters. The Baron had died last year leaving only Sophia and the children in residence.

The main entrance to Easton was in the south west side of the estate though the grand Easton Neston Gate, a huge stone arch topped with Fermor's coat of arms and flanked on either side by four Corinthian pillars. But, as Lambert was approaching from the north, he chose to enter through the more common north west gate which consisted of two ten foot high stone pillars for coaches along with twin side gates for pedestrians. The road snaked up through thick woodland that occasionally parted to provide a glimpse of open meadows. The road eventually forked, straight ahead leading to the west entrance to the main house, Lambert took the left fork which led to the stables where he could rest his horse.

Horse and rider were, by this time, exceptionally weary after over a week of continuous travel. He was hungry and tired, but he knew that he must first see the Duke. The Duke was on his way to Kiveton and, if he kept to his schedule, should have arrived at Easton that very day. The Duke would be due to depart tomorrow so it was urgent that Lambert speak to him this evening.

So, having given his horse over to the stable staff, Lambert rushed over to the main building. The building itself was of a rectangular shape, originally intended to have flanking north and south wings, but these were never completed. It was of a modern, palladian design, each side consisting of two floors of nine windows which reached from floor to ceiling. Lambert crossed the large, square courtyard in front of the house and entered through the main doors.

He found himself in the Great Hall. High, bare walls reaching up to the height of the house with vestibules to either side fronted by Corinthian columns. A servant came across to greet him.

"I'm John Lambert, steward to the Duke of Leeds. It is urgent that I speak with the Duke, if he has arrived, and Lady Sophia."

"Certainly, sir. The Duke arrived earlier this afternoon. They have just eaten and are now in the Drawing Room. If you would follow me."

The servant led the way through the Hall and through some large doors on the far side. The Drawing Room was heavily decorated with huge tapestries of medieval women in orchards or lovers reclining by lakes. Numerous landscape paintings hung along the panelled walls. A plethora of various pieces of furniture were situated around the room, clustered around the mighty windows, the fire or a harpsichord that occupied the far corner.

Lady Sophia and her father were sitting near one of the windows, admiring the view in the summer evening light. The view was of a gentle parkland as far as the eye could see. Directly ahead a large parterre was peppered with sample topiary. Beyond it, a large, bell shaped pond fed a dramatic fountain that sprayed water into the air in a sparkling cascade of pure white. The pond merged seamlessly with a larger body of water, seven hundred yards distant, that created the illusion of a massive canal, as wide as the house, and unerringly straight, advancing towards the horizon – the Long Water.

"Isn't it amazing, father," gushed Sophia. "There's a meadow between the pond and the Long Water but, from here, the eye is deceived and they appear as a monstrous canal. I think Wimbledon would definitely benefit from a water feature such as this. Don't you think?"

But before the Duke could answer, Lambert interrupted. "Pardon the intrusion, your Grace, my Lady."

"John!" said the Duke, startled. "What are you doing here? You're meant to be in Kiveton."

"I have just returned from there. I am afraid I have bad news."

"Please take a seat, John," said Sophia. A concerned look had appeared in her eyes.

Lambert sat in a chair next to them. "You were correct, Lord Carmarthen has taken up residence at Kiveton. I arrived at the stables, but I was refused entry to the house itself by the servants. I was informed that their instructions were to allow no one to enter the house without Lord Carmarthen's authority. I suggested that they should obtain that authority with haste and so Carmarthen was informed. He then, apparently, declined to permit me to enter. I told them that this was your Grace's house and Lord Carmarthen had exceed his authority in not permitting a servant of your Grace to enter. Lord Carmarthen then appeared, armed, and informed me, in no uncertain terms, that I should vacate the premises immediately. I decided that I was unlikely to be allowed access to the house so I departed and came directly here."

"The base scoundrel!" stormed the Duke. "Who does he think he is? It's not his house to permit or deny access to anyone. He lives there on my favour. Kiveton is my house. I built it. I will not be denied entry by that wastrel."

"Father, don't upset yourself." said Sophia. "I'm sure my brother can be persuaded to comply with your wishes."

Lambert said, "He was very insistent. In fact, his words were that he would shoot your Grace or any servant of your Grace who tried to enter."

The Duke's anger forced him from his chair. "He's gone too far this time! I have always been too lenient with that boy and this is the result. I excused his failings. Settled his debts. Apologised for his behaviour. I blamed myself for his shortfalls only for him to fall further. But this...this...is...too..."

The Duke froze where he stood. A confused look clouded his face. His hand rose up to his heart as he suddenly collapsed to the floor with a loud thud.

"Your Grace!" exclaimed Lambert rushing towards him as Sophia screamed. Lambert turned the Duke over onto his back. The old man was obviously in a lot of pain, his features were crumpled with it and his breath was a staccato drumming. "Your Grace! Can you hear me. Try and lie still."

Lambert hurriedly undid the Duke's clothing, which seemed to help, and the agonised Duke began to calm slightly. Lambert picked him up in his arms and carried him over and laid him down on a lounger. The Duke looked as pale as cotton.

Sophia rang for assistance and, when the servant appeared, said, "Fetch a doctor immediately. The Duke is unwell." Then she rushed back to stand over the prone Duke, her hand over her mouth as if to stifle a wail. Her eyes filling with tears. "Father! You shouldn't get so upset," she muttered, mainly to herself.

The Duke had quietened to some extent, but still could not speak and was in obvious discomfort. "John..." said the Duke, so softly that is was difficult to hear.

Lambert leaned nearer, "Yes, your Grace? I am here. Lady Sophia is here too. Don't stir yourself. Try to rest. "

"John...I meant to tell you...." said the Duke with some effort.

"Tell me later," replied Lambert. "There will be time."

The Duke's hand gripped Lambert's arm. "I want William moved...to Harthill."

Lambert's forehead creased as he thought for a second, "You want me to exhume Lord Danby?"

"Yes..." gasped the Duke. He started to shake uncontrollably. Lambert laid across him, trying to quieten him, but the shaking grew worse until it became monstrous convulsions that threatened to throw him onto the floor from where he lay. Lambert gripped him tightly as the Duke's body flexed angrily and spittle foamed madly from his mouth.

Sophia screamed in panic and Lambert's mind grappled frantically for a cure, but he didn't know what else he could do.

The convulsions ceased and the Duke tensed into an unnatural shape as rigid as iron. His breath wheezed from him in a final rattle and then he collapsed back onto the lounger. Inert, lifeless, his eyes wide, unblinking and staring upwards at a distant heaven.

Lambert reached over and closed those frightful, wide eyes then rose slowly to his feet. Sophia was sobbing violently. Instinctively, he held open his arms and she, just as instinctively, came to him. His arms enclosed her protectively.

29th July 1712

The vegetables were growing well at Horseshoe Cottage. Every alternate young lettuce was ready for picking to create space for the others to grow. They were quite a delicacy, fresh and sweet. They were also growing exotic vegetables such as potatoes. Peregrine had never eaten them before as they were generally regarded as poor man's fare and only fit as animal feed. But he found they grew easily, cropped regularly and could be cooked in a large variety of ways and were always wholesome. They were still planting out peas, turnips and spinach to be cropped later in the year. And the remaining crops of cabbages, onions, swedes and leaks all needed regular watering and thinning. So it was a busy time.

Peregrine found that he enjoyed it immensely. He derived a lot of pleasure from watching a combination of seeds, water, sunlight and a little effort slowly transforming into food. He had never experienced such a direct connection between his efforts and what he ate. The idea of sustaining yourself instead of being reliant on an army of others gave him a feeling of freedom he had rarely felt before.

It amused him to wonder what his Aunts would have thought if they could see him now. Hands grimy with soil, clothes and shoes dirtied. Sweating and toiling like a garden labourer in the hot sun. They would probably consider he had lost his mind. From their point-of-view he probably had. But, from his point-of-view he felt that he had regained a sense of sanity and order. He had come round to the idea that it was important to find your place in the world. And that place may not necessarily be the one you were born into.

Elizabeth came into the garden and shouted him. "Pen, there's someone here from the Hall. For you."

He nodded, stopped what he was doing and went inside. The servant from the Hall stood in the kitchen of Horseshoe Cottage. Peregrine was startled by it for a moment. The servant did not belong in those surroundings. He was dressed in a clean, tidy uniform. The blue and gold trim stood out in a room otherwise devoid of colour. He was from one world and the cottage belonged to another. The juxtaposition was jarring.

"Lord Osborne?" he asked as Peregrine entered.

"Yes, I am," replied Peregrine as poured some water into a bowl and washed his hands.

"I have been instructed to fetch you to the Hall. I have a horse outside for you."

"Do you know why?"

"That is all I have been told. It is a matter of importance."

"Alright. Give me five minutes to get cleaned up."

So, five minutes later the servant went out to the horses. Peregrine turned to Elizabeth and kissed her. "I will see you later and tell you what this is about."

She looked worried, "Yes. I hope everything is alright."

He smiled and climbed onto the spare horse the servant had brought and, together, they rode up towards the Hall. It was nearly a month since Peregrine had received a beating at the hands of his father. He was now almost fully recovered, his bruises had gone, but he still felt the occasional twinge from his back. However, riding up to the Hall still stirred a sense of dread and imminent danger. Questions kept rising to the surface of his mind.

Was his father still there?

Was he still drinking?

What was all this about?

They dismounted in the stable yard, handing their horses over to staff and then they proceeded into the house. The servant led Peregrine up to the Drawing Room even though he could have easily found his way there unaided. The servant had been given a task to complete and he couldn't consider it done until Peregrine was in the room.

As Peregrine entered he saw that his mother and father were already there. No one else was present. Peregrine entered and took a seat near, but not close to either of them. They themselves were sat some distance apart. His father's eyes were on him continuously, but he seemed calm and sober.

Lady Bridget began. "Alright, now we are all here. I received a letter this morning from Sophia at Easton. She tells me that the Duke of Leeds passed away three days ago while staying with her."

"Yay!" shouted Peregrine's father with a large grin and started pouring himself a brandy.

Lady Bridget gave him an evil look but otherwise ignored him. "Apparently, he was on his way here and had stopped there for the night. He had convulsions and died very quickly and suddenly. There was nothing they could do. "

Peregrine sighed, "I suppose he was old, but he always seemed so full of life. " His grandfather had been a presence for the whole of Peregrine's life. It was difficult to realise he was gone. "He told me when I came home that he planned to live a long time yet."

"Alas, it was not his choice to make," said Bridget sadly. "But, yes, it was inevitable."

"It's the best news I've had for a long time," said Peregrine's father.

"Are you incapable of any respect?" said Lady Bridget savagely.

"Not really. Not for him. Anyway, this solves a lot of my problems."

"What do you mean?" asked Bridget.

Peregrine's father took a gulp of brandy. "All my life I've been under his boot. Even when I finally threw him off, he could still try to get his way because he always had all the damnable money. Because he was always the Duke of Leeds and he owned everything. Well, not any more. Now I am the Duke of Leeds and I'm no longer dependent on him for money because it's all mine now. So, good news indeed!"

What a disaster, Peregrine thought to himself. His father had a reputation for spending other people's money with frivolous abandon and now he had inherited a fortune. Technically, his father had just become one of the country's most powerful men, but Peregrine suspected that there would not be many people making their way to his door as they had to grandfather's.

"Yes," said Lady Bridget. "We are all elevated to greater titles with the sad demise of the Duke. As you say, you become the 2nd Duke of Leeds and I become the Duchess. Even you, Pip, are now the 2nd Marquis of Carmarthen."

Peregrine said, "What about the funeral arrangements?"

"John Lambert is arranging everything. It is expected to be

on the 8th August at Harthill."

"Well, I won't be going," said the new Duke grumpily. "And I won't have the body brought here either. Or that Lambert. He can take it directly to the crypt at Harthill."

No, you didn't go to your son's funeral either, thought Peregrine angrily. *I wonder if anyone will go to yours?*

"There's something else," said his mother. "William's body is being exhumed from Westminster and is to be interred at the same time as the Duke at Harthill."

"Well, that's good," said Peregrine. "William always deserved to be at Harthill."

"It was your grandfather's dying wish. John is arranging that too."

Peregrine's father rose from his chair and picked up the brandy bottle. "So, is that it?"

"Yes," said Lady Bridget solemnly. "That is all the news I have."

"In that case I shall take my leave. The new Duke of Leeds has some celebrating to do." Holding his brandy bottle in one hand and a glass in the other, Peregrine's father left the room.

Lady Bridget turned to Peregrine. "Have you had a change of heart? Does this news affect anything?"

"In what way?" asked Peregrine.

"You're now the Marquis of Carmarthen, don't you think you need an heir?"

"I'm going to have child in a few months. Whether it's an heir or not is really up to you."

"I cannot allow you to marry her," said his mother sternly. "You know that."

"But I won't marry anyone else." he replied. "If I'm only going to have children with Elizabeth then, if you want an heir you'll have to permit us to marry."

"And make your harlot into the Marchioness of Carmarthen? Think what you are asking, Pip. Can you see her going to masked balls at Welbeck Abbey? Can you see her entertaining landed gentry or members of Parliament? Can you see her bringing up her son to be a Duke of Leeds?"

His eyes fell to the floor. He could envisage all those things. What he couldn't envisage was Elizabeth actually wanting to do them.

"No, you can't see it, can you?" his mother continued. "And that is because, whatever title she acquires and however wealthy and powerful her husband, she will always remain what she started as. A blacksmith's daughter. However desirable it may be you cannot turn your dog into a race horse. It remains a dog."

Peregrine got out of his seat. "Mother, I hope you'll forgive me, but I am in no mood for one of your lectures." He turned and walked out of the room.

He walked down the hill to Wales. As he walked up to Horseshoe Cottage Elizabeth came out and ran towards him.

Her eyes looked at his face for some sign of what had happened. "Well? What was it all about?"

"My grandfather has died," he said simply.

"I'm sorry to hear it, Pen," she said with feeling. "But you weren't close, were you?"

"No, not really," he admitted. "I don't suppose it changes much. Except my father is now the Duke of Leeds."

"Your father? Oh, of course, he would be." They entered the kitchen of Horseshoe Cottage and sat at the table. "So, your father, who beat you so badly, is now the master of everything? He now owns Kiveton Hall?"

"Yes, that's true. He's now the 2nd Duke. "

"You used to say that your grandfather owned everything and that the other members of your family were just resident in your grandfather's house. But that isn't so now. The rooms that you occupy are now in your father's house. You get your income from him."

"Yes," said Peregrine. "My father has always been careless with money and now he has been handed a fortune. Grandfather knew this. He told me once that he hoped that I would be carry out the responsibilities of the Duke. He knew my father would be totally unreliable. He looked to me to be the Duke in all but name. I suppose I've let him down too."

"They ask too much of you," said Elizabeth.

"And you too," he answered softly. "If I am supposed to act like a Duke, then the woman I marry would be expected to act like the Duchess."

Elizabeth laughed. "Oh yes. I can really see me pretending to be the Duchess of Leeds! What would that make Henry and Susanna? Baron and Baroness? Oh no. If I told Pa he'd think I was having a laugh."

"That's what my mother said. That it wouldn't work."

"I think she might be right."

"Then we cannot be married then?" he asked quietly. "Our baby will be base? Illegitimate?"

Elizabeth became suddenly serious. "I don't see any other alternative, Pen. If I was to marry you I would become, what? Countess of Danby?"

"Marchioness of Carmarthen," he said. "Now grandfather's dead I am the Marquis."

"And our baby? What would he or she be?"

"If he is a boy he would be the Earl of Danby, as I was."

"And has being the Earl of Danby made you happy, Pen? Is that the sort of thing you would wish on our child?"

"No," he replied. "If I am absolutely honest I would do anything to prevent him having to endure what I have had to endure. If anything, I would hope he would grow up in a loving family, as you have, and be happy. When I think about it, I could wish nothing more for him than to carry on his mother's family tradition...and be a blacksmith."

She took both his hands in hers and looked at him straight in the eyes. "That means we have some very difficult decisions to make and some significant hardships to endure. But that is what it means to be loving parents."

8th August 1712

The family congregated at Kiveton Hall for the day. Many had arrived a few days before. Apart from his mother and father, his two sisters had also arrived. Mary with her husband, Henry Somerset, and Bridget with her husband, the Reverend William Williams. Then there were his three aunts, Sophia, Anne with her husband, Horatio Walpole, and Bridget with the Reverend Philip Bisse.

Peregrine had never known the hall to be so full of people. They toured the gardens, played on the bowling green at the bottom of the South Lawn, went riding in the park and could be found regularly walking round the Saloon or Great Hall. The Hall, which Peregrine was accustomed to always feeling so empty suddenly felt so full. It was oddly reassuring, as if the place had been granted a lease of life, as if it had finally come into its own and was fulfilling the role it was always designed for.

Mealtimes had become much more crowded affairs too. Breakfast literally filled the Garden Room with people. The evening meals could be held in the rarely used Dining Room with everyone sitting round the huge table there. Peregrine's father never made an appearance at all. He was never mentioned. Everyone acted as if the 2nd Duke had died along with the 1st and had been erased from history to boot. Peregrine himself made an effort to be at all meals, although he often wondered why, as he was mainly ignored. But he found that he did have a fascination with listening to the conversations of others, even if they didn't involve him. He almost felt like a spy at times, invisible but silently eavesdropping on the little secrets that others gave away.

On the day of the funeral all the families coaches were gathered in the stable yard. The yard, usually so empty, was filled with coaches, horses and coachmen. Tom Crowther was running around administering to various stable staff. Oddly, the coffin of the 1st Duke, which was the reason for all this activity, was notably absent. No one dare risk a confrontation with Peregrine's father so the coffins would be delivered directly to the church along with John Lambert, who had spent the night in an inn in Worksop.

It was all very odd. A fact that Peregrine found vaguely amusing. It was typical of the family, he thought to himself.

At the allotted time the coaches all pulled out in procession from the stable yard and turned left down the hill from Kiveton. They went slowly down towards the crossroads with the Anston and Wales road, but crossed directly over towards Harthill. The road ran straight southwards, between small hedgerows which marked the boundaries of wheat fields. Soon those fields would be filled with people, busily bringing in the harvest, but for now they were expanses of gold, shifting and swaying in the wind. The road rose up a small incline, then over the crest and down the other side towards the small hamlet of Harthill.

The village lay on the very southerly edge of the Kiveton estate on a small hill from which it presumably took its name. The coaches entered the village, passing the old farm buildings on the right of the road, before ascending the hill into the village proper. The cottages closed in on either side of the road, their high walls creating a sense of enclosed space that seemed more pronounced when entering from open countryside. They passed the side road that led to Thorpe Salvin and, on the left, directly ahead was Harthill church. The church was set slightly above the road, raised behind a six foot wall and on the top of the hill giving the already high building a commanding presence. It stood in large, open grounds peppered with gravestones. It had a square bell tower and castellated roof over the nave.

As the coaches pulled up they saw that two hearses were already there. One holding the coffin for the 1st Duke which had been transported up from Easton Neston. The second contained the slightly older coffin of Peregrine's brother, William, the former Earl of Danby. It had been exhumed from St Margaret's in Westminster and transported up from London. At the 1st Duke's dying wish that they would both be interred in the family crypt.

The family left their coaches in the road and went silently into the church. The church had been built by the Earl of Warren in the eleventh century. The interior formed a substantial edifice with seating for around three hundred. The nave and tower was heavily buttressed with huge stone pillars. The North Aisle, where the alter stood, was separated from the nave by three Norman pointed arches set on stone pillars with octagonal heads. Stained glass windows mounted in arched, stone frames shone a myriad of vivid colours. Beyond the North Aisle was the chancel which led to the Lady Chapel which held the vault of the Dukes of Leeds.

Once everyone was seated the two coffins were brought in by two teams of bearers, walking in slow, mechanical steps. The coffins were laid, side by side, on the altar at the front of the church.

The Rector, John Hewyt, formally adorned in black and white robes, rose at the front and proceeded to read the ceremony for the interment of the bodies.

Then, as had previously happened at William's funeral, Philip Bisse went to the front and delivered a eulogy. He spoke briefly regarding William, a life in which so much hope had been invested now cruelly extinguished at such an early age. Then spoke at some length regarding the significant contribution the 1st Duke had made to the country.

The two teams of bearers then carried the two coffins through into the Lady Chapel where they were placed inside the family vault with the 1st Duke's wife and parents.

Finally, William is placed in the family vault, thought Peregrine grimly. *As he should have been from the start. Yet another Osborne family debacle.*

As the congregation filed out to their waiting coaches John Lambert came over to Peregrine.

"So sorry to bother you, my Lord, on this day of all days, but as you know I am not allowed to enter Kiveton and I must speak with you."

"That's alright, John," said Peregrine. "And thanks for all your efforts in arranging everything."

"It's my honour," he replied with a smile. "But, I must now start carrying out the details of your grandfather's will. So I need to head straight to Wakefield and then back down to London. When everything is finalised I will need to speak with you regarding the details. I am due back in Wakefield on the 30th August. Can we arrange to meet at Kiveton on the following day?"

"Yes, of course," said Peregrine bemused. "It sounds like you expect to spend most of this month either in the saddle or in a coach."

Lambert smiled. "As I have for most of the last three weeks already. I'm unsure which will wear out first, me or my horse."

"I don't know what this family would do without you, John." said Peregrine honestly.

"It's a pleasure,." he replied. "I shall see you in Kiveton on the 31st then."

"Aye, see you then."

Peregrine turned and joined the others as they walked slowly back to their carriages.

14th August 1712

Summer was a busy time for the Kiveton Estate generally. It was harvest time in the fields where Wheat and Barley needed to be brought in. There was a lot of it and the longer it stayed in the field the more chance there was that early Autumn rain would spoil it. The farms did not have sufficient labour to achieve the harvest, so they supplemented their workforce with seasonal labour where ever it could be found.

Most men, women and a lot of children in the villages were recruited. All the members of the Mirfin family customarily worked on the farms in Summer, as did most of the villagers. It was a communal activity and it felt good to work alongside your neighbours for the common good. It was also well paid, for the small period of time it lasted, and attracted many workers from outside the village - so the usually small populations rose during these weeks.

But it was hard work involving arduous leaning to perform the cutting, and then back breaking bending to gather up the sheaves. The morning work wasn't too bad, but by midday the weather could be hot then the work became sweaty and dusty.

Peregrine has realised that for the next few weeks he would see less of Elizabeth and her family as the harvest would take up most of their day and leave them too tired to do much else but sleep. The best time would be Sundays. Traditionally a day when work was reduced and the Mirfins, like everyone else, usually went to church. During early harvest time they kept to the same routine. As the season advanced, if the work left to do was still significant, they may have to work Sundays too.

When his mother was staying at Kiveton she usually went to Harthill church with any of the family that were in residence. Peregrine often joined them, but not always. He had never seen his father at a service, or for that matter in a church under any circumstances, and he would have been surprised if he did. As harvest had started, Peregrine had begun going to Wales church. His family never went there but, since the Mirfin's did, it was a good chance to see them.

As it was a church day Peregrine dressed finely in royal blue with gold edging. He wore a gold waistcoat with white embroidery, white breeches, a deep royal blue coat and three pointed hat and black knee length boots. He rode Theseus down to Wales, unsaddling him and leaving him at the stables at the blacksmiths before walking over to the blacksmith's cottage.

As he walked in Susanna said, "Whoa, you've made an effort, Pen. You look every bit the Lord of the Manor."

"Why, thank you," said Peregrine, bowing to her. "Might I say, Susanna, you look very fine yourself." She was wearing a new, bright yellow dress laced up the front **which he had bought her recently.**

Elizabeth was wearing her dark blue dress. "We're wearing the same colour, Pen."

"The same dress you wore when I first saw you," said Peregrine. "My favourite."

"Perfect," said Susanna. "You go together just like a couple should."

Elizabeth examined him closely. "Yes, you've brushed up well," she said approvingly. Then, haughtily, to everyone else, "The Marquis of Carmarthen will be escorting me to church today."

"Lucky girl," said Susanna. "I only get Henry the blacksmith."

"And you're lucky to get that," said Henry, who was also dressed in his best clothes.

Robert said, "We'll be the best dressed family there. As long as we look better than the Pinders, I'm happy."

"Oh not the Pinders again, Pa," moaned Elizabeth.

"Jack Pinder borrowed a shilling off me and has never mentioned it since."

"Well, you have. Every time you see him."

"Of course. Nothing wrong with my memory," he said.

"He is getting on now, I thought he told you that he'd leave it you in his will?"

"Not quite," said Robert bitterly. "He actually said I'd get it over his dead body."

Elizabeth shook her head and decided to change the subject. "Are we ready then?"

They agreed they were. Peregrine offered Elizabeth his arm and, together, they all walked up the lane to the church.

John Hall, the curate, greeted them at the entrance and welcomed them heartily to the service. Peregrine was not a regular attendee so Hall didn't recognise him, but at that time of year, he didn't recognise a lot of the people that came to church. There were so many migrant workers in the village during the Summer that attendances increased significantly. The church in Wales had seating for less than two hundred, which was usually sufficient, but during Summer it was at capacity.

Peregrine enjoyed the service. He wasn't a regular church goer and, if he was honest, he was more of an observer than a believer, but he found that being with people who were enjoying themselves was very infectious. He sat next to Elizabeth, holding hands and so close together that he could feel her leg against his. Susanna sat on his other side, singing enthusiastically along with everyone else. Henry was next to Elizabeth and, beyond him, Robert. Robert, in particular, seemed less than impressed with the hymns. Henry more so, but he seemed too self conscious to let others hear his singing voice. But they all seemed happy to be there, almost euphoric.

I can't give this up, he thought to himself as his thoughts drifted. *I can't and I won't.*

With the service over, they all slowly filed out of the church into the morning sun. John Hall shook their hands as they left, thanking them for attending and wishing them a good day.

As they went of the church yard and into the lane, the family turned right to head back home. But Elizabeth pulled Peregrine's arm to stop him.

"Let's go for a walk, Pen," she said. "Just up to the top of the hill."

"Of course, I'd love to," he replied happily.

The rest of the family continued down the lane, but Peregrine, with Elizabeth on his arm, began walking up. Thatched cottages lined the sides of the road as they climbed the inclined road to the top of the hill. After two hundred yards the road levelled out into a flat, open area. The road continued along for another hundred yards.

They stood together right on the edge where the ground dropped away down into the Rother valley, giving a expansive view into the valley and the low hills beyond. Directly ahead was the dense forest of Norwood, hugging the valley side downwards. Where the woodland grew sparse could be seen the plumes of smoke from the cottages in Westthorpe where it occupied the near bank of the river Rother. On the other side of the river the ground rose gently towards Renishaw and Eckington. The end of Yorkshire and the Osborne estate and the beginning of Derbyshire.

A welcome waft of cool air came up the valley, blowing across their faces that were hot from the walk.

"I've been thinking," said Elizabeth slowly as she continued to admire the view. "Working in the fields all day gives me plenty of time for that. We always knew that we would only have a few months this Summer. Then things would change. That was the deal and that was what I, we, accepted. That we would have this time together and then you would have to marry. It was always clear from the start. You were an Earl then - now you're the Marquis of Carmarthen. An arrangement had to be made. And it was. And we accepted it. Reconciled ourselves to it."

"That's all changed," he replied. "You're having our child. I want to marry you."

"You can't marry me. And I don't want you to. Not because I don't love you, because I do. But because of what it would do to our child. If it's a boy it would turn him into an Osborne heir, like you, like your brother, maybe even like your father. If it's a girl it would turn her into an heiress like your sisters or your mother. I don't want that future for a child of mine. None of the people in your family are actually happy with their lives. They should be, they have everything in abundance, except love. That seems desperately short and I want our child to have that. Even if it means giving up everything else."

"I agree," he said slowly, also continuing to look ahead. "I have to protect you and our child. Even at immense cost to myself."

She sighed, "Which brings me to you. I want to carry on as we are, seeing each other, loving each other and bringing up a child together."

"Me too. But they won't allow that..."

"But this is where we are going wrong," she interrupted,

turning to face him. "We must play them at their own game. Your family can do what they want because they wield tremendous power and influence. If you want to do what *you* want then you must accumulate power and influence too. You must become the Duke they want you to be because, once you are, it will no longer be a question of what they allow. It will be what you command."

"It would mean giving up you."

"No. Not if you don't want to. If the Duke of Leeds chooses to see a blacksmith's daughter and raise their child, who is going to tell him he cannot? Would they have told your grandfather what he could and couldn't do? No. He told them what he was going to do. And that is what you must become or you will always be at their beck and call."

"But how?" he asked helplessly.

"By doing what your grandfather tried to tell you a long time ago when you first came back from Europe. Become the Duke in everything but name. That's what he told you, so you say. That he couldn't rely on your father, even though, inevitably, your father would acquire the Duke's title. He needed you to be the Duke your father can never be. They need the Marquis of Carmarthen to take control, because they know the 2nd Duke would never be able to. And once you have control, you can do anything you want. And that includes being part of my life and your child's life. Your grandfather had confidence in you. I have confidence in you, Pen. It's time to have confidence in yourself."

"You think I should marry this Elizabeth Harley?" he asked quietly.

"Yes. For the same reasons that she wants to marry you. Not because she loves you, or even likes you, but so she can get what she wants. And you have to marry her so we can get what we want. The Marquis of Carmarthen needs a powerful wife and she's as good as any. She'll do all the entertaining and socialising that I would never be able to do. Not for you, for herself. And we'll let her, because the more powerful you become the more secure we become."

"Marrying her is one thing. Having a child with her is another. I'm not sure I could ever..."

"That's someone else's problem," she said dismissively. "Not yours or mine. We have a child. We don't care about the Osborne inheritance because our child won't inherit it. If someone else cares about it, it's up to them to figure out a way round it."

"You make it sound so simple," he said.

"It's not simple. It's very hard. But it's not impossible. For the first time, I see a way through."

"Alright," he said resignedly. "I'm going to do whatever you want me to do. As long as you are with me I can do anything...."

"I'll always be with you," she said and kissed him.

Chapter Thirteen

Elizabeth woke with a start and felt a brief disorientation – where am I? Then it all came flooding back and she knew. She was in Peregrine's four poster bed in the Green Room at Kiveton Hall. The blankets that wrapped round her were warm and snug. The pillows under her head were so thick and soft she felt like she was laying on fluffy clouds. She felt his body against her naked back, one arm under her shoulders, the other draped across her waist. He had asked her to come back with him to the Hall last night and spend the night. He needed her support last night and he needed her with him this morning. She had agreed.

She felt him stir and awaken. "Good Morning," he said in a low tone. "Oh, I love waking up with you. Have I ever told you that?"

"You may have mentioned it once or twice," she replied.

"I want to wake up with you forever."

"Forever is a long time."

"Well, for the rest of my life, then."

"*That* I think we can manage," she said.

"Promise?"

"Definitely. Didn't I mention? My husband is the Marquis of Carmarthen. What he says, happens."

"Your husband?"

"Well, sort of. At the moment, at least. Occasionally, he's someone else's husband - but that's just his work. He's always mine really."

"Sounds like he's devoted to you."

"Oh he is. And I am to him. We're madly in love. Marriage – that's just an arrangement between families. Nothing to do with us."

"You are so right!" he said, pulling his arm out from under her. "But now it's time to get washed, dressed and go for breakfast."

"Go for breakfast? Can't we have it in here?"

"We could," he said as he pulled on some underclothes. "On any other day we might. But today, we have to face the world."

"We?" she said, sitting up in bed startled. "You want me to go to breakfast? Downstairs? With your family?"

"Probably just mother. But, yes. No more hiding."

"Oh God," she exclaimed, jumping out of bed. "I need to get ready then."

Peregrine was ready to go down to breakfast in about ten minutes. Elizabeth took nearly an hour. He waited for her restlessly. He wasn't quite sure what she was spending so much time doing, but it seemed to involve a lot of rearranging hair and looking at herself in a mirror. But finally she emerged.

She was just wearing her normal clothes, she didn't have any other at the Hall. But they looked very tidy, very prim, without a single hair out of place.

"How do I look?" she asked nervously.

"Like manifest Heaven," he replied.

"Hardly. But it'll do." She took a deep breath to steel her racing nerves then reached out and grabbed his hand in a tight grip. "Right. Let's go."

He opened the door and went out into the South Pavilion corridor. He led her through the twisting passages until they reached the large doors of the Garden Room. He gave her a comforting smile and squeezed her hand in reassurance and then flung the doors open.

To Elizabeth it was as if they had entered some magical cathedral space. The morning sun streamed through the windows in a blaze of light. It reflected off the veined, white marble floor, illuminated the pale green, flowered wallpaper with floodlit beams. The central table was set with a cornucopia of colour, familiar and exotic fruits in overwhelming abundance, entire loaves and a choice of cheeses. It was more food than Elizabeth had ever seen in one place.

She stood, frozen to the marble. The table had only one occupant who sat at the very top. Lady Bridget had finished her breakfast and seemed to be looking at some papers as they entered. She looked up with a surprised expression, her brow quickly furrowing.

"Pip," she said, as she quickly banished her surprise and regained her composure. "What a treat this is to see you for breakfast. How...unusual."

Peregrine led Elizabeth by the hand over to the table where they took two seats next to one another.

"Good Morning, mother," he said. "We thought we would join you for breakfast."

Elizabeth was staring out of the windows at the extensive terraces, the Long Drive that led down through the parkland to Anston church. The distant hills and, on the horizon, the towers of Thorpe Salvin. It seemed so huge and, the bigger it was, the smaller she felt.

Peregrine placed some assorted fruit on their plates. He picked up a long, yellow fruit and expertly peeled it and took a bite of the revealed flesh. "Banana," he explained to Elizabeth. "Have you seen one before? Try it. They're delicious." She shook her head silently. "That's melon, very sweet. And oranges we grow ourselves. Peaches, you can eat it like an apple, but watch out for the stone. Grapes, of course, and cherries. And figs, they are my favourites, to eat it you...oh, just do what I do. "

Elizabeth had seen grapes and cherries before, the occasional orange, but everything else was new to her.

"An entire education on a plate," said Lady Bridget with a touch of sarcasm.

A servant asked what they wanted to drink. "Tea!" they both said at once. Peregrine laughed. "Yes, tea for two."

"So, she has acquired a taste for tea?" commented Lady Bridget. "How indulgent."

"My name is Elizabeth."

"Um, yes, I think you've mentioned that before."

"Then please have the courtesy to use it."

"I don't need lessons in courtesy from you."

"You need them from someone," replied Elizabeth angrily.

Lady Bridget sighed, "Pip, why have you brought her in here? You know that I indulge your *hobbies*, but there are limits to my endurance. Do you have to parade your deficiencies before me like laurels?"

"No. You can always leave," said Peregrine. "But, before you do, we have a question for you. Is the Harley marriage still on?"

Lady Bridget looked surprised. "As it happens I haven't informed the Harleys yet. I was hoping, apparently forlornly, that you might change your mind."

"Good," said Peregrine. "Because I want to go ahead with it."

"You want to..." she began, looking even more startled. "I don't understand. I thought you were totally opposed to it? Primarily because you, she, was having a child..."

"*We* still are," said Elizabeth.

Lady Bridget ignored her and spoke to Peregrine. "So, why is *she* here?"

"Elizabeth is the one who has asked me to go ahead with the marriage."

Lady Bridget looked at Elizabeth. It was as if she saw her for the first time. "You have asked him to marry Elizabeth Harley?"

"Yes," replied Elizabeth as their tea arrived.

"Why? I thought you wanted him to marry you?"

Elizabeth sipped her tea. "No, I don't want to be part of this family. We certainly don't want our child to be. But Pen does need a wife."

Lady Bridget looked at Peregrine. "And you are alright with this?"

"Yes," he said sipping his own tea. "I detest Elizabeth Harley, but that's no reason not to marry her. You and father can't stand each other either."

Bridget turned to Elizabeth, "And you are prepared to give him up?"

Elizabeth smiled, "I'm not giving anything up."

"Oh, I see," said Lady Bridget. She thought for a while and then said, "I may have underestimated you."

"I hope so," said Elizabeth.

"Alright. Well, that's a step forward then," said Lady Bridget. "We'll let things go ahead as planned at Christmas." She rose from her seat and went round the table. She paused, "Enjoy your breakfast...Elizabeth." She left them alone in the Garden Room.

Elizabeth felt like she could exhale for the first time since entering the room.

"I think she likes you," said Peregrine and they both laughed.

Elizabeth held up a fig, "Now, how did you say you're meant to eat these things?"

They finished their breakfast at a leisurely pace. Now they were on their own in the Garden Room Elizabeth felt that should relax and enjoy her surroundings. She realised that it was probably the first time she had been completely relaxed at Kiveton. Her first trip there had been stressful, sneaking into the Saloon only to be confronted by Peregrine's sister Mary. The second time was when he took her on a tour, but even then she had felt out of her depth, conscious that she shouldn't really be there. Then there were the times when they had surreptitiously sneaked into his room. She had felt safe while with him, but there was always that uneasy feeling that what they were doing was illicit and, at any time, they could face discovery and censure. Even when walking or riding in the grounds she hadn't felt completely at ease. Surrounded by the obvious testimony to wealth and power beyond her dreams, how could she feel like she belonged?

But today, in the Garden Room, having confronted and resolved their differences with his mother, for the first time she felt like she had won a respite. For the first time, with Peregrine sat beside her, she felt that she did have a right to be there. While Kiveton still belonged to a different world to the one she inhabited, and she could never feel at home there, nevertheless, the edgy sense of imminent detection was gone. She felt she could justify why she was there and had no reason to explain herself to anyone.

After breakfast they toured the Hall once again. Retracing the steps they had taken several months earlier, the Saloon, the Gallery, the Great Hall, the staircase with *The Creation of Pandora* ceiling, the Dining Room. Everything was the same as before, unchanged, the pictures looked as beautiful, the statues equally impressive, the staircase took her breath away just the same. But, between them, the whole world had shifted on its axis. Where before he was the Earl of Danby, so high and aloof, and she was the over curious local girl from the blacksmith's cottage, now she was just herself, walking with Pen. Her Pen.

They didn't live here. Their home could never be here. Home was somewhere down the hill in Horseshoe Cottage. But they still had shared memories of Kiveton, a growing fondness and a feeling that they needed to care and preserve it. They would never have met if not for Kiveton – so they owed it that much at least.

In the afternoon they went into the Library. Elizabeth had never been in there before. She had always loved books, but she had only ever seen a handful. The Library had entire walls full of them. Six shelves stacked with books of every colour, size and description. More books than she could imagine ever existed or that she could read in her entire lifetime.

"These are all the travel and history books," said Peregrine, indicating a huge number of books on the middle shelves. "You'll probably find something interesting. Europe, of course.

But also the Holy Land, Asia Minor and the New World. One or two on China, I think."

"These are mythical places," she said. "I don't even know where most of them are."

"Speaking of mythology, the classics are all on the top shelf over there."

"And Shakespeare?" she asked coyly.

"Um, lower shelf on that wall," he pointed. "We have most of the plays, *Venus and Adonis*..."

"And the Sonnet about Summer?"

"Yes, all the Sonnets. I think that's Sonnet Eighteen..."

"You quoted that one when we were at Roche Abbey."

He grinned. "Yes. That was a great day."

"It was when we created our child," she said. She looked at him closely.

"Really? How can you know?"

"The dates are about right. And it would be nice to think so."

"Aye, it was a great day," he mused. "And how is he or she?"

"Fine. As far as I can tell." She rubbed her stomach, "Starting to get a bit of a bump now. Bigger breasts too," she added with a laugh.

He bit his lip. "This isn't a good time for me to be going to Wimbledon to get married. You must write to me and tell me what's going on and how you are."

"Alright. Just make sure you're back by March. That's when it's due."

"Of course. I'll be here - even if I have to walk it."

A servant came into the room. "My Lord, Mr Lambert has arrived. He is in the stable yard."

"Oh, right," said Peregrine. "I'll come and meet him." He turned to Elizabeth, "I'll go and meet John. Last time he was here my father wouldn't let him in the house, I think they need me there to provide some authority before he'll feel comfortable coming in. Are you coming along?"

"No, it's alright," she said. "I'll stay and look at some books."

"Alright. See you later." He left with the servant.

Elizabeth turned and drew out the book of Shakespeare's sonnets and opened it carefully. She flicked through a few pages then decided she preferred travel and carefully closed the book and put it back on the shelf. The Library door opened.

"Did you forget something?" she asked, turning. But it wasn't Peregrine.

A tall, middle aged, bald man stood in the doorway. Despite his fine clothes he looked dishevelled. "Well, well, what have we here? A book thief, perhaps?"

Her heart started quickening. There was something vaguely threatening in his tone or manner that she didn't like. "No, not at all. I'm a friend of Pen..I mean the Marquis."

The man laughed harshly. "That's not very likely. Pip has no friends."

He took a slow step into the room. There was something about the deliberate way he did it that made Elizabeth feel suddenly quite exposed.

"You're his father," she said slowly.

The man smiled, continuing to walk slowly forward. "Yes," he said, elongating the last syllable into a snake hiss. "I am the Duke. You've heard of me?"

"Yes," she said, stepping backwards as he advanced.

"Nothing good I expect. Pip doesn't hold me in a very high regard."

"I wouldn't know."

"Oh, I think you would. Shall I hazard a guess who you are? My wife mentioned that he was involved with one of the local girls. Is that you?"

"Yes. I am Elizabeth," she said with as much assertiveness as she could muster.

He grinned, "See, I guessed correctly. So, do I get a prize?"

"No," she said flatly. She suddenly realised her back was to the wall. "He should be back any minute."

"So what? He knows what happens when he interferes with me. He's probably still got the bumps from last time. No, he won't be bothering us. No backbone, you see. His grandfather sucked the spirit out of him years ago. He spent too long in places like this. Reading his books!" he spat the words out.

Elizabeth decided the best thing she could do was attack. "His grandfather valued him higher than he did you, Admiral! He called you a loser who only knew how to spend other's money, but could never hold onto any of his own."

He stopped coming forward. "You know nothing about me!"

"Your father called you an inebriated no-mark destined for penniless oblivion!"

"Well, he was wrong there. I've inherited his fortune." he said defensively.

"And how long will you keep it?" replied Elizabeth.

He paused then grinned. "You are trying to upset me. That's a very dangerous thing to do with someone like me. I run on a very short fuse. Ask any of my crew." He sat on the edge of a table, between her and the door. "Women have always interested me. They remind me of horses. Initially, so wild, so untamed and so full of spirit. But, to be of use, they have to be trained. That wildness has to be suppressed, that spirit... broken. My experience is that can only be achieved with the application of overwhelming force..."

"Keep away from me," said Elizabeth as aggressively as she could manage.

He laughed and got to his feet, starting to come towards her. "Or what? This is my house. This is my estate and these are my servants. They would not dare to interfere. No one will assist you. You are alone. Your only salvation is in complete and unconditional surrender..."

"You are wrong about everything you just said, father," said Peregrine who was standing in the open door.

The Duke laughed, "And here he is! The hero of the hour come to rescue the fair maiden. You read too much. You're just an annoying pup barking at my heels." He turned angrily with gritted teeth and shouted, "Until I kick you away!"

"A hero? Not me, father. I prefer the odds to be more in my favour."

John Lambert and two other servants stepped through the door and stood behind Peregrine.

The Duke laughed. "These lads? They belong to me! And, as for that piece of shark shit Lambert, what is he doing here? I told him I'd shoot him next time I saw him."

"These are my men, father. And this is my house."

"Like Hell it is..."

"The Marquis is correct," said John Lambert, keeping his eyes on the Duke. "The 1st Duke's will leaves this house and estate to Lord Carmarthen here, not you. I have been to Wakefield and signed it over."

The Duke roared angrily, "I'm going to tear your eyes out..." But then he stopped.

John Lambert had drawn a pistol and was pointing it directly at the Duke. He drew the hammer back with a loud click.

Peregrine said, "Unlike you, father, I'm not a military man, but John assures me that, from this range, he will be able to blow a reasonable hole in you, if necessary. In self defence, of course. " The Duke froze, but his face twisted with ill concealed rage. Peregrine continued. "I have a wager with myself. That, despite your bullying, military bravado, deep down you're as much a failure at being a naval captain as you are at everything else. And, to use your own words, when faced with overwhelming force, it is *your* spirit that breaks. You are a coward, sir. But feel free to prove me wrong."

John Lambert took aim.

With great effort, the Duke's anger subsided. "And what do I get in this will?"

Lambert kept the pistol aimed at him, but said. "Wimbledon House will be placed in a trust managed by the Earl of Abingdon on behalf of a number of beneficiaries including the Marquis and the Earl of Oxford. Some annuities will be paid to some family members, faithful servants and clergy. The rest, including the whole of Kiveton and the majority of the financial assets, are to go to the Marquis. You will receive nothing."

The Duke roared, but he dare not move. "But I am the Duke

of Leeds!!"

"Yes," said Lambert. "You retain the title for life. For what it is worth."

Peregrine said, "I assume you have no funds of your own, and you have already spent most of mother's money. So I will grant you an annuity..."

"You! You expect me to live on handouts from my own son?"

"Unless you would rather I didn't..."

"No, no," said the Duke. "An annuity would be...most agreeable. Considering my depleted funds."

Peregrine smiled, "I thought it might be. But there are conditions."

"Conditions?"

"There are many and I will change them from time to time without notice. Violation of any of them will cause your annuity to be stopped. There is only one you need concern yourself with presently. This is now my house and you are no longer welcome in it. John will arrange accommodation for you locally. But I want you out. Tonight. And you must never return."

His father cooled then, and with visible effort, smiled, weakly, "Pip..."

Peregrine fixed his eyes on the Duke. "Get out of my house."

His father sighed, marshalling all the dignity of the navy admiral that he was, he raised himself to his full height, bowed his head, clicked his heels, turned and left.

Lambert released the hammer of the pistol. "Will he go?"

Peregrine nodded, "Yes, he's been dependent on others money all his life. He knows the routine. Are you staying here tonight, John?"

"If I may. It's been an eventful day. I'm quite tired."

"Thanks for everything, John," said Peregrine. "Get some well earned rest."

Lambert left with the other servants.

Finally, Peregrine turned to Elizabeth.

Elizabeth said, "So, your grandfather really did mean what he said. That he'd make you the Duke in everything, but name.

Even while your father was alive."

"Yes. Looks like you don't have to worry about being evicted any more. I now own the whole estate. Including Horseshoe Cottage. So you can keep that forever. " But his face suddenly clouded. "Do I still have to get married?" he asked hopefully.

She smiled and put her arms round his neck and he held her waist. "You may be rich, but your wife is going to bring her status and social standing and add it to yours. She's going to make you powerful too. No one's going to care about the Duke of Leeds when the Marquis of Carmarthen has all the money and influence. Which means...no one is going to be able to tell us we can't be together. Not even your mother." Her eyes narrowed. "I hope being rich and powerful isn't going to change you, Pen," she said with a worried expression.

"Of course it will, " he said. "For a start, whenever I stay at your house I want bananas and figs for breakfast."

"Well, you can bring them, your Lordship."

They laughed and hugged each other, feeling very happy indeed.

6th December 1712

Slowly the seasons had turned into Autumn. The hot sunny afternoons toiling in the fields gave way to cooler, cloudier skies. The golden crop fields were cut, collected, threshed and taken to the mills to be stored and turned into bread. Grass fields that had dried under the heat into hay were cut and formed into bales for animal feed through the winter.

As the end of the harvest had approached, celebratory parties erupted, apparently spontaneously, across the villages. Slowly, as the Summer work wound down so did the populations as the transient workers began to make their way home. After the frantic activity of the Summer the estate began to wind down to a more sedate, and more normal, pace. The activities, that had been suspended while the Summer harvest drained the village of labour, began to reopen and resume.

Robert and Henry fired up the furnace every day. Tools that had taken a battering during the Summer now needed fixing or replacing. There was plenty of smithy work to be done. Elizabeth and Susanna concentrated on getting up to date with many household tasks that had been neglected.

Peregrine visited most days and, as Autumn ripened, he usually brought lots of fruit and vegetables. The kitchen gardens at Kiveton were overloaded with a glut of produce and were only too glad to reduce their stock. The plot at the back of Horseshoe Cottage had been just a productive, with an explosion of vegetables. Peregrine was really quite proud of his achievements in the plot to say he had never done it before. He found a tremendous fascination in watching plants grow from a seed, sun, soil and some water into a a thriving, healthy crop that you could consume. There was a kind of miracle in it.

John Hall, the curate, must have thought so. On one of his infrequent visits he had inspected the abundant plot while Peregrine, Henry and Robert were busy in it.

"You and God have worked wonders in this garden," he announced proudly.

"Aye," replied Robert ruefully. "He didn't do so well when he had it to himself."

Peregrine found them to be simple, happy times. His mother spent less and less time at Kiveton. She had adopted some responsibility for his marriage preparations which required her to be in Wimbledon. When she wasn't there she had decided to spend more time at Aldbury Manor in Hertfordshire, a manor left to her by her father. Her occasional visits to Kiveton were largely to discuss marriage or some other duty. The 1st Duke's insistence that he be the Duke in everything but name involved a lot more than just marrying Elizabeth Harley, there would be social engagements to arrange and attend. His mother informed him that a date had been set for him to be elevated to the House of Lords, 25th January. He didn't actually know what he would do there, but his mother had advised it would be a good idea to try and keep up with current affairs, such as Queen Anne's deteriorating health.

Peregrine and his mother had arrived at a kind of truce. Elizabeth had been correct. While ever he fulfilled his obligations, even if only for appearances sake, then his mother would leave them alone. His mother seemed resigned to the fact that Peregrine would never be a dynamic Duke, carving out a name for himself in history and guiding the country. He was just not that sort of person. Peregrine got the impression that his mother was already looking beyond him, and had pinned her hopes on the 4th Duke. Peregrine just needed to, first of all, get married, and then have a son. The first part of that, he was also resigned to. The second, he had some serious reservations about. Of all the aspects of his wedding that most worried him, the prospect of the wedding night worried him most of all. And every night after that too, if he was honest.

Elizabeth was very cavalier about it. As far as she was concerned, she didn't care whether Elizabeth Harley had a child, so Peregrine shouldn't either. Who cares if they never slept together and there never was an heir. Peregrine could see her reasoning, but couldn't help thinking that, in a lot of peoples eyes, that was the entire point. Even the Harley woman herself was prepared to, literally, lay down for the cause. They expected him to do the same and he knew he wasn't strong enough to fight them.

The knowledge that, in the not too distant future, he would be married and have to face these issues one way or another, detracted from the present like a spot on the sun. As every day grew a little bit shorter than the day before so his worries grew a little bit larger. Gentle breezes gave way to cold winds. Refreshing showers became persistent drizzle and the verdant leaves lost their sheen and crisped into brown decay. So the first clouds of Peregrine's future began to darken his days like an approaching, distant storm. Until, eventually, the first hard frosts of winter sprayed the hedges and fields with cold crystal and Peregrine knew Christmas would soon be upon them.

As the Christmas season began, one morning Peregrine ordered that his coach be made ready and boarded it in the stable yard. Under Peregrine's direction the coach made its way down into Wales. It turned right at the crossroads in Wales and made its way down to Horseshoe Cottage, but instead turned right into the blacksmith's yard and pulled to halt. The door opened and Peregrine got out dressed in his best blue and gold coat and waistcoat. He carried a series of parcels into the cottage kitchen.

Susanna and Elizabeth were in the kitchen. They wished him good morning and Elizabeth kissed his cheek.

"You're all dressed up," she commented. "Going somewhere nice?"

"Hopefully," he said mysteriously. "Today's a special day."

"It's St Nicholas Day!" interrupted Susanna with excitement. "We're getting some presents later."

Peregrine grinned, "Well, I'm giving mine early. Can you go and get Henry and your father?"

"Alright," said Susanna with excitement and went out to the forge where they were working.

"So, are you going to tell me why you're all dressed up?" asked Elizabeth.

"Not yet," he replied. "Soon."

Susanna came bursting back in and Henry and their father followed along afterwards. They all sat down by the table. Peregrine remained standing.

"It's the start of Christmas," said Peregrine. "Time to give gifts to those who are important to us. And, believe me, no one is more important to me than you four. I can say, with all honesty, that meeting you all last Christmas changed my life. And probably saved it." He felt himself beginning to choke up, "So, before I get too emotional, let's open some presents! Starting with the head of the household."

He passed a large wooden box over the Robert. "Well, thanks, I wasn't expecting anything...." He opened the box and was greeted with the sweet scent of tobacco.

"Cigars. From the new Spanish plantations in the Caribbean. Reputed to be the best smoking tobacco in the world."

Robert took out a cigar and smelled it lovingly. "It certainly smells very good. Thanks a lot. I'll enjoy trying them. One a week, I think, to make them last."

Peregrine took one box out, leaving another four large parcels on the table and floor. "All those are yours, Henry," he said.

"All of them?"

"Yes, all of them."

Henry tore the wrapping off one, revealing a gleaming white waistcoat. Another parcel contained some fine, light brown breeches. Another, some black knee length boots. And the final one a bottle green jacket with gold patterned edging.

Henry was wide eyed, "These clothes are too good for me. I've never had anything so grand."

"Then it's about time," said Peregrine. "A complete outfit. For special occasions."

Susanna said, "If Mary Parkin sees you in that you are never going to be free of her!"

They laughed. Peregrine passed the final box over to Susanna. She took it with excitement and, with a big grin, opened the lid.

Her mouth fell open and she just stared.

"Got nothing to say?" asked Peregrine with a smile.

She pulled it carefully out of its case and held it up in her hands. It was a gleaming silver necklace with a silver butterfly wing clasp which held a teardrop shaped gem. The gem shone with strands of blue, green and red.

"It's the most beautiful thing I've ever seen," said Susanna.

Peregrine went round the table, gently took the necklace from her and put it round her neck, fastening it at the back.

"It's nine carat silver. The gem is a black Opal, from Africa."

"It must be worth a Queen's ransom," said Henry.

"No, not quite," said Peregrine with a smile. "But I'm sure the Queen would like it. Which is her bad luck, because it's for the second best girl in my life."

Susanna turned and threw her arms round him, "Thanks, Pen, thanks."

"I can't wait to see what the first best girl's going to get," said Elizabeth coyly.

"Ah, for that you need to accompany me. I have a coach waiting outside."

"Oh no," said Elizabeth with a grin. "You could have warned me."

"Now where would be the fun in that?" said Peregrine. "Shall we go?"

They went out of cottage and climbed into Peregrine's coach. Despite herself, Elizabeth was beginning to feel pretty excited, especially as the coach drew away and she waved madly back at Susanna, Henry and Robert who were waving her off.

"So, what's all this about, Pen?" she demanded as she sat back in the coach.

"A surprise," was all he said.

"I've got you something, but it's back at home. I wish I'd got you more now..."

"We are not competitors. What you've already given me is priceless."

"We're not rich like you. It makes me feel...inadequate."

He laughed. "No, I'm the one who is inadequate. You're the one that saved me, remember? You are the lodestone of my life. Without you, I am lost."

The coach went up towards Kiveton Hall and pulled into the stable yard. Peregrine got out and then took her hand and led her into the Hall through the North Pavilion. Once in the main building they entered a door that Elizabeth had never been through before. They were in a small, vestibule waiting room. It was completely bare apart from one chair in the corner.

On the chair was laid a dress. It was as white as snow with a square neckline, sleeves from shoulder to elbow which ended in ruffles. It had a quilted petticoat embossed with flowers and leaves. Around the neckline was a three inch wide border of white lace and, sown into the lace, an abundance of small sequins that caught the light and radiated a delicate rainbow of colours.

"You have a blue dress and a green one. Now you have a white one," said Peregrine.

Elizabeth touched the lace and sequins. "It's beautiful. Very intricate. It looks... expensive.

"Nottingham lace inset with mother of pearl," he said.

She said helplessly. "I don't know what to say. Or how to thank you."

"Well, then do me a favour. Put it on," he said. "And then follow me." He opened a door in the far wall and disappeared through, leaving her alone.

She shrugged and started taking her petticoats off. Minutes later she was only dressed in a shift and then she started putting on the white dress. She was now six months pregnant and had a very visible bump, but the dress seemed to have been created with it in mind and fitted her perfectly. She spun round, noting how the dress moved as easily as she did. It felt wonderful and, as she looked at the shimmer, it made her feel so very special. She loved it.

She opened the door and followed Peregrine.

He was waiting on the other side and took her hand as she came through. "Welcome to the Chapel."

She looked round. The Chapel was a square room with four rows of oak pews separated by a small aisle. The room itself was double height, the bottom covered in walnut panelling. Above that the walls were covered in colourful frescoes depicting biblical scenes. On the far wall was an ornate alcove largely made of white marble carved with statues of old testament figures. It rose to the full height of the room, the top half centred with a painting of Jesus washing a disciples feet. Set in the alcove was a marble altar.

Peregrine led her down the aisle of empty pews to the altar.

He took her hands and said, "Officially, we cannot marry. But, unofficially...Well, what's the point having your own

Chapel if you can't get married in it? "

"An unofficial marriage?" she asked quizzically.

"Yes. I want us to make a promise to each other before any other promises are forced from me. This one will be first, and it will diminish and annul the significance of anything that comes after. Between us, where it matters, we will be married." He gripped her hand tightly, "So, Elizabeth Mirfin, will you marry me?"

She looked at him and smiled. "Yes, of course I will."

He took a small box out of his pocket and passed it to her. She opened it slowly, inside was a ring mounted with a square cut, deep purple blue gem.

"Amethyst," he said. With her hands in his and, looking directly at her, he began. "I, Peregrine Hyde Osborne, take thee, Elizabeth Mirfin, to be my wedded Wife, to have and to hold from this day forward, for better for worse, for richer for poorer, in sickness and in health, to love and to cherish, till death do us part."

She replied, with some assistance, "I, Elizabeth Mirfin, take thee, Peregrine Hyde Osborne, to be my wedded Husband, to have and to hold from this day forward, for better for worse, for richer for poorer, in sickness and in health, to love and to cherish, till death do us part."

He took the Amythyst ring and placed it on the ring finger of her left hand.

"With the power vested in me, by myself, as the Marquis of Carmarthen, I now pronounce us Husband and Wife."

She grinned broadly, "You may kiss the bride."

7th December 1712

It was a cold December morning. Gloomy, leaden skies were pregnant with the promise of rain. A strong wind shook the trees, torturing their creaking branches and blowing any piles of dessicated leaves into spinning whirls of auburn.

With his baggage already loaded, Peregrine gave a last

backward glance at Kiveton's North Pavilion, then turned and boarded his coach. The two horses raised up slightly on their back legs for traction and pulled the coach out of the stable yard. They turned left down the lane and then continued on towards Wales crossroads where they turned right. It pulled up outside Horseshoe Cottage.

Peregrine climbed out, his heart heavy, his mood dark. He walked up to the door, opened it and walked into the kitchen. Elizabeth and Susanna were sat round the table and looked up as he entered.

"Pen!" said Susanna. "Elizabeth says you're leaving? That you won't be here for Christmas?" She sounded distraught.

"Yes, I have to leave," he said sadly, fighting an odd lump that had suddenly appeared in his throat.

"For how long?"

"I, err...don't know," he admitted reluctantly.

"But you're coming back? You've got to come back. You're family now," she replied.

"I'll be back as soon I can. I'm just not sure how long that will be. But a few weeks..."

Susanna jumped up and ran over to him, putting her arms round him and hugging him. He hugged her back, looking over her head at where Elizabeth was still sat at the table, staring ahead. As he watched, Elizabeth stood up, turned and then came rushing over. He held out an open arm and she hugged him and her sister.

"Do you have to go?" said Susanna tearfully.

"I have to. But I'll be back, have no fear of that. If I have to crawl on my hands and knees from Wimbledon I will. This is my home now."

Elizabeth looked up at him. "I want you to know that whatever you need to do in the next few days... I'm alright with it."

"I'm not doing anything except turn up for the ceremony," he insisted.

"You say that now, it might be different when you're there. With her. And surrounded by everyone else. I just want you to know that it's alright. Do whatever you have to do to come home. We'll be waiting."

He hugged them both. "I shall see you after Christmas. Promise. " He let them go and turned round and went back out to his coach.

Elizabeth and Susanna stood, arm in arm, in the doorway watching his coach pull away.

Susanna asked "Is this the hurt you once told me I'd have when Pen leaves?"

"Yes, I'm afraid it is," said Elizabeth.

"Are you hurting too?"

"Yes, I am."

"Alright. We'll hurt together then. And wait for him to come back."

"Yes. We'll wait. And hope he comes back."

16th December 1712

Peregrine's wig made his head itch. He had always avoided wearing them if he could, but he couldn't get out of it this time. It was his wedding day. The light blonde wig was a mass of curls that tumbled down his back and lightly touched his shoulder. He had made sure it was the very last part of his costume that he donned. For the first few minutes he had been fine, but then his head got hot and the itching started. He just knew he would spend the rest of the day fighting the urge to scratch his head.

And his new boots hurt his feet. They looked fine. The polished brass of the spur fittings gleamed against the thick, shiny black leather. They rose all the way up his legs to end above his knee. Perfect for riding, painfully uncomfortable for walking.

He quite liked his new waistcoat which was a pale yellow with a fringe of dark blue embroidery. His tunic was bright scarlet with gold braiding. Once he had it all on, he had to admit that he did look impressive. He had to, everyone else would be wearing their most expensive outfits.

He made his way down to the large entrance hall in Wimbledon House. There were already lots of people milling around. Mainly servants, but a few wigged dignitaries turned as Peregrine entered. He didn't know them, but they were undoubtedly important people that he aught to know.

Henry Somerset waved him over. Henry was dressed in a mixture of different shades of grey, quite restrained by his standards. "Ah, good, you're here! And on time too," he said. "I've been charged with getting you there on time. Well, making sure you get there at all, actually. On time would be nice too, if we can manage that."

His wife, Lady Mary, slapped his arm. "Stop putting ideas in his head, Henry."

"There's still time," he said to Peregrine with a grin. "We can jump on the horses and be out of here before anyone notices."

Mary scowled at him, "And leave me to face Mama's vitriol? No, thank you! Pip, stay right where you are!". She noticed Peregrine's worried look, "Cheer up. We're only joking."

He smiled, "I know. I was just thinking about something." Actually, he was wishing he was two hundred miles away in Kiveton.

"Ah, thinking," said Somerset. "We have a cure for that." He reached into an inside pocket and pulled out a small flask which he passed over to Peregrine. "Brandy. Guaranteed to get the nerves under control."

Peregrine opened it and took a large sip.

"Just be careful with that," said Mary. "If you two can"t stand up in the church it will be so humiliating. Although it would be quite funny!"

Peregrine passed the flask back. "Thanks. That's better. When do we go?"

"Right now," announced Somerset.

They went out of the front door of Wimbledon House, over the dry moat, between manicured knot gardens and into the courtyard where their horses waited. A black one for Somerset and a grey mare for Peregrine. They climbed up into the saddles then waited while the other guests got into their carriages which were waiting nearby. Finally, Peregrine and Somerset led the way out into Wimbledon village followed by a caval-cade of coaches.

It was a cold, Christmas day, the sky was full of leaden clouds that threatened rain, but so far it had remained dry. A wind blew into their faces as they rode, biting Peregrine's fingers with the promise of frost.

They turned right on leaving the House and followed the road for a mile down to St Mary's church. They rode down the side of Wimbledon Park, beside black, bare trees through roads wet with last night's rain. Past the church which stood in a large area of trees and grass attached to the main Park. When they reached the junction with the main road they turned right into the church's driveway. St Mary's was a grey stone church with a large spire. The church was surrounded by trees. At the end of the driveway were four robust, stone gateposts topped with stone pyramids. They left the horses and continued up the drive on foot. They entered through the large, wooden doors into an entrance hall and then into the main part of the church. It had a large nave flanked by a dozen stone pillars which supported a series of norman pointed arches. The nave was filled with several rows of pews, many of which were already occupied.

Peregrine and Somerset made their steady way between them to the front of the church then sat down and waited. Peregrine felt the nerves beginning to build, all eyes seemed to be upon him and it was not a situation he was accustomed to. He found that he was confident in small groups, but that confidence diluted as the group grew. With Elizabeth he was perfectly at ease, and even with her family. But, now, with hundreds of eyes looking in his direction all he wanted to do was go into a room of his own and close the door. He realised that his new role as the Marquis was a very public one and he, as a very private person, was simply not suited for it.

After some time everyone suddenly rose to their feet and

Peregrine did likewise to stand rather uncomfortably waiting. He knew why they had risen - his bride had arrived. He saw the commotion from the people sat nearest the door, heard the increased buzz of anticipation, but he himself could see nothing for the crowd. He waited, tensely.

Finally, Elizabeth Harley drew next to him. He had not seen her since his visit to Brampton. Then she had always been dressed very casually, often for riding or some physical activity. Now she was dressed very differently. He didn't recognise her immediately. Her long hair was pushed up, pinned into place and held perfectly in a series of voluminous folds. Her eyes shone like beacons from dark eye shadow, their every glance emphasised by eye liner. Her long lashes caught his attention and refused to release it. How had he not noticed them before?

She wore a dress that glittered under the diffused light, appearing to shimmer as if made of silver. It was cut to a square neck with sleeves ending in a series of flowery folds edged with gold ribbon. The front and the neck of the dress were decorated with fine needlework depicting different coloured roses, as if someone had thrown a mixed bouquet across it and, where each flower fell, it had transformed into a picture. A dazzling necklace of diamonds was draped, almost casually, around her neck, three rows deep of interlaced jewels and then, hanging from the bottom, a single conical gem, pointing to her cleavage.

He felt dazzled by her. Almost unable to look anywhere else. She looked at him, held him mesmerised, but he read no affection in her eyes. He saw confidence and pride. A deep satisfaction in her own ability to enthral and arouse.

On the other side of her, her father, Robert Harley, seemed to fade into insignificance even though he was also dressed in a crescendo of colour.

The priest went through the service. At the appropriate moments, Peregrine and Elizabeth made their promises until finally, the Reverend declared them to be married. She turned and gave him the full effect of her captivating eyes then inclined her face to his and he leaned forward and kissed her. She tasted as sweet as rosehips, her lips against his were as smooth as if he were kissing silk. He had never kissed her before now, and he felt a pang of regret that he hadn't. She was intoxicating.

As she drew away she smiled sweetly. But he saw a flash of something else in her eyes, before that merest slip was wiped away to leave him wondering if he had imagined it. He knew he hadn't. For a second he saw the flicker of mocking amusement. He knew then that, behind the elaborate show, somewhere inside she was laughing at him. With that realisation he felt his spirit wither.

She captivates like Aphrodite, he thought to himself. *But she stings like a viper.*

After the service, they made their way out of the church. The six bells of Wimbledon church began to ring their deafening celebration. A group of drummers, specially assembled for the occasion, began to drum their raucous applause. The happy couple were greeted by a cheering crowd, Peregrine's own extended family, the Harley's and also a good helping of unknown people of influence. They all grinned their widest grins and beamed their brightest smiles, but as Peregrine looked at them, they all seemed curiously fake. Like actors playing parts or wooden manikins dancing on their strings. What did they really think? Why were they really here? The entire enterprise was an elaborate show. The truth was so deeply hidden that even the participants could no longer find it.

Peregrine played the part that had been assigned to him. He kept his arm around Elizabeth's waist. She held herself so close to him it could be easily mistaken for affection. They beamed back at their guests their obvious happiness at the most glorious day of their lives. When they were joined in holy matrimony forever.

Afterwards, they rode back to Wimbledon House where a series of tables had been laid with a gargantuan feast. A mouth

watering selection of meats, fruits, cheeses and assorted vegetables. Larks, hawked that very morning, were cooked and
served along with several dozen pheasant. And drink in overwhelming abundance, gallons of Brandy, cases of Viana white
wine, more cases of Viana claret, gallons of Arrack and hogs-
heads of sherry.

Elizabeth sat next to Peregrine at the top of the table. Her
father sat on her other side. She spent most of the time speaking and laughing with her father, but occasionally spared a few
choice words for her new husband. Peregrine's mother sat next
to him, which dampened his mood even further.

As the day wore on, the meal ended and more serious drinking began. Music was provided by a band and the dancing
started. The dancing was formal, groups of people pirouetting,
skipping in unison and clapping hands at predetermined moments It was all very *arranged,* when Peregrine compared it to
the chaos of the Twelfth Night celebrations back in Wales. He
knew these dances better, but on balance found that he longed
for those informal shindigs back home.

Home. How he longed to leave and just go home. Back to his
Elizabeth and his friends. To immerse himself in their simpler,
more honest existence and wash away the stench of this depravity and deception.

In the back of his mind some trepidation lurked. The formal
events were either finished or the end was in sight. But the
main event still remained. This was his wedding night. But a
lot of things were wrong. When he looked at his new wife,
she shone like an enticing vision of paradise. On one level he
couldn't help but respond to her physical lure. But she had
hardly noticed him at all, had barely spoken any words to him
all day. When they danced, when they held each other closely
in the presence of others she switched on an illusion of joy and
affection. But, once free from others scrutiny, she switched it
off just as easily and reverted to a cold remoteness. Like a mask
she assumed and dropped at whim. Peregrine found it unnerving and hard to predict what would happen next.

As the night grew older she eventually caught him completely by surprise and leaned over to him. "Shall we retire for an early night, my love?" she asked.

He was thrown by her sudden change in gear and was lost for words.

Before he could reply, his mother did on his behalf. "Yes, you two get along. This night will go on for a while yet. And it is your night, after all."

"Then we will," replied Elizabeth. "We've had a wonderful time. Thanks so much for arranging all this for us."

"It was a pleasure," replied his mother, casting a suspicious eye on Peregrine.

Elizabeth took hold of his hand, rose from chair and led him away from the table and out through a back door. They were in one of the staircase towers of Wimbledon House. Ahead, the stone stairs spiralled away up the tower. Without hesitation, she started climbing and, dumbly, he followed. Dressed in her glistening silver gown she was like a fairytale princess leading her prince lover up through the castle. Two flights up, she took him through a door in the wall. They emerged into a candlelit corridor, full of wooden panelling and low ceilings. Without stopping, she pulled him along by the hand and, then, after they had passed two doors, she suddenly stopped and opened the third.

She pulled him into a lavish room where rich, bright tapestries of lovers reclining in pastoral surroundings were hung against panelled walls. In the centre of the room a giant, four poster bed dominated the room. She turned to look back at him as she entered. Her smile was radiant and alluring. It melted his reservations as he felt a familiar heat rising. She closed the door behind him and then went to stand in front of him.

"So, here we are," she said softly. "Alone at last. How did you think I looked today?"

"I never realised you could be so beautiful. You astounded me."

"Good enough for a Marquis?"

"Without a shadow of a doubt."

She drifted around the room, dominating the space. "Elizabeth Osborne, Marchioness of Carmarthen. Oh, I love the sound of that! It sounds so...regal. Don't you think so?"

"The name suits you. You fit the part."

"I do, don't I?" she said suddenly. "It's like I was destined to be this." She stopped and said casually, "Can you help me take my dress off?"

"I, er..."

"There are some clips round the back. I need someone else to unfasten them."

She turned round and stood patiently waiting. Hesitantly he went over to her. He saw what she meant, a series of metal clasps ran down the top half of the back of her dress. He reached out for the first. His hands seemed suddenly sweaty. As he fiddled with the topmost clip, the back of his hand inadvertently stroked her neck and she moved her head slightly in response. Her skin was so smooth. His mouth was suddenly dry.

He opened the first clip then began the second. Steadily he worked his way down, while she presented herself patiently, until finally the last clip came free. She pulled at the arms and the dress fell off her in a single piece and, with agile grace, she stepped out of it.

She turned to face him with a strange smile playing across her face. She was wearing a very tight shift, much tighter than any he had seen his Elizabeth wear. It hugged the outline of her body, the fabric so thin it was possible to discern the underlying light and dark patches of her body beneath.

She was still wearing the fabulous necklace she had been wearing all day. Still facing him, and with her eyes locked on him, she reached up, putting both arms behind her head to unfasten the necklace. As she reached up, her breasts were thrust forward, the tight shift hung on them like wet cotton, revealing their pertness. Presenting them to him. Offering them.

She took off the necklace and dropped it on the floor by her white stockinged feet.

"Do you like what you see?" she asked as she started slowly walking towards him.

"Y...yes," he replied falteringly.

"Do you want to see some more?" she asked.

A small voice in the back of his mind yelled no, but he heard himself say "Yes."

She was standing in front of him, so close he could hear her breathing, feel the warmth of her body next to him and smell her scent. She reached her face up to him, her lips drew very close to his without quite touching.

She whispered, "Are you glad you married me?"

"Yes," he breathed helplessly.

"Good," she whispered, but slowly drew away. Her voice grew louder, shattering the tenderness of the moment. "Because I just needed you to know that."

"What?" he said in a weak voice and a look of complete confusion on his face.

"Always remember that, on our wedding night, you wanted me and you were glad you married me. It was *me* that didn't want you! Now get out."

"I don't understand," said Peregrine, his mind spinning with confusion. I thought you wanted...a child?"

"My father does. And I always give him what he wants. But you don't , do you?"

"I..." he didn't know what to say. She was right, actually.

"Until a few moments ago you didn't want to bed me at all. What were you going to tell me? Sorry, I know I married you, but I can't sleep with you because I love someone else? Well, you don't treat me like that! Even if you are the Marquis of Carmarthen. I'm telling you that *I* can't sleep with *you* because I utterly despise you. Now go. Get out! You're in the room next door."

"You have no intention of sleeping with me," he said in disbelief. He was staggered. It was meant to be him saying that to her. He sighed and, in shock, turned and made his way back to the door.

He opened it slowly and then blinked in disbelief. His father stood there. "Evening, lad," said the Duke nonchalantly. "Problems in the bedroom? Well, what are father's for if not to sort out their sons problems."

He pushed past Peregrine into Elizabeth's bedroom. Peregrine felt like the world was spinning wildly out of control. He shook his head. "I don't understand."

"She prefers older men, lad," said the Duke in an almost comradely tone. "Always has. She'd bed her own father if she could, but, well, I'm about the same age. She was never going to be happy with someone two years younger than herself. Sleep tight, lad."

The Duke closed the door. Leaving Peregrine out in the corridor. Slowly he turned to make his way to the bedroom next door, only to find his mother standing outside it.

"Is all this your doing?" asked Peregrine.

"Of course," admitted his mother without a trace of guilt. "It seemed like the best solution."

"Best? For who? To have my own father bed my wife on my wedding night?"

"But I thought you didn't want to?" She asked innocently. "And he did. And she did. It seems to please everyone. Or have you changed your mind....again?"

"No. Yes. No, oh, I don't know any more."

"Well, you have a think about it, Pip, then I think you'll see that it makes perfect sense. The Harley's and us want an heir and, this way we'll get one. Alright, you won't be the father, but near enough, because your father will be. And you've married her, so when the child's born everyone will assume it's yours. The Harley's won't say anything and neither will your father. I'll be raising any children with the Harley's, here in Wimbledon. If it's a boy he'll grow up to be the 4th Duke."

"And what about me? Cuckolded by my own father! To have a son who is really my half-brother!"

"That's just details," said his mother dismissively. "You'll fulfil your duties as the Marquis of Carmarthen with your wife faithfully at your side – as far as appearances go. But that shouldn't take up too much of your time. You'll be elevated to the House of Lords at the end of next month. But most of the Lords don't turn up anyway so your absence won't matter. You can go back to Kiveton, live with your...with Elizabeth...and watch your real child growing up. So, you see, it really does work for everyone."

"I suppose," he acknowledged reluctantly. It would be good to go back to Kiveton. "I can't help thinking that history is going to judge us very harshly for this."

Lady Bridget smiled. "I doubt it. Haven't you realised yet? We write history."

14th February 1713

The coach wheels spun alarmingly in the snow as it clambered up the slight hill on the Todwick Road. Peregrine didn't care. As the days had passed in his journey up from Wimbledon, so his excitement had steadily grown. With every mile he counted nearer to home he felt another part of his soul being healed. He had been diminished by the Christmas in the same measure that the one a year previously had elevated him. By the end of January he had felt worn and bone weary.

He mused on what a difference that year had brought. He had barely known Kiveton then. It was a distant, remote place, vaguely remembered from childhood. A monument built by his grandfather, but surrendered to his father then abandoned by him. By the time Peregrine had returned, it had become his mother's uncontested domain. But a year on, all was transformed. His grandfather was dead and his father banished. His mother now seemed determined to spend most of her time in either her manor in Aldbury or at Wimbledon. Her focus had shifted, she was now concerned mainly with producing an heir, something which no longer involved Peregrine. Something she could manage much better in the south.

Which left Kiveton strangely vacant. Now his family had been largely purged from it, Kiveton, with its treasures and extensive grounds, seemed powerfully alluring. It was far away from all the people he had, quite honestly, had his fill of. But reassuringly close to the people that mattered to him most.

It was early evening and as dark as midnight as Peregrine's coach drew past the woods surrounding Todwick. Kiveton Hall came into view and he felt his spirits lift further. The imposing wall of the stable block was to his left and, beyond it the stable yard gates. The coach didn't turn in, on Peregrine's instruction it continued. Past the windows of the North Pavilion, flickering with homely candlelight while the servants had their evening meals, busied themselves with light tasks or made their way to their accommodations. Past the large entrance courtyard and, behind it, the imposing presence of the main building, now largely unlit. Without visitors or residents and with the daily maintenance duties finished for the day, it waited patiently to be awakened. For someone to appreciate it for the magnificent work of art that it was. Peregrine realised he was the best person to do that. He was more knowledgeable about its contents and grounds than anyone he knew. And he had the resources to keep it intact and let it survive for another generation.

His coach drove past the South Pavilion where his rooms were located. Where he felt most at home. Where he and Elizabeth had first experienced each other's intimacy. He had not fallen in love with her there, that had happened when he first saw her on Twelfth Night. They had not reached the zenith of their relationship there, that had been in the Summer sun at Roche Abbey. But those innocent moments in his Green Rooms at Kiveton had been the building blocks of their love for each other.

His coach continued down the road along the smooth, untarnished snow that now filled the South Lawn. The coach turned right at the crossroads, towards Wales. Two miles further it turned again into the lane that led to the blacksmith's yard. It clattered noisily into the yard, Peregrine flung the door open and jumped out. Straight away the coach started turning round and making its way back to the stable yard at Kiveton.

Peregrine stood alone, in the dark, his boots ankle deep in snow in the blacksmith's yard. He took a deep breath and trudged up to the door of the blacksmith's cottage. And knocked.

"Who's that now," came Robert Mirfin's voice from inside. Peregrine smiled to himself. The door opened. "Oh, it's you, Pen," said Elizabeth's father. "Come on in. We're just having some broth."

He entered the kitchen. It was thankfully warm after the cold journey. Henry was sat at the table, spooning broth into his mouth. Susanna was messing with cooking pots. They both stopped as he entered.

"Oh, Pen's here!" exclaimed Susanna. She put down the pot she was holding, ran over and threw her arms round him. "I knew you'd come back. Because you promised you would."

"Yes, I'm back home now. For good this time," said Peregrine with a huge grin.

"Good to see you, Pen. Elizabeth's over at the other place," said Henry.

"She was feeling tired, I think," said Susanna. "She's due soon."

"Alright, I'll go over there," said Peregrine. "See you later."

He ran over the road to Horseshoe Cottage. He didn't knock. He just opened the door and went in. Elizabeth was in the kitchen, just about to put some wood on the fire. She threw the wood down and ran over to him, throwing her arms round him and kissing him.

"Careful, careful," he said. "In fact, you better sit down and I'll sort the fire out."

"I'm alright," she said with a grin. "I'm just so glad you're back."

"Me too," he said, making her sit down. "And just in time by the look of it."

"How long are you back for?" she asked demurely.

"For good," he said with a broad grin.

"Really?" she asked hesitantly. "I know the idea was that once you were a Marquis, once you were married, you could do what you wanted. But I had my doubts."

He put some wood on the fire then sat at the table next to her. "You were right. You're always right. I went down to Wimbledon. I got married. I did what they wanted. Now they can leave me alone."

"But what about having an heir? How are you going to....?"

"Other members of my disreputable family are dealing with that issue," he said scathingly. "Let them get on with it. God knows, I had a low opinion of them before, but the last few weeks have taught me that there may be no limit to the depravity they'll conceive to achieve what they want."

"So, you're off the hook?" she asked carefully.

He smiled. "Aye. I may have to put in the occasional appearance or attend a social event with my lovely wife, but apart from that...I'm here, with you. And the bump."

"And Kiveton?"

"It's my house. I'll live there...and here. Mother's down in Wimbledon with my wife."

She held his hand, her eyes growing cloudy with tears. "Well, I couldn't be happier. It seems to have all worked out."

"Yes," he said slowly. "It's all worked out. Just one more thing..."

"What?"

"Happy St Valentines Day," he said.

She reached over and hugged him. "The best present ever!"

Reluctantly, he had to admit maybe mother was right. It was the best solution for everyone.

24th February 1713

"You're wearing a groove in the kitchen flags," complained Robert Mirfin as Peregrine paced up and down in the blacksmith's cottage kitchen.

"Sorry," said Peregrine worriedly. "Keeping moving seems to help," he said as he continued pacing.

Elizabeth had been in labour over at Horseshoe Cottage for hours now. The menfolk had been evicted over to the blacksmith's cottage to await word. Susanna and the midwife had remained with Elizabeth. So far there had been no word. Peregrine realised he wasn't very good at waiting.

"Sit down and have a cup of tea," said Henry who was sat with his father at the table.

"I've lost count of how many I've had already," replied Peregrine.

"Well, sit down anyway."

"Tried that. Didn't work. We've not heard anything for ages. Do you think I should go and see what's happening?"

"No!" exclaimed Henry and his father simultaneously.

"Aye, you're right. Don't want to put them off if they're busy. On the other hand, what if they need help?"

"Sit down, please, Pen, you're making me dizzy," said Henry. "They don't need help. And, if they did, it's not the sort of help you're likely to be able to provide."

"How about a beer?" asked Robert. "Or a brandy. I've still some left, I think."

"No thanks. I need to keep my head clear. " He sat down in a seat at the table. But he didn't look very relaxed.

His mind was rushing off down lines of thought he didn't like. Of course, he hoped the child was alright. But it might not be Many weren't. He'd heard stories. Some bled out. Others were born dead. Some lived only long enough to be held.

And what about Elizabeth? Labour was long, arduous and painful. Often it wasn't survivable. He couldn't lose Elizabeth now, not now, after they had been through so much and reached an agreeable place. Elizabeth had to live...even if the child was lost. Otherwise, what would become of him? Losing Elizabeth was also not survivable...

The kitchen door burst open and Susanna charged in, grinning, "It's a boy!"

Henry and Robert cheered.

"Elizabeth? Is she alright?" asked Peregrine.

"She's fine," said Susanna. "No problems. They're just tidying things up over there."

Robert opened his box of cigars, "This calls for one of these," he said, passing them round. "Well done, lad," he said, slapping Peregrine on the shoulder.

"I really did very little," admitted Peregrine sheepishly.

"Well, congratulations, anyway," said Henry, shaking his hand.

"Can I see her?" asked Peregrine. Almost pleading.

Susanna smiled. "Of course you can. Come with me."

It was late evening and bitterly cold, but thankfully the snow had cleared away. They ran over to Horseshoe Cottage, into the kitchen and then up the stairs.

Susanna held him back at the door. "I'll just make sure she's decent," she said and went in closing the door behind her. She reappeared a few seconds later. "You can come in."

Elizabeth was sat up in bed, she looked dishevelled and exhausted.

But wonderful, thought Peregrine.

She was holding a bundle of blankets and, there wrapped snugly, was a round little face with a little flat nose. His eyes were completely closed as he slept soundly.

"Meet your son, Pen," said Elizabeth.

"Your son," said Peregrine. "I was just glad I could help."

"I'm calling him Matthew after my favourite verse in the bible. Matthew, Chapter sixteen, verse twenty-six. For what is a man profited..."

"...if he shall gain the whole world and lose his soul?" finished Peregrine. "That's my favourite too."

Chapter Fourteen

9th May 1731

Peregrine adjusted his waistcoat in the mirror just outside the Drawing Room in Kiveton Hall. It was one of his favourite waistcoats, but it no longer seemed to fit him properly. It's a problem he had been having for a few years now. Clothes that he had worn perfectly well for years all seemed to be unaccountably shrinking. He made another attempt to get the top button of his waistcoat to fasten then lost patience and gave up. He would just have to leave it.

What did it matter? He was only meeting his mother anyway. It was one of her regular six monthly visits from Aldbury. She had quickly got into the habit of visiting just before Christmas season and then again at the beginning of May. Often the purpose of the visit was to update him on the state of the estates finances, but usually it was to allocate him some tasks and put some dates in his calendar for the next few months. There were people to visit or, occasionally, visitors might come to Kiveton. Some dates in a social calendar that he never saw and cared about even less.

It was a routine he and his mother had developed shortly after he married Elizabeth Harley. Mother had been in Wimbledon most of the time and he was in Kiveton. Mother felt they needed a schedule or they would lose touch.

He still thought about Elizabeth Harley from time to time.

Disagreeable though she was, his lasting image of her was how beautiful she looked on their wedding day. He would have been relieved not to have had to marry her, but once he had seen her, he felt insanely jealous to lose her so quickly and so easily to his own father. It turned out they had been seeing each other for weeks before the wedding. It was all planned, no doubt by his mother.

His father had got her with child by February, just a few months after the wedding. The child was a boy, born in November 1713, just eight months after Peregrine's real son, Matthew. So mother and the Harley's got their heir. Thomas Osborne, Earl of Danby from the moment of his birth. The future 4th Duke. So the 2nd Duke had definitely fulfilled his part of the bargain. Peregrine's mother took the boy under her wing, Peregrine had only seen him briefly. She had him educated in Westminster.

Sadly, poor Elizabeth had died shortly after giving birth, aged twenty-three. Peregrine felt sad about it. He couldn't ever say that he liked her, and she certainly didn't like him, but that was no age to die. She had literally laid down her life to give her father a Duke as a grandson. Somehow, for all her shortcomings, Peregrine couldn't help feeling she deserved better than that.

A year after marrying Elizabeth Harley, Peregrine was a widower. His mother tried her best to find him another bride, but since he made no attempt to promote the family socially or politically, their standing waned.

He eventually sold Wimbledon House in December 1717. With his wife gone, himself living as a recluse in Kiveton and his mother and father in Aldbury, they had no use for it. Besides, they needed the money.

Few saw an advantage in pairing their daughters to the Osborne's fading fortunes. A suitable match proved virtually impossible. But not *completely* impossible.

Charles Seymour, the 6th Duke of Somerset, was a big friend of the family. His house of Petworth had copied many of the interiors from Kiveton, including the *Creation of Pandora* staircase. When his daughter, Anne, was suddenly expecting a child, there was the possibility of a scandal. He needed to get her married quickly, and he wasn't fussy about who to. So Peregrine's mother arranged for him to marry Seymour's daughter, Peregrine thought it was a ludicrous proposition. In truth, it was a desperate concession and a sign of how low the value of the Osborne brand had sunk. But, it was pointed out to him that it was just like the Harley marriage. Get married to legitimise the child, then he would never have to see her again. It would help the Duke of Somerset and his daughter. And he was very rich and he would be very grateful.

So Peregrine had married her, in September 1719. It had been a bizarre, small, simple ceremony. As usual, Peregrine gritted his teeth, got on with it and then went back to Elizabeth. The only sanity in an insane world.

He was later told that Anne had the child successfully, but that it died as an infant. Anne herself died a couple of years later. And Peregrine found himself a widower again by 1723.

He had assumed that was the end of it as far as marriages went, but his mother was persistent. So, four years later he had married again. This time to Juliana Hele. She was nineteen and he was thirty-four. She was ambitious heiress, but she craved a title. Which was about the only thing Peregrine could offer her. The first time he met her was on their wedding day, but he had to admit he liked her and they got on well. It was a marriage of convenience. There was no physical side to the relationship, she was happy to play the part of the Marchioness of Carmarthen and he was happy to let her. She didn't mind that he lived in Kiveton or that he had another family there. He suspected she was having affairs of her own, but he didn't mind that either. It was an arrangement that suited them both.

Throughout all this, the only constant thing, the anchor of his life, had been Elizabeth. She still lived in Horseshoe Cottage. She occasionally visited him at Kiveton, but more likely he went to Wales. They acted almost like a normal husband

and wife – except that they lived in separate houses. Together, they had brought up Matthew to be an eighteen year old young man.

Matthew had been baptised in Wales church a month after he was born. His father was officially recorded as unknown, Matthew's status as *base*. There was no getting round it, Peregrine's mother had never relented on allowing Peregrine and Elizabeth to marry. But everyone knew that Peregrine was the father. Matthew himself regarded Peregrine as a sort of stepfather or uncle who was always there while he was growing up. They had never told him that Peregrine was his father, their view was the less association Matthew had with the Osbornes the better. So he had grown up learning to be a blacksmith like grandpa Robert and uncle Henry. They had never taken Matthew to Kiveton Hall.

Peregrine's life with Elizabeth hadn't been all plain sailing though. There had been ups and downs.

The worst was when Susanna had died ten years ago. She died suddenly and unexpectedly from an internal haemorrhage. She was twenty-four. Everyone was devastated, but it hit Peregrine particularly hard. Nothing, apart from losing Elizabeth, could have hit him harder. He had grown to love Susanna immensely and her loss was a pain he carried with him constantly. It took him a very long time to get used to her not being around. He didn't think he would ever be able to say he was over it.

But there had been lots of good times too. Mary Parkin's persistence had finally paid off and Henry agreed to marry her. She was twenty-three, he was twenty-nine. It had been a really enjoyable family wedding, unlike the debacles of Peregrine's own weddings.

Susanna dying had spurred Peregrine on to take Elizabeth somewhere he had been promising to take her for years. Henry being married had also allowed them to leave young Matthew with someone. They went on a tour of Italy, visiting all the places she had previously only read about. Milan, Genoa, Florence, Rome, and Venice. They had been gone for a year, but it had been the tour of a lifetime.

All these thoughts passed through Peregrine's mind as he made his way to the Drawing Room to meet his mother. He was more relaxed about meeting her than he had been for years, thanks to Juliana. Since he had married her, he no longer had to worry about some bizarre marriage plot his mother had dreamed up – he was already married.

Peregrine's father had died two years ago at which point Peregrine had finally become the 3rd Duke of Leeds. Juliana had automatically become the Duchess of Leeds, a fact that seemed to give her immense pleasure. She had married him in order to be a Duchess and now she was. Peregrine was happy for her. In fact, Peregrine was pretty happy all round as he went into the Drawing Room

Meetings with his mother always made Peregrine feel nervous. They were always like being taken in to meet royalty. It always took him back to the rare visits his mother made when he and William were children and they were led in by nanny to meet her. He was thirty-nine now, but the same feelings always surfaced.

"Pip! Come in," said his mother as he entered. As usual, she was sat in a chair by the fire. "I've asked for some tea while we have a chat."

He went over and lowered himself into a chair opposite her. "Morning, mother. Did you have a good journey?"

She frowned as she sipped her tea. "I loathe the journey up from Aldbury. But I suppose it is necessary. Are you used to being the Duke, yet?"

He took his tea and shrugged, "It isn't really that important to me. But It's made Juliana very happy. Whenever, I'm with her she seems to love being called Duchess of Leeds."

"Well, that's something then. That's what she married you for after all."

"Yes, quite. Juliana and me get on well," he said taking a gulp of tea. " I leave her alone, she leaves me alone. We meet up at official functions. She's pleasant company."

"There are rumours she's seeing that sporting friend of yours, Charles Colyear."

"What if she is? He's good company too. We all get on well. Good luck to them."

"That's very understanding."

"I love Elizabeth and Matthew. I'm only married to Juliana. She understands that."

"Matthew? Ah yes, your other...son."

"I only have one son, remember?"

"What about Thomas?"

"He's father's and Elizabeth Harley's, as you well know."

"Technically yes," she admitted. "But legally he's your heir."

"Yes...but...bu..." he suddenly struggled to speak. He didn't know why. Then he found his hand holding the tea cup relax of its own volition causing the tea to spill on the floor. The effect spread quickly, he fell back into the chair, unable to get up even though he dearly wanted to. His muscles refused to obey him. Fear flooded him like cold water trickling through his veins.

"It will take a few minutes," said his mother icily. "Or, at least, it did with your father when I used it on him. But it's quite effective."

Only his eyes could move. He looked at her, puzzling, pleading..

She continued casually. "You've been a big disappointment to me, Pip, as I'm sure you realise. The men in this family are meant to be leading the country, not wasting their lives on some blacksmith's trollop. We didn't accumulate all this by being country bumpkins. Your father was less than perfect, but at least he had his uses. But, I have really struggled to find a suitable role for you and now I don't think there is one.

"I think it's really best for all concerned if we simply forget about the 3rd Duke of Leeds. Pretend you never happened and just move to the 4th Duke as soon as possible. Thomas is eighteen now. He's been educated in private school in Westminster. This year he will be going to Oxford. He'll be a very different sort of Duke to you, Pip. The sort we always really wanted.

"And I'm afraid there'll be no room for your trollop and her bastard in the new world either. We'll have her evicted from that cottage as soon as possible. She's an abomination I simply cannot endure any longer.

"You see, Pip, I have to think in the very, long term. In generations. And now we're going to move to the next generation. You only have one more part to play. You will perform that final duty that befalls all Dukes. You will die."

Peregrine felt a sudden, excruciating, stabbing pain in his heart. He wanted to yell, but he had no voice. He wanted to cringe, but his face would not obey. A tear formed in his wide open eyes and trickled down his frozen cheek. And his eyes stared forever, unseeing, at his mother.

Epilogue

Peregrine Hyde Osborne, 3rd Duke of Leeds is recorded to have died suddenly from unknown causes at the age of thirty-nine. He was interred in the Osborne family vault at Harthill.

Peregrine's mother died in 1734, three years after Peregrine. She was buried at Aldbury in Hertfordshire, a manor she inherited from her father and where she lived in later life. Her husband, Peregrine Osborne, 2nd Duke of Leeds, is buried with her. They are the only early Duke and Duchess of Leeds not to be interred in the Osborne family vault.

Peregrine's third wife, Juliana, married long time friend Charles Colyear, 2nd Earl of Portmore, seventeen months after Peregrine's death. She had no children with Peregrine, but went on to have four with her second husband. She continued to call herself the Duchess of Leeds even after she remarried.

Peregrine's only heir, Thomas, succeeded his father and became 4th Duke of Leeds six months after his eighteenth birthday. He was educated at Westminster School and then Christ Church, Oxford. He received a Doctorate of Civil Law in 1738. He became a Lord of the Bedchamber and Justice in Eyre south of Trent in 1748. He was made a Knight of the Order of the Garter and was sworn of the Privy Council of Great Britain. He became Justice in Eyre north of Trent in 1761 and Deputy Lieutenant of the West Riding of the County of Yorkshire. He married Lady Mary Godolphin in 1740 and died at the age of seventy-three in 1789.

Peregrine's brother-in-law, Henry Somerset, died three years after marrying Peregrine's sister, Mary. She remarried John Campbell Cochrane, 4th Earl of Dundonald. She died seven years later, in 1722, aged thirty-four.

John Lambert continued to be a highly trusted steward to the Osborne family. He served the 1st Duke, Peregrine himself and then Thomas, the 4th Duke. He was held in such high esteem that his full length portrait was hung at Kiveton. It is the only portrait belonging to the Osbornes that is not of the family, royal family, political associates or by a famous artist. He died at the age of seventy-three and was interred, with the Dukes of Leeds, at Harthill in 1754. The entry in the register reads *"A gentleman universally beloved in his life and lamented at his death."*

The Dukes of Leeds continued to occupy Kiveton for the rest of the 18th century until the 6th Duke moved the family seat to Hornby Castle, near Bedale in North Yorkshire. His father, the 5th Duke, had acquired Hornby through marriage.

The South Pavilion of Kiveton was demolished in 1800. The rest of Kiveton Hall was steadily demolished over the next twelve years. The gardens were destroyed. The trees in the park were removed and the park was turned into farmland in 1808. The entire estate was eventually partitioned into plots and sold progressively over twenty years from 1927. All that remains is Kiveton Park's boundary wall, still enclosing the vast acreage which now forms Kiveton Hall Farm.

Robert Mirfin lived with his son, Henry, for the rest of his life. He died in 1735 at age of seventy-five.

Susanna Mirfin never married. She continued to live in Horseshoe Cottage with Elizabeth and Matthew until she died in 1721, aged twenty-four. She was buried at Wales church.

Henry Mirfin married Mary Parkin in 1722 and continued to be a blacksmith in Wales. They had eleven children. He named his second daughter Susanna. He died in 1760, aged sixty-seven. He was buried in Wales church yard. His gravestone is still visible behind the church, against the wall.

Elizabeth Mirfin and her eighteen year old son, Matthew, were evicted from Horseshoe Cottage. For a while they lived with her brother, Henry. But they eventually moved to Woodhouse, four miles away on the other side of the River Rother, where Matthew earned a living as a blacksmith. Elizabeth lived with Matthew for the rest of her life.

She had always promised Peregrine that, whatever happened, she would always wait for him. He had told her, as long as he knew she was waiting, he would return.

So she waited.

She never married and never had any more children. She died in 1759, aged seventy, and was buried at Handsworth church.

Matthew continued to live in Woodhouse. He married Mary Jones in 1742. He died, aged sixty-two, and was buried at Handsworth church.

Matthew's son, John, followed tradition and learned to be a blacksmith by working with his father. After his father's death he moved to Wales. He was buried at Wales church.

His son, Henry, also became a blacksmith and lived and died in Todwick.

His son, Lubin, was a taylor in Aston. In later life, he looked after the horses at Aston Hall. His gravestone is in Aston cemetery.

His son, Joseph, became a carpenter with his brothers. His gravestone is also in Aston cemetery.

He had a son, Cyril, who had a son, John.

John's son, Andrew, wrote this book.